THE

MICHELANGELO

DECEPTION

A Novel

DON MIKKELSON

Mikkelsen Publishing, Inc

The Michelangelo Deception

Published by Mikkelsen Publishing, Inc.

This book is a work of fiction, although it does contain factual information, which, when quoted directly, is indicated by citations. Paraphrasing of some non-fiction works is acknowledged in the text. Historical narration is used to provide context for fictional characters and events. Names, characters, businesses, organizations, places and incidents are either the product of the author's imagination or are used fictionally. Any resemblance to actual persons, living or dead, or actual events is entirely coincidental.

ISBN: 0615433782
ISBN-13: 9780615433783

For

Doug

Steve

Todd

Mark

Golden

The Poetry of Michelangelo—Clements, 1965 (p. 295)

Rend thou the veil, O Lord, break down this wall,
Which by its hardness keeps retarding so
Thy holy sunshine, in the world gone out.
Oh, send the light so long foretold for all,
To thy fair bride, that so my soul may glow,
And feel thee inwardly, and never doubt!

"Problems cannot be solved on the same level of consciousness that created them."

— **Albert Einstein**

"**Events, occurrences,** happenings, conditions, circumstances—are all created out of consciousness. Individual consciousness is powerful enough. You can imagine what kind of creative energy is unleashed whenever two or more are gathered in my Name. And mass consciousness? Why, that is so powerful it can create events and circumstances of worldwide import and planetary consequences." ***Conversations with God***

LETTERS TO THE EDITOR

June 12, 2005
Mountain Lake Press
Mountain Lake, Wisconsin

SUBJECT: *A modern-day Martin Luther?*

I am wondering when we will be blessed with a modern-day Martin Luther. In 1517, Pope Leo X issued a papal bull modifying the sale of indulgences: a vicious scam that involved people avoiding the horrors of purgatory through various means. The purpose of the change was to raise money for continuing the rebuilding of St. Peter's Basilica.

On 31 October of that year, Dr. Martin Luther—a priest and professor of Theology at the University of Wittenberg, Germany—posted his famous Ninety-five Theses on a church door, thereby challenging the Church leadership to debate the issue. They refused. In 1521, he was excommunicated from the Church sparking an era in history known as The Reformation.

Today, we need someone who will challenge the outrageous corruption condoned by a series of recent popes who have openly defied common decency by their associations with the Mafia: a fact well-documented in recent books and newspaper articles. And now we are seeing cover-ups that range from the priests to the bishops to the cardinals and the pope himself: I speak of the pederasty scandals that involve thousands of priests and tens of thousands of children—some as young as four years old. Like the sale of indulgences, this is the straw that has broken the camel's back. Enough is enough!!! We need a new Martin Luther.

Joey Larksfield
Mountain Lake

PROLOGUE

Monday: 11:25 p.m. Mediterranean Sea

The USS Abraham Lincoln languishes in the wine-dark sea a mile off the Italian coast, ten miles north of the Leonardo De Vinci International Airport near Rome. The fighter pilots are asleep: *no training tonight.* On the flight deck, seven trembling helicopters await Captain Ferguson's signal to lift off.

When the order comes, the choppers, like dancers practicing their pas de sept, will assemble above the carrier, bringing their kabuki maneuvers into formation, ready to deliver—to the Vatican—five NATO Special Operations Teams protected by two United States Marine Corps assault helicopters.

The Captain of the carrier is as calm as a Buddhist monk in deep meditation.

She couldn't hear the desperate scream launched from the depths of her being. She struggled. But the huge, gloved, left hand crushing her face did not budge. In his right hand, the assassin held a pistol—with silencer—an inch from her forehead—and fired.

The day following the early morning murder, Italy's leading daily newspaper, *Il Repubblica,* reported the death of a nun, an employee at the Vatican Bank. She was found in her bed with a bullet wound in her forehead and a rock in her mouth—a Mafia hit . . . and a warning.

Chapter 1

Maria Martinovna Luderenko fastened her seatbelt and settled in for the long flight home. She removed her low pumps and covered her feet with cotton slippers. She wore a V-necked, light-purple sweater and three-quarter-length, tan, cargo pants.

She had been in Russia for three years. Burned out on affairs with older, married men—a business woman—she was bored with her job as a financial manager for a Russian/American computer manufacturing company. She looked at her watch: 10 a.m. Tuesday. The flight would be on time.

The night before, she split with a German businessman; it occurred, but not as planned. They were to meet at the bar of the Baltschug Kempinski Moscow hotel—located on the banks of the old Moskva River—with views of the Kremlin, Red Square and St. Basil's Cathedral. The bar was an alternative to meeting in her room—for reasons he understood. He didn't object. He knew what was coming.

She sat at the bar waiting for him. He was late. The room was empty except for an older, white-haired man sitting at the end of the bar sipping a beer.

The bartender, tall and husky, looked like a bodybuilder. His head shaved, he sported a closely cropped mustache with strings descending around his mouth forming a fashionable sling that held his whiskered chin in place.

He seems like a gentle soul, Maria thought, *but one you would not mess with on a busy night.* He wore a collared, short sleeved, light green, elegantly patterned, silk shirt, khaki pants and brown alligator shoes.

"Dobre vecheris," he said in Russian, laying a thin, round, leather coaster on the bar.

"Good evening. Vodka-on-ice. Do you have Belvedere?" Maria asked in Russian, while removing a cigarette from her handbag. "Konechno," he replied, reassuring her as he held a lighter under her cigarette and watched her inhale. Exhaling, she said, "Spacebo."

She's in her twenties, he thought. Her appearance suggested Varangian ancestors who lived in the ancient state of Kievan Rus in the area of the modern Ukrainian capital.

He prepared her drink. *A perfect specimen*, he mused: *tall, shapely, with blond, straight hair, dusting her shoulders. Her face is chiseled out of Viking stone.* As he turned around to place the drink on the coaster, he noticed her grey flannel pants, and a dark-gold, short-sleeved, Badgley Mischka shirt. He could not see her tawny, Jimmy Choo, spike-heels.

A middle-aged man, with a newspaper tucked under his arm, sat down next to Maria's window seat in the business-class section of the cabin. After settling in and declining a complementary beverage, he opened the Moscow Times and began reading. Maria glanced at the headline:

POPE DIES PEACEFULLY AT VATICAN

In the bar, Maria and the bartender chatted. Finishing her drink, she sensed something unfortunate was about to happen; someone was staring at her.

She had not noticed that a married, middle-aged businessman—wearing a dark-blue, business suit over a white shirt open at the collar—staggering slightly—had slipped into the bar and taken a seat at a table behind her. He came up to the bar, leaned over the bar stool to her left, placed his left hand on the rim of the bar, turned to his right, looked at her, and said, "Haven't we met some where before?" slurring his words in English.

Maria ignored him.

"Hey, haven't we met somewhere before?"

Maria looked at him and replied in English, "Close your eyes, open your mouth and stick out your tongue."

"What?"

"You heard me," she said with a smile. "Do as I said."

"Well, okay," he said thickly, thinking, in his foggy state, she might have an erotic surprise for him. He looked at her, closed his eyes and did as she requested.

She lifted her cigarette, placed it over his tongue, tapped it and watched the hot ashes fall.

He swung to the left, grabbed the rim of the bar with both hands and spit the ashes, mixed with saliva, into the face of the bartender as he raised his head from below the bar where he had reached for a towel.

"You dumb bastard!" the bartender screamed in English, as he grabbed the man by his lapels. He lifted Maria's tormentor and sent him crashing into the table and chairs behind her barstool.

"Now, get the hell out of here, before I cut off your balls and stuff them in your mouth."

The gray-haired man at the end of the bar laughed; the bartender was not amused.

The philanderer struggled to his feet and staggered to his room. Maria stared at her hero as he wiped his face with a towel.

"You speak English," he said, throwing the towel into a nearby hamper.

"I should," she replied. "I'm an American."

"But you speak with a Russian accent."

"As do you, but you're not an American."

"Correct. But I've spent over half my adult life in the States," he said.

"How did that happen?" Maria asked, declining his offer for a re-fill.

"It's a short story. I went to the States with my parents—a teenager. After college and a brief stint in the Soviet Army, I joined the Russian Foreign Service, returned to the States and worked in New York for a few years."

"So, what are you doing here, a bartender with all that education and training?"

"I told you," he said, glancing over his shoulder as he reached for another beer for the gentleman at the end of the bar, "it's a short story. What about you?"

"It's shorter than yours. What's your name?"

"Igor."

"Goodnight, Igor." She laid a 1,000 ruble bill on the bar. "My name is Maria. Thanks for castrating that moron for me. I'm going to my room. I have a long, nonstop flight to the States tomorrow. If someone asks about me, tell him I left with someone else. Will you do that for me?"

"Of course!" he said, with a smile, wiping a glass and placing it in the rack overhead. On her way out, she re-arranged the scattered chairs and tables.

The next morning she found Igor's business card taped to her door:

Igor Yavolinski
C O N S U L T A N T
C-7-900-77-34 igor@center.tx

On the other side: the same in Russian. Next to the business card was a note: "He never showed up."

In the plane, Maria dialed her home number in the States. "Hi Mama. It's Maria. I'm at the Sheremetyevo airport near Moscow. I should be home around midnight, your time tomorrow."

"That's wonderful, my dear. I made arrangements for someone to leave the Mustang for you at the Minneapolis/St. Paul Airport. We have great weather. You can pick up the keys at the Hertz counter. Sammy has a friend who works there and he said he'd be happy to hold the keys until you arrive. Is that okay with you? He can't wait to see you."

"Well, I feel the same way. He's such a wonderful character. Getting the keys from the Hertz counter should work well. I'm dying to see you again."

"Same here, Sweetie. I'm so excited. I won't be able to sleep until after you are home—safe and sound. As you know, I'm a 'night hawk' and don't go to sleep until after mid-night anyway."

"I'm excited, too. And by the way, thanks for staying in touch with your emails; they have been a source of strength for me. I love you so much."

"Well, thank you, my dear. I love you, too. We can chat when you get here. Okay?"

"Yes. See you when I get home. Bye!"

Without making eye-contact with her seat partner, Maria pulled down the window curtain, punched her pillow into shape, and closed her eyes.

Chapter 2

Maria Martinova Luderenko's German/Ukrainian heritage probably had something to do with her childhood character: a spunky, no-nonsense personality.

In 1930, over a million German-Ukrainians lived in what was called The Ukraine: a Republic of the Soviet Union. Six years later, about one-fourth of them, mostly farmers, had vanished due to Stalin's three-pronged campaign to punish what he perceived to be rebellious farmers—a danger to his rule. His methods: deliberate starvation, deportation and shooting.

Thousands died of starvation due to a deliberate campaign on the part of the Soviet authorities to strip farmers of their crop-seed, farm animals and any grains or vegetables they had stored for their survival. Scavenger teams went from farm to farm and village to village stealing or destroying everything that looked like food. Anyone caught hiding food was shot.

The deportation was partially a deception, deliberately concocted by the authorities to make it easier for them to murder thousands of peasants. Many of the people—who were deported to Siberia and the Russian Far East—died of starvation and exposure. Crammed into box cars with no food or water, only the hardiest souls could survive the trip. Bodies were dumped from the trains as deaths occurred.

Maria's great grandparents, German-Ukrainians, were among the tough ones who made it to the Magadan Gulag in the Russian Far East where Maria's grandfather, Ivan, was born in 1936. Shortly thereafter, her great grandfather was shot for being a "Kulak," a rich farmer, in the Communist Party's view. He talked openly about someday owning a couple cows and maybe some chickens and a pig. He was poor, but even talking about being "rich" was dangerous.

The trauma Maria's great grandmother endured during the trip to the Russian Far East, the unforgiving winter weather, and now the senseless murder of her husband goaded her to rebel. She joined an underground resistance movement. She and her co-conspirators, betrayed by an informer, fled and hid in a cave. The NKVD, predecessor to the KGB, dynamited the entrance.

In 1952, Maria's grandfather, Ivan, escaped the Magadan Gulag and fled to Vladivostok, a seaport, geographically similar to San Francisco, on the Russian Far East, Pacific Ocean coast.

He joined the navy and met a clerk, Olga, who worked at the Headquarters of the Russian Pacific Fleet. They were married and had a son,
Martin, born in 1954 the year after Stalin died. A tall, blond, sturdy man
with a determined demeanor, Martin—eighteen—joined the army in
1971.

Because of his considerable talents as a soldier, Martin was selected for
officer training in 1974, was commissioned in 1977, married his fiancé, Ludmilla in 1978, and rose rapidly through the ranks during the Afghan war. Ludmilla attended college at the Vladivostok State Pedagogical Institute, graduated with honors, and earned certification to teach English in an elementary
school. Ludmilla remained in Vladivostok teaching school while her husband
served in Afghanistan.

Their daughter, Maria Martinovna, was born at a naval hospital in Vladivostok on June 19, 1981. In Russian schools, students began formal training
in English at the fifth grade, but Ludmilla vowed that her children would
be exposed to English from the time they were born. Medium height and
weight, with light brown hair, Ludmilla's hubris often infuriated Soviet
bureaucrats.

Upon being promoted to Lt. Colonel in 1985, Maria's father attended the
Malinovsky Tank Academy in Moscow for two years and then did a two-year
tour of duty as the commander of a tank battalion in Afghanistan.

Luderenko was decorated for heroism twice: once for pulling two of his
wounded soldiers from a burning tank, seconds before it exploded; the second
incident involved racing his command tank through an anti-tank minefield into
heavy rocket and mortar fire to rescue an infantry platoon from a Mujahadin
ambush.

In 1990, Luderenko was assigned to a Tank Brigade near Dresden, East
Germany following his tour of duty in Afghanistan. His wife and daughter
accompanied him to his new assignment.

While Maria's father rose in the ranks of the Soviet Army, Gorbachev"s
Glasnost i Perestroika liberalization policies plunged the USSR into political and
economic turmoil. A looming military defeat in Afghanistan compounded
Gorbachev's problems as the USSR plunged toward disintegration.

Chairman Gorbachev announced the dissolution of the Soviet Union on
December 25, 1991. By early 1992, hundreds of thousands of military personnel and their dependents were being withdrawn from Eastern Europe.

Facilities to accommodate returning army and air force personnel did not exist. Some of them were dumped in open fields when the planes landed, leaving the commanding officers to fend for themselves, their troops and their families.

At a Russian military base outside Dresden, Germany—one hundred miles due south of Berlin—Lt. Col. Luderenko guided the 211 remaining soldiers of his under-strength tank battalion into a giant, troop-transport plane.

Confident that all of his men were present and dressed in cold-weather uniforms, he helped his wife, Ludmilla, and ten-year-old daughter, Maria, into the plane. Luderenko whispered to Maria: "Soon we will be back on Russian soil and everything will be okay." She did not feel reassured, but offered him a weak smile and stared at her shoes. Two hours later, the plane landed on a frozen field.

The temperature inside the plane had been warm, but outside the weather had plunged to well below freezing. A slight breeze caressed elm and birch trees nearby. A full moon welcomed them back to their Motherland.

"Stay close to me," Luderenko said to his wife and daughter as they disembarked.

"Papa, what are we going to do? Where are we going?" asked Maria, feeling a flutter in her chest.

"I'm not sure, but I'll think of something. Nobody told me we would be landing here." His wife, Ludmilla, squeezed her daughter's hand: a silent reassurance.

Luderenko shouted, "Commanders, get your troops into formation." After telling Ludmilla and Maria to stay put, he went to the cockpit and confronted the pilot—"What the hell is going on?"

The pilot shrugged his shoulders and said, "Orders, Sir—to land anywhere near Moscow." *'If you land at an airport, you will be arrested,'* they said. "The airports are inundated with returning troops and families."

"Where are we?" Luderenko asked.

"Somewhere south of Moscow. That's all I can tell you. Sorry about that, Colonel. I have my orders."

Those dumb bastards—from Gorbachev and Yeltsen on down—they're the ones who should be arrested, Luderenko thought.

"Okay, I know the drill," Luderenko said. He returned to his troops.

Watching the soldiers scramble into formation, Luderenko contemplated his next move.

I should march my troops to the Kremlin, set up camp there, and let them figure out what to do with my troops and family. While he was considering that unlikely option, Major Sidorov approached and saluted.

"Sir, the troops are in formation. What do we do now?"

"Good question, Major," Luderenko replied, returning the salute. "I couldn't find out where we were going before we left Dresden and now all I know is that we are in the middle of a field near Moscow."

Looking around and slapping his hands together, Luderenko muttered, "Damn, it's cold. Those buildings over there,"—pointing toward a cluster of trees to his right-rear—"they look like an aristocrat's dacha. Check them out and see if anyone is there. Maybe they would let us use their phone."

"Will do, sir!" Major Sidorov saluted and ran toward the trees. In less than fifteen seconds, he was back.

"Sir, that's Chekhov's Estate. I was stationed at a base about twenty-five kilometers from here while I attended communications school. It's a museum. I visited it a couple times. Maybe we could march to the base and stay there. I know the way. That road over there will take us to the freeway that heads north to Moscow. The base is off to the left about three kilometers. It'll take us several hours."

"Thanks, Major. Good idea. You take the lead. I'll let the troops know what we are doing. My family and I will bring up the rear."

Standing before his battalion formation, Luderenko shouted, "Comrades of the mighty Soviet Army. It has been my honor to command you for the past two years. Tonight, under the full moon, we will march to a nearby Army base; we will do it with honor and dignity.

"We will seek accommodations there until we can muster out of the Army. I congratulate you for your courage and discipline during this trying time in our lives. When we arrive at the base, we'll make formation until I can make arrangements for our stay. Major Sidorov will lead the way. My family and I will bring up the rear. Major Sidorov, let's move out!"

Several hours later, nearing the base, Sidorov led his troops through a small village with gravel roads. As they approached the entrance to the base,

Maria noticed a huge round sign: twenty feet in diameter and one foot thick. Made of wood covered with tin, it had a huge, painted-red, hammer and sickle in the center, the symbol of the Soviet Union, which no longer existed. The red paint had faded and the tin was soiled, as if they were mourning the death of a great nation.

The sign was illuminated by a single floodlight. Blocking entrance to the base was a green wooden fence ten feet high, split by a drab, green, steel gate guarded by a soldier. He was protected from the elements by a small guard shack adjacent to the gate.

"Stay here with Mama," Luderenko said to his daughter. I'll talk to the guard and see if he can help us."

"Do you think we will be able to stay here tonight, Papa?" Maria said. "I'm cold and tired."

"We'll see, Malyskha, my little teddy bear," he said. She loved her Papa more than ever because she was seeing him in action doing things she never could have imagined.

While Sidorov brought the troops into parade formation, Luderenko approached the guard who snapped to attention, saluted and said, "Good evening, Sir!"

Luderenko, returning the salute, said, "Good evening, Corporal." What's your name?"

"Corporal Kavorsky, Sir."

"I'm Lt. Colonel Luderenko. I'm the commander of a tank battalion that was stationed in Germany." Motioning over his left shoulder with his head, he said, "We came from Germany and need a place to sleep."

The Corporal's eyes widened. "Sir, d-d-d-did you walk all the way from Germany?"

The troops roared with laughter.

Luderenko stifled a smile and replied, "No, Corporal, we didn't. I need to speak to the base commander."

"I'll need to contact my sergeant, Sir."

"How long will that take?"

"I don't know, sir. He's probably asleep and his phone is out, so I can't call him from here."

"Then go get him."

"But, Sir, I can't leave my post. I would get court marshaled, or," he gulped, "or worse." His voice cracked.

"You go get your Sergeant and I will take responsibility for your post duties until you and the sergeant return."

"But, Sir . . ."

"That's a direct order, Corporal. Go or I'll shoot you," Luderenko said sternly. "My men and family are cold and tired and need a place to sleep; we marched twenty five kilometers; I'm in no mood to argue with you."

"But . . ."

Luderenko pulled his pistol from the holster, pointed it at the Corporal and said, "It's your choice: a bullet or an errand for me."

The Corporal hesitated, briefly, chose the latter and disappeared through the gate.

Luderenko walked over to his wife and daughter who had taken it all in. "You weren't really going to shoot him, were you Papa?" Maria said, sincerely, loud enough for all the troops to hear.

"Of course not, my dear; I was going to do more: I was also going to roast him and eat him for dinner," he said with a wink and a smile at his wife.

Another roar from the ranks.

In a few minutes the Corporal led a man Maria recognized as someone very important through the gate. He wore a gray, double-breasted trench-coat and a round, military hat with gold braid on the bill. He carried himself with dignity and the demeanor of a man who did not tolerate fools—medium height and muscular, with a grand mustache.

Recognizing the General, Major Sidorov shouted, **"atten-HUT!"** order-ing the troops to come to attention. He turned and saluted. The General returned the salute. As the general walked toward Luderenko, they exchanged salutes. The general offered his hand and said, "I'm General Petrovsky, the Commanding General."

"Sir, this is my family. I'm Martin Ivanovich Luderenko, a commander of a tank battalion that was stationed near Dresden, until today. We flew in this evening and were dumped in an open field over by Chekhov's estate . . ."

"Excuse me for interrupting, Colonel." Turning to the Major, he said, rais-ing his voice, "Please put your men at Rest."

The major shouted: "REST!"

Turning to Luderenko, he said, "Now, what did you say your name is?"

"Lt. Colonel Martin Luderenko, Sir."

The General's eyes narrowed. "Didn't you get decorated in the Kremlin a few months back for heroism in Afghanistan?"

"Yes sir, I did."

The General saluted him. Then motioning to Ludmilla and Maria said, "And this is your wife and child?"

"Yes Sir, they are."

"Well, in front of your family and your troops, I extend my congratulations for your heroism in battle and the medals you received. I was in the audience that day."

The General turned to Luderenko's wife and child, introduced himself, put his hand on Maria's head and said, "You have a very brave father, young lady. You have every right to be proud of him."

"I love him very much," Maria replied. Pointing to the corporal, she said loudly, "Papa almost shot that corporal over there."

The troops exploded in laughter. The General looked at the terrified corporal and smiled and said, "Relax, Corporal, no one is going to get shot tonight."

Turning to Luderenko, the General said, "The Officer of the Day told me you are looking for a place to stay tonight—for your troops and family. Is that correct?"

"Yes sir, it is. You see . . ."

The General raised his hand to interrupt. "You don't need to fill me in on the details; I am aware of what is happening and I can assure you that you and your troops can stay here until we figure out the next step."

Maria heaved a sigh of relief and hugged her mother.

"General, I . . ." As he started to speak, Luderenko was interrupted by blinding headlights approaching from the village.

When the car stopped on the other side of the hammer and sickle sign, he could see that it was a chauffeured, government car—a black Zil sedan—used by high ranking government officials. The driver stepped out of the car and hurried around to the other side and opened the rear door.

Lieutenant General Dimerov struggled to move his oversized body out of the rear seat, stood by the car, looked around, caught General Petrovsky's eye, walked over to him and waited for a salute.

General Petrovsky stared at him, his arms hanging loosely at his side.

Flummoxed, General Dimerov looked around—"What the hell is going on here, General?"

General Petrovskey recognized the intruder with three stars on his epaulets as a Lt. General in the KGB's Third Directorate (military), outranking *him* by one star. Such blatant insubordination—failing to salute a senior officer—was unthinkable to Dimerov. It had never happened to him in his thirty-three years of military service.

General Petrovsky knew him to be amongst the most insufferable of the highest ranking officers in the KGB. Not all KGB officers were of his ilk. Most of them were honorable men, serving their country with dignity.

General Petrovsky stifled a strong impulse to tell General Dimerov to "piss off."

General Petrovsky's failure to salute, and respond immediately to General Dimerov's question about what was going on, roiled Dimerov.

"*Well, General?*" Dimerov snapped.

"These men, their commander and his family are here looking for a place to stay. They are evacuating from our base near Dresden. They were dumped in a field over by Chekhov's estate. The Colonel and most of his men are brave, decorated combat veterans of Afghanistan.

"They marched over here because they don't have anyplace to go. I told them we have plenty of room for them here until we can figure out the next step. Our training was cut in half when the country collapsed so I had to send hundreds of students home."

General Dimerov turned red in the face and fulminated, "Are you out of your mind General? Do you know what goes on at this base?"

"Well I should, General. I am the Commanding General."

"Yes, which makes me all the more concerned with what I'm seeing. Do I need to remind you General, that this is the most highly classified base in all of Russia? We train soldiers and airmen to operate the missile defense system that protects Moscow, and *the Kremlin*, from a nuclear attack. You can't bring—how many men are there?"

General Petrovsky looked at Luderenko for an answer.

"Two-hundred-eleven, sir."

"You can't bring 211 men who have been living in Germany for several years into this highly secure base. It would be an extremely serious breach of national security. Don't you realize some of them may have been recruited by West German and American agents for espionage in our country? And you want them to enter this base for an indefinite period of time? *It will never happen, General,*" he shouted.

Maria clutched her mother around the waste, buried her head in her abdomen, and started to cry.

Major Sidorov and the rest of the officers and men were cocky, combat veterans who had served in Afghanistan, and had seen their buddies killed and maimed. They were enjoying the confrontation between the generals at the entrance to the anti-missile training base. But Major Sidorov was the only one who saw what was coming down.

Moving carefully, he went to the rear of the formation, motioning two of his more athletic company commanders to join him.

"Listen," he said to them in a whisper, "I served with General Petrovsky, when he was a colonel and I was a lieutenant and I can see where this is going with that buffoon."

Looking at one of the captains, who looked like a bulldog, he said, "Get a man out of the rear ranks and post him over by the Zil and stay with him. Don't let the driver standing by the sedan move that car under any circumstance. Do you read me?"

"Loud and clear, even though you are whispering," the bulldog hissed, smiling.

Looking at the other captain, who had an aura of an aristocrat, and who eagerly anticipated a little action, the major said, "Stay close to me when we return to the formation and follow my lead. This is going to get ugly."

"Yes sir."

"Okay, move quietly," Sidorov whispered.

The major and his more sophisticated captain returned to the front of the formation. The driver snapped to attention when the bulldog and a trooper came over to the Zil; he knew better than to speak while standing at attention.

Maria's mother was trying to comfort her daughter who was hanging on to her and sobbing. Without warning to her mother, Maria broke away and strode, like a proud peacock, over to General Dimerov and shouted at him; **"I hate you! You are a bad man. Why won't you let us go to bed and sleep?"**

The troops could feel adrenalin roiling their blood, as if they were about to go into battle. They recognized a hot contest when they saw one and were prone to cheer when they saw an underdog break loose and gain an advantage over her opponent.

A roar of delightful cheers—like a crowd going wild when the home team scores the winning point at the last second of a game—shattered the icy mood, as if on cue from a fussy, orchestra conductor's baton.

Assaulted by the little girl's words and rebellious cheers, General Dimerov reacted as though he had been struck by a blinding dust-devil. He staggered back, almost lost his balance—recovered, and lurched forward toward Maria looking like a mad bull charging a toreador's red muleta.

Chapter 3

Within the KGB, the Third Directorate enforced political correctness. Officers of the directorate were placed in every echelon of the armed forces down to the company level of the fighting units and all other military organizations: land, sea or air. KGB officers reported directly to KGB headquarters in Moscow through their own chain of command.

For example, in the tank brigade to which Lt. Col. Luderenko's battalion belonged, there were nearly four thousand personnel; nineteen were KGB officers, some of whom were in Lt. Col. Luderenko's battalion—one for his headquarters and one for each of his three tank companies.

Besides criminal investigations (for example, for losing secret documents), the KGB officers had responsibilities for ensuring political reliability of the armed forces. They provided daily instruction to ensure political correctness and communist ideological convictions; they monitored official as well as personal telephone conversations and correspondence. They also maintained an extensive network of informers, recruited from among the soldiers of each unit.

Operational commanders, especially in the combat units, loathed the KGB leeches, who sucked them dry with their oppressive presence—their duplicitous natures. Everyone, at every level of command, knew informers were amongst them, but rarely knew who they were. A slip of the tongue could ruin an officer's career; the same could bring severe retribution for an enlisted man.

KGB officers could override a commander's tactical decision with impunity, provided they were not in trouble with their own superiors. Their overriding concern was their own careers. Some of the most brutal, most merciless, and occasionally, the most corrupt officers, rose to the highest ranks.

As General Dimerov lunged toward Maria, Major Sidorov made what—in the National Football League—would be called an illegal cross-body-block at the General's knees from the right rear. Simultaneously, the refined captain slammed into the General's upper torso from the left, driving him away from Maria and onto the ground. The General's hat was still rolling when the captain stood and placed his foot on the General's back.

The bulldog captain near the Zil kept a close eye on the chauffeur. The Sergeant didn't move an eyelash.

Maria's mother ran up to retrieve her daughter from the melee.

General Petrovsky looked at Luderenko with a strained smile, winked his approval, held his left hand down parallel to the ground, signaling Luderenko to stay put and let him handle the situation.

He walked over to the trapped general, who looked up and shouted to General Petrovsky: "Tell this bastard to take his foot off my back. I'll have you all shot, including that little bitch."

He got no further. The polished captain stood up and kicked him in the kidneys which elicited a gargantuan fart, sending the troops into another gust of laughter.

Maria, her head buried in her mother's abdomen, turned and looked at the troops and laughed through her tears, which caused some troops to tear-up because of the courage she had shown. Now she was one of them.

One of the officers resolved that one day the little girl would get a reminder of the courage she had shown on that cold, dark night in front of that dilapidated hammer and sickle sign. One of KGB officers in the ranks was thinking . . . *revenge*.

General Petrovsky handled the situation from there. He put General Dimerov in the base brig for the night, reminding him that the moment the Soviet Union collapsed and turned the corner away from totalitarianism toward democracy, he had lost his job. His days of pretentious, ass-like behavior amongst the troops were over. He ordered the General's chauffeur to take the Zil and report back to the motor pool at the Kremlin.

The General invited Luderenko and his family to stay with him and his wife in their quarters.

The following morning at breakfast, after small talk about the weather and what he would do with General Dimerov: He would be given a ride in one of the trucks going to Moscow that day. Then, General Petrovsky had a question.

"Would it be possible for you to stay a few days? I think it would be better for you, Colonel, to stay with your troops until we can be certain that they are properly deactivated from your battalion."

Maria spoke first. "I want stay here forever!"

The adults all smiled. "Well, my dear child," said the general, "I'm sure your parents have other plans that would be much better for all of you."

Ludmilla said, "That is very kind of you General. How long will we be here?"

"It may take a two or three weeks to get everything sorted out. Do you think that would work for you?" looking at Luderenko and his wife.

"The reason I asked is that as soon as I found out we would be returning to Vladivostok, I contacted the school principal where I taught before we went to Germany. He has an opening for the term that starts in a couple weeks. But I would like to get back there, get settled in our apartment before school starts."

The General looked at Luderenko.

"Well," Luderenko said, "I should probably stay as long as it takes to ensure my troops are properly mustered out of the Army. I suppose Ludmilla and Maria could go back as soon as transportation can be arranged and I could go soon thereafter."

"If that is acceptable to you Mrs. Luderenko, I am certain that can be arranged. We have military flights from a nearby airbase every other day to Vladivostok. Tell me when you want to go. The next one leaves tomorrow. I'll see if I can get you on that flight."

When they left the base the following morning, Maria told General Petrovsky that he was the nicest man she had ever met—besides her papa; no one would ever be as nice as he.

On the tarmac next to the plane, Luderenko hugged his wife, kissed her goodbye and then picked up Maria and gave her a special, long hug and kissed her as tears flooded his eyes. He put her down and watched as they boarded the plane; he stayed until the plane was in the air and out of sight.

He held on to the last moments with them as long as he could and then said out loud to himself, "Well, in this world, anything is possible." He had been wondering if he'd ever see them again.

His wife had once said, referring to their daughter, "I sometimes wonder if you love her more than you do me."

He had not replied, but he had a vague awareness that there was some substance embedded in her statement. In Afghanistan, he had heard rumors that his wife had been seen with other men. But he disregarded them as being the dirty-work of some disgruntled soldier in his command who had been recruited by the KGB into the informer network. Still . . . .

Chapter 4

In the early 1960's, Nikita Khrushchev, Chairman of the Communist Party of the Soviet Union, initiated a massive, housing-upgrade project. Five-story apartment buildings popped out of the ground like popcorn on a hot griddle. They appeared with amazing regularity, a mute testimonial to Soviet keenness for massive construction projects.

Each building had a stairwell and a tiny elevator; mail boxes lined one wall in the small lobby of each building. A massive, steel entry door provided protection from foul weather and intruders.

Every apartment had a bathtub and a sink in a small room; next to it was a toilet in a narrow, three-by-six-foot chamber. The kitchen had a one-half-booth built into a wall behind a tiny table; a gas stove, and a small refrigerator; a mini-laundry washer stood on the opposite wall.

A door in the kitchen led to a ten-by-ten-foot bedroom. A twelve-by-ten-foot multi-purpose room served as living, family, dining, and bedroom spaces. All apartments had double entry doors: the outer—wood with padded, faux leather; the inner: a heavy steel door with a peep hole and a lock. Two doors provide added insulation and reduced noise transference between the hallway and the apartment.

The doors opened into the apartment to a small entry with coat hangers on the wall to the right opposite the bathroom door on the left. A box held slippers which were exchanged for shoes upon entry. The multipurpose room was located opposite the entry door. The kitchen was down a short hall to the left, beyond the bathroom; the entry to the bedroom was opposite the stove, to the right.

The apartments were dubbed "Khruschevski": ubiquitous, with cracker-box-like architecture. Construction of the new apartment houses extended across the Soviet Union from St. Petersburg in the west to Vladivostok in the east.

During the next several decades people living in large cities were able to move out of eighteenth and nineteenth century shacks into modern apartments with indoor toilets, hot and cold running water—when it was hot . . . and running—electricity and sometimes a small balcony, often used for drying clothes.

A month after Ludmilla and her daughter returned to their "Kruschevska" in Vladivostok, a substitute teacher came to Ludmilla's classroom with a note from the Principal. She stared at the woman. "Why are you delivering this note? What's going on?" She could feel a knot developing in her stomach.

Usually, student monitors carried notes; this was highly unusual. "The Principal has arranged for me to take your class for the rest of the day. He didn't tell me why. He asked me to tell you to come to his office."

"Did he say why?"

"No."

With a worried look on her face, Ludmilla gave the substitute the plans for the rest of the day and departed.

"What's going on, Mr. Levorov?"

"Well, I'm not sure. All I know is that I received a phone call from the Pacific Fleet Headquarters here in Vladivostok ordering me to have you report to their Personnel Department. They said they have a telegram for you regarding your husband. They said it was urgent. I thought he was in the Army."

"He is. He was due back any day now, but the nearest Army base is several miles north of here, so it's possible that urgent messages would be sent through the Navy. But why would there be an urgent message. Is there something wrong?"

"All I know is what I've told you. You have less than two hours before the navy offices close. You had better get going. Take your daughter with you and don't bother to come back."

In the car, Maria asked, "What's happening Mama?" She did not like the anxious look on her mother's face.

"I don't know, Malyskha." That's why we are going to the Naval Headquarters—to find out."

Maria made a fist and pounded her chest.

"What are you doing? Why did you do that?"

"I feel funny in my chest sometimes. If it gets really bad and I feel like I'm going to faint, I pound on my chest and it stops."

"Are you sure you are okay?"

"Yes, Mama. I'll be fine. I miss my Papa," she said, staring at her mother.

"I know, dear, so do I."

They walked up the massive stone steps leading to the Naval Headquarters on Aleutskaya Prospect and entered the personnel office lobby.

A middle-aged man in a security uniform sat at a desk at the entrance. He checked Ludmilla's identification and waved her in.

More than the number of students in her fifth-grade class sat in the waiting area: about thirty. A removable sign "BACK IN ONE HOUR" perched on the service window counter.

It was a little more than an hour before closing time, and almost two hours since lunch-time, the intended purpose of the sign.

Ludmilla's heart sank. The frustration she was accustomed to, rose to an unusual level. In Russia, when life and death matters were not at stake, the typical response to such situations was: "It's Russia." The epithet expressed a profound resignation to the frustrations of daily existence experienced by Russians. Long delays in getting anywhere with the plodding bureaucracies was one thing, but what lay behind it was another: surly clerks, barely functioning services, bribery—the list goes on.

But this was not a normal situation to Ludmilla. "How long has that sign been up there?" she asked, looking at no one in particular in the waiting room.

"About an hour. They are taking their fifteen-minute afternoon break," a man said, sarcastically.

"Spacebo," Ludmilla said, thanking her informer.

She went up to the window and could see clerks at their desks—all women. She knocked on the window to get their attention. No one looked up. She knew the drill, but with due respect, gave them a second chance to respond. She knocked again. Nothing. She picked up a metal trash container and banged it on the counter. One clerk looked at her and went back to chatting.

She stepped away from the window, picked up a chair and threw it at the window, sending shards of glass flying into the room. The clerks ducked to avoid injury, hurling harsh obscenities at her.

Someone in the waiting room shouted to the security man: "Do something, you idiot, before she turns on us." Another said, "If there were another window, I'd throw a bigger chair through that one; this woman has tits!" A smattering of chuckles rippled across the room.

The security guard, checking a woman in, didn't look up. She, looking frightened, turned and walked out the door.

"It's not my job to stop riots; I only check people in and out," the security guard said, looking at the waiting-room crowd.

While the glass was still flying, a naval officer entered the office at the far end. He walked to the service window and confronted Ludmilla.

"What the hell are you doing?"

"I came here to pick up a telegram. I'm told it has an urgent message. Do you know anything about it?"

"No I don't, but the way I'm feeling now, I'd probably hold it for a couple weeks if I did. Do you know the penalty for destroying state property? You could go to jail."

"Oh, for god's sake, Commander, that horrible time in our lives is over. These citizens have much better things to do than sit and wait for your clerks to get off their dead asses and do their jobs."

Maria began to cry.

The Commander stared at her. "Is this your daughter," nodding to Maria. "Yes."

"I would think you could set a better example for her than getting angry and throwing a chair through the window."

"Then you're a part of the problem in there. Where can I get the telegram?"

"You'll have to wait here. Security?" The Commander said, sticking his head through the broken window and looking at the guard. "Take this woman's name and address."

"Yes sir," he replied.

By the time Ludmilla had given her name and address, the commander was at her side handing her the telegram. It had been opened.

"You can go. There will be no charges brought against you," he said in a sympathetic tone. His attempt to relieve her stress did not reassure her. She felt a little dizzy, but recovered quickly.

Ludmilla put the telegram in her handbag, thanked the Commander, took Maria's hand and walked toward the car. *Whatever the news, it will have to wait until we are home.*

When the Commander walked back through the office, he pointed at the civilian supervisor and said, "I want to see you in my office immediately. "The rest of you," he said, gesturing, "clean up this mess. Anybody, who leaves work before all of our citizens are served, will be fired."

Special Operations Forces (SOF) have operated in varying sizes and formations, with a wide variety of missions throughout the history of warfare. Generally, the missions were to achieve disruption behind enemy lines by hit-and-run attacks and acts of sabotage. Other significant roles were reconnaissance: to locate enemy positions, strength and weapons capabilities.

An early, special-operations force, the Knights Templar, was established in the Middle Ages in Western Europe by Christian military units to protect pilgrims traveling to and from Jerusalem. Later, in several of the Crusades, they operated against Muslim Army units, attempting to steal supplies or seize valuables held by their enemy. The warriors were known as fierce fighters, which, at their peak, numbered between fifteen hundred and two thousand.

Another eighteen thousand members of the Knights Templar, which became a religious order of the Catholic Church, served in support roles of various kinds, including businesses and rather sophisticated banking systems for the secular rulers of the time. Their presence was an integral part of the Church throughout Europe and during the Middle East for two hundred years.

The French branch of the organization was disbanded when King Philip IV arrested the Knights Templar under his jurisdiction on Friday, October 13, 1307, an unlucky day for those arrested; this is said to be the origin of the superstition that any Friday the 13th is an unlucky day. The Knights Templar throughout Europe soon suffered the same fate.

During the Napoleonic wars, rifle and sabotage units (referred to this day as "sappers") had roles in reconnaissance, assassination, and clandestine destruction of enemy positions. During the French occupation of Vietnam, Vietnamese military resistance units adopted the "sapper" designation.

The Viet Cong R-37 Sapper Battalion was active in the Da Nang area of Vietnam during the French occupation and remained active until the Tet Offensive in 1968, when its commander was wounded and captured as his battalion was decimated.

As war weapons and materiel became more sophisticated, the demand for more effective unconventional warfare increased. Today, most countries, with any significant military power, have Special Operations Forces (SOF). The United States has major special operating forces in each of its four branches of service, far out-distancing any other country in scope and sophistication.

As a general rule, Special Operating Teams are the basic combat operating teams of larger special operating groups or brigades. Teams consist of about fourteen enlisted men, a couple of sergeants, a warrant or leading petty officer, and two or three commissioned officers.

The teams' missions and the make-up of personnel specialties vary, depending on the branch of service; but generally, operational deployment includes reconnaissance, airborne assault, direct action operations, infiltration and exfiltration by air, land and sea—raids—and recovery of personnel and special equipment.

Following the attacks on New York and Washington in 2001, NATO countries realized the need for coordination and eventually the establishment of a NATO Special Operations Force that could serve the needs of the NATO Alliance more efficiently than relying on individual countries when crises arose within NATO's ambit.

C h a p t e r 5

Upon arrival at their Khruschevska apartment, Ludmilla entered the bathroom to read the telegram, which came from the Headquarters of the Department of the Army at the Kremlin.

She had renovated her bathroom. She knocked out the wall that separated the toilet from the bathtub and the sink, and replaced the tub with a corner shower stall. That left enough room along the wall by the shower stall for a narrow multi-level, chrome covered shelf.

"We regret to inform you that your husband, Lt. Col. Martin Ivanovich Luderenko died on Wednesday in an airplane accident near Irkutsk. Please contact your nearest Army base for details and any follow-up that is necessary."

She stared at the words as if they had no meaning. Despite the fact that General Dimerov's job with the military ended with the collapse of the Soviet Union, he was still a respected—however malodorous that was to Ludmilla— member of the KGB . . . later renamed the FSB. From the moment he was brought down by her husband's officers, she feared the worst; now her worries were over. Her husband had been murdered. She would learn later that General Petrovsky also died in the crash of the sabotaged, executive jet.

Since the Navy commander handed her the telegram in an open envelope with words and a demeanor that implied his condolences, she had been rehearsing how she would tell Maria her father was dead. She had come up with nothing. And now Maria was pounding on the door. "Mama, please open the door."

"The door is unlocked, Malyskha."

Maria pulled the door open and saw her mother sitting on the toilet stool with the seat cover down. Her head was in a towel and she was crying.

She lifted her head and looked at Maria. Tears were rolling out of her eyes onto her cheeks. Her tears were for Maria, not for the sadness she felt because of her husband's death. She had already mourned him for a month because she was convinced General Dimerov would exact a horrible revenge. She felt helpless to do anything about it.

But, what to do about her daughter who would be devastated by the news of her father's death? She had no idea. And now, time was pressing in on her like a humid, hot, summer day.

"Don't cry Mama. I know you are crying because Papa is dead. The angel told me I would be a little sad and that I would miss my Papa a lot. But not be too sad because Papa is with her in heaven, which is where everyone goes when they die."

"What are you talking about?" her mother retorted, sniffling and wiping away her tears. Raising her voice, she said, "What do you know about angels? You've never been to church. You don't know anything about religion," her mother sobbed. Why didn't you tell me?"

"An angel came to me in a dream last night and told me. I cried a lot; I didn't want to believe it; that's why I didn't tell you. I still don't want to believe it, but that's what the telegram is about, isn't it?"

"Yes."

"Well then, everything will be all right. We will have to go on without Papa."

Ludmilla threw the towel aside and took her daughter in her arms and held her, tenderly rubbing her back. "I'm so sorry. I wish there were something I could do to bring him back. He was such a good man—a good Papa."

"I know Mama." Maria replied, staring at the shower stall, wistfully. Tears fell from her cheeks.

Several months after her husband's death, Ludmilla invited a man she had been dating to dinner at their apartment.

It was September, the most beautiful time of the year in Vladivostok. The rest of the year is, in general, miserable: extreme cold during a long winter; chilly, overcast drizzle in the spring, with scattered clouds and rain, during a warm summer . . . and chilly, but pleasant in the fall.

His name: Vadim, derived from an old, Russian word that means "dispute." When her mother introduced them, Maria thought he looked like a weasel, even though weasels are among the cutest animals extant. Vadim smiled— insincerely—and told her she was a very beautiful child.

It was the shape of his head that reminded her of a weasel: round with a low forehead, pug-ears, a big nose and a bald head. His appearance was one thing, but her intuition frightened her. The contrast with her Papa was striking; Maria wondered about her mother's judgment: *What on earth is she doing with this guy?*

Maria assumed he was trying to win her over so she would not oppose her mother's involvement with him.

During dinner, he got drunk; nastiness followed. He said to Ludmilla: "I know you think you are better than I am because you have an education and work in a school. I'm just a laborer on a road repair crew. You think that, don't you?"

"Of course I don't, Vadim. If I did, I wouldn't spend time with you and wouldn't have invited you to dinner."

"Oh, yeah," he said sneeringly, "the only reason you invited me here was to get her". . . looking at Maria, "approval." She doesn't like me, and you knew she wouldn't like me. Isn't that so?" he asked.

"I don't know what you are talking about, Vadim. You are talking nonsense. You've had too much to drink. I think it's time for you to go home."

"Oh sure. That's what you always say: 'You've had too much to drink,'" he said, in a falsetto voice, waving his head back and forth. "Well, I'm not buying your bullshit anymore!"

Maria's mother asked him, politely, to leave.

"I'll leave when I'm ready to leave. Got that? You uppity bitch!"

"We can talk about this tomorrow, if you want to. You are not going to talk like that in front of my daughter."

"So . . . who's going to stop me? You? This little pipsqueak? The two of you couldn't throw out a wimpy cat."

His behavior rounded what looked like a curve toward violence.

After gentle coaxing by Maria's mother, he decided to leave peacefully, although reluctantly.

He gave Maria a menacing look on the way out, as if to suggest she were responsible for the trouble.

Maria had seen the man before and she didn't like what she saw. But she couldn't remember when. That night, she was awakened by a dream. Trying to go back to sleep, she remembered where she had seen her mother's friend, Vadim. It was at a food market.

She and her mother were standing in line to buy tomatoes and cucumbers when a man came up behind her, cupped his hands over her eyes, pushed his knees into the back of her knees, disengaging them. She almost fell. Maria remembered her mother being very displeased with his juvenile prank in a public place. It happened while her papa was in Afghanistan.

The morning after the dream, Maria said to her mother: "I don't like Vadim. I wish you would stop seeing him."

She didn't stop. She continued to date him, but she didn't invite him to their apartment again.

A month after the dinner, she had a bruised eye when Maria went to the kitchen for Sunday breakfast. "What happened, Mama?"

"Oh, I ran into a coat hanger at a restaurant last night." But Maria wasn't buying the explanation. Maria didn't think much more about it until a couple weeks later, when, on a Friday night, someone knocked on their door—the inner steel door.

Her mother looked through the peep-hole to see who was there. It was Vadim. He was drunk.

"Let me in," he screamed.

"You're not coming in, she said loudly. You're drunk and I don't want to see you anymore. I told you several times. It's over, Vadim. Go away!"

"Please, Ludmilla? I'll stop drinking. We'll go on picnics together with your daughter. I miss you. I'm so lonely," he pleaded.

"I've heard all that before, but you always go back to drinking and acting like an ass."

"I'll get you for this," he screamed.

A babushka, living in the apartment next door, came into the hallway. "Shut the fuck up! I can't sleep with all this screaming."

Vadim, swaying, looked at her, whacked the stocky, white-haired, old woman across the face and sent her reeling back into the apartment. She slammed the door to prevent him from coming after her. Ludmilla had seen it all through the peephole.

She saw Vadim leave the hallway and start down the stairwell. A few moments later, a banging on the steel door made a sound that could only be produced by a heavy rock or concrete object. Ludmilla went to the door and looked through the peephole. Vadim was back. Babushka, again angry, watched what happened through her peephole.

As Ludmilla backed away, Vadim slammed the huge rock against the peep-hole.

The steel, peephole-cylinder insert holding the magnifying glass in place, shot from the door like a bullet and struck Ludmilla between the eyes with devastating force.

Vadim saw her fall backward and hit the floor face-up. He saw Maria come out of the multi-purpose room as he turned and fled toward the stairwell.

Chapter 6

The USS Abraham Lincoln is deployed with the United States Fifth Fleet's Area Of Responsibility (AOR) to support Maritime Security Operations (MSO). MSO promotes stability and global prosperity. These operations complement the counter-terrorism and security efforts of many nations and seek to disrupt violent extremists' attacks or to transport personnel, weapons and other materiel.

The United States has become increasingly entwined in the economic and security issues with the rest of the world. Her security depends upon protecting overseas interests as well as encouraging peace and stability around the globe. Forward presence, by the U.S. aircraft carrier battle groups and amphibious ready groups, helps accomplish this mission. When the word "crisis" surfaces at the White House, the first question the president asks is: "Where is our nearest carrier?" "Crisis" includes political, military and humanitarian assistance operations.

A Carrier Battle Group (CBG)—operating in international waters—does not need the permission of host countries for landing or over-flight rights. Nor does it need to build or maintain bases in countries where our presence may cause political or other strains. Aircraft carriers are sovereign territory for any nation.

A relevant fact is that most of the surface of the globe is water. This characteristic is not lost on our political decision-makers, who use the Navy aircraft carriers as a powerful instrument of diplomacy, strengthening alliances or answering the call to assist in a crisis.

Vadim flew down the five flights of stairs. *She looks like she's dead and I could be charged with murder.*

In a restaurant on their first date, Ludmilla had gone to the ladies' room and left her purse on her chair. He saw her key ring out of one corner of his eye and out of the other a slab of cheese that resembled a bar of soap. *Eureka!*

Before she returned, he had impressions of the car and house keys, had split the cheese bar in half, stuffed the impressions in his pocket and was chewing on the last of the remaining cheese when she sat down.

"Great tasting cheese," he said, chasing it with a swallow of vodka, looking at her sideways.

When he was much younger, he worked at an auto repair shop. He would take a bar of soap, make impressions of customers' keys, make keys from the impression, and steal their cars. It was easy; he kept a record of their addresses. For a price, he would turn the cars over to "chop shop" owners, who would strip the cars and sell the spare parts.

It struck him, half-way down the stairwell; *I have the keys in my pocket. I could steal her car! If she's dead, she won't need it and if she isn't? Well, I'll be long gone before she knows it's missing.*

He reached the building exit and headed for the rear where Ludmilla parked her car.

"Shit! It isn't here! Looking three-sixty, he didn't see it anywhere. He ran to the front to see if she had parked it on the street or at an adjacent Prawdoocty: a convenience store. That's where he found it. *No more public transportation for me,* he thought.

He unlocked the door of her Lada, jumped in and slipped the key into the ignition with a twist. *Pieces of junk!! The key works in the car door but not the ignition! Not to worry. I'll hot-wire this mother-fucker! I'm an auto mechanic, for crissake!*

Which he did; he was on his way.

Nearing his home on a wide boulevard, lightning struck again. DAMN*! I've got a key to the apartment and that little bitch is a witness to my murder . . . if her mother is dead. I could get in and kidnap her, or if I have to, kill her too, before she can identify me.* Impulsively, he twirled the steering wheel, sending the Lada into a wild U-turn and headed back to Ludmilla's apartment.

Sitting in his police car under a shade tree, Anton washed down the last of his sandwich with a bottle of beer.

For five years, he sat in this same spot, eating a kolbasa sandwich and drinking a beer or two, waiting for the moment when something would happen that would make it possible for him to impress his boss.

Right before his eyes, some crazy bastard in a green Lada made an illegal U-turn in the middle of the block, forcing a car to swerve up onto the sidewalk and crash into a light-pole.

Spring, summer, fall and winter—he left his engine running for just this moment. The chase was on. This was his moment! Anton, whose name in Greek means "go into action," went into action.

He knew how to conduct car chases, *professionally,* because he had seen them in American movies. He knew everything: how to box them in; how to make them spin out; how to be restrained in pursuit; how to be careful in a shootout not to kill any bystanders. He knew it all and he was about to take that criminal down.

Excited, he pulled into the street without looking for on-coming traffic, forcing a car to swerve and hit a car parked on the opposite side of the street.

He forgot to turn on the red/blue flashing lights. He was chasing a criminal who did not know he was being chased.

Maria heard the screaming and horrendous blast that sent the peep-hole crashing into her mother's forehead. *Now what?*

She ran to her mother, screaming, "Mama, Mama . . . are you all right?" She knew the answer before she stopped screaming; she could see the severe wound the peephole "bullet" had made on her mother's forehead.

She knelt beside her and looked at her face. She was already turning blue; there was no sign of life. *None.*

"Mama, Mama," she said, picking up her head and holding it in her arms. "Please don't die, Mama, *please!"* Tears rolled down her cheeks.

Maria put her mother's head down gently and lifted her right arm to check her pulse. She couldn't find one, but wasn't sure where to put her finger. She checked her own pulse for a clue and tried it in the same spot on her mother. *Nothing.*

She ran to the phone and dialed "0." When the operator came on the line, she shouted: "Operator," she said, crying, "Someone has killed my mom, but I'm not sure. I'm eleven years old. I need help! Can you help me, please?"

"Where are you? What is your address?"

Maria gave her the address and said, "Please hurry. I don't know what to do. My name is Maria." She wiped her tears with her sleeve.

"I'll notify the ambulance service and police immediately. Stay where you are. I'll get someone on your line to talk to you while you wait. Is that okay?"

"Yes, but please hurry. I'm so scared."

Chapter   7

"Go into action" Anton—in hot pursuit, holding onto the steering wheel, his knuckles white—stared at the green Lada, three car-lengths away.

He had pulled out his revolver and placed it on the seat beside him, but it had fallen onto the floor in one of his frantic braking episodes. With every swerve, the pistol and beer bottles made glass and heavy-metal music. The sun was in its denouement of the warm summer day.

Anton had watched a few American cowboy movies: his favorite—The Lone Ranger. He was fascinated by fast-draw artists. He practiced his fast draw for years. His colleagues all conceded: he was the fastest draw in the East—The Russian Far East, that is. But he had never drawn in anger; maybe this was his chance.

He wished he were riding Silver, or Trigger or Champion, instead of this aging nag. He had shopped for a silver bullet for his pistol, but was disappointed; people had no clue what he was talking about.

He was gaining on the green Lada and getting close enough that he, in his professional judgment, decided that a quick "tail-flicking maneuver" would send the criminal into a tail spin, forcing him into some tight spot that would allow a quick-draw and arrest of the criminal; "suspect" was not in his vocabulary.

The Lada slowed and made a U-turn as Anton was initiating his tail-flicking maneuver, denying Anton his prized moment of heroism. What was worse, his engine began to sputter and died, leaving barely enough time to follow in a U-turn and make it to the curb in front of a Khruschevska apartment. He had run out of gas.

As he rolled to a stop, he saw the Lada driver stop near the entrance of the apartment house set back from the street about thirty yards. The criminal jumped out of his car and raced toward the entrance. Anton ran in hot pursuit.

Half-way to the apartment house, he reached for his pistol.

"Damn."

He retrieved his pistol from the car and ran toward the apartment house as two police cars were pulling alongside the Lada.

What are those bastards doing here? This is my case. One was Lieutenant Nikitin; the other a patrolman named Titov.

"What are you doing here, Petrov?" the lieutenant asked.

"I was chasing a traffic violator. He made an illegal U-turn on Lenin Pros-pect. I was getting ready to issue him a "tail-flicking maneuver" when he pulled in here and ran into this apartment.

"What was he wearing?" Nikitin, a former Spetsnaz Special Forces officer, asked.

"A red shirt and black pants," Anton replied.

"Someone murdered a woman here a few minutes ago," Nikitin said. "The woman's eleven-year old daughter is in the apartment, alone at the scene of the crime. Be careful; he could still be here."

Anton's adrenalin reached stratospheric heights. He did the quickest draw of his life and assumed a combative stance: bent knees, both arms outstretched to steady his two-hand grip on his pistol, and surveyed the area with extreme care, moving his weapon from left to right and back again, like a pendulum on a grandfather clock.

"For god's sake Petrov, put that damn thing away," Nikitin said.

With Petrov calmed, the lieutenant said, "Titov, stay out here and keep an eye on the fire escape. Petrov come with me. When we get inside, I'll take the elevator to the fifth floor. The apartment number is 512. You take the stairway. Detain any man you see inside the apartment house or anyone on the fire escape. Are my instructions clear?"

Both patrolmen replied in the affirmative.

Chapter 8

Maria hung up the phone and returned to her mother, hoping she might find her alive. She was not.

My God! I have no parents and no relatives that can take care of me. Where will I go? What will I do? What will become of me?

These questions, bombarding a dark, crystal ball, temporarily paralyzed her thinking—but not for long. She pulled herself together and began prioritizing what she needed to do.

First: survival. But how? She had seen her mother placing money in her "home banking account." Russia was opening banks to the public, but they were not for her mother.

She went to the glass enclosed cabinet in the multipurpose room, reached behind a row of books and pulled out a jar stuffed with ruble bills. She had no idea how much money was in there; she didn't have time to count.

She retrieved a sizeable wad of bills and put them in a plastic bag. She lifted her skirt and stuffed the roll of bills in the crotch of her panties. She didn't bother with the change.

She put her mother's key chain in the side pocket of her jacket hanging on the wall. The car would be of some value. She had vague thoughts of leaving Vladivostok. Vadim would be a threat the rest of her life.

The babushka next door could be of some help, but Maria hardly knew her—didn't even know her name. She had borrowed a tablespoon of butter from her for her mother and had introduced herself at that time, but if the babushka mentioned her name, she didn't remember it. *She is a recluse and rarely comes out of her apartment.*

She found a bed sheet and covered her mother's body, telling her she loved her as she placed the sheet over her head.

If Papa went to heaven to be with the angels, I'm certain Mama has gone there, too. She felt better—until she heard a key being inserted into the steel door. She looked at the door and saw Vadim staring at her through the hole in the door. She froze . . .

Chapter 9

Maria Martinovna Luderenko stirred, opened her eyes and looked at the video screen monitoring the flight from Moscow to San Francisco. They had passed over St. Petersburg, over the Scandinavian countries, Greenland and were well within the Arctic Circle.

She lifted the window curtain and looked down. She saw the sun—traveling with them—backlighting the cracks in the ice, creating a lively tableau that took her breath away. At nearly six hundred miles per hour, at 35,000 feet, the backlighting created a pas de nivata aqua: shining cracks dancing on the ice within the boundaries of the sun's reflecting orb.

When the sun hit an opaque surface, the dance paused, and resumed when the back-lighted ice reappeared. The "Calm of the Angel," a phrase she had adopted to identify the "angel experience," washed over her. The divine tableau, framed by her window, lasted for almost an hour.

When the sun's graceful dance with the cracks in the ice ended, she glanced at her seat-partner's book:

SURVIVORS OF PREDATORY PRIESTS

The "Calm of the Angel" vanished.

Chapter 10

While the plane was crossing the Canadian border and heading toward San Francisco, Sammy was finishing his chores in the barn. In her exchange of emails with Maria, Pat had not mentioned that they had bred Dana the year before because they wanted to surprise Maria with a foal when she returned from Russia.

The colt had the same dark-brown color as Dana, including a white, diamond-shaped spot on his forehead. Sammy was energized about Maria's return and even more thrilled that they would surprise her with a colt.

He knew she would be delighted by this addition to her family. If she had come a couple months earlier, she would have enjoyed seeing Dana mothering her colt. But that was not to happen since they would be weaning the colt from Dana shortly before Maria's arrival.

Chapter 11

Maria froze . . . but only momentarily.

She ran to the kitchen and picked up a long, sharp knife, went into the bathroom and locked the door.

Vadim twisted the key several ways, moving it slightly in and out each time; it wasn't working. He could see the sheet over Ludmilla's body and knew that he had killed her. The only witness to his crime—he thought—was Maria. His only hope was to kill her, but how?

He heard the elevator going down. It could be someone descending, or they could be waiting on a lower floor to go down . . . or up.

He had taken a chance on going back to the apartment before the cops arrived. His risk factor was rising like a rocket headed for outer space. He tried the key a few more times, gave up and headed for the stairwell. As he descended to the first landing, he heard the elevator doors opening.

Anton had made his way up to the third floor landing when he heard footsteps: *descending*. He drew his pistol and stood on the third floor landing in his ready-to-fire, both-hands-on-the-pistol stance—pointing his pistol up the stairs.

Vadim was moving fast. He descended to the fourth floor landing. Looking down into the barrel of a police pistol pointed at his head, he became a marble statue before the officer exploded.

"FREEZE!" Anton screamed, in a high-pitched voice, quickly modulating to a very low, menacing tone; his pistol shaking, Anton continued, "Don't move, or I'll shoot!"

Vadim could spot a phony from the moon. He started toward Anton . . . one step . . . another step . . . another step.

"I'll blow your head off!" Anton shouted, lowering his aim to Vadim's knees. His shaking hands inadvertently pulled the trigger.

"*Click*." Then, "*Click . . . Click . . . Click*," in rapid succession, as Vadim pounced on him like a mountain lion on a sleeping deer.

Anton had forgotten to load his pistol before leaving home that morning.

The decline of the three last steps gave Vadim the momentum of a hurricane hitting a coast at 200 miles an hour. He slammed Anton up against the wall, put his hands around his neck, and pressed with his thumbs. Anton's face swelled and turned purple.

Lieutenant Nikitin heard the ruckus below; he descended, cautiously, with his pistol drawn.

From the fourth floor landing, he said, calmly, "This is Lieutenant Nikitin. Release the officer or I'll shoot."

Vadim hesitated. "You can't shoot me without hitting him."

"BAM!" Nikitin knew more about the human skeleton than Vadim. He aimed at his lower spine.

Vadim screamed, fell back onto the steps and then forward onto his chest.

Nikitin came down the steps . . . calmly, and put a bullet into the back of Vadim's head. "You okay?" he asked Anton, who was gasping for air.

"Of course, sir!" he said, in a raspy voice, shaking into a posture of bravado. "We showed that bastard, didn't we?"

"Yeah, we did," Nikitin replied. "Go get Titov. We have a couple bodies to take care of. I'm going up to make sure the girl is okay."

Nikitin looked through the hole in the door. He tried the door handle. The door was locked. "This is Lieutenant Nikitin of the police department. Are you okay in there?" Silence. "If you are okay, please speak up. The murderer is dead and I'm here to help you."

Maria had heard the scuffling and shots, but she had no idea who did the shooting or who got shot, if anyone. She did know it was not Vadim talking; it was the voice of a stranger, but she wasn't taking any chances.

"Come on! Open the door!" Nikitin screamed, pounding on the door.

The babushka next door heard the shots and Nikitin's pleas. She could see him through her peephole.

Babushka opened her door and said, "I'm her neighbor. The girl's name is Maria. Do you want me to talk to her? I saw the bastard slam that rock into Ludmilla's door. Is the girl's mother okay?"

"She's dead." Nikitin said and introduced himself. "See what you can do."

"Maria, this is your neighbor. It's okay. That monster is dead and you are safe. Come and open the door."

Recognizing Babushka's voice, Maria relented. She came out of the bathroom, opened the door and threw herself into the arms of the police officer and started to cry.

"My mama is dead," she whispered through her tears.

Babushka put her hand on Maria's head and said, "You are safe now."

Nikitin released her gently, held her shoulders, looked at her and said, "You seem to be about the same age as my daughter."

"I'm 11," she said, wiping away her tears. "Thank you for rescuing me. I was terrified!"

"I'm sure you were," Nikitin said. "I'm sorry it took a while to get here."

Anton and Titov arrived.

Turning to Babushka, the lieutenant said, "Did you see what happened?"

"Yes. I saw that idiot slam a rock into Ludmilla's peephole and then head toward the stairwell."

"What was he wearing?"

"A red shirt and black pants."

"Good. Thank you. I shot the right man. Titov, call the coroner and the undertaker. You know the drill. I'm going back to the station." Looking at Babushka, he said, "Can you look after this girl?"

"Yes, officer, I can. Thank you for all you have done. I was worried about my neighbors after seeing that creep treat them the way he did. Come, Maria, to my apartment until the officers are done. You can stay with me tonight."

"Go back to your patrolling, Petrov," Nikitin said, with a nuance of disdain in his voice.

Chapter 12

Maria—exhausted—wanted to sleep. Babushka re-arranged the multi-purpose room into a bedroom. Maria fell asleep quickly. She kept the money and keys under her pillow.

Babushka, after making a light breakfast, said, "Maria, what do you want to do?"

"I'm certain of only one thing: I want to leave Vladivostok. Maybe go to Khabarovsk. I'm not sure about Khabarovsk. I haven't had time to think about it. It's just a vague feeling I have."

"Do you have relatives or friends of your mother you could stay with here?"

"No, I don't. I want to leave immediately. Like tonight."

"But why? You must have friends at school to say goodbye to; they might want to throw a party for you or something."

"That's why I want to leave tonight. I don't want any of that. I want to leave. This morning, after I woke up . . . well, I was wondering if you would like to have Mama's car. It's mine to give away. Do you have a driver's license?"

"Well, yes I do. I had a car a couple years ago, but it broke down and I didn't have enough money to repair it. But isn't this a little sudden? Don't you want more time to think about what you should do?"

"No, I know what I want to do. I want to go to Khabarovsk. Tonight. On the train. It leaves at eight p.m. Will you go with me to Khabarovsk on the train? I will give you the car and you can have the apartment, too. Mama purchased the apartment when we came back from Germany. It is of no use to me."

"My goodness. This is so sudden. I don't know. What will you do in Khabarovsk?"

"I have a friend at school who lived at an orphanage in Khabarovsk after her parents abandoned her. She said she liked it better than living at home. Now she's living here. She told me the name of the orphanage.

"Can you go with me and make sure I'm admitted and have a safe place to stay? Will you do that for me if I give you the car and the apartment?"

"Well, I don't know. I . . ."

Interrupting, Maria said, "We have time to prepare for the trip today. We can take the overnight train to Khabarovsk. It leaves at eight p.m. You could be with me tomorrow. You can return home the following day. A train leaves Khabarovsk at eight p.m. tomorrow night. Mama and I visited there a couple times."

Babushka agreed to Maria's plan. They slept well in their two-bed compartment on the trip to Khabarovsk.

The orphanage was located on the highway to Komsomolsk, about half way between a regional airport and the train station. They took a taxi to the orphanage.

Maria said to Babushka before they went in, "Let me handle it, okay?"

Babushka agreed. She hadn't quite recovered from the sudden turn of events in her life. After all, she was sixty-eight years old, hard of hearing and feeling other assaults of old age on her body and mind.

"May I help you," said a medium-height woman with short black hair. She looked like an Italian movie star Maria had seen in a romantic role. In her mid-thirties, she wore spikes, dressed professionally in a knee-length, black, wool skirt coordinated with a white, silk, collared shirt. She had stepped into the hallway when she saw Baba and Maria enter the orphanage to her right.

"Yes, Maria said. "I want to join your orphanage."

"And you are? Madame," speaking to Babushka.

"Well," Baba said to the director, wringing her hands, "I'm Maria's . . . her, ah . . . guardian . . ."

"She's my neighbor," Maria interrupted. "My mother was murdered yesterday in Vladivostok and my Papa was killed in a plane crash near Irkutsk last February. Baba is helping me until I can stay with you at this orphanage. My friend, Nastya, told me about it. She says you are—*really*—a nice person."

"I see," said the director, eying them skeptically. "I'm Anya. My name means 'Grace of God,' she said with a smile, looking at Maria, "and you are?"

"I'm Maria Martinovna Luderenko. Where do I put my things? This is Baba. That's all you need to know about her because she's going back to Vladivostok tonight."

We're going to need all of Anya we can get to make it through this, Baba thought.

"I see," said Anya. "It might not be that simple. We have a waiting list. It will be at least a year before we can admit another child. Do you think you can wait that long?"

"Could I speak with you privately in your office?" Maria asked.

"Uh, well . . . yes, I guess so. You don't want your guardian to meet with us?"

She pulled Anya aside and spoke in a hushed tone. "No, she's getting old and gets nervous in situations like this, so I think it would be better if she stayed out of the details. But, first, I have to go to the toilet."

"It's down three doors to your right," Anya said. Maria returned to where Baba was waiting.

"Baba, please come with me. I may need your help." *I don't want her talking to Anya and screwing everything up,* she thought.

"This is the door to my office. I'll wait in there," Anya said.

Maria headed for the bathroom with Baba in tow.

"Go ahead and pee if you have to, Baba. I'm going into this stall."

Maria went into a stall, lifted her skirt, reached into her panties and took half of the ruble bills from her plastic-bag "bank" and placed them in her coat pocket. She put the remaining bills back in the bag and then into the crotch of her panties. When she came out, Babushka was straightening her hair in the mirror, still looking a little nervous.

"It will be okay, Baba. Don't worry. Let's go."

Anya was waiting for Maria in her office. Babushka took a seat in the waiting room.

"Anya," Maria said, after pulling the blinds shut. "I can't wait a year. Maybe this will help you make up your mind. Let's say you discovered, while I was taking a pee, that there is a mistake that someone has made and that you have a vacancy after all——starting today. She pulled the wad of money out of her coat pocket and handed it to Anya.

Oh, my God . . . do we have a winner here! Anya thought.

"Now . . ."

"Anya," Maria interrupted, sitting on the edge of her chair.

"Hold it. Let me see what we have here."

Anya looked at the wad of money and began counting. It was over fifteen-hundred dollars in rubles, more than she earned in six months.

"Where did you get this?" Anya asked, with a puzzled look.

"Well, I didn't steal it, if that's what you're thinking. I took it out of a jar in the cabinet after my mother was murdered yesterday. I'm an only child so I thought it belonged to me. Don't you agree?"

"Uh, yes . . . this is . . . highly unusual." She fiddled with the wad of bills, not knowing quite how to proceed. She put the money back in the drawer, locking it while trying desperately to think of what to do next.

"Now . . . what did you say your name is?"

"Maria."

"Yes—Maria—well; Maria, when we adults make agreements of this nature, it's not something we discuss with our friends, or anyone else."

"You mean the police, right?" Maria grinned.

Anya coughed, "Uh—well, yes I suppose so. But there aren't any laws against helping a homeless child find a safe and loving place to live, so I don't think the police will need to be involved. Don't you agree?"

"Excuse me," she said, before Maria could answer.

Anya picked up the phone and asked her deputy to come to her office.

Her deputy was a play-by-the-rules person. Anya thought, *this was going to be . . . a . . . ah . . . an interesting discussion.* So she straightened her back and waited for Larisa, whose name derives from Latin and means "sea gull."

Larisa came flying around the corner in the hallway, bending into the curve like a bicyclist on a sharp turn in a mountain race. Except she didn't look like an elegant bird. She looked more like a lumbering, obsolete, T-34 Russian tank. She entered Anya's office and eyed Maria suspiciously. *Usually, I'm the one to see new candidates first,* she thought.

"Larisa. Thanks for coming in. This is . . . uh . . . Maria," looking at Maria for reassurance that she had the name right. "Her father was killed in a plane crash a few months ago, and you did say your father is a decorated war hero, didn't you, Maria?" Continuing, again without giving Maria a chance to respond, Anya said, "Well . . . also her mother was murdered a couple days ago. I know this will seem highly unusual to you Larisa, because I know <u>you</u> <u>know</u> we have a waiting list . . ."

"Anya . . . ," Larisa interrupted, loudly.

"Larisa, please hear me out and don't interrupt," she said sternly. "I've been thinking about that attic we cleaned out a couple months ago and wondered if we couldn't put some insulation up there, clean the place and make room for another child . . ."

"You mean *this* one," said Larisa, interrupting angrily, and nodding toward Maria.

"Yes, *this* one," Anya responded, firmly.

"How much was the bribe this time?" Larisa asked, pushing the envelope.

Maria exploded with laughter.

Anya felt miserable. *Where the **hell** is this going?*

Larisa started to say something, but she didn't get the first word out.

"Listen you old fart," Maria said, when she stopped laughing, "I don't think you realize how much I resent your accusing me of bribing this beautiful, merciful, compassionate young woman who is just doing her job."

Anya grabbed her hair with both hands and slammed her head on the desk, waiting for someone to speak.

It was Maria again. "I demand an apology: first, to your boss, and then to me. Don't you realize what you just said?"

Usually, Larisa handled confrontation easily—up to a point, but she could see she was losing this one.

"I'm out'a here. You can fix up your own damn attic."

"Yea," said Maria, after the door slammed, "she approves. Does that mean I'm in?"

Anya lifted her head and looked up . . . smiling.

"I . . . think so."

Gathering her wits and picking up the pace a little, Anya said, "Would you like to go to work here? I could use someone like you on my staff. How old did you say you are?"

The eleven-year-old replied: "Thirteen."

In the hallway, Maria gave her mother's keys to Baba and said goodbye.

Babushka waddled down the hall toward the outer door. She left the building shaking her head, muttering: "fuck a pig . . . fuck a pig."

Chapter 13

Maria's time passed rapidly. Anya fixed up the attic to make room for her, but Maria insisted that she have no more space than other children and that the privileges and responsibilities remain the same for her as anyone else.

Occasional spats with Larisa broke wind, but they managed to keep interactions on a civilized plane, in spite of the odium.

Maria had adoption on her mind from the day her mother died. West Germany, she noticed, was different from Russia; from what she had seen in American movies, East Germany seemed more like her Russian home. Germany would be closer to the Russia she loved. Still . . .

Because of her father's connections and Gorbachev's perestroika and glasnost, she had access to Western culture through American movies, music and books. She was obsessed with anything "American." She made up her mind: adoption by an American couple.

She continued the English lessons she had started in Vladivostok and was improving by the hour. She spent a lot of time on English grammar and increasing her vocabulary . . . and talking with English-speaking visitors. Interactions with foreigners were humorous, delightful . . . and appalling.

She had figured out the drill, in terms of what to say and what not to say when being scrutinized as a prospective adoptee by PAP's (Potential Adoptive Parents). But the "drill" did not apply to her; she spoke up when encounters with PAP's careened into daffy, vertiginous answers to questions posed by eager, anxious and naïve Potential Adoptive Children (PAC's).

A middle-aged couple came from America to meet the children and answer any questions the PAC's might have. About fifteen children were gathered in the lunchroom asking questions.

One six-year-old asked where babies come from. The couple looked at each other, as if to say, *You can handle this one.*

The mother cleared her throat and said, "Well, babies grow in the mother's stomach—bobbing her head as if that would sugar-coat her lie—and then, when the time comes, the mother gives birth to the beautiful baby. You were all beautiful babies at one time, weren't you?" she said, with a strained smile.

The children stared at her.

Maria stood and piped up, "So, let me get this straight. You say the baby grows in the mother's stomach, right?"

"Yes, my dear."

"Well, if that's the case, how does the baby get out of the mother's stomach? The hole is too small at the bottom of the stomach."

The wife squirmed. The husband shifted his feet as his face turned red.

"Well, I didn't exactly mean *stomach* . . ."

"Well then, what *did* you mean?"

"I meant in the tummy, where the stomach is, like right here," patting her abdomen.

"So how does the baby get in there? Do you chew on something and swallow it and then the baby grows?"

The husband was getting dizzy.

"Well, not exactly like that, but something like that, yes."

"*What?*" Maria asked loudly. "Why can't you just say the father places the semen in the mother during intercourse and then the baby grows in the uterus, and at the time of birth, the baby exits via the vagina? Why can't you just tell us the truth? My mother did; she told me. I don't think any of us here want to be adopted by parents who tell such outrageous lies."

Some humorous and delightful interactions were fun and informative, but Maria was becoming impatient. She wanted to move on. She had all the documentation she needed and now it was up to Anya and the PAP's to make a good match.

The day finally came when it was Maria's turn to begin meeting prospective parents. The parade started with a slick looking couple from California who seemed to have it all: Good looks, intelligence, a fancy home, three cars, well-educated—the list goes on.

Anya, and the committee involved in the process, thought this might be a good match for Maria. But it wasn't. Maria wouldn't even talk to them. She didn't like their looks. By looks, she meant they didn't look like sincere people—sincere about life, in general or even sincere about their own happiness in particular.

With them, it seemed to be all about status symbols. In their home, she would be an icon of the couple's compassion for poor Russian children—little more.

Other couples came and went without coming close to a match, but then one day . . .

"Maria, come with me," Anya said. "There is someone I want you to meet." They walked to Anya's office . . . silently.

"Maria, this is Mr. and Mrs. Leo McCarty. They are from America. Minnesota. They are farmers and have shown an interest in you, based on your file and your picture. Mr. and Mrs. McCarty, this is Maria Martinovna Luderenko." They shook hands.

Speaking to Anya, Mrs. McCarty said, "Please call me Pat. My husband's name is Leo. Maria, we are happy to meet you."

"I want you to be my parents," Maria said.

"But Maria, they might want to get to know you a little . . . talk with you . . . you know . . . what we do here," Anya said, pleading mildly.

"If they don't know they want me, then I don't want to go with them. But I don't think that is the case. I think they already know that I am the one for them."

"Well, why don't we ask them . . . Mr. and Mrs. McCarty . . . er' Pat and Leo ah. . . What do you think?" Anya said, brightly, as if a sunburst had enlightened her thoughts.

Pat spoke first. "I knew before she did that she was the one and I suspect my husband had the same reaction. Did you, honey?"

"Yes, of course. My only question is to you, Anya . . . Can she go home with us tomorrow?"

"What?" Anya asked. "That is impossible. As you know, there are certain legal formalities that the authorities in our country require, and that takes time. America has similar requirements as well. It usually takes several more weeks, even months before all the requirements are met."

"Isn't it true that everything has been done that needs to be done, so far as American requirements are concerned?" asked Leo.

"Well, yes. We've had everything ready for some time, but as I said, there are documents that need to be in order on our side before she can leave."

"It's nine o'clock in the morning. Our plane leaves tomorrow for the States. Isn't there something that can be done?" asked Leo.

"As I . . ."

"Anya," Maria interrupted, "may I speak to you alone?"

"Well . . . I . . . uh . . . Mr. and Mrs. McCarty? Is that okay with you? Would you mind waiting in the outer office?" Anya asked.

"Of course not," they reassured her in unison, and left the office as Maria closed the door behind them. Anya returned to her desk, as Maria reached over and closed the window blinds.

Oh boy, here we go again, Anya thought.

Maria lifted her skirt, reached into the crotch of her panties and pulled out her plastic bank.

"I gave you half of the bills the last time we did this, but I didn't realize that I gave you all the small bills." After removing the remaining bills from the plastic bag, she said, "here are the large ones," as she placed them on Anya's desk . . . over three thousand dollars in rubles. Do you think that will get me out of here tomorrow?"

Anya, in a maladroit move, plopped into her chair in shock. She sat staring at the wad of bills.

She didn't bother to count them. She picked them up, put them in the drawer, locked it and sat staring at the door for a moment.

"Maria, would you please ask Mr. and Mrs. McCarty to come in?"

Maria reset the blinds, opened the door and invited the McCarty's in.

"Well, ah . . . Mr. and Mrs. McCarty," Anya said, standing near the door, turning her head sideways and stroking her hair, trying to think of something intelligent to say.

"I think I can fix this . . . I mean, not *fix* . . . I mean I think the problem can be . . . uh, . . . *solved* . . . uh . . . her going home with you tomorrow morning . . . **yes!**" she said, with a smile, nodding her head to punctuate her decision.

Having scaled *that* unpleasant hump, the pace picked up. "I'll put my deputy on it right away," Anya said, brightly. "We should have your papers ready by the time you leave for the airport tomorrow morning."

Maria slammed Anya with a big hug, and turned to hug her new parents. "May I call you Mama and Papa? She asked. "Of course," they replied in unison.

Chapter 14

Exiting the Minneapolis/St. Paul Airport—Leo driving—Maria in the passenger seat and Pat in the rear behind Leo—they proceeded west into the countryside on Highway 62. They passed small-grain fields that had already been harvested, and corn fields turning from shimmering green to brown. This early September evening was warm, with a little breeze under scattered, billowing clouds.

Farm buildings, surrounded by trees, each looking like an oasis, passed, as if on parade, on both sides of highway.

Maria noticed diversity amongst the buildings that populated each homestead: some large, some small, some with buildings that looked like smoke stacks on old, coal-burning, steam-powered ships.

Leo could read her mind: "Silos," he said "To store silage and grain: The larger ones hold grain which is sold when the price is right. Some of the smaller ones hold silage."

"What's silage?" Maria asked.

"Usually, it's ground, green corn stalks or some other green stalk and leaf that ferments and tastes delicious to cattle and sheep," Leo answered. The explanations of less obvious details had begun.

The airports, beginning with the Inchon International Airport in Korea, followed by the San Francisco International Airport, and finally the Minneapolis/St. Paul Airport, were familiar sights that did not need explanation, but their size and modernity were something of a shock, which Maria did not reveal.

Maria noticed horses grazing and asked if every farmer had horses.

"Actually, very few, but some do for pleasure and recreation," Leo responded. Keen to change the subject, he said, "Is there anything you like to eat, especially . . . or cannot or don't like to eat? We can stop on the way home."

"No . . . thank you," Maria replied. She was thinking about horses.

"It's not much farther and we will be home," Pat said. They were about twenty minutes west of the airport and would turn north off the wide, paved highway on to narrower, Highway 7, and then make a right onto a gravel road that led to the driveway of their farm.

The driveway connected with the road at the beginning of a curve that veered to the right.

It extended down a mild slope, about a quarter of a mile toward the buildings in a grove with a creek running through it. From the curve in the road, their old, two-story farm house could be seen, sheltered within the grove.

As they entered the driveway, Pat said, "Well, Maria, here we are. This is your new home."

Maria did not respond verbally, but the response within recalled the angel informing her of her father's death: A profound tranquility washed over her, reassuring her that the decisions of the previous day were immaculate. She began to cry.

Sensing what Maria felt, Leo and Pat had tears running down their cheeks when the car stopped in front of the garage. They sat in silence, wiping away their tears with the tissues Pat provided from the back seat.

Maria spoke first. "The only thing that could be better than this is if you have a horse!"

They all laughed and got out of the car.

"We have something to show you. Come with us to the barn," Pat said. They walked in silence toward the barn, Maria searching their opaque faces for clues.

Leo opened the small side door and waited for Maria and Pat to follow.

Maria screamed. She jumped up and down and ran to Pat and then Leo, hugging them. Pulling away, she turned and ran a short distance to the stall where a dark brown filly stood . . . wondering . . . *What is going on?*

"She's yours to name," said Leo. A brown beauty with a white diamond on her forehead, it was as if the girl and her horse had known each other forever.

Maria slept in the barn with her head on the filly's neck that night. Leo was up several times during that night to make sure their daughter was safe.

She named her horse: Dana—pronounced "Donna"—which is a diminutive of a Russian name, Bogdana, which means: "Given by God"

In the days following Maria's arrival at the farm, Maria and Pat exchanged stories about their lives. The evening after she arrived, they were chatting at the dining room table after Leo had gone to bed. Pat told Maria that Leo had taken over the operation of the family farm when his father died. She had worked as an airline attendant for a few years after high school and met Leo through a mutual friend. "It was love at first sight for both of us," she said, smiling.

"Did you get married immediately?"

"Two weeks later. I wanted to wait. He said, 'What for?' So . . . we sort of eloped," she said, airily, moving her head back and forth with her arms reaching for the ceiling.

"What does that mean?" Maria asked.

"Oh, it means you don't bother with all the fuss and expense of a big wedding. You go to a judge and he marries you. We went to Las Vegas."

"Where?"

"It's a city out west, in Nevada, bordering California, ah . . . in the desert . . . which has casinos . . . entertainment of all types. Things like that. You can get married quickly. Get a marriage license one minute and you're married the next."

"Did you have a good time?"

"You *betcha!*" Pat replied.

Maria told Pat about her turbulent life, although she didn't brag about her bold behavior during her transition to the orphanage. She was proud of her father . . . and her mother, who was anything but a shrinking violet. She spoke mostly about how she enjoyed being a part of a loving family who remained close and respectful of one another during the incredible events that involved her country's collapse.

Behind Pat was a picture of a soldier on the wall. Maria asked about the picture.

"That is our son," Pat said. "He was killed in the Gulf War. Our country invaded Kuwait to drive Iraq out. Every night he was over there I prayed for his safety before I went to sleep."

"One night, as I was praying, I received a message which said; 'He has come to live with me.' It wasn't a voice. It was a message that came to me in a very clear and gentle way. There was no doubt in my mind that the message came from God and that I would be visited in the morning by the casualty assistance officers.

"The next morning, I made cookies and coffee so I would be prepared to greet the officers and help them get through the job they had to do. At nine-thirty that morning, they came and we chatted for a while and they left. I feel so sorry for the men and women who get such duty. He was such a good boy."

Half way through the story, Maria was crying. "How old was he?"

"He was nineteen years old that year, 1991."

"I'm so sorry."

"He enlisted to see the world. He wasn't interested in college. He liked farming and the plan was for him to take over the farm when he got out of the Army. But that was not to be."

"Was he married?"

"No. He had girlfriends, but I'm sure he would have married and had children.

"When we learned about adopting, we decided that's what we wanted to do, even though we are an older couple. Leo is fifty-five this year and I'm fifty-three."

"Do you think you would have adopted me if your son had lived?"

"Of course, I don't know. His death left us without an heir. We hadn't really thought about adoption before he died. But what I do know is we are so happy to have you as our daughter now."

Maria told Pat about living in East Germany until the collapse of the Soviet Union and how she learned about the death of her father through the angel. They agreed that these experiences are rare.

Pat said that since the message about her son, she never doubted the existence of a higher being, but she had serious doubts about the Catholicism she grew up with and had stopped going to church. Her husband had never attended church.

Maria confessed that she knew almost nothing about religion because it had been banned in the Soviet Union. "As you know," she said, "I haven't had a lot of time to reflect on religion."

Yet, she told Pat she became curious about it after the appearance of the angel and that curiosity persisted. She said the appearance of the angel altered how she thinks about death; the knowledge that they lived on in a spiritual realm of some sort, was comforting. She said she wanted to know more about why such experiences are so powerful, but she did not know where to start.

"Well, I suppose you could start by going to church in town. There are several churches; I think at least five, including the Catholic Church I was attending. If you like, we can visit some of the churches on Sundays and you can decide what to do from there."

"I'll think about that. I'm tired. I loved sleeping in the barn with Dana last night, but I will sleep better in my bed, I'm sure. So I won't be doing that very often. And I think Papa didn't get much sleep worrying about me."

Pat laughed and said she agreed. I can tell he already loves you very much and wants to take good care of you. He wants to show you the farm sometime soon, but it will be on weekends, since you need to start school next week. We live only three miles from town—Sylvan Lake. I'll take you there Monday to get registered. Since we are retired, we will drive you to and from school until you are old enough to drive yourself."

"When will that be?"

"When you are sixteen," Pat said, with a smile. "Sleep well."

"You too, Mama."

In the days following Maria's arrival at the farm, Pat, Maria and Leo continued to exchange stories about their lives.

For Pat and Leo, farming served their desires and needs well. The rains came on time, the weeds and pests had been eliminated using herbicides and pesticides, and the harvests provided an escalating accumulation of wealth, enhanced by increased land values.

Leo managed money and investments carefully. Their wealth was well into millions of dollars, but their lifestyle had not changed over the years. They had taken a few trips around the United States, Canada and to other foreign countries, but preferred home.

During the year prior to Maria's arrival, Leo renovated the horse and cow barn combination, which consisted of dirt floors, stalls and mangers for the horses and the concrete floors, gutters and stanchions for the cows . . . and a hayloft.

The barn, built in the early 1900's, accommodated twenty milk cows, and six horses, with stalls for eating and sleeping. It needed to be raised from its foundation, a new foundation built, the concrete part of the floor removed and the horse stalls and cow stanchions removed. New studs, supporting the barn superstructure, provided the stability of a new building.

The dirt floor would be covered with a cushion of straw that could be removed when soiled. A couple stalls, large enough for an adult horse, were built along one side of the barn, and two stalls for a foal, each having properly sized Dutch doors. In each stall, Leo installed a modern equine flooring system that included sturdy foam, with a non-porous polymer cover, that sealed to the side walls—a five-star comfort zone for a horse. One area was constructed with a hot-and-cold-running shower for horse grooming.

Feeding and watering conveniences were installed. A lean-to on the left side of the barn was used for holding supplies and equipment needed to care for the horse. Two cupolas perched at the top of the A-framed roof. Leo installed a climate control system.

The barn was painted fire-engine red with white trim. Two sliding doors to the rear of the barn allowed easy transition to the corrals that Leo had built behind and to one side of the barn. The corrals consisted of enclosures made of heavy wood, with rounded features, to prevent injuries. One corral was circular for training purposes while others were of varying sizes to be used when the horse was not in the pasture grazing. A couple light poles with flood lights stood amongst the corrals.

Chapter 15

In the nineteenth century, railroads, rivers and lakes attracted the attention of entrepreneurs seeking places to build a town to serve the surrounding homesteaders' needs. The westward expansion spawned hundreds, and eventually thousands of small communities that would take advantage of transportation links to product resources and markets.

Early settlers named their town Sylvan Lake because of its location—on Sylvan Lake. A railroad would follow within two years.

Minnesota is known as the "Land of Ten Thousand Lakes." More than sixty towns and cities include "Lake" in the community's name.

Into the late 1950's, train engineers stopped in Sylvan Lake for lunch, not only because their schedule allowed it, but the town had the best restaurant on their route. They left their coal-burning, steam engine spitting and sputtering at the local depot while they ate lunch.

Standard fare was a hot roast beef sandwich, which included mashed potatoes and gravy atop a slice of white bread, a vegetable and all the coffee one could drink; the price of lunch included your choice of homemade pie—all for $1.25.

Established in 1855, the town grew to about three thousand inhabitants, large enough to have avoided school consolidations with surrounding small towns that are not large enough to support a viable school system of their own. As such, Sylvan Lake possesses one of the best rated school systems in the state. And Maria was poised to take full advantage of that thrilling reality.

Thus, Sylvan Lake became Maria's anchor for her sizeable ambitions. It seemed as though the opportunities had no limits; she was determined to use them to her maximum advantage.

After a few days of testing, and because of where her birthday fell on the calendar, the school authorities determined that Maria belonged in the eighth grade of the middle school . . . even though her age group would suggest the seventh grade. Schools in Russia place a strong emphasis on math and science classes; Maria, being one of the top students in all of her classes, tested out a year or two ahead of her peers in Sylvan Lake.

She made the basketball teams in both middle school and high school; sports were a welcome relief from her—at times—intense intellectual labors.

She joined the debate squad and contributed to several competitive honors received by her teams.

She was thrilled by the depth and breadth of the curriculum and extra-curricular activities, which included vocal and instrumental music. She joined the girls' chorus and mixed chorus, was chosen to perform as a soloist in those groups and sang solos in musical performances at various festivals that occurred during the school year.

From her perspective, Minnesota earned its reputation for having excel-lent public school systems. A Lutheran elementary school and a K-12 Catholic system played important roles in the Sylvan Lake culture, as well.

Invited by one of her girl-friends to join a karate club at a local karate training center, she accepted with enthusiasm.

By her junior year in high school, she had morphed from a lanky adoles-cent into a mature, young woman. She earned the respect of her peers and teachers at school.

Summers were always welcome, not only for relief from the winter that seemed to last forever, but because she could spend more time with her horse, Dana.

During the first few winters, Leo took care of Dana most of the time, but she was not neglected by Maria. She sometimes bundled up and slept in the barn next to Dana. On weekends she groomed her and went riding when the weather permitted.

Summertime, a few girl-friends would come over on their horses and they would ride into the meadow to a small lake. They packed a picnic lunch and hung out, talking about the cute boys at school—went skinny dipping, and lay in the sun to dry off. Then, go off again, diving into the lake, dunking and splashing each other in the cool water. Toward evening, they raced home. They took turns winning.

Occasionally, during the winter on clear, moonlit nights, Maria invited some of her classmates, including boys, to a skating party on the lake.

Upon Maria's arrival at their farm as their newly-adopted daughter, Leo drew up plans for a new three-car garage. He had helped his father build a chicken coup and a pig pen building, both of which stood empty. Thus, he knew how to lay a foundation, build a garage, and install electri-cal outlets.

He felt no urgency to finish. He spent time with his buddies in town every week, discussing local issues and national politics at a local restaurant. He traded off with Pat, driving Maria to and from school—he, driving his pickup, she driving their sedan.

Those moments alone with Maria were Leo's favorite times of the day. Sometimes they were silent during the trips and other times they engaged in animated conversations. Occasionally, she would help her dad with the garage, knowing that someday *her* car would be sheltered there also. For years it seemed like that day was an eternity away, but she was beginning to feel like time had warped into a speed demon.

Chapter 16

In the lingua franca of rural Minnesota, not all was "peaches and cream" for Maria during her high school years.

During the fall semester of her junior year, Father O'Reilley, who had transferred to St. Sebastian Catholic Church in Sylvan Lake six years earlier, heard from his parishioners about a high school concert in which Maria had sung, "Ave Maria." They said she sang as beautifully as she herself was beautiful—and almost as beautiful as the Madonna, herself. "She is the daughter of Leo and Pat McCarty," they said.

Examining church attendance records, Father O'Reilly learned that Pat stopped coming to church several years before he arrived; Leo had never attended church.

All over the country, attendance had been declining in mainline churches, especially where there was not a significant influx of immigrants from Latin America. Bishops were encouraging their priests to do what they could to get the backsliders to return.

Father O'Reilly decided to encourage Pat to return; maybe their daughter would follow. He called to make an appointment to see them at their farm.

After he introduced himself and some pleasantries, Father O'Reilley said to Maria, "I heard from some of my parishioners that you sang a solo, 'Ave Maria,' at a high school concert the other night.

"They say they had never heard it sung more beautifully. I'm wondering if you would be willing to come to our Church on Christmas Eve and sing 'Ave Maria?' You look like your mother, I think," Father O'Reilley said, glancing back and forth between them.

"Well, actually . . ." Pat started to say.

Maria interrupted. "I think I look more like my father, don't you, Mama?"

Pat paused long enough to realize what Maria was doing: She didn't want to get into the adoption drama with a stranger. "Well, yes, of course you do."

"To answer your question," Maria said, "I'm not a member of your church, and I don't intend to be. Wouldn't my singing a solo at your church be a problem for your congregation?"

"Oh, I don't think so," he responded, "I often have outsiders come to perform in various ways: sing a solo; we had a Lutheran clarinet quartet come and perform last Christmas; it's part of reaching out to the community. What do you think, Mrs. McCarty? Would that be okay with you? Wouldn't you and your husband like to come and hear your daughter sing? Maybe that could be a start toward attending church on a regular basis. What do you think?"

"Well, I suppose the singing part of your question would be okay, if it's okay with Maria. What about it, Sweetie?"

"I don't want to make a decision right now. We'll let you know. I want Papa in on the decision. He'll be home this evening and we'll talk it over with him."

The decision was that she would grant the priest his request, but she wanted to do a rehearsal in the church so there would be no surprises on Christmas Eve.

A week before Christmas Eve, she walked to the church on a Friday afternoon after school. Pat would pick her up at four.

Father O'Reilley greeted her at the door. They walked to the front of the church. Father O'Reilley pointed out where she would stand: at the center, in front of the altar, two steps up from the church floor and back about five feet from the steps. She would sing a cappella. "Could you sing it through once or twice for me?" he asked.

"Certainly; I'm not sure you are aware that I sang Schubert's 'Ave Maria' lyrics. They were taken from Walter Scott's original—from the 'The Lady of the Lake.' I sing in German. Storck did the translation from English into German."

"Well, thank you Maria, I didn't know that. Please proceed," he said with a smile, and went and sat in the front pew to her left.

> **Ave Maria! Jungfrau mild,**
> **Erhore einer Jungfrau Flehen,**
> **Aus diesem Felsen starr und wild**
> **Soll mein Gebet zu dir hinwehen.**
> **Wir Schlafen sicher bis zum Morgen,**
> **Ob Menschen noch so grausam sind.**
> **O Jungfrau, sieh der Jungfrau Sorgen,**
> **O Mutter, Hor ein Bittend Kind!**
> **Ave Maria!**

"Wonderful! Bravo, Maria. You have her name, don't you?"

"Yes, I guess I do."

Rising from his seat and walking toward Maria, Father O'Reilley said: "Now Maria, I've seen 'Ave Maria' sung with gestures. You know, like raising your arms at certain points in the lyrics to emphasize the meaning of the words? Would you like for me to come up and show you what I'm thinking?"

"Well, I suppose that wouldn't hurt, if that's what you want. What the hell, it's your church isn't it?"

He coughed; "Well . . . I guess it is . . . Yes."

He stood behind Maria.

"Okay, proceed. I'll hold on to your elbows and lift them up when you come to the part that I think would enhance your already impressive performance."

Ave Maria! Jungfrau mild,
erhore einer Jungfrau Flehen

As Maria started the next line, "Aus diesem Felsen...," Father O'Malley pushed on her elbows moving them up high as though she were gesturing to heaven, and held them there to the end of the line.

"Okay, good," he said. "Now start over and do it yourself."

Ave Maria! Jungfrau mild,
Erhore einer Jungfrau Flehen,

As Maria started *Aus deisem Felsen* . . . she raised her arms, as if reaching to heaven—and then he struck; he grabbed her breasts with both hands, cupping them, massaging them.

Maria grabbed his left wrist with her right hand, dropped to the floor onto her right knee while twisting to the left, and threw him over her back to the floor. He landed on his back. In a flash, she stood up and placed her left foot on his neck. "What the hell do you think you are doing?" He moved his left arm.

"I wouldn't do that if I were you." Father O'Reilley's face was purple.

"I'll release you and walk out of here. But if you make a move toward me, I'll shove your nose into your brain. Blink twice if you understand me."

He blinked twice. Maria stepped back. He didn't move. Calmly, she walked down the aisle—without looking back—toward the narthex, went out the front door, sat on the steps and waited for Pat.

Chapter 17

Maria's seat partner had mixed nuts scattered on the tray in front of him; he munched on them as he was reading the sex-abuse book. Looking at Maria and pointing to the nuts, he said, "Want some?"

She looked at him, smiled and said, "Sure, why not?" She took some cashews—her favorite.

"Interesting title," Maria said, motioning toward the book.

"Yes . . . interesting book . . . nearly finished. I live at the Vatican, but had no idea this scandal was as pervasive—both historically, and institution-ally—as it was and is. Sex abuse of children and its cover-up goes back to the beginning of the Church and continues to this day from the smallest parishes all the way to the pope's office."

"You live at the Vatican?"

"Yes, I'm one of the Swiss Guards."

"You are? Those guys with the striped pantaloons and the funny hats?"

"Those are my guys," he replied with a smile.

"But you look a little old . . . I mean, you don't look *old;* you look older than the guards I've seen at the gates and doors. I've been on a couple of tours there."

"Well, yes . . . I am older. I was a guard at the gates several years ago, but now I've moved up the ranks and don't need to do that anymore. Most of my men on the gates are your age or younger."

"My men? Are you in charge of the guards? Are you a sergeant?"

"Yes. I am in charge of the guards, but I'm not a sergeant. I'm the com-mandant, a colonel . . . the guy in charge. I worked my way up through the ranks."

"Wow! I'm sorry. You look too young to be a colonel."

"Well, I'm 47. I need to stay in good shape. I'm responsible for the safety of the pope and his minions."

"Why are you on this flight from Moscow to the states? I mean, you aren't lost, are you?"

He laughed. "No. I'm not lost. My name is Fritz Isenberg. What's your name?"

"Maria. So . . . are you lost?"

"Actually, no. I'm traveling to the States to visit a sister who lives in San Francisco. She's been there for twenty years and this is my sixth trip to visit her and her family. I came by way of Moscow this time because I've known about the Tretyakov Galleria for many years and always wanted to visit and see the old, Russian icon paintings of the twelfth to the sixteenth centuries.

"For some reason I fell in love with Russian Icons that I've seen in people's homes. When I learned there was an entire floor of the Tretyakov dedicated to the icons, I had to see them. What about you? You speak with a Russian accent."

"I was born in Russia and adopted by a wonderful American couple when I was twelve years old. I've been in Moscow for two years and am returning home to see my mom. My dad died a few years ago, so she's alone, misses me and I miss her. I'm looking forward to seeing her again."

Chapter 18

In January 2002, The Boston Globe reported that a local area Catholic priest, John Geoghan, had molested dozens of children over a period of several years, that his superiors had transferred him to a half dozen parishes, knowing that he was a child molester, and that Church officials had systematically covered up his crimes.

The scandal created a firestorm that reached across the United States to numerous countries around the world where priests were being exposed as unrepentant pedophiles. Eventually, over 150 victims would come forward accusing Geoghan of molestation. The youngest victim at the time of the crime was four years old.

In response to the blistering heat felt by the United States Conference of Catholic Bishops, a National Review Board was established to assess the bishops' progress in implementing remedial sex abuse programs that had been adopted at a conference in Dallas.

On June 14, 2002, former Oklahoma governor Frank Keating was appointed Chairman of the National Review Board charged with the assessment. One year later, he resigned from the review board shortly after Los Angeles Cardinal Mahony had criticized him for comparing some church leaders to the Mafia.

In his resignation letter, he said that some of the bishops were offended by his remarks, but that he would not apologize because they were statements that reflected his feelings. He insisted that resisting Grand Jury subpoenas, hiding the names of clerics involved, dissembling on matters of such grave importance was characteristic of a criminal organization and not that of the Catholic Church to which he belongs.

In a draft survey, reported by CNN.com, and released February 27, 2004, over 4,500 priests had been accused of sexual abuse between 1950 and 2002. More than 11,000 allegations of sexual abuse by priests were recorded. The report was based on a nationwide survey of church records, and was compiled by the John Jay College of Criminal Justice.

The numbers are not the entire truth; they are low, according to a director of Survivors Network of Those Abused by Priests. The editor of the National Catholic Reporter stated that "the scandal is not just about sex . . . It is a

scandal about the abuse of power and trust, and a breach of faith with people."
Over the next several years, the number of priests accused of sex abuse in the
United States had risen to over 5,000.

The abuse of power and trust reaches all the way from priests, through
the bishops, archbishops, and cardinals (located in numerous countries) to
the papal office in Rome. Numerous articles and books, addressing sex abuse
and abuse of power in the Roman Catholic Church, have been written in
recent years—too many to list. Here are some of the book titles: *The Vatican Exposed: Murder, Money, and the Mafia; Betrayal: The Crisis in the
Catholic Church; Sex, Priests and Secret Codes: The Catholic Church's
2,000-year Paper Trail of Sexual Abuse; Survivors of Predator Priests;
Confronting Power and Sex in the Catholic Church; Lead Us Not Into
Temptation: Catholic Priests and the Sexual Abuse of Children.*

Chapter 19

On a cool, clear, breezy, Monday afternoon in early March, the spring semester of Maria's junior year, Leo stopped in front of the high school, waved his arm, and hollered to Maria, "Over here!" Maria walked slowly, not seeing Leo's car, but finding him sitting on a new, silver and black, Harley-Davidson motorcycle. She walked up to Leo, kissed him on the cheek and said, "Golly, Papa . . . is this your second childhood, or what?"

"Well, sort of, I suppose. When I was a kid, my dad had an old, army-surplus motorcycle that he purchased after World War II and I always loved riding that thing. *And,* I've wanted one ever since; so I thought it was about time I fulfilled my dream. Do you like it?"

"I love it!" she exclaimed. "Can I learn to ride it someday?"

"Sure," he said, "I've been thinking of teaching you to drive a car one of these days . . . on the gravel roads around the farm where the cops won't see us. And we can do the same for this thing. Jump on and hold on tight."

"I'd love that," Maria said.

"How was your day?" Leo shouted, as they pulled away from the curb.

"Oh, the usual . . . lots of classes; no big dramas today."

"I've got an idea," Leo said. "I noticed on the way to town this afternoon that we have new neighbors. Would it be okay if we stop and introduce ourselves?"

"Sure," she replied.

The McClellan's, living about a half mile from Leo and Pat's home on the gravel road to town, sold their farm, built a new home in Sylvan Lake, and moved in shortly after Christmas the previous year. They sold their farm to the Youngstads who were moving from western Minnesota.

When they reached the short driveway, the family dog came to greet them with full-throttle barking, alerting his masters that visitors had arrived. Leo pulled into the yard and stopped in front of the house.

A heavy man, in his mid-fifties—with graying blond hair—wearing dark-blue, denim overalls, a light blue, cotton shirt, a red baseball cap, and a gray jacket, emerged from the barn about forty yards to their right.

Leo and Maria dismounted and petted the dog, which had calmed down, and was wagging its tail in delight. His day would not end with the usual boredom. Leo and Maria waited for their neighbor by the motorcycle.

Leo spoke first. "I'm Leo McCarty and this is my daughter, Maria. We live about a half mile down the road," nodding to the right, as he offered his hand. "Welcome to Sylvan Lake."

"I'm pleased to meet you both," shaking hands with both of them. "I'm Ole Youngstad. I've heard a lot of good things about you. I was on my way in to have a cup of coffee and a cookie or two. My wife is baking them, so she might have some . . . fresh out of the oven. Do you have time to come in and meet her and my son?"

"That would be a pleasure," Leo replied. "Is that okay with you, Maria?"

"Of course," she said.

In the kitchen, Ole introduced his wife and son: "Mary and Sammy, this is Leo and Maria, our neighbors the McClellan's told us about." Sammy, about Maria's age, sitting at the table eating a cookie with a glass of milk, looked up and smiled.

Mary, slender and petite, with black hair—wearing a red and blue print dress covered with a blue apron—took a towel and wiped her hands before greeting Leo and Maria.

"I'm so glad to meet you," Mary said. "Is your wife with you?"

"No," Leo replied, "I guess I should apologize for that. I was in town to pick up Maria from school and decided to stop and say hello on the way home. We'd like to have you over for dinner some Sunday afternoon as soon as you are settled. Pat, my wife, has mentioned she'd like to do that."

"That would be wonderful. Let us know. Come, please sit down and have some coffee and cookies," she said as she pulled a couple chairs away from the kitchen table. "They're oatmeal/raisin—the favorite around this house. Do you take sugar or cream in your coffee?" Leo replied, "Both, thank you."

Maria said she'd prefer milk instead of coffee. "Coffee gives me heart palpitations, and I wouldn't sleep."

"Okay. Sammy loves cookies just out of the oven," Mary said, "don't you, honey?"

"Yes, and don't call me honey," he replied, with a smile. He took another bite of his cookie. His full head of coal-black hair, with bangs, lay over his forehead, combed to the left. Round, steel-rimmed glasses perched precariously on his nose. His dad often said it was easy to see who the boss of the house was by the color of Sammy's hair: his mother dominated in more ways than one.

Ole grew up a Norwegian Lutheran, but when he married Mary, her Catholic priest insisted that he marry them, and that Ole convert to Catholicism and rear their children in the Catholic Church. He agreed to go through the mumbo-jumbo of the marriage ceremony because he wasn't about to abandon the only woman he loved—or ever would love—because of some tedious religious rules.

He wasn't much of a Lutheran anyway; what difference did it make. So they got married; she went to church and Sammy attended Sunday school until he was confirmed in the faith and then he stopped going to church as well. The family lived peacefully when it came to religion; they didn't talk about it.

They chatted for a while. The Youngstad's moved from a smaller farm they had sold the year before and were moving up to a farm with pasture and more arable land. They wanted to raise some cattle and sheep, perhaps some chickens and a few pigs. That would keep them busy during the long Minnesota winters.

Leo and Maria thanked their new neighbors for their hospitality and all agreed to get together sometime soon to get better acquainted. Leo offered his assistance to Ole: "Any time you need it," he said.

Father O'Reilly made a routine pastoral call to the Youngstad's farm on a Sunday afternoon a couple weeks later. When Ole learned the pastor was coming, he told Mary it was her game, and he didn't want to play. At the appointed time, he disappeared.

Sammy's mother, Father O'Reilley could see, was immediately impressed by his caring and compassionate personality. He picked up on Sammy's developmental disability quickly. Combining those two bits of crucial information, he didn't waste any time trying to build trust with the Youngstad's before he made his first move to take Sammy into his evil lair.

"Mrs. Youngstad," Father O'Reilley said, "Sammy seems like such a nice young man. You know," he lied, "I let my yard-work man go last week, so I'm wondering if Sammy would be interested in coming over once a week to mow the lawn and maybe, during the winter, do some light cleaning around the house. I would be happy to come and pick him up and take him back home, if that would work for you and Sammy."

"Well, I'm sorry his father isn't here to help with the decision, but let's ask Sammy what he thinks."

"I don't know, Mom, whatever you think."

"Well, Father O'Reilley, let me talk to my husband and we'll let you know."

Two weeks later, Father O'Reilley picked up Sammy on a Saturday afternoon and took him to the rectory, the priest's residence adjacent to the church. The house was made of the same red stone that was used to build the church in the late eighteen hundreds. A two-story house with four bedrooms, a living room, dining room, a kitchen, two bathrooms and a basement provided ample room for the priest and visitors.

The first two times Sammy was there, they spent most of their time talking, but Sammy did most of the listening, responding only when asked a direct question. He did some yard work, but not much.

The third week, Father O'Reilley, approaching his mid-forties, told Sammy that he was not feeling well and that he wanted to go upstairs and lie down and rest. He asked Sammy if he would come with him to give him a back rub because that might make him feel better. Sammy agreed . . . reluctantly.

Father O'Reilly pressed a button on his tape recorder. Beethoven's Fifth Symphony saturated the atmosphere. It begins with a four-note "V" for victory, Morse Code beat: dit, dit, dit, daaa; dit, dit, dit, daaaa, which the BBC used to introduce broadcasts during WW II. Father O'Reilley stripped naked and lay face-down on the bed.

Sammy hesitated.

"What's the matter, Sammy?"

"Well, I . . . "

"Sammy. This is the way God made us. This is the way we come into the world. We have beautiful bodies, but because of Eve's sin, we are ashamed of our bodies. But with faith in God, we can overcome that. Don't you agree?"

"Uh . . . "

"I knew you would. So go ahead and start. Take some lotion from that bottle, rub it on your hands, and rub my back."

After a short back rub, Father O'Reilley turned over onto his back. He had an erection and could see that Sammy was disturbed.

"Don't worry, Sammy," he said, "God always takes care of us. You did study your catechism and get confirmed in the church, didn't you?"

"Well, yes but . . . "

"That's okay Sammy. I wanted to make sure you understand how God's love comes to us through the Pope and his bishops and priests, who are God's representatives on earth. Also, if you don't obey your priest, you are going to hell. Did you learn that, Sammy?"

"Well . . ."

"So, you can show your love for your priest, God's representative on earth, by doing what he asks you to do. Do you think you can do that?"

"I . . ."

"Well, put your mouth over my . . . what do you call your . . ."

"You mean, prick?"

"Yes . . . that's good enough. Put it in your mouth and move your tongue around it and move in and out. By doing that, you will be pleasing God and you will go directly to heaven; won't even spend time in purgatory."

"I don't know . . . "

"Sammy! Do what God tells you to do, or you'll burn in hell!" Father O'Reilley said, raising his voice.

Father O'Reilley ejaculated in Sammy's mouth. Bewildered, shocked and sickened, Sammy pulled his head up, looked at Father O'Reilley, coughed and unintentionally spit the semen into Father O'Reilley's face.

"YOU FOOL!" Father O'Reilley yelled, reaching for a Kleenex. "Don't *ever* do that again! You hear me?"

Sammy ran to the bathroom to wash his mouth and in the process threw up in the sink.

On the way to the farm, Father O'Reilley told Sammy that he should not tell anyone what had happened. If he did, his parents would die, leaving him alone.

The first time Maria saw Sammy at school he was eating by himself in the lunch room. Medium height and weight, he wore a black, V-neck wool sweater, over a red, plaid, cotton shirt tucked into brown, corduroy pants. He wore varying colour combinations of similar clothing, sometimes wearing blue jeans and a gray sweatshirt.

Maria noticed that Sammy always found a spot in the lunch room where he could eat alone. *He always ate by himself in the lunch room—every day—what's up with that?* She thought. She began to notice other oddities. He walked the halls alone. His beatific smile never left his face. Maria's thoughts drifted in and out about Sammy; *what makes this guy tick?* She thought.

Like Maria and Bubba, Sammy was "different"; all three attracted attention as no others: Maria, a foreigner, with a peculiar accent and a track record of stunning successes; Bubba, a foreigner of sorts, also—from Tennessee—southern drawl, football star, 220 pounds, a crew-cut, and a gait that signaled "muscle bound."

Bubba's tendency to play the school bully in Tennessee did not thaw like the winter ice in Minnesota. Bubba was different, true, but he didn't make the connection—didn't see the irony—of his being "different" while attacking others who, to him were "different," and therefore legitimate targets of his harassment and bullying.

He hung out with his football buddies, who were fascinated by his athletic flair and his considerable contributions to their team's successes. His entertainment value to them was priceless; they liked playing tricks on him. Bubba's arrogant behavior gave added-value to his buddies' entertainment.

Last year, they dared him to pat the sexy English teacher on the butt. His suspension, the final week of the football season, reduced the season's winning record by one, spoiling an undefeated season. The coach did not think the butt-patting episode was funny, but Bubba's buddies roared with laughter when it happened.

The coach was fired, allegedly for failing to control the behavior of his players, but everyone in town knew it was because he didn't have an undefeated season. Football in Sylvan Lake was big.

Maria didn't hang out with any of the school cliques; she lunched, walked the halls, and chatted with whomever: it could be the cheerleaders, a study partner, drama team—that's what she did; no rigid routine with other students. Enigmatic Sammy was another matter.

By mid-April, Maria's observations of and interest in Sammy's odd behavior produced a demanding curiosity; it was time to find out what was going on beneath that charming smile and excessive shyness.

She went to his table—carrying her lunch tray—and asked if she could join him for lunch. He said, through his smile, "Sure," and continued to toss down his soup without looking up.

"Do you remember me?" she asked, placing her tray on the table across from his. He continued eating, his smile showing between each gulp.

"Yup." he said, grabbing a piece of bread. Maria sat across from him.

"How do you know who I am? You didn't even look up."

"I didn't need to. I saw your blue-jeans."

Maria looked down, just to make sure. For the first time in her life, she was flummoxed. *Wow, I was right. This guy is interesting.*

Sammy buttered the bread, added peanut butter and strawberry jam—still smiling. "I know all about you. I see what you wear every day. Bubba doesn't think I know how to read, but I can make out what's going on with you through the school newspaper. You are like a baseball player: a star.

"I know a lot about baseball," he said, taking a bite of his sandwich. "Do you know who played the longest, professional-league, baseball game? You don't need to answer: nobody does. It was the Triple A, Pawtucket Red Sox and the Rochester Red Wings: 1981—thirty-three innings."

He continued, without looking at her. "You are very beautiful. You'd better be careful coming over here like this. Bubba will get you." Sammy was still smiling when he finished eating his sandwich. He guzzled a pint of milk and grabbed an oatmeal/raisin cookie.

Taking a bite of the cookie, he said, "You ever heard of Sandy Kofax? My dad says he is the greatest pitcher of all time; saw him pitch a no-hitter one time. People argue about who's the greatest of all time—a lot of it based on the numbers—but Dad says it's not only numbers; it's also 'class' that makes players great. Like Willy Mays. He wasn't just a great player, he was an entertainer.

"When a high, fly-ball came directly to him, instead of standing there waiting for the ball to arrive, he ran in a big circle and caught it on the run. My dad says that sometimes that was necessary in order to get more power on his throw to home plate, but usually it was simply to entertain the fans. My dad says that's what makes a great ballplayer the greatest."

Sammy looked all around Maria, but never directly into her eyes.

Every time Maria joined Sammy for lunch, it was the same. He sat and talked while they both ate, telling her fascinating details about baseball: the players, unusual games, strikes—not the bat swinging kind, but when the players refused to play until they got what they wanted. Sammy didn't understand all the strike details. He thought they were stupid and not worthy of his attention.

Toward the end of the semester, Bubba had had enough. "What's up with Maria spending so many lunch hours with the dummy?" Bubba asked his buddies at their lunch table. "Do you think Young**stud** is doing her?"

One of the gang, noticing the lunchroom supervisor was nowhere in sight, egged him on: "Why don't you go over and find out?"

Bubba screwed up his courage and decided to do just that.

Out of the corner of her eye, Maria saw Bubba coming.

Ignoring Sammy, Bubba stood by Maria and looked down at her. She looked up at him.

Without saying a word, he formed a hole with his left-hand thumb and index finger. He poked his other index finger through the hole in his left hand—repeatedly–bowed his head slightly, while nodding toward Sammy; he raised his eyebrows, asking her to answer the question.

Maria stared at him in disbelief. She stood up. Looking past Bubba toward the gang on the other side of the lunch room, she bellowed: "Hey fellas! Bubba is using sign language. Did some **guy** bite off his tongue?"

The gang roared . . . slapping each other on the back and giving "high fives," while the other 200 students laughed and snickered. One of the gang yelled back, "What does the sign language say?"

"I don't know," Maria shouted, as she stood and faced the gang. "It looks like this!"

The entire room erupted in laughter; the gang provided harmony with howls of "OOOOOO," piling it on Bubba, who was turning into a flaming torch.

"I'll get you for this!" Bubba hissed, as he passed by Maria toward the lunch room door. Maria turned and gave him the finger; it was a private gesture; no one else saw it.

Sammy continued to eat during the incident, smiling as usual, ignoring what was going on around him.

Chapter 20

Thursday June 19, 1997 finally arrived: Maria's sixteenth birthday.

At breakfast, Leo said to Maria, "Would you like to go for a ride with me to Hutchinson this morning?"

"I can't imagine why," Maria responded, coyly.

"Oh," Leo replied, picking up on her playful response, "I had something special on my mind; not that it's a big deal, or anything like that." He sliced some bacon, placed it on the egg already resting on an English muffin, covered the egg and bacon with the top half of the muffin, took a hefty bite, and began chewing.

A flash of lightning, followed by a clap of rolling thunder, echoed through the massive black clouds that had been gathering since midnight.

"Maybe we'll get enough rain to break the drought," Pat said, when the thunder stopped. "I'm sorry to interrupt. Please continue."

"Well," Leo said, wiping his mouth with a napkin as he stopped chewing, "I thought that since we have such a big pasture, we could go to the cattle auction and buy a calf . . . maybe start raising a few head of cattle. I've been thinking about that for a long time, actually."

"And how long might that be?" asked Maria, flashing a radiant smile, glowing like the aura on the Madonna.

"Well, not *that* long, really. I made it up," he replied, smiling broadly. "How would you like to go get your birthday present?"

Maria jumped out of her chair and ran to Leo, kissed him on the cheek, and gave him a big hug. She did the same to Pat.

"It's been a while, hasn't it, Sweetie?" Pat said. I'm glad the long wait is finally over. Do you remember talking about that the night after you arrived?"

"How could I forget, Mama?"

Looking at them, she said, "Thank you so much. You have been such wonderful parents; I've been in awe at your love for me all these years. Now, Papa, did you say we are going to buy a calf, or a car? I'm not sure I understood."

The growth of Hutchinson—to a population of about 13,000—had forced many surrounding small-town businesses to close because of the ambush that came with the decline of the railroads, and incline of the automobile, the inter-state freeway system, and airlines.

Large grocery stores, pharmacies, car dealerships, department stores— the list seemed endless—had forced many, but not all, small businesses to close in Sylvan Lake; a couple of car dealerships were among the casualties. Someone had opened a used car lot, but it didn't last very long. All towns surrounding Hutchinson, indeed the entire Midwest, were affected by the metamorphosis that transformed much of the United States from the 1960's on.

A red, Ford Mustang convertible: That's what Maria wanted; Pat and Leo approved. The big day had arrived. Pat wanted this to be a special day for Maria and her dad. She loved the way they had become close friends over the years: Maria always respectful, but not always agreeing . . . he protective, but trusting to the point where Pat felt, at times, he was a little too lenient. But, so far, their strategies, rearing this delightful teenager, had worked well and nothing would change.

The trip to Hutchinson lasted less than an hour.

About half-way there, Maria asked Leo about the possibility of Dana having a colt.

"I was wondering if you would ever ask that question. I've had it on my mind since we brought her to our farm, shortly before you arrived. You might have noticed that I rebuilt the barn with that eventuality in mind. But I didn't want to mention it because I didn't want you to feel pressured into taking on that responsibility. It would be a lot of work: giving attention to, building and maintaining a bond with two horses. I'm delighted you asked."

"Well, I thought I'd mention it to see what you think. I'm not thinking about doing that immediately, but maybe someday when I have fewer responsibilities at school. I am happy to hear you like the idea. I think it would be a lot of fun."

The lightning passed, but dark clouds lingered; the rain they wanted did not come.

As they entered the car dealership lot, Maria screamed with delight.

A salesman, watching for Leo's car, drove around the corner into Maria's sight, in a new, red, Mustang convertible, bearing a broad white banner, with red lettering, blaring: "HAPPY BIRTHDAY – MARIA."

All of the formalities had been dealt with the week before, so there was little to do but sign papers and be on their way. Maria wandered around the showroom amongst the new models waiting for Leo to hand her the keys. A middle-aged couple looked at a convertible; two salesmen and a saleswoman were standing by to answer questions.

A man in a black suit, with his back to Maria, asked several questions about a black, luxury sedan.

Father O'Reilley! Maria's face turned ashen.

Papa and the office manager emerged from his office at the other end of the showroom. Leo beckoned Maria with a wave of his arm. As she approached, he said, "Is something wrong?"

"No, not really, just the monthly curse, I think," she said. "I think it's a little early. Better that, than late, right Papa?" she said with a smile.

"Well, I guess so," he said, as he pulled her into a hug, comforting her, in spite of her bravada. As he released her, he put his hands on her shoulders and said, "I love you so much! And by the way," he said with a mischievous look in his eye, "I forgot to remind you about your driver's license. I assume you have it with you."

"Oh, Papa," Maria said, her face and voice feigning deep disappointment and surprise, "I thought you had it with you. Remember? You told me you had taken care of *everything*." She reached out to hug him with a deep affection she had not felt before. "I love you, too, Papa."

"I'll see you at home. Mama wanted me to stop at the grocery store on the way home. Now, go get in that ugly car and get out of here," he said with a smile.

She walked toward the side door of the showroom. As she reached to push the door, she heard a thud and a woman scream. She turned around. Leo lay face-up on the floor.

Chapter 21

"So, I guess that book has some special significance for you, since you are charged with guarding the pope and his cardinals," Maria said to her seat partner.

"Yes. This pederasty scandal has exploded like an atom bomb. I stay very busy with my responsibilities.

"I'm not in the rumor-mill loop. I couldn't play favorites or take sides in all the gossip they say goes on, even if I were in the loop, because I need to stay focused on my job. I answer to my bosses in the Swiss Army, but I also am sworn to protect and defend the pope.

"I'm almost finished with the book. If you'd like to have it, I'll give it to you before we leave the plane."

"Thanks. Yes, that would be fine. I'm not much into religion, but this does sound interesting."

Fritz finished the book. After the plane landed and was taxiing to the terminal, he handed the book to Maria. "Here's my business card. I've put my personal cell phone number on there. If you ever get to Rome, give me a ring. Maybe we could go to dinner."

"Thanks. I don't have much to offer you, unless you use these." She pulled a pack of cigarettes from her hand bag and held them up. "I'm quitting smoking. I acquired two bad habits in Russia: smoking and not using a seat belt.

"A lot of people do the first and almost no one uses a seat belt. I can stop smoking easily; I really don't like it and wonder why I ever started. As for the seat belt habit—well, it might take a while to make it as automatic as it was when I left the States to go to Russia."

"I don't smoke. Toss them in a trash receptacle at the baggage claim area. It was a pleasure meeting you."

"Thank you for the book. It was a pleasure meeting you, also. Sorry, I don't have a business card that would do you any good. I won't have an American cell number until I get home, so can't help you there. I'll take you up on the offer for dinner, if I'm ever in Rome."

"Great. It's been a pleasure."

Chapter 22

Before Maria reached Leo, Father O'Reilley had knelt beside him and was speaking in a language she did not understand. Leo lay on his back, his body rigid, his face contorted in profound trauma, signalling what Maria had learned in her health classes: cardiac arrest.

She yelled at Father O'Reilley, "Get out of the way!"

He continued mumbling. Maria grabbed his right shoulder with both hands, yanked him backward and sent him sprawling across the floor.

Grabbing Leo's nose with her left thumb and index finger and his chin between her right thumb and fingers, she asked one of the salespeople to start pumping motions on his chest.

A salesman called 911 and was talking to a dispatcher.

None of the men moved, but the woman did. She knelt beside Leo's abdomen. They started their rhythmic efforts to revive Leo.

The priest sat up and shouted, "He'll go to hell if you don't let me administer last rites!"

Maria ignored him.

They continued the resuscitation procedure until the paramedics arrived a few minutes later. Their sophisticated equipment didn't work. Leo was dead.

Maria stood up, beat on her chest a couple times, walked to a couch and sat down. The saleswoman, in her mid-twenties, sat beside her and offered her condolences. "My name is Megan. Are you okay?" referring to the chest pounding. Maria—crying—nodded, answering Megan's question. Megan took her in her arms and held her until she regained her composure.

"I loved him so much. He was so good to me. I will miss him terribly." Megan remained silent.

The manager of the dealership went to his office and asked someone to call the mortuary. He came back and sat on the other side of Maria. "Do you have a pastor I can call to help with the situation?" he asked, sympathetically.

"No we don't. I will tell Mama. I want to go home and be with her. But I would like to ask a favor of you. He always said he wanted to donate his body to the University of Minnesota Medical School. He made arrangements several years ago.

"Would you mind telling the mortuary to take his body there? If there are any problems, call us at home. Mama and I will come for his car tomorrow."

"**You know, sweetheart,** when you left home this morning, I had a vague feeling I would not see Leo again; I am not *that* surprised, but of course, deeply saddened.

"I loved him more than I can explain. But," she said, with a weak smile, "We will go on without him. He lives on in our hearts and has gone to a spirit-world we know exists. For that we can be grateful. You and I are luckier than most people I know."

"I know," Maria replied. The "Calm of the Angel" had taken over half-way home. "I asked him on the way to Hutchinson this morning if he'd thought about Dana having a colt. He said he'd had it on his mind for many years, but was waiting for me to bring it up. I wish I'd mentioned it earlier."

"Well, we can still do it if you want to. Your "Gift from God" still has a few more years for colt bearing, so whenever you decide, we can do something about it."

Chapter 23

Summer vacation—between Maria's junior and senior years—had started when Leo died. After a brief mourning period, Maria and Pat made plans for life without him; they weren't complicated, but they did need to have an understanding about who would do what.

Pat would shop for groceries and make the meals, as usual. She would pay the bills. They would share the house cleaning. Maria would take care of Dana, making sure she was fed properly, exercised regularly and monitor her health and wellbeing. That was a major undertaking that would need some adjustment when she went back to school in the fall.

With her papa's passing, Maria thought about what would happen when she returned for her last year of high school. Pat and Dana didn't know each other, which might sound strange, but the fact is that horses become very dependent on leaders: either another horse, or a human master.

They depend on their leader or leaders to protect them, much like parents protecting children. Thus, Maria was the only person left to provide aid and comfort to Dana. She had to figure out before the end of the summer what to do about that . . . not longer, because she would be very busy at school.

Pat waited a month before opening her husband's will. Ten years earlier, Leo and Pat decided to sell the crop-producing land and keep the pasture and the farm buildings for themselves. Leo left Maria two million dollars in T-bills, C-D's and mutual funds, which yielded about ten thousand dollars a month.

About half of that yield went into an interest-bearing savings account and the rest was hers to spend. One million dollars went to Pat with enough yield each month for whatever needs she had. When she passed on, whatever remained would go to Maria.

Maria wondered if she could have a normal conversation—any conversation—with Sammy outside of school. Maybe they could have a real conversation if they spent some time together during the summer. *I have an idea,* she thought. She learned Sammy had a horse because when the Youngstad's came for dinner earlier that year, the subject came up.

As soon as their lives at home had settled down, she drove over to the Youngstad's. Sammy's mother was delighted to see her. She and her husband had heard from Sammy and others about Maria's interest in him at school. They heard a lot about her from Sammy.

Mary invited her in for a cool drink. Sammy and his dad were in the meadow fixing a fence. The weather was hot and muggy: lemonade hit the spot. They chatted for a while about what Maria was doing during the summer and what Mary was doing at home; "I stay very busy with a huge garden," she said. "Fortunately, Sammy is willing to help."

"Speaking of Sammy," Maria asked, "do you think it would be okay for Sammy to come over some Sunday afternoon and go riding with me; maybe pack a picnic lunch and go to the pond for an afternoon in the shade? I would like to get to know Sammy a little better. I'm thinking of asking him to help me with my horse, Dana, when we go back to school in the fall. I won't be able to devote as much time with her as needed. Do you think that would be something Sammy would like to do?"

Mary responded: "I'm sure you know by now that Sammy has some developmental disabilities. They seem to be mostly academic issues. He is slow, mentally, and sometimes it takes a while for him to catch on to what is happening. But when he does catch on, he never forgets; but other than that he is a good boy.

"He can take care of his own horse very well and seems to love horses as much as anything—besides baseball, of course," she laughed. "I think he might enjoy helping out. When he comes home we can discuss it."

Everyone agreed it would be a good idea for Sammy and Maria to get together the following Sunday. Sammy showed up on his horse, ready for an outing.

The ride to the pond became a moving feast with mother-nature on the menu. They bounced along at a slow trot. Scattered clouds, delectable to the eyes, gave them occasional relief from direct sunlight. A soft breeze caressed them like a Mahler symphony on a sentimental, moonlit night. Grasshoppers popped out of the knee-high grass, keeping a rhythmic pace with the horses' hoofs. Birds, communicating in their special ways, became their aural dessert.

Sammy wore blue-jeans and a white, tank shirt. Maria wore three-quarter length, cotton pants, a halter and a straw hat that dangled on her back.

They dismounted at the lake and took refuge under a large shade tree. Maria spread a blanket, while Sammy secured the horses in the shade of another tree; they had been trained to stay close to where the reins were dropped, but felt free to graze on the lush, green grass.

Maria was determined to have a real conversation with Sammy. She had no idea what would happen out here away from the social pressures endemic in a high school milieu. She would wing it.

They ate in silence; finished, they sat cross-legged: she looking at him; he staring at the blanket, fiddling with the knife they used to cut the cheese.

"What are you thinking, Sammy?"

Silence.

"Sammy. I think you are cute."

Silence.

Maria had considered dropping her halter to shock him into some kind of response—any response. Instead, she dropped her halter, shimmied out of her pants and panties and raced toward the lake and made a flying leap into the cool, clear water.

Acclimated, she shouted to Sammy to join her, in his shorts, if he preferred. He stared at her.

She did a few breast strokes, back strokes, and her favorite, a side stroke, before she returned to the shore and back to the shade-tree. Sammy sat staring at the blanket.

She sat down next to him and looked at him. Maria had absolutely no interest in having sex with Sammy. That wasn't even a remote possibility, for more reasons than she could count.

Maybe her compassion for him was misguided; she didn't know, but she had thought about it. All she knew was that somewhere behind that thick wall of emotional protection was a sensitive young man who needed a friend and if she had to do something bizarre to shatter that barrier, she would be happy to do it. She knew he adored her and, on some level, loved her for her courageously . . . openly, reaching out to him in full view of their peers.

"Sammy, have you ever felt a girl's tits?"

He shook his head.

"Want to feel mine?"

He shook his head.

She reached for his hand and raised it toward her right breast . . .

"Don't touch me," he shouted, simultaneously bursting into tears. "I don't want to touch you!" he said, becoming more agitated by the moment.

"Sammy, I'm sorry if I offended you. I was only trying to open up communication for us . . ."

"I don't want you to touch me!" he interrupted, "That priest . . ."

Maria remained silent, looking at him, until the sobbing stopped. He wiped the tears from his face, coughed, and sat looking at the blanket.

"That priest, what? . . . Sammy," she said, gently.

"I don't want to talk about it," he said firmly.

"I think you should."

"I said I *don't want to talk about it!*" he shouted.

"The priest at your church molested you, didn't he?" she asked quietly.

"No . . ." he paused . . . "He *is* molesting me. It's been going on since we arrived. He told me it would save my soul and that if I told anyone, my parents would die, leaving me alone."

For the first time since they met, he locked eyes with her. His secret was out.

"Sammy, he molested me, too, and . . ."

"NO, NO, NO! Not YOU Maria."

He started to cry again.

Maria took him in her arms and stroked his hair. He put his arms around her, held her tight and wished he could stay that way for eternity.

"Well," Maria said, "Finally, we have something to talk about." They both laughed.

They were still laughing when the sound of a galloping horse and a **"yeeee ha"** pierced the air like a bolt of lightning. It was Bubba.

He reined in his horse, hung with his left foot in the stirrup, his left hand on the saddle horn and his right foot dragging on the ground. He hit the ground with both feet before the horse stopped. He dropped the reins and walked toward Maria and Sammy. Maria scrambled for her halter and panties.

Chapter 24

Igor Yavolinski, the bartender who saved Maria from the advances of an inebriated, American businessman that night in a Moscow hotel, played his cards close to his chest with strangers—especially women. The KGB taught him how beautiful, young women can incapacitate a man's rationality as fast as a shooting star slices through the night sky.

At times, it interfered with his carnal desires; still, he believed what he was taught. An impromptu lay can be a very high price to pay if the tag includes death, dismemberment, or worse: unintentional betrayal of one's comrades.

Unlike a lot of his colleagues in college and the KGB, he had no problem giving his lust for women the heave-ho in tempting situations; he felt an intense distaste for intimacy with strangers. He wanted emotional and intellectual familiarity prior to sexual intimacy.

Igor was born in Moscow in 1966 to a father who was an officer in the KGB, and to a mother who was educated as an accountant. He was thirteen years old when his father was assigned to the Soviet Embassy in Washington, D.C. He graduated from an Arlington, Virginia high school in 1983 and American University in Washington, D.C. four years later. He was commissioned a second lieutenant in the Soviet Army and trained as a tank commander. In 1989 he was assigned to a Soviet tank brigade in Dresden, Germany.

He returned to Russia with his brigade after the collapse of the Soviet Union, whereupon he joined the Federal Security Service (FSB—for Federalnaya Sluszhba Bezopasnosti) . . . the successor name for the KGB.

He was working undercover as a bar attendant when he met Maria the night before she returned to the United States. He retired from the FSB three years later.

His job in the FSB involved contact with the new intelligentsia and entrepreneurs of the liberated Russian people. Some of his acquaintances had become very wealthy and possessed an insatiable thirst for fine cars and beautiful women. Igor became a pimp—for fine cars.

Some clients were not satisfied with the latest model luxury cars; they collected, rebuilt and restored cars from around the world. They created minimuseums in Moscow and St. Petersburg and then charged admission for public viewing.

Not willing to buy cars sight-unseen, the oligarchs hired intermediaries to be their "eyes": to travel, find and buy the cars that quenched their appetite for shiny, antique cars and hotrods; that's how Igor became a liaison for the Russian nouveau riche of Moscow and St. Petersburg. Italy—a captivating country—offered intriguing opportunities Igor couldn't resist.

Chapter 25

"You won't need your panties for what I'm going to do to you. We are going to fuck and Sammy can watch," Bubba said as he walked past Sammy.

"What's this Sammy, Do you screw with your pants on?" slapping Sammy on the back of the head. "I knew you were odd, but I didn't think you were that weird. Maybe you can't get it up, so you were just sucking on her tits, is that it?"

Maria struggled to get into her panties as Bubba walked toward her. She had her right leg almost in and was hopping on her left.

"Well, my pale, wildwood flower, have you been *de-flowered* yet?" Bubba sneered, approaching her.

She was stumbling, trying to get her other leg into her panties when he grabbed her and threw her to the ground, falling on top of her. His 220 pounds was too much for her.

He could feel her relax.

"Bubba," she said, softly. I'll let you screw me if you will let us both go when it's over."

He laughed hysterically. "Oh, so *now* you are a sweet little pussy when you don't have a lunch-room full of punks laughing while you're making me look like a fool.

"Well, I'll tell you what, you little bitch, this ain't going to be your average Saturday night screw. This is going to be a violent rape that you won't forget as long as you live . . . and the way I feel right now, you ain't got long to live."

He reached down, unzipped his pants, pulled down his shorts and was on top of her preparing for a violent thrust, when he felt a razor-sharp knife slicing the right side of his neck, below his jaw. He slapped at the knife; instead of driving it away from his skin he drove it further into his neck, severing his carotid artery.

He rolled off Maria, frantically trying to stop the bleeding. "Help me," he shouted. "You sonofabitch Sammy; you tried to kill me!"

He passed out. Maria tried to stop the bleeding, but it was impossible. He was dead.

Chapter 26

The Monday following Bubba's death, Father O'Reilley picked up the Minneapolis Star Tribune. The far left column headline read:

Sylvan Lake Football Star Murdered

Two Sylvan Lake High School students slit the throat of Bubba Barbar, a football star, on a farm near Sylvan Lake Sunday afternoon. Because the alleged killers are minors, their names were not released. The students were arrested and released to the custody of their parents after being interviewed by police and posting $100,000 bail bonds.

A district attorney is investigating the circumstances of the alleged murder. Few facts are known, but a source, who asked for anonymity, because she was not authorized to speak about the case, said that the two minors would probably be charged with second-degree murder, and could stand trial as adults. No further details were available at press time.

The following Saturday afternoon, Father O'Reilley, sitting on the porch of the rectory reading the local newspaper, heard the phone ringing. He walked to his study and picked up the phone.

"Father O'Reilley, here."

It was Archbishop McDuff. "Tell me something," he said, angrily. "What did I demand from you when I transferred you from Trapville several years ago? You don't need to answer. We both know what I'm talking about. Are you aware that you are about to be deposed in that football star's murder case out there?"

"Your Eminence, I have no idea what you are talking about. What do I have to do with the murder? What's going on? Why are you calling me? Does my bishop know about this? He's my direct boss."

"He isn't handling it because I've lost confidence in him. He's the one who talked me into letting him transfer you to Sylvan Lake.

"Your name has been mentioned as the priest who abused the two children who are accused of the murder. The defense attorney is alleging that one of them is a child with developmental disabilities. The boy is alleging that you have repeatedly molested him for the past several months.

"The attorney claims that the child's anger boiled over when he saw the football player—what's his name—Bubba, or something like that—trying to rape a fellow student and threatening to murder her. He slit the guy's throat in a heroic act to save his friend's life; that's what the defense attorney is saying. Who knows what the truth is?"

"Eminence, I assure you . . ."

"We don't have time to argue about this. I told you when I transferred you that I would have you excommunicated if I ever heard another complaint about child molestation. I've protected you twice and this is the thanks I get from you. How many others have you abused since you've been in Sylvan Lake?"

"Your Eminence, this is news to me. Have you had any complaints from anyone else in Sylvan Lake? Have you?"

"No, I haven't, but given your record of having been accused of abusing over 15 children in the last 17 years, suggests there is enough fire where this smoke is coming from and I can't afford to take any more chances with you.

"You know as well as I do that we can't allow any of these cases, including this one, to go to trial. A jury could bankrupt my archdiocese . . . create a public relations nightmare."

"Your Eminence, I don't see how my being deposed, if it should happen, has anything to do with the fears you are expressing. First of all, I've done nothing wrong; secondly, I'm not the one on trial here; thirdly, a couple of snot-nosed kids are on trial and will probably end up in prison. How does that end up costing our archdiocese money?"

"Listen, I'm not going to argue with you. We don't have time. It's already cost my archdiocese over a hundred million dollars settling child abuse cases. Do I need to remind you that several of the cases were yours?

"I've been on the phone to the Vatican. The Prelate in charge of the Congregation of Doctrine and Faith has been approached by the head honcho of the Legionaries of Christ who is intervening on your behalf."

"Your Eminence, how did they find out about this in Rome?"

"I don't have time to talk about this any further. Cardinal Juarez has asked the pope to promote you to bishop immediately and then transfer you to the

Vatican where you will have diplomatic immunity and can't be deposed or involved in the trial.

"Here's what you have to do. First, don't breathe a word of any of this to anyone. Do you understand?"

"Yes, Eminence."

"Second, I'm coming out there tomorrow morning for the eleven o'clock mass. You will assist me in the mass, after which I will announce that, because of your outstanding service and your potential as a future, high-level leader of the Church, you are being promoted to bishop and being transferred to Rome, immediately, to replace a bishop who died of cancer this week. I'll tell your parishioners that a priest from a neighboring town will serve them until I find a replacement.

"You will say goodbye to your parishioners during the service and then leave with me to go directly to the Minneapolis/St. Paul airport for your flight to Rome. A Vatican gendarmerie agent is arriving tonight to accompany you back to Rome, to make sure you get there; I don't want you on the loose.

"You will be a prisoner inside the Vatican. If you leave, the Italian authorities will arrest you and extradite you to the United States. We are doing this to protect ourselves, *not* you. Don't muck it up! Do you understand? You keep your mouth shut and I'll see you tomorrow morning."

Sammy and Maria were indicted and tried for second degree murder. Pat found an attorney in Louisiana with experience prosecuting predator priests to handle their defense; currently in private practice, he previously practiced law as a county defense attorney.

The defense case consisted of: (1) the facts as Sammy and Maria stated them (2) Pat's testimony that Bubba came to her house wanting to speak to Maria. Unaware that Maria and Bubba had clashed at school, she told Bubba where he could find her and Sammy; (3) Sammy's heroic act to save Maria's life resulted, partially, from repressed anger—due to repeated molestation by a priest—being released when he saw Bubba on top of Maria threatening to rape and then kill her. In the attorney's words, Sammy "saw" the priest on top of Maria; and (4) Father O'Reilley's flight to Rome, to avoid prosecution, was credible evidence that he had been molesting children in Sylvan Lake.

The prosecutor, a devout Catholic, asserted that the case centered on a couple teenagers murdering a student who caught them having sex.

His rationale for the murder was that Maria, being a star amongst her peers, couldn't tolerate the potential damage to her reputation, which would be inevitable if the community learned that she was exploiting her lofty position to have sex with an innocent victim of her carnal desires.

The prosecutor contended that there was not one scintilla of evidence that Father O'Reilley had physically abused either one of them. Maria's testimony, that he had molested her, was, he asserted, a red-herring to draw the jurors' attention away from her own murderous actions.

The prosecutor emphasized their lunching together frequently and the extremely damaging testimony that Maria was naked when Bubba discovered them embracing under the tree. He asserted that they were having sex, but when Bubba showed up, Maria lured Bubba into a compromising position and ordered Sammy to slit Bubba's throat to conceal their secret.

Sammy and Maria were acquitted.

Chapter 27

Sammy and his parents decided that he should not attend school anymore because they knew that he was making little progress academically. Sammy did not want to return to school because he knew he would be taunted by students' cruel comments.

For Maria, the situation had changed dramatically. Dealing with trial preparations vetoed any thought of continuing the dizzy pace she had maintained the first three years of high school. She decided to attend Hutchinson High School to avoid creating a stir at Sylvan Lake High. She would attend classes, come home, do her homework and spend time with Pat and Dana.

She had no regrets. She was grateful that she lived in a country where—at least in the United States—there is hope of justice when you get in trouble with the law.

After Father O'Reilley's escape to Rome, she realized there was no such system of justice in the Vatican City State.

Maria asked Sammy to spend more time at her home. Besides needing help during her last year in high school, she wanted him to help while she attended the University of Minnesota. Her senior year in high school was uneventful.

Comparing her four years earning a degree in Financial Management at the University of Minnesota with her earlier life, recalled rides at a recreation theme park—roller coasters and horse carousels. While attending the university, she lived at home and commuted to her classes in order to spend as much time as she could with Dana, Pat . . . and Sammy, who had moved into their home to help care for the horse. She eschewed all extra-curricular activities and concentrated on her studies while attending college.

Chapter 28

Maria retrieved the keys to the Mustang from the Hertz counter, picked up her luggage, and found the car in the covered parking lot. She put the top down and headed home. For Maria, a warm, summer night in Minnesota caressed her heart like few other experiences.

Stars sparkled brightly on the moonless night. The Mustang, without the protective top, brought memories of her borrowing Leo's motorcycle to go to a baseball game the Friday night before he died. About a half-hour drive going west from the airport, Maria turned north.

She had given her red Mustang to Sammy when she left for Russia. He could drive it to Sylvan Lake and back and forth between his parents' farm and Maria's home, but didn't feel comfortable driving it beyond that range due to the many complexities that he would face in faster and more congested traffic.

She swung right onto the gravel road that led to the driveway of the farm. She was getting excited to see Pat after being gone for two years. About a half-mile from the farm driveway, she realized she was racing down a rural, gravel road as though she were weaving through Moscow traffic . . . trying to stay ahead of everyone else. *It's a habit I will work on breaking* . . .

"Damn!" . . . a horse jumped out of the ditch into the headlights. She spun the steering wheel to the left, but clipped its right rear flank as the car skidded toward the ditch . . . .

A high school boy—driving home from a date in Sylvan Lake—lived about five miles beyond the McCarty farm. He squinted. *What the hell is that?* His foot lifted from the accelerator and moved to the brake. He saw automobile headlights, but they were in the ditch to his left, the light-beams piercing the sky like searchlights at Hitler's Nuremberg rally.

"Ah, shit!" He swerved to miss a horse lying in the road as he approached the lights. Stopping between the horse and the lights, he reached for his cell phone and dialed 911.

"Nine-one-one. What's your emergency?"

"I'm out here near the McCarty farm. There's been an accident. It looks like a car rolled over . . . a Mustang, it looks like. There's no one in the car. There's a horse in the middle of the road."

"Which McCarty farm?"

"It's the one south of Sylvan Lake about a mile, and about two miles east on the first gravel road south of town."

"I'm at a call center forty miles from Sylvan Lake," the dispatcher said, "and don't know that area. I'll transfer you to the highway patrol in your area and they can help you. Please stay on the line."

"Minnesota Highway Patrol. How can I help you?"

"I'm near the McCarty farm Southeast of Sylvan Lake. There's been a car accident. The car is in the ditch and there's a horse in the road. It looks like the car hit the horse, because the horse is injured and can't stand up."

"Is anyone injured?"

"I don't know. I'm walking around looking for who might have been in the car. I don't hear anyone and I don't see anyone."

"I'm sending medical assistance and will dispatch a couple patrolmen to the scene right away. Where exactly are you? Are you alone?"

"I'm between the overturned car and the horse lying in the road."

"Are you alone?"

"Yes. Wait . . . I found someone. Oh, my God!! She's that McCarty girl they put on trial for murder a few years ago. She looks all messed up! She's unconscious."

"Can you see if she is bleeding? Don't move her, but see if you can tell if she is losing a lot of blood."

"It doesn't look like it. Her face is scratched and has some blood there. But I don't see any other blood."

"Can you feel her pulse?"

"Let me see. She has a very weak and erratic pulse. It's skipping beats."

"Okay, as I said, don't try to move her. Can you tell how her breathing is? Can you see her chest rise and fall with the breathing?"

"I don't see her chest moving, but she must be breathing, because she is still alive."

"Where is your car?"

"It's in the road—between me and the horse—with emergency lights flashing and the headlights on."

"Good. There isn't much more you can do for her at this point. Paramedics from the Sylvan Lake will be there soon."

"Yes, I can see their flashing lights now."

"Okay. Don't stray too far from where you are so you can direct the patrolmen and the paramedics to the McCarty girl. But look around the area there to see if there was anyone else in the car. In the meantime, I'll send someone out from Animal Control to take a look at the horse."

Maria looked down . . . fascinated and a little confused. She was above the scene of an accident at night, peering down on a horse, lying in the road. It was Dana; *she came out to welcome me home.* The Mustang was upside down in the ditch, with the headlight beams piercing the sky.

She could see her crumpled body in the ditch, not moving. Dana attempted to stand, but fell back on her side. Two highway patrol cars and an ambulance sped toward the scene with lights flashing. A boy went to meet them before they got to the accident.

Curious about her body, she desired a closer look and, instantaneously, was beside her body. She wondered about her mother, and instantaneously was in their farm-house kitchen looking at Pat who was sitting at the kitchen table reading a book.

Maria moved freely . . . wherever her thoughts took her. Pat put the book down and looked around; she shrugged her shoulders and went back to her reading.

Maria watched a medical emergency helicopter land near the ambulance; the crew placed her body on a stretcher and into the helicopter. One of the patrol cars drove toward the farm house and the other stayed with the horse. The boy headed east in his car.

Pat heard a knock on the door.

"Good evening. Are you Mrs. McCarty?"

"Yes, I am. Is something wrong?"

"I'm sorry to have to tell you this, Mrs. McCarty, but your daughter has had a very bad accident about a half-mile down the road from your driveway.

She is being airlifted to the University of Minnesota Medical Center because it appears her injuries are very serious. They are trying to stabilize her vital signs on the helicopter. She hit a horse. Do you own a horse?"

"Oh, for land's sake! I wondered what the ruckus was all about! Why, yes we do. But will Maria be okay?"

"As I said, I don't know. All I know is what the paramedics told me. The ones from Sylvan Lake said that her injuries were too complicated to be treated locally, so they are sending her to the university medical center."

"Oh, my goodness . . . Well, it couldn't be our horse," Pat said, "because we keep her in a pen behind the barn. Can you go with me to the barn to see if it's our horse? I'm sure she is in her pen."

"Sure. Let's take a quick look. We'll need to know whose horse it is before we can do anything. The horse has at least one shattered leg and will need to be put down."

Walking toward the barn, Pat said, "I'm worried. Maria was coming back from Russia and was supposed to be here by now. Oh, my goodness . . . Oh, no!! Dana is not in the pen! The gate is open! How could that happen? I don't understand."

"Who takes care of the horse? Could they have forgotten to close the gate?"

"Sammy, a neighbor boy, but he is always very careful about . . . Oh, wait! We had a problem with the corral lights. We had an electrician out here late this afternoon who fixed the lights.

"I saw him go in through this gate and he must have come back out the same way and didn't make sure the latch was firmly in place. The mare is a little nervous because we are weaning her colt from her and she must have nudged the gate and it opened. Oh, my God. Maria will be devastated."

"I'm sorry, Mrs. McCarty, for both your daughter and the horse. We'll have to stay with the horse until we can get Animal Control to come and take her away. I'll call a tow truck to take the car to a body shop in Sylvan Lake.

"I need to get back there because we need to conduct a preliminary assessment of the accident scene. Is there anything else I can help you with? Do you have a way to get to the hospital?"

"Well, I do drive, but not into the city. I'll call my neighbor and ask him or his wife to take me to the hospital. Thank you for your assistance. Oh, my goodness!"

Hovering above her body and the hospital staff in the emergency room, Maria watched, with interest, as they hooked her up to machines while still lying on an orthopaedic stretcher and trapped in a huge, removable, body-stabilizing cast.

She wondered about Pat and was beside her and Ole in the hospital waiting room.

Traveling at incredible speed through a tunnel, headfirst toward a tiny light that expanded slowly, she saw lights flashing in small circles all around; an ear-shattering, screech-like roar accompanied her as her life experiences flashed like a video on fast forward before her eyes. The light slowly expanded into a pale, yellow-gold cloud as the deafening noise abated.

The cloud saturated her consciousness with a far more, awe-inspiring serenity than the "Calm of the Angel." Pure, unconditional love enveloped her. That was it: no "beings," no room, nothing: only the gold cloud and love. She wanted to stay forever. But the moment she felt that desire, she received a communication, which was very clear, and unequivocal. "*You must go back. You are God's Messenger.*"

The doctor walked into the waiting room.

"Mrs. McCarty?"

"Yes! I'm over here."

"Please come with me." They entered a small, private room.

"Mrs. McCarty, I'm Dr. Wilkinson. I'm supervising the ER tonight. I understand you are Maria Luderenko's mother. Is that correct?"

"Yes, I am. She's going to be alright, isn't she?" she said with a confident tone in her voice.

"I wish I could be that positive, but I'm not. Your daughter has multiple injuries: her lower spine is severely damaged, she has a broken right arm and her upper left leg has been shattered and she has some internal injuries.

Apparently, she was thrown out of the vehicle and it must have hit her as it rolled. She is very lucky to be alive. I'm not sure we can save her. But if we do, she may never walk again. She has been unconscious since the paramedics picked her up. When she will regain consciousness is anyone's guess. We'll do our best to save her."

"When can I see her?"

"Probably not for several hours. She is heavily sedated and will need several surgeries as soon as we have her vital signs stabilized. It will probably be tomorrow afternoon before you will be able to see her, but I wouldn't count on it."

"Okay. Well, thank you, doctor, for doing what you can to help her. God bless you!"

"Thank you."

Back in the waiting room, Ole said, "How does it look?"

"I think she will be okay, but the doctor is being very cautious about what he says. He isn't as optimistic as I am. We need to talk about how to break this news to Sammy."

"I know," said Ole. "He'll be very upset. We need to get back to your house before he wakes up this morning. When can you see Maria?"

"I won't be able to see her until tomorrow afternoon at the earliest, so we might as well go home. I agree; we need to talk about how to handle this with Sammy."

Sammy blamed himself for the unlocked gate, but recovered quickly and demanded that he be allowed to stay with Maria and talk to her—even if she was unconscious—as soon he was allowed in the ICU.

Several days passed before he was allowed to sit with Maria during the night. He talked as long as he could stay awake. He'd drift off to sleep in the stuffed chair, wake up and begin talking again about anything that came to his mind: baseball, how he took care of Dana, how he missed her.

After a week, he was too tired to continue.

His last night would be Friday, the last day of September.

Sammy was very lonely that weekend. He missed Maria terribly. All he could think about was her waking up and getting well.

Chapter 29

"SAMMY! WAKE UP! It's Maria on the phone. She wants to talk to you," Pat hollered from downstairs. Sammy turned on his nightstand light and looked at the clock. It was five a.m. He picked up the phone.

"Hello Maria, is this really you?"

"Well, silly boy, whom did you *think* it would be, *Madonna*?"

"Maria . . ." Sammy started to cry. ". . . I . . . I . . . don't know what to say."

"Well, you could welcome me home, for one thing."

"Are you okay? I mean . . ."

"I will be okay, Sammy. The doctors said I will recover. I might have trouble walking, but you know me Sammy. They can't keep me down forever. Right?"

"Yes . . . right.

Mrs. McCarty, when can I go see Maria?"

"We'll go right away."

"We're coming to see you right away, Maria. I need to go."

Chapter 30

Two weeks after the pope died, the Conclave of 116 cardinals met in the Sistine Chapel in the Vatican and selected Cardinal Marcus J. Madsen, the first African-American (and first American) to rise to the papacy and the first African to hold papal office since the fifth century; three from Northern Africa had served as popes prior to Madsen's selection. He took the name Immanuel.

Pope Immanuel called a meeting for eight a.m. the Monday following his Friday coronation. He summoned ten cardinals. (1) the President of the Pontifical Commission for the Vatican City State; (2) the five cardinals appointed to the commission; (3) The Secretariate of State who directs and coordinates the congregations and councils of the curia; (4) and the three cardinals that head the three tribunals: The Apostolic Penitentiary, the Roman Rota and the Apostolic Signatura.

He was assembling his two Chiefs of Staff and his top generals to let them know who was in charge and what his intentions were—should there be any doubt. That's one way to describe the situation. However, the pope and his minions are often referred to as the king and his princes, resembling more of a feudal monarchy than a military organization.

According to protocol, the pope does not enter a room until all are seated. The cardinals, in their black cassocks with red fascias wrapped around their waists and wearing red caps and white collars, rose as the pope entered the library, the room where the pope receives foreign dignitaries. The library was chosen deliberately to impress upon his cardinals the magnitude of the situation; it was punctuated by the pope's gravitas, which most people agreed was not unlike that of an astronomical black hole that swallows galaxies.

"Please be seated, gentlemen."

Seated at the head of a rectangular, polished-oak conference table, the pope folded his hands and looked around the table to see who was present. He saw eleven cardinals who, only a few days ago, were his equals; today all of them were his subordinates.

"There have been rumors circulating," he said, with an air of modesty, but steely, self-confidence, "about how I would run this place. We are gathered here to dispel any doubts.

"I can assure you that I will not contact any of your subordinates directly for any reason. I have observed how debilitating that is to the morale of our Vatican bureaucracy and it will stop as of this moment. That should help buck up your spirits and those of your subordinates.

"I will hold each of you accountable for your respective areas of responsibility—for the morale and all other professional matters. You will hold your current positions until you prove to me you are not as outstanding as I think you all are."

The gathering was an impressive group, indeed. The President of the Pontifical Council of the Vatican City State is the administrative power-broker of the VCS: a 108-acre territory, within which the Vatican City State and Holy See operate. The President is responsible for the physical, material and administrative functions of the Vatican

The Holy See is an idea, not a place: it is the authority for the pope to govern the Church—of approximately one billion baptized Catholics worldwide—through his cardinals, bishops and priests.

The *Roman Curia,* as opposed to the Vatican City State, is the instrument through which the pope administers the Roman Catholic Church. The offices are separated by two functions—legalistic governance and promotional—the former under the rubric of "congregations": the latter under "councils."

The Roman Rota is the busiest tribunal. Most of its business is annulments. This is the office to which Cardinal O'Reilley was assigned upon being promoted to "red hat" status shortly before Pope Immanuel's predecessor died.

An unprecedented assignment such as this, raised red-cap eyebrows because only Monsignors—priests with an administrative title—are assigned to the Roman Rota. But the previous pope wanted to protect the cardinal from the Minnesota legal system and needed a post where Cardinal O'Reilley would do the least harm; he assigned him to "oversee" the auditors in the Roman Rota.

The Apostolic Signatura is the supreme court of the church and is composed of six cardinals and four bishops. The Vatican gives lip service to protecting the rights of parishioners, but there is no independent judicial system in the Roman Catholic Church as in western democracies.

While Catholic Church apologists are prone to boast that their judicial system has the longest history of survival in human experience, others wonder if any such system is worth boasting about: The Catholic Church's history of flagrant violations of legal justice and human-rights abuses is as long as the history of their judicial system.

That fact was sufficient to put Pope Immanuel on the warpath: he had no idea how hot the war would get; he didn't care. He had spent a lifetime preparing for this war and now it was on.

"We have a lot of work to do, gentlemen. The lackadaisical ambiance in this place is over. I have a lot on my mind this morning and respectfully ask you to hold your questions for some future meeting. I am telling you my expectations up front for your benefit and serious consideration."

Cardinal Madsen's promotion to the papacy seemed enigmatic to anyone informed about Vatican culture and politics; for others, he was merely another pope, except of course, for the stunning fact that he was of African descent and an American to boot.

What happened? Vatican insiders, journalists in the know, and bishops around the world knew that the most recent popes had systematically replaced nearly all the cardinals with conservative, orthodox-leaning archbishops. Cardinal Madsen was one of the exceptions. He charmed his way up the Vatican hierarchy, despite his reputation as a hardheaded free-thinker. Some joked that he was the token "leftist" amongst the College of Cardinals.

Marcus J. Madsen was born in 1946 and grew up in Oakland, California, and was baptized in a Catholic Church a couple miles from the University of California campus at Berkeley. A stocky, athletic, young man earning top grades in high school, he earned a full-ride football scholarship to attend Berkeley.

He arrived at the Berkeley campus in the fall of 1964, the beginning of a student revolution that spread around the world. The Free Speech Movement at Berkeley was led by students who had gone to Mississippi and other southern states the previous summer to take part in the non-violent demonstrations against institutional discrimination that seemed intractable. They came back, used what they had learned about non-violent protests, and catapulted the Free Speech Movement into the faces of university administrators.

The University had banned political activity on campus: *We are an academic institution, not a political activist's training camp!* But the students saw things differently and organized mass-demonstrations to make their point. They wanted their constitutional rights respected: *A state university campus is a public place where we can freely exercise our rights to freedom of assembly and free speech!* They faced down the administration and won. They called it a demonstration of pristine, participatory democracy.

The Free Speech Movement was the spark that ignited a decade of student unrest that roiled universities around the world. Anti-establishment sentiment, a generational gap, political upheaval, communist/capitalist confrontations and disintegration of cultural and moral values, had many young people unhinged—mentally, morally and spiritually.

It was a decade of experimentation by young people who sought alternatives to the mental, moral and spiritual anchors of their parents. Their acting-out ranged from radical confrontations—intellectual and physical—to massive illicit drug and sexual experimentation, to flaunting their independence with outrageous behaviors and unconventional dress codes.

To be sure, a minority of students went to the extremes seen on TV screens all over the world. At Berkeley, a minority of leftists occupied the vanguard of the counter-culture/New Left movements, while a majority of the students took their educational pursuits seriously.

Radical politician-students, hell-bent on taking control of the tens of thousands of dollars doled out to student governments each year, were repeatedly defeated by moderate voters on campus.

Marcus J. Madsen was one of the students who had grown up in a working-class family and appreciated the chance to get a top-flight education at one of the most prestigious universities in the world. He eschewed the drug culture and the hippie phenomenon at Berkeley, but he was keenly aware of the underlying moral and political issues that disturbed a significant segment of students. He participated in the demonstrations, but was not a leader in the protest movements.

He had visited relatives in Mississippi and Alabama and seen the colored/white drinking fountains and restrooms and the inequities that separated minority populations from the white majority, who held the political and institutional power.

He didn't need to go to the South to see and experience such moral abominations because California still had its share of racial issues. He believed that a spiritual regeneration was needed to attack the underlying problems that all Americans—indeed the world—faced; he was determined to dedicate his life to *that* cause. Following graduation from Berkeley, he entered the Seminary of the North American College in Rome.

He was ordained four years later, returned to America, and received a scholarship to pursue a doctorate in religious studies at Columbia University in New York.

Five years later he was awarded his doctorate, moved back to California and began his career as a pastor of a medium-sized parish in San Francisco and taught at the University of San Francisco, a private Catholic university. While in San Francisco, he was promoted to bishop and several years later, archbishop.

Upon his promotion, he moved to Rome and held a temporary professorship at the Pontifical Angelicum University, where seminary students take some of their classes as part of their training for the ministry. He was promoted to cardinal and assigned to the Congregation of Catholic Education, Vatican curia.

"I do not want to waste your time," the new pope said. "And I don't want you or your congregations and councils to waste time. Starting next Monday, a week from today, the hours of work in your dicasteries will be from eight o'clock in the morning until five in the afternoon, Monday through Friday, with an hour off for lunch.

"Working half-days, a centuries-old tradition has ended. I expect you to inform your employees immediately after this meeting so they will have time to make the adjustment.

"Second. I want recommendations from each of you—this is not a group effort—regarding what needs to be done in our bureaucracy, the curia, to make it a joyful place to work. All of you have worked here for many years and know what I am talking about.

"Third, I want an analysis of the underlying issues that have brought our Church to its present crisis; include in your assessment what can be done about whatever conclusions you come up with.

"We don't need to quote what our numerous critics have said about the Catholic Church, the Vatican bureaucracy, the horrors of our history, and how we now face a crisis that is as much of a challenge—or more so—than the crisis we faced at the time of the Reformation. Why? Because we know that most of what our detractors say—within and outside our Church—has a lot of merit.

"If you wonder what I have in mind when I refer to a crisis, here are a few clues: (1) Sex abuse by thousands of our priests all over the world resulting in tens of thousands of victimized children, a fact compounded by the reality that a cover up by priests, bishops, cardinals and even popes has been underway for centuries and continues to this day; (2) Twenty percent of our parishioners here in Rome—the so-called "City of God"—attend church regularly; (3) the situation is worse in France and Germany: ten percent of all Catholics attend mass; (4) Churches are closing at an alarming rate in many of the major countries of the world, especially America. (5) Over 100,000 of our priests have left the ministry in recent years. (6) Our Christian doctrine is being challenged by new revelations about who Jesus of Nazareth really was and what he really said and did; (7) We live in luxury here in the Vatican, parading around in gilded robes and hats, the cost of which could feed thousands of starving children; (8) We seem to think that pageantry/ceremony is some kind of evidence of our authenticity—a substitute for decency, respect for each other, and humanity at large; (9) Catholic popes and apologists exult that St. Peter's Basilica proves the Catholic Church holds a preeminent authority over all religions . . . that it is the most glorious structure ever applied to the use of religion; I wonder about that; (10) We have a religious doctrine and a governance process that are relics of the past, making one man the supreme authority over all his subjects, which has resulted in abuses of power that rival that of humanity's worst totalitarian regimes **. . . Think:** *mass murders of men, women and children, burning women at the stake, relentless pursuit of "heretics" (which continues to this day), mafia connections, and financial scandals . . . you name it;* (11) Our Church was founded on a doctrine of fear and terror, specifically chosen to intimidate and terrorize: *fear,* that we might not live up to the requirements of the faith we fabricated out of Judaism and the life of a man named Jesus of Nazareth; and *terror*, that if we violate any one, or many of the 800 rules we have in our catechisms, we will spend an eternity in hell.

"In secular, totalitarian states, terror ends with a bullet in the back of the head; in the Roman Catholic Church, the terror never ends because we face the possibility of spending eternity in hell; tragically, our highest value—retaining the pre-eminence of Catholicism over all other religions—outweighs providing a religion that expresses the love and joy our Creator has for us.

"If any of what I have mentioned here is a surprise to you, wake up!

"I haven't mentioned all of our problems; I'm sure some of you can cite many more, as can I. I'm here with you this morning to tell you that our apostolic soiree, characterized by arrogance, corruption, callousness, and disdain for humanity, is over.

"From this moment forward, you will start earning your pay and your title, or you will be dismissed.

"All pageantry and ceremonial events will be cleared through me before planning begins. I am cancelling all foreign trips until further notice.

"Cardinal O'Reilley. Please come to my office at eleven Wednesday morning."

Looking angry, Cardinal O'Reilley said, "Your Holiness, may I ask why?"

"No, you may not. Apparently you have a short memory. I said at the beginning that I was not taking questions." The pope continued. "I want solutions to the problems I have mentioned and I expect each of you to give me your analysis of the problems that have produced the crisis and what to do about them. I will give you a hint as to how to proceed.

"The problems I mentioned are symptomatic of contradictions that exist in our system of governance and our magisterium—our authority to teach the truth. You might start by asking: what is the truth? I want your analyses on my desk within six months. While you are doing your papers, see what you can do about making life in this place a little more pleasant for yourselves and your subordinates.

"I will expect a report from each of you by the end of the day today that you have informed your employees of the new working hours. Now, let's all get back to work."

"Well, how did it go, Holiness?" asked Father Sandusky, as the pope entered his office.

Pausing after the office door closed, the new pope said, "I did all the talking. I had a digital recorder on, so we'd have a record of what I said for our files." He handed it to Sandusky. "Transfer it to our computers so I'll have access to it when I need it.

"Before I forget, have a computer and printer installed in my office, with the keyboard and monitor on my desk and the printer behind me on a table that will accommodate it and a couple feet of space on either side for convenience when copying. You might need to move the safe over a couple feet to make room for the printer. And set up an email account for me also.

"Back to your question: My two main purposes were to let them know who was in charge and also give each of them an assignment, which by the way, I would like to have you participate in as well; it was to analyze what got us into the crisis in which we find ourselves, and, secondly, what to do about it. Frankly, I don't expect to receive thoughtful responses, but I want some of them to see how inane their thinking is. Compared to what? To your analysis.

"You are highly educated at prestigious institutions, including Columbia University in New York, in the area of religious studies. I know your analysis and recommendations will be of great value. Your specialty in your doctoral program was the history of early Christianity; is that correct?"

"Yes, Holiness."

"Okay, then. Here's what I want you to do. I want you to give a brief history of the conflicts that arose in the early Christian Church; then, relate that to what we know today due to the revelations we now have from the discoveries of the *Gospel of Judas* and the *Nag Hammadi Library*, and the controversial, *Conversations with God*. I am aware of these recent revelations, but haven't had time to read them, not to mention study them.

"I anticipate you will come up with some very interesting data that will be useful to me as I look at opening up the Church to new ideas and restructuring the bureaucracy.

"I've given the cardinals six months to come up with their analyses and recommendations. Shoot for a year as your timeline because you will need that much time, given the task. When we get the cardinals' analyses, I'll give them to you for use in your paper. Can you do that for me?"

"Of course, Holiness. That sounds like an interesting project."

"Now, after you have put what's on the recorder on a computer, read it so you will know what I said and what my expectations are."

"Will do, Holiness. Is there anything else?"

"Not for now. Thanks." Pope Immanuel stepped toward his desk, turned, looked at Father Sandusky and said, "Oh, . . ." knitting his brow, "yes there is. See if you can find and recommend a young, recently ordained priest to come and work with us as another secretary. I will need two of you. See if you can find someone with advanced study in finance and accounting."

"Will do, Holiness."

Father Sandusky had been the previous pope's personal secretary. He was tall, with an egg-shaped head, which was ameliorated by a full head of blond hair and penetrating, blue eyes. Rising to a position as the pope's secretary did not necessarily guarantee a shot at the papacy, but for the right person, it didn't hurt; Father Sandusky was praying he would be an exception to what was customary: that most personal secretaries didn't have a chance to become pope.

Chapter 31

"**Cardinal Penelli.** This is the pope. Are you free to come over to my office?"

"Yes, Holiness. I'll be right there." Penelli entered the office.

"Have a seat. What is your title," the pope said, gently.

"President of the Pontifical Commission. Basically, I'm responsible for the administration of all financial and logistical matters pertaining to the Vatican City State. Their commission has sixteen offices. I have about 1500 employees, nearly a hundred of them priests. I have nothing to do with the administration of the Vatican Bank."

Leaning back in his chair, the pope said, "And did you hear what I said yesterday about wanting a report that you had informed your employees about the change of hours?"

"Yes, Your Holiness, I did."

Leaning forward over his desk, folding his hands, the pope proceeded. "Well, you may have been in the habit of ignoring what your boss told you in the past, but I won't tolerate it. Why didn't you report as instructed?"

"Your Holiness, with all due respect, I am in the habit of doing my home-work before I bother my "boss," as you say. I did inform my people of the new change in hours, but there was an-uproar and nothing got done yesterday. I wanted to see what happened today, so I could make a more in depth report on what the ramifications—of what you ordered us to do—would be. I have the report with me."

"I understand you may have worked that way in the past. But I am warn-ing you that that is not the way you will work for me. Is that clear? What you have done is tell me I don't know what I am doing, so you will save me from my own ignorance. When I ask for a report by the end of the day, that's what I mean. What does your report say?"

"It says I have told my employees what you told me to tell them, and it also contains many reasons why this is not a good idea. That's it." He handed it to the pope.

"Okay, thanks. Now, I understand your financial affairs are in a mess. You have one month to prepare a report on what the difficulties are, what your operating budget is, and how you plan to solve the problems. Is that clear?"

"Yes, Holiness, it is. If I need guidance, should I see Father Sandusky?"

"Yes. And stay in touch. You are dismissed."

The pope pressed a button on his phone.

"Yes, Your Holiness."

"Can you come and see me?"

"Certainly, I'll be right there."

"Have a seat Cardinal Moretti," the pope said gently. "And the office you hold is?"

"Secretary of State. I am the head of the Secretariat of State, which has two sections: (1) *Sostituto*, which is responsible for general affairs, correspondence, and the language desks. (2) *Secretary for Foreign Relations*, which is self-explanatory. The Sostituto section coordinates with the twenty offices of the Curia, a term which, as you know, in ancient Rome, referred to the seat of the Roman Senate. I handle religious and church affairs, as opposed to the administrative affairs of the Vatican State. Totaled, there about one hundred employees under my authority."

"You have a huge responsibility, don't you?"

"Yes, but I have a lot of dedicated people to assist me. So I feel comfortable in my job."

"So comfortable that you think you can ignore my orders? In other words, violating your vow of obedience? You heard what I said yesterday about how things will be done around here. Right?"

"Yes, Holiness, I did."

"And you heard that I wanted a report from you that you had informed your employees about the new working hours starting next Monday? Is that correct?"

"Yes, Your Holiness, that is correct."

"Then, why didn't you do what I told you to do?"

"I don't have any employees who work for me."

"Tell me, Cardinal Moretti. Do you supervise any employees?"

"Yes, and they have employees who work for them, but I don't. I assumed it was those employees you were referring to. So I didn't make a report."

"I see, Cardinal Moretti. And I presume that is the way you are accustomed to working around here. Is that correct?"

"Yes, Holiness, I take my responsibilities very seriously. And I do exactly what the Holy Father tells me to do."

"Well, in that case, why didn't you tell your supervisors to pass on what I told you to do?" asked the pope.

"My supervisors are not *'employees',*" Cardinal Moretti said, with a twisted emphasis on *employees*. "They are priests, high-ranking servants of God. I thought you should go to the supervisors of our working employees—not cardinals—and tell them yourself so they would know where the message came from.

"It will be very painful for many of our employees to do what you are telling us they must do. If you insist on our carrying out this mandate, there will be serious repercussions that you can't now imagine. I'm only trying to help you out, Holiness."

"I see. Well, I tell you what, Cardinal Moretti. I'll help *you* out . . . right out the door. You're fired."

Cardinal Moretti stared at the Pope.

"Get out of my sight, Cardinal Moretti. It's not your poor understanding of how a bureaucracy works; it's your arrogance in trying to explain away your avoidance of a distasteful task that bothers me. *Leave* . . . before I call the Swiss Guard to escort you out."

Cardinal Moretti rose, turned, walked toward the door, turned around and said, "You're not playing with fire, Marcus, you are playing with a volcano."

"Cardinal Moretti. I'll give you one week to move out of your apartment here in the Vatican. Where you go is your business. But when the week is up, you will not be welcome here. If you show up, I will have you arrested."

Cardinal Moretti turned toward the door, opened it, and smiled at the Swiss Guard, who took the door from his grasp. As he turned left and headed down the corridor toward the elevator, he met Father Sandusky, who stopped and greeted him with: "Good morning, Your Grace. How did your meeting with our new pope go?"

"He fired me."

"He what? He fired you? Are you serious?"

"Of course, Father Sandusky. It's not a joking matter."

"Well, I don't know what to say. I was looking forward to working with you."

"The only way that will happen now is if the pope dies and the elector cardinals call me back to be their pope." He stared at Father Sandusky.

Father Sandusky flinched, not knowing what to make of the stare. He felt a twinge of horror, but only a *fleeting thought* that Cardinal Moretti was suggesting something Sandusky didn't want a *second thought* about.

Recovering, Father Sandusky asked if there was anything he could do: meaning now that the man was fired, did he need help packing, finding a place to live or whatever? Cardinal Moretti replied, vaguely, that he would get in touch if he needed any help.

"Is this Cardinal Conti?" the pope asked, holding the phone.

"No, this is his associate, Archbishop Lam. Who is this?"

"This is the pope. May I speak to Cardinal Conti?"

"He took the day off. Is there anything I can do for you, Holiness.

"Yes, come to my office immediately."

"Yes, Holiness. I'll be right there."

The Swiss Guard held the door as Archbishop Lam entered the pope's office.

"You work in the Congregation of Doctrine and Faith, as I recall. Is that correct?"

"Yes, Holiness."

"I've watched your career for years. I've been impressed. You are now a Cardinal. We can take care of the formalities later. Starting today, you will be the Secretary of State. I just fired Cardinal Moretti. I don't have time to waste.

"Ask Father Sandusky what I said at our meeting yesterday. He has a transcript of what I said. Take the actions I have directed. In addition to what Father Sandusky will tell you, I want you to prepare a report on all the financial aspects of your new office, including but not limited to, your operating budget, real estate holdings and such. If you need clarification along the way, talk to Father Sandusky. Is that clear?"

"Yes, your instructions are clear, but Holiness . . . I . . ."

"Don't bother. Go and do your job. We have a lot of work to do around here." The pope looked down at his paperwork, looked up and said, "We don't have time to waste."

Chapter 32

Upon Bishop O'Reilley's arrival in Rome, he went to the Vatican and did not leave the premises for two years in order to avoid being arrested for his crimes in Minnesota. He knew the courts there had issued warrants for his arrest and that Italy does have an extradition provision in its code of law.

Because he was getting restless, and wanted someday to wear the red cap, he decided to risk arrest. He left the Vatican three times a week to attend a university in Rome where he could get a doctorate in canon law (J.C.L.). *Most likely,* he thought, *prosecutors in Minnesota have decided to move on to more urgent and less complicated cases that did not involve arrest in a foreign country and eventual extradition.*

He graduated, was promoted to archbishop, and continued to "oversee" the annulments, the most important of several functions of the Rota.

Based on what Pope Immanuel knew about O'Reilley—which wasn't much other than his incompetence—it wouldn't be long before he could fire him with some sort of justification.

The biggest obstacle he faced in getting rid of Cardinal O'Reilley was his close ties with the Legionaries of Christ who wielded enormous power in the Church. He would wait until he brought out his big guns aimed at solving the crisis in the Church to take on the Legion. That could be years away.

Based on the notorious bureaucratic custom of "kicking employees upstairs" when higher management wanted them out of the way, but for whatever reason, couldn't or didn't want to get rid of them, Pope Immanuel reasoned that the higher the rank O'Reilley held, the lower the risk of his doing any harm would be. He silently thanked the previous pope for taking care of that onerous task: promoting O'Reilley to cardinal. But that didn't stop him from holding Cardinal O'Reilley responsible for the office he held.

At eleven a.m. the Wednesday following his first meeting with the cardinals, Pope Immanuel stood half-way between his desk and the office door when the Swiss Guard let Cardinal O'Reilley in. He walked stiffly toward the pope, knelt as the pope held out his hand for the cardinal to kiss the papal ring. O'Reilley, still angry at the slight he experienced in front of his colleagues at the meeting Monday morning, looked up as he kissed the ring and tried to stare down the pope; it didn't work.

The pope withdrew his hand, turned, and walked slowly around his desk and sat down. O'Reilley stood in place where they had met, waiting for the pope to invite him to have a seat. The pope took his time making a gesture with a wave of his arm toward the chair on the left.

"The reason I want to talk to you is that I have learned that you have over a thousand annulment applications waiting to be processed. Is this correct?"

"Yes Holiness. And there will be a lot more than that if you take away my employees."

"What makes you think I'm taking away your employees?"

"You told us to announce that the hours are changing. My people won't stand for that. They'll go on strike instead. Then you will have taken away my employees."

"I see. And what will you do then?"

"I'll have to wait until they come back. By that time I'll probably have twice as many annulments waiting to be processed."

"How many years have you held your oldest application?"

"The oldest is over eleven years."

"Are there many like that?"

"Not many, probably not more than a dozen."

"And what is your average turn-around time for annulment applications?"

"I would say about six months."

"So a young couple, say in Peoria, Illinois, who want to get married, but need an annulment, must wait for you to do your job, is that correct."

"That's correct, Your Holiness. We don't have enough staff to get the job done efficiently."

"So, how many hours do your employees work each week?"

"Well, they are supposed to work thirty six hours, but most of them have family, and other things to take care of and end up working a lot less. It's been that way for decades, if not centuries."

"And what have you done to get them to work the hours for which they are getting paid?"

"Nothing. It's the way things are around here and all the offices are the same."

"And it didn't occur to you to take the initiative to get the backlog of work done? Is that correct?"

"Holiness, I see where this is going. I don't think you understand . . . "

"I think you are right. I don't understand how someone of your rank can sit on his dead ass and do nothing when there are hundreds of people all over the world waiting for a decision from your office.

"I'll tell you what I do understand and it's this. As of this moment, I am suspending all policies and procedures you follow to get these annulments processed. You *will* do whatever it takes to get those annulment applications approved and out of your office in thirty days."

"But, that is impossible. They all need to be analyzed . . ."

"The pope interrupted, raising his voice. "That's not what I meant! What I said is I want those annulment applications out of your office and going back to their applicants in thirty days.

"If that means simply taking a stamp and slapping "APPROVED" on the front of the application without any further processing, then do that. In fact, that's what you will need to do to accomplish what I have ordered done in the time required. If you simply throw them in the trash can, I will find out about it and I will excommunicate you. Is that clear?"

"Before you can excommunicate me, I will have you removed from the papacy and excommunicated for giving me an unlawful order."

"You may have a doctorate in canon law, but I have studied canon law also. So long as I occupy the Office of Peter and the Chair of Peter, I cannot be removed from either, for any reason, unless you can prove I have done something immoral. Yes, priests, bishops, cardinals and popes can be removed from offices for acts of immorality. I think your failure to process annulments in a timely manner is immoral.

"Have you considered the harm you are doing to the thousands who wait months for you to do your job? Our canon law has no basis in morality. It was created by old men for the purpose of maintaining the power of the church over its people, especially women. Now, that's something to think about when you start talking about immorality."

"Well, I have made some arrange . . ."

"This discussion is over," the pope interrupted. "Go back to your office and do what I told you to do. If you don't meet the deadline and have proof from our postal service that all thousand, or whatever the number is, have been sent to the applicants, I will fire you the following day. Is that clear?"

"I hope you have a couple of your American Army divisions behind you, because you will need them to survive what you have already started."

"Now, you are sounding like Stalin, when he asked about the power of the pope . . . 'How many divisions does he have?'

"I have the power of our people with me. They want something done to heal our Church. I've seen surveys of our parishioners, and in one large American city, thirty percent of the Catholics wanted to separate from Rome. Does that tell you anything? I'm not sure what we can do, but I'll do my best. I assure you, I will do whatever I think is morally right, as I see that right. I'll send a memo to all concerned cancelling the annulment policy. Now get out of here and go back to work."

Chapter 33

A Swiss Guard held the door open as Father Perfecto Gonzales entered the pope's office. He wore a black cassock, white clerical collar, black socks and black dress shoes. Bushy, black, curly hair framed a round face, accented by large, brown eyes on either side of a well-sculpted nose.

Father walked straight forward. The new pope, sitting at his desk, was busy with paperwork in an open, manila folder. The priest walked to the front of the desk and stood staring at the pope. After what seemed like a ten-inning baseball game with no hits, the pope looked up and glared at the priest.

"Please stand up! I don't want my visitors to come to me on their knees!"

"Your Holiness, I am not on my knees. I am standing on my feet," he said with a big smile. I'm four feet, ten inches tall."

The pope stood up, leaned far forward, looked at the priest's feet and said, "So you are. Your shoes need shining," and sat down. "What brings you here this morning?"

"Your Holiness . . . "

"Excuse me. You don't need address me with 'Your Holiness' with every sentence you utter. It wastes time and I don't have time to waste. Why are you here?"

"I was told you wanted to interview me . . . by Father Sandusky, Your . . ."

The pope stared at him. "He said he was sending someone to interview for the Assistant Secretary position."

"That would be me, uh . . . Holiness."

"What's your name?"

"Perfecto."

"You're hired. With a name like that, I can't miss."

"Your . . . uh . . . what am I supposed to do?" Perfecto asked with a big smile.

"First, find a place to live. There's an apartment down the hall from mine next to Sandusky's. Get moved in, get settled and then come back to see me." The pope went back to his paperwork.

The pope looked up. "Well, are you going to stand there the rest of your life? Or are you going get to work. We don't have time to waste!"

"Yes, Your Holiness." Perfecto said with an even bigger smile.

The pope glared at him until Perfecto turned around and walked toward the door. *It looks like I'm on the fast track!* Perfecto mused.

The pope smiled and folded the file labeled, "Father Perfecto."

The file contained Perfecto's academic record. Perfecto grew up in West Los Angeles, the son of a UCLA history professor; his mother: a medical doctor at the UCLA Medical Center. He graduated from UCLA with a bachelor's degree in business (summa cum laude), an MBA from USC, and a Ph.D. from UCLA in financial management. He graduated from the North American College Seminary in Rome and was ordained the week before he met the pope.

Clerical positions in the Roman Catholic Church are held by carefully vetted appointees, but no one ever applies for a position. When a position comes available, superiors are asked to nominate several candidates based on personal knowledge and recommendations of others who know the potential candidate.

In Father Perfecto's case, the only record they had was his academic record. Father Sandusky had made some phone calls to some of his professors and confirmed that his psychological stability and personal relationships were as outstanding as his academic record.

Chapter 34

Cardinal O'Reilley went back to work, picked up the phone, and called the Regional Legion of Christ headquarters in Rome.

"Father Morales here."

"Father Morales. This is Cardinal O'Reilley. How are you today?"

"Fine. And you?"

"I wish I could say the same. I've already had two meetings with the new pope. If these meetings are any indication of what is in store for the Church, we need to start marshaling our forces against this maniac.

"Within about three hours of his reign, he has called into question the core doctrines of the Church, has initiated a sweeping review of our Church history as a means of determining how we got ourselves into what he calls a crisis, has radically altered employee work schedules, and ordered me to violate long-standing rules within the Code of Canon Law."

"Is that all?" Father Morales laughed.

"It's not a laughing matter. Is the director in? I'd like to talk with him. And, by the way, who are you? I don't recognize your name."

"I'm new here. I'm the General Administrator for this regional office. Our General Director of the Legion's headquarters in Connecticut, Father Pablo Nunez, comes once a month. Currently he is on a month long tour to several countries where we have operations. I'll leave him a note to call you, if you like."

"Do you have his phone number?"

"Yes. I'll send you an email with the General Director's itinerary and include the phone number."

"Thanks for your help."

By the time O'Reilley got off the phone, he had calmed down. He ate lunch at his desk, while reading the newspaper. His lunch hour over, his eyes fell on his checkbook. *Ah, shit!! NOW what am I going to do?*

He grabbed his cell phone and punched a speed-dial number. A raspy voice answered. "What the hell are you doing waking me up this early in the morning?" It was 1 p.m. in the afternoon.

"It's urgent! We need to meet this evening. Something has happened. I can't talk now. The usual place. Ten-thirty p.m."

Cardinal O'Reilley dialed the Opus Dei headquarters in New York.

"Opus Dei headquarters. How may I direct your call?"

"This is Cardinal O'Reilley in the Vatican. May I speak to the Monsignor Lopez?"

"I'll connect you."

"Lopez."

"Monsignor Lopez. This is Cardinal O'Reilley in the Vatican. How are you today?"

"Fine . . . and you?"

"I'm well, but I have an urgent request . . . "

"I understand our new pope is raising hell over there," Lopez interrupted.

"To put it mildly, yes. That's why I called. I'm sure you have your sources in the Vatican, so I won't go into details. The point of the call is that we need to do something before he brings down the house. We have a war on our hands. I'm a member of the Legion. I'm thinking we should get together and see what we can do to stop him."

"Don't you think that is a little premature? He's hardly had time to get settled in. I think we should wait until the entire deck of cards is dealt; he has only thrown out the first round of cards. We need to see what hands we are holding before we make our first move, if any at all."

"If we do that, it might be too late! Look, I don't want to get into an argument with you. I see you don't get it . . . how serious this is. If you think Luther's rebellion was a big deal, you're about to witness an uproar that will make the Reformation look like the egg-roll on the White House lawn at Easter time. I tell you what . . . I'll call you back when you've seen what I'm predicting. Maybe then we can have a constructive conversation."

"Yes, I agree. I think that's an excellent idea. The first thing we need to do is find out who our enemies are and what they are up to. Good idea, Cardinal O'Reilley. Keep me informed. Talk to you later."

Cardinal O'Reilley put down the phone, sat back and stared at the ceiling, deep in thought. *These two organizations have the power to bring down this pope, and they are ignoring me. Someday, I'll be able to say, "I told you so, but you wouldn't listen."*

C h a p t e r   3 5

Wednesday afternoon, two days after Pope Immanuel held his first meeting with his top cardinals, Pope Immanuel called in the two cardinals having responsibility for all Vatican employees: the President of the Vatican City State: Cardinal Penelli; and the Secretariat of State, responsible for the Curia, Cardinal Lam.

"I understand my order to change the working hours has caused a stir amongst our employees. Is that correct?"

"Yes. Correct, Holiness," the two replied, simultaneously.

"What's going on?"

Cardinal Penelli, responsible for most of the affected employees, spoke first. "I'm sure you expected there would be some resistance to this move. The hours, for decades if not centuries, have been quite lax . . . generally not enforced, which makes it virtually impossible to get anything done in the afternoon. I won't belabor all the problems associated with such nonsense. Bottom line is that the employees are threatening to go on strike if the order is carried out. If they do, that would cripple our operations. Do you agree with my assessment, Cardinal Lam?"

"Yes, I do. The two of us have been sharing what's going on in our respective areas and the reactions of our employees are the same. I'm quite sure they will go on strike Monday morning."

"Okay. Fine," the pope said. "Tell them that anyone who doesn't show up for work Monday morning at eight a.m. will be fired. We'll deal with extenuating circumstances relating to no-shows as they arise.

"Keep records of who shows up and who doesn't and have form letters, prepared by your staff, for you to sign and mail to those who fail to show. Use your own judgment if someone is a few minutes late as to whether they get a termination letter; it'll depend on the plausibility of their excuses. Any questions?"

"If they all, or nearly all, don't show up, what happens then? We won't have anyone to do the work," Cardinal Lam said, quietly. "And what about the thousands of visitors who pass through here each day? What will we do about that?"

"Excellent questions, Cardinal Lam. That's why you are now a cardinal. Obviously, the priests on your staff will not be going on strike, *obedience,* being one of their vows. We'll pull in as many priests, living and working in Rome, as we need to get our work done: clerical or whatever.

"I am told there are about fifteen thousand priests living in Rome. I don't know what all of them are doing, given the fact that almost none of our parishioners attend church. Draw from that pool."

"But, Holiness, they probably won't want to come to do clerical work and so forth. They are priests, trained to do God's work amongst our people," Cardinal Penelli said, gently."

"Well, so they are. I consider clerical work to be God's work, also. So you find out who they are and order them in here. If they refuse, remind them that it's an order from the pope and they took a vow of obedience, and we all know what dire consequences that has for those who disobey. Work through the bishops. If you have any problems with the bishops carrying out these orders, fire them and we'll take care of the paperwork later.

"Now, ask the commander of the Swiss Guards to come and see me. I need to talk to him about what's going on.

"Which reminds me; we should cancel the museum and gardens tours, starting next Monday—for a month—until we get all this sorted out. Get ahold of all the tourist agencies we do business with and inform them of my decision. They will need to give the tourists who already have tickets a refund. Any more questions?"

The two cardinals looked at each other and smiled. "Your Holiness, we'll do as you say," said Cardinal Penelli. "Will that be all?"

"Yes. Thank you for coming. Let me know what happens Monday morning."

"**Colonel Eisenberg,** thank you for coming over to see me. How was your vacation?"

"Wonderful, Holiness." I loved seeing the iconography in Moscow and enjoyed my time with my sister in San Francisco."

"Good. Well, I wanted to talk to you as soon I learned that we could be in for some interesting times around here. You probably heard rumors that there is a devil who has become pope: that would be me. Well, so be it. I'll deal with it, but I will need your help.

"A rumor has reached me that one of my top ranking cardinals wants you and your Swiss Guards removed from the Vatican. It wouldn't take a quantum physicist to figure out what's up with that. Without you and your small army here to protect me, my detractors would reduce resistance to their perfidious intentions by about ninety percent.

"It is difficult to say who our 120 internal Vatican security force would back in a showdown between me and some rebellious cardinals. I know I can count on you to cover my back as I carry out reforms. So I want to assure you that you and your men will be here as long as I'm pope."

"Thank you, Holiness. I really appreciate your support. But I'm a little worried about what's going on with some of the cardinals who oppose what you are doing. Some of the cardinals have suggested you might be in danger."

"Ah, yes. Well, we are in grave danger from the moment of conception and on up to when we go to our heavenly reward, however long that might be. So I don't worry about things like that.

"Now, having said that, you should have gotten the message by now that I have changed working hours for Vatican employees, but, of course, that does not apply to you and your employees.

"We will probably have a strike on our hands Monday morning. What will happen is any body's guess. I have ordered my chief cardinals to take measures to keep our operations going by bringing in local priests to replace the strikers.

"That could mean several hundred priests coming on board as soon as we can verify the identity of each one. Once that is done, they will replace our clerical staff.

"We need to wait and see if our 130 Corps of Gendarmes, our police and security personnel will strike also. If they do, they won't be re-hired, but non-security clerical staff and others like them will be re-hired eventually. We'll hire a completely new security force if necessary.

"From what I've seen in the square and our screening for tourists inside the tourist reception area, terrorists could strike at any time. I've been talking to our Italian friends and our staff about my concerns. I have ordered the end of all tourist visits, starting next Monday, until we get this personnel situation under control.

"My cardinals are working to inform the tourist agencies. All of our employees associated with the tourist operation, who do not strike, will be re-assigned until the strike ends. Work with Cardinal Penelli on any problems you encounter. And don't hesitate to come directly to me with any concerns or for assistance you may need. You work directly for me. I am your boss, not one of my cardinals, but I'm sure Penelli will work with you on the day-do-day matters.

"Do you have any questions?"

"Not really, Holiness. You have covered the waterfront. If I can be of any assistance on any matter, let me know."

"Thank you. I will certainly do that. Now, I must get back to work. And again, welcome back."

Chapter 36

The Monday morning following Father Perfecto's first meeting with the pope, he stood before the pope's desk waiting to be recognized. The pope looked up. "Have a seat, Perfecto."

"Thank you . . . uh, Holiness." He said, as he walked to a chair to the left of the pope's desk.

"Are you moved into your apartment?"

"Yes Holiness."

"Good, because I've got some things I want you to do. I'm not certain at this point what will happen, but it's always better to be prepared for any eventuality. Would you agree with that, Perfecto?"

"Oh, yes . . . Holiness. I was in the Boy Scouts. In fact I was an Eagle Scout. So I know and practice the Boy Scout motto: 'Be Prepared.'"

"Okay, good. You and I are going to have some fun. Here's what I want you to do. There's a fella that lives in a small town, just north of Castel Gandolfo, off to the west from Via Appia, the road that takes us down to Gandolfo. I forget the name of that small town. Maybe I have his business card."

As the pope searched for the card, he continued talking. "It's only about fifteen miles south of here, depending on how you go. He and I were buddies when I was at Berkeley. He owned a chop-shop and we used to drink a few beers together now and then. I knew him from high school.

"He dropped out and started his own business: a chop-shop. You know, taking stolen cars, removing their serial numbers, removing the parts and selling them on the black market, that kind of thing. He'd take wrecked cars, chop them in half and weld on the other half from another wreck and sell it. Made some good money. But, got busted.

"After a stint in prison, he decided to move here and opened a legitimate chop-shop, creating hot rods out of old cars—you know, for racing and dressing them up with modern parts, chopping the roofs down, things like that.

"Yet, he always dreamed of inventing something related to cars that would stun the automobile industry: something that no one has ever thought of. So he's been working on that while he makes a living at his shop.

"I mean his auto repair shop to keep him in spending money when there's a dry spell in selling his restored cars. He had some pretty bizarre ideas.

"Okay, here it is . . . his card," he said, leaning to his left and handing it to Perfecto. His name is Tyrone. "You go out there and introduce yourself and tell them the pope sent you. He'll know who you mean," said with a wry smile. "And while you're out that way, stop by and check in at Castel Gandolfo. You ever been there?"

"Yes, Holiness . . . once as a tourist. Beautiful place."

"I agree. Now, you go out there and tell them the pope sent you. If they give you any guff, just call me at this number . . . put it on your card there. You got it? It's my cell phone. Good.

"Now, you visit my friend at the shop. You go out there and introduce yourself.

"Do you have a cell phone? If so, give me your number before you leave. Do you have a car?"

Perfecto nodded *yes*. "It's an old Volkswagen, a Beetle. I purchased it while I was at the seminary."

"Okay then. I want you to drive in and out of here, meaning the Vatican, several times a day. Where you go is your business, but I want you to make two or three trips to Gandolfo a week. Get an office for yourself down there and do whatever suits your fancy when you're there. Stay there for a few hours, overnight or whatever, even two or three days.

"What you do while you are there is your business. If anyone asks what you are doing at any time, your reply will be: 'God's business.' Repeat it ten times if you need to, but that's all you are to say. I don't care if it's outsiders or cardinals. Got that?

"Now, one more thing. There's a reason why I hired you besides your being a nice, congenial guy. You have all that education and training in business and finance. Right?"

"Yes . . . Your . . ."

"Fine. Now, I've asked the two cardinals in charge of finance and property accounting to give me reports on what's going on in their areas of responsibility. Their reports are due in a few months. When I receive them, I want you to analyze them for me and give me some insights about the reports. But before then, I want you to get some context for what you will be doing in the finance and accounting areas.

"I want you to read some books and give me a synopsis of each, highlighting the important points made in the books. I don't have time to read them. That's one reason I hired you. That way we'll both get some context we'll need to deal with the problems we face in this place.

"I have a list here." The pope reached into a desk drawer and pulled out a list of books. "I've run across them somewhere. I kept a list of them, hoping someday being able to take the time to read them. But you know how that goes. Being a cardinal in this dysfunctional place takes twice the work it would in any place that has some semblance of order and efficiency. Here, they don't know what those words mean.

"Anyway, I digress. Here's the deal. Here's a list of books that I have given to Tyrone. Some of them are very critical of the Catholic Church in general and the Vatican in particular. He's ordering them online, and will have them for you to pick up from him. Right?" Perfecto nodded affirmative.

"Good. We'll be getting into some serious business here in a few months and things could get nasty and I want to protect you as much as possible. But I need your help . . . big time. Got that?" Perfecto smiled and nodded.

"Okay. So you pick up the books from Tyrone at his shop. There are people around here who are wondering what you are up to, so don't be surprised if they try to find out what's going on. They might be staking out Tyrone's place some months down the road.

"We don't want them to know that you are walking out of his place with books in your arms. So, when you go there, call Tyrone in advance and let him know when you are about fifteen minutes away and he'll be in his hotrod showroom waiting for you.

"There's a door in the rear for his airplane. Drive in. He'll give you three books; when you return the three you have read, pick up another three. Do that every time you visit so you get into the habit and won't screw up a few months down the road when screwing up won't be an option. Got that?"

"Yes, Holiness," Perfecto said, enthusiastically.

"Okay. For starters, peruse the list and leave it here with me. I read the dust-covers and concluding remarks of a couple of them. I extracted and put on paper a couple paragraphs from those two books that I'm also giving you.

"They bracket the subject matter spectrum in the books you'll be reading; that should give you a good motivational boost to read all of the books on the list.

"John Cornwell, the author who investigated what he calls the mysterious death of Pope John Paul I, says that we aren't surrounded by a bunch of crooks, assassins or gangsters here in the Vatican, which is, of course, comforting news.

"However, he says we do suffer from a host of dysfunctional characters which makes life very unpleasant in this City State we call the Vatican. He describes their crimes—not as "murder," "major theft," and "fraud," as some have suggested, but has a laundry list that looks like this: "equivocation," "economy of the truth," "mental reservation," "petty ambition," "pusillanimity," "denigration," "cynicism," a lack of "kindness" and common "charity." Nevertheless, he reports he found men of holiness and prayer.

"Okay . . . here it is," the pope said as he handed the list to Perfecto.

How to Save the Catholic Church (1984) Greeley/Durkin; *A Thief in the Night: The Mysterious Death of Pope John Paul I* (1989) Cornwell; *Lead Us Not Into Temptation: Catholic Priests and the Sexual Abuse of Children* (1992) Berry; *Papal Sin: Structures of Deceit* (2000) Wills; *The Catholic Church: A Short History,* (2001) Kung, (Catholic theologian); *Modern Inquisition: Six Prominent Catholics and their Struggles with the Vatican* (2001-2002) Collins; *Betrayal: The Crisis in the Catholic Church* (2002) Boston Globe Investigative Staff; *The Vatican Exposed: Murder, Money and the Mafia* (2003) Williams; *Vows of Silence: The House of Power in the Papacy of John Paul II* (2004) Berry/Renner; *Survivors of Predatory Priests* (2005) Handlin; *A People Adrift: The Crisis in the Roman Catholic Church* (2005) Steinfels; *Sex, Priests and Secret Codes* (2006) Doyle, Sipes and Wall.

"Here are the excerpts I mentioned," the pope said, handing a paper to Perfecto.

EXCERPTS

Number One: Paul Williams', *THE VATICAN EXPOSED: Money, Murder, and the Mafia,* (2003)

The back flap of the dustcover states the following: "*Based on his years as a consultant for the FBI, Williams produces explosive and never-before-published evidence of the Church's morally questionable financial dealings with sinister organizations: over seven decades! He examines the means by which the Vatican accrued enormous wealth during the Great Depression by investing in Mussolini's government; the connection between Nazi gold and the Vatican Bank; the vast range of Church holdings in the postwar boom period; Pope Paul VI's reliance on reputed international Mafia chieftain Michele Sindona as the Vatican banker; a billion-dollar counterfeit stock fraud uncovered by Interpol and the FBI; the "Ambrosiani affair," called "the greatest financial scandal of the twentieth century" by the New York Times: the mysterious death of Pope John Paul I;*

most recently, profits from an international drug ring operating out of Gdansk, Poland; and much more."

Number Two: Paul Williams', *The VATICAN EXPOSED: Money, Murder and the Mafia* (2003)

Williams' concluding remarks about his book state: "*The accounts in these pages are not exaggerations and have not been subjected to editorial amplification for popular consumption. They are matters of recorded history. They have been captured on camera and kept as evidence in crime labs, police files, and even Holocaust museums. They have been documented by leading historians and journalists, such as Richard Hammer, David Yallop, Claire Sterling, Nick Tosches, and John Cornwell. They have been broadcast by reporters and news commentators throughout the world even though the matter has not captured the major attention of the media. Such matters cannot be treated as matters of no substance or importance. They have impacted all aspects of life—moral, spiritual, political, and economic—at the turn of the twenty-first century.*"

"Any questions? Are you clear on what I've told you?"

"Yes . . . Holiness . . . uh . . . okay, I got it!" Perfecto said with a big smile, after glancing at the material.

"Okay, that's it. Now get to work and . . ."

"DON'T waste time . . ." Perfecto interjected.

The pope reared back in his chair, roared with laughter, and said, "You and I are going to get along just fine."

Pope Immanuel picked up the phone and called Cardinal Gerhardt Wagner, the President of the Supervisory Commission of Cardinals, which is responsible for supervising the activities of the Vatican Bank. "Can you come over?"

"Certainly, Your Holiness."

After pleasantries, the pope said to Cardinal Wagner, "The reason I've asked you over is that I have something I want you to do. I want you to provide me with copies of your annual reports going back ten years. If you have them on computer discs or portable drives that would be fine.

"If you don't have them in your computer, you can provide them in hard copy. I expect to see everything a bank's board of directors would want to see in an annual report in a capitalist democracy."

"Your Holiness, we are not a capitalist democracy and therefore our bank does not operate that way. We have a supervisory council of five financial experts with banking experience from around the world. They oversee the bank and appoint a lay director general, who actually runs the bank. He is the 'president' of the bank, in our system. They appointed our current president, Mr. Lidano Russo, a banker who was recommended by Opus Dei.

"The supervisory council is appointed by a commission of seven cardinals—of which I am the president—which in turn appoints the council members. The commission of cardinals is appointed by the pope, who owns the bank under our system. You are a very wealthy man, Your Holiness," Cardinal Wagner said, with a smile.

"Okay. Well, I tell you what. Give me, the owner of the bank, a detailed accounting for all the funds you manage in my bank so I will be able to see what's going on over there. I'd like to know if you ever cleaned up your act. By that I mean: Do we still do business with the Mafia?"

Cardinal Wagner burst into laughter. "Your Holiness, we don't *do business* with the Mafia . . ."

"Excuse me for interrupting, but that has been going on for decades and was, by some well-documented accounts, still going on a couple years ago. I want to know if it is still going on."

"Holiness, I'm not the one who produces these reports. We have a supervisory council of experts who review them regularly and we rely on them to keep the president of the bank in line . . . that is, in compliance with our banking statutes."

"So the oversight commission of five cardinals . . . what do you do, if you don't do what your titles suggest you do?"

"Oh, we meet occasionally to deal with the most important things, like our relations with public opinion and the banks interactions with the dicasteries here in the Vatican. We approve the balance sheet and where the money goes, and all that, but we don't spend a lot of time second-guessing the experts who oversee and run the bank.

"We put a lot of trust in them, and don't interfere. We provide an annual report to the pope that everything is running smoothly and he signs that he has seen the report and then that paper is filed in my office. It's all rather simple, really."

"Would you consider doing business with the Mafia one of your 'important things', as you say, if that was going on?"

"Well it isn't, so there is no reason to be concerned, is there, Holiness?"

"Have you read Paul Williams' book *The Vatican Exposed: Money, Murder and the Mafia?*"

"Your Holiness, I don't read comic books."

"Well, I haven't read it in its entirety, but I've read enough of it to know there is incontrovertible evidence that the Mafia was very involved in the scandals that broke out in the early nineteen eighties.

"As recently as 1999, twenty-one members of the Mafia were arrested in Palermo for conducting an online banking scam with the cooperation of the Vatican Bank. Despite the arrest and convictions, Italian investigators were prevented from looking into the Vatican Bank's role in the scheme.

"In 2001 the *London Daily Telegraph* identified the Vatican bank, along with other 'cut-out' countries, as being one of the major places in the world for laundering underworld cash. The latter two incidents happened on your watch. Did you investigate what was going on?"

"No. There was nothing to investigate since we weren't involved."

"I see. Well, I tell you what. From this point forward, you won't be involved in banking matters, because as of this moment, your oversight commission and the supervising experts' council are hereby abolished. I'll deal directly with the bank president. Letters will go out to all concerned tomorrow informing the community of my decision. How old are you?"

"Sixty-eight, Holiness."

"Old enough to retire. You are retired as of this day. You have been derelict in your responsibilities in that you haven't investigated well-known facts about the operation of the bank you are supposed to be overseeing. It seems recent popes have been misled by your cavalier attitude. That approach does not fly with me because sooner or later the craft will crash and burn. You are dismissed Cardinal. Good luck in your retirement."

Chapter 37

Pat and Maria sat at the kitchen table on a Sunday evening, three months after the accident. Sammy had turned in at his usual eight-thirty bed-time; the new colt had been bedded down. A fireplace flame flickered, casting shadows across the living room, which Maria could see from the kitchen.

"I think I'll name him Bog, the other half of Bogdana," Maria said. "That way they both had and have names that mean 'Gift from God.' I haven't told you that I knew when I woke up that Dana had died in the accident. I saw her lying in the road, trying to get up and I knew then she wouldn't make it.

"Horses with broken legs have to be put down because they can't lie down to heal as can we humans and some other animals, and they can only be put in slings to hold them up if they have relatively minor injuries that don't require long term healing."

"But Maria, how could you have seen Dana lying in the road when you were unconscious?" Pat said.

"Well, that isn't all I saw. I saw the whole thing: the car upside down with the light beams piercing the night sky, the boy who came upon the accident, the highway patrol cars, an ambulance with its red lights flashing, my body lying in the ditch and the para-medics placing me in the medi-vac helicopter. I also saw you reading a book, sitting here at the kitchen table." Maria smiled and watched Pat's reaction.

"My dear, you had a near-death experience! I was sitting at this table reading before I was informed of the accident. I remember feeling as though someone was looking at me. I put the book down, looked around. Nothing. I went back to reading. So, it was your spirit."

"Yes. I was here."

"Was that all that happened?"

"No, it wasn't." Maria went on to describe how she had been pulled through the tunnel, her life passing before her, the light that grew from a small dot to an angelic cloud of love, and the message she had received while there: "You must go back. You are God's messenger."

"There have been hundreds of such experiences reported. Are you aware of that?" asked Pat.

"Well, I have heard the term, but never paid much attention to it. Yet, I can tell you it was more real than what we are experiencing right now. I thought the 'Calm of the Angel' experience was quite something, but this experience has had me in a dither ever since I woke up. I don't know what to make of it. *I*, am God's messenger? I have no idea what it means, not to mention what to do about it."

"Have you had any thoughts on the matter? I know you and I have been very busy with your therapy sessions and all that, so we haven't been able to talk. Thank God you are able to walk and will recover completely.

"Most of what you tell me is not atypical of such experiences. But not everyone gets instructions. Really, the experiences range all over the map. None of them are exactly the same, but most of them have some of the experiences you describe."

"I was waiting until this moment to tell you. Yes, I have been thinking about it all the time. One thing I can say for certain is this: I'm looking forward to dying. The feeling of being engulfed by such all-embracing love, sense of well-being, and extreme desire to not let go of it, has me a little puzzled, to put it mildly. And I have absolutely no idea what the charge to be 'God's messenger' means. Do you?"

"No, my dear heart. No, I don't, but I feel like crying for joy at the experience you describe. I've read somewhere that that is who we really are, in our souls, pure love, unconditional love. I must tell you, in all my years, I've never had such an experience. In my humble opinion you are extremely fortunate to have had such an experience, despite the problems you've encountered."

"You know, Mama, I feel exactly the same way, because my life will never be the same. Now I know there is that part of my being, what do you call it? Uhmm . . . a soul. But what confuses me more than anything is that I don't feel that way now and haven't since I woke up. What I *feel* is something like the 'Calm of the Angel.'

"I don't go around saying to myself: 'Oh, I feel the 'Calm of the Angel,' but there is a sort of gentle awareness that . . . that is who and what I am. Why can't I, why can't you and I, why can't all humanity feel the bliss that I experienced all the time? If we did we would have heaven on earth. And I really mean that. I wish there were some way I could wave a magic wand and create that feeling for everyone. Wouldn't that be wonderful?"

"Yes. But it won't happen. Still, there must be something you can do to move us in that direction. Wouldn't that be why you are 'God's messenger?'?"

"I suppose so. I wish I had a clue where to begin."

Chapter 38

The pope had weathered the storm resulting from the change of work hours. Priests were brought in for a couple months while the anger dissipated, until the employees accepted their new hours, and a pay raise and increased benefits had been implemented. His Holiness's drastic action, taken to break the logjam of annulment requests, and eliminating the requirement altogether, succeeded.

He cut back on ceremonial events, allowing only those he considered unavoidable. He continued his audiences in the Square, but reduced them by half. He knew that a lot of the people attending were curiosity buffs, who valued little more than seeing a world leader up close, a phenomenon that had disappeared in recent years amongst secular leaders, due to security threats.

The temporary interruption of tourist visitations to the museums and gardens created many headaches for the tourist industry. The crisis was over in a couple months and the museums were re-opened.

Grumbling—about the pope's requirement that selected cardinals were ordered to assess the Church's state of affairs, and that he had ordered his personal secretary, Father Sandusky, to do the same, but take a year to get it done—continued throughout the year.

Father Perfecto had those who were close to the pope scratching their heads. *What is this guy up to?* When the pope was asked, he said: "God's work."

The cardinals, who had the six month deadline for their analyses and recommendations, were on time.

"Well, Father Sandusky," the pope asked, a couple months after the deadline, "What is your assessment of their papers?"

"Pretty much a bell-shaped curve. Some are quite well done, but not particularly insightful, nor especially helpful. The majority are mediocre, and some wouldn't have received a passing grade in my junior high school English class. The worst was Cardinal O'Reilley's; he can't write a complete sentence, which precludes writing a coherent paragraph, not to mention a paper."

"I'm not surprised by what you say," said the pope. "I presume their papers reinforce in your mind the importance of your project. Anything to say at this point?"

"Being scholars, we know that whenever one gets into a project such as this the task becomes daunting very quickly; every time one discovers new material, three or four new sources need to be examined. I have been able to use some of the material provided by the cardinals' papers, but for the most part, they are useless.

"From where I've been and where I'm headed in my research, I can see why you are doing what you are doing. Some of what I'm finding could challenge our Church doctrine. I hope you have a thick skin when you see what I produce, because you will need it. When word gets out about my analysis, it won't be pretty around here."

"Father Sandusky, I've been preparing my entire life for this opportunity to see what can be done. I don't know what the result will be. Still, I'm not afraid of this process, nor am I afraid of the outcome."

"Okay. It'll take another month or so to have a final analysis ready for you."

"Fine. There's no rush."

Chapter 39

The billowing clouds foreshowed a cold-front passing through Rome the day Perfecto made his first trip to Gandolfo. The fall weather had been unusually warm, but now it appeared the winter months were muscling their way into their rightful place.

Leaving the Vatican, he passed east of the Square and merged onto Gregorio VII on his way to Via Aurelia, which took him to the beltway, where he headed south past Fiumicino International Airport and then circled around to the east and exited on Via Appia—south—toward Castel Gandolfo.

He turned right onto a side-road that led to his destination: a small town, where the pope's friend, Tyrone, lived and worked. His GPS mapping-guidance system worked perfectly. He arrived at Tyrone's shop on the northeast edge of town and parked in a small parking lot in front of the repair shop.

He walked toward a car with the hood open: a man, in blue coveralls, leaned over the front fender, his back toward Perfecto. The car appeared to be an old Fiat, a popular Italian car that had a bad reputation, in terms of performance, yet, in recent years, had corrected the problems. The older ones kept Tyrone busy.

Perfecto walked past the front of the car on his right and stood watching the man working on the car. "Are you Tyrone?" he asked.

"That would be me. Want some work done on your car?" he asked, without looking up or stopping what he was doing.

"It could probably use a lot of work. But that's not why I'm here. The pope sent me." The morning had slinked to afternoon as he drove up.

Tyrone looked up at Perfecto, straightened up slowly and rubbed his stiff back into shape. "Getting old is not for sissies!" he remarked, as if to himself. Then he looked at Perfecto. "So you're that blackbird Skip has been telling me about."

"Blackbird?" Perfecto responded.

"Yes, that's what the Romans call the hundreds of priests in their black cassocks as they fly toward the Vatican every morning."

"And who is Skip?"

"That would be the pope, my son. That's who he is to me," Tyrone said, as he grabbed a shop towel, wiped his hand and offered it to Perfecto in a cordial greeting. "Skip has told me about you and that I could expect you. He said he wanted to warn me so I wouldn't shoot you. He knows I don't like priests," he said, grinning. "Pleased to meet you, son."

"It's a pleasure to meet you, too," Perfecto replied, with a big smile, looking up at Tyrone, who towered over him. Tyrone, an African-American, well over six feet tall, with a build that looked like it could lift a Buick and twirl it in a breeze, had white hair that gleamed in the sunlight. "Why do you call him 'Skip'?"

Tyrone laughed. "Because when we were in high school, he skipped classes all the time. Never could take the boring stuff they were dishing out. He had been reading books since he was four years old and knew more than the teachers about their respective subjects. Same was true in college, I'm told.

"I'm hungry. Have you had lunch? I am finishing up here. I'll do a couple things so the owner can pick up the car when he comes later today. If you haven't had lunch, we'll go as soon as I'm done."

"Sounds great to me," said Perfecto.

They walked down the main street toward the Pizzaria. The ordering line formed parallel to the glass-enclosed counter, which was about chest high to most people. Behind the glass was an array of pastries, arranged attractively, on two shelves.

They could take a seat at a table, where they would be served by waiters, or they could stand in line to place their orders—stand and eat at shelves on the walls of the restaurant. If they sat down, they would pay slightly more. Tyrone and Perfecto sat at a table.

"You know, me and Skip, we did a little hell-raising when we were in high school—some dating, but we mostly liked to hang out with the boys. Drink a few beers after a basketball or football game . . . just hang out and have fun.

"It was prior to all the uproar at Berkeley, so I didn't get involved in any of that because I didn't go over there to school like Skip did. But I did go over there to see him sometimes. He never did get involved in their radical politics or anything like that.

"Underneath all his light-hearted acting out, he was a deadly serious young man; he wanted to make a difference in the world. He chose religion as his horse to ride, and I chose cars. I wanted to make a difference in cars and he wanted to make a difference in the world." Tyrone laughed. "Quite a pair, huh? Don't know if we'll realize our dreams."

"Well, I don't know about your dream, but it seems the Holy Father has realized his. The percentage of priests who become pope must be less than one tenth of one percent. Hasn't his dream been realized? And I'm not going to assume yours hasn't just because you say so. You seem like a very modest person to me."

"Thanks, Perfecto. I repeat; we haven't reached our goals. You see, it's like this. For Skip, he couldn't give a rat's ass about being pope."

Perfecto exploded in laughter.

A waiter came to take their orders: a large pizza with sausage and pepperoni and a couple beers.

"The thing is," Tyrone continued, "he despises all that pomp and ceremony and those pretentious, ass-kissing cardinals over there. Oh, there are . . . I'm sure there are some sincere, well-meaning red-caps and bishops, as Skip was when he was one of them.

"Yet, too many of them are all caught up in what Skip sees as an abomination, a vile spectacle that detracts mightily from what the love of God should be about. For him, that whole priestly bureaucracy in the Vatican is all about gaining power, for the sake of having power.

"He has always known that. Yet, he was able to play the game to acquire the power needed to do what he thinks needs to be done . . . "

"Which is?"

"To discover what Jesus was really all about and then do something about it. He isn't sure about that quest, but he is hell-bent on finding out. That's not so unusual for popes, by the way. Some popes have written books about "the search for Jesus," as if they don't know where he is or how to find him. Some of them seem to think they can find him in words, by analyzing scripture and quoting other books ad nauseam.

"But Skip has other ideas, now that he has a staff that can do the research necessary to sort all that out, I think he will have some success. But I wouldn't bet on the outcome.

"You see, if he comes to conclusions that are anathema to the Catholic Church, his conscience will force him to take action and that would cause major problems for him, his staff at the Vatican and the whole world. It would rival the chaos that Luther caused, or worse."

"Why are you telling me all of this?"

"Because if he didn't want you to know, he wouldn't have told me. He sees you as a major player in his dream to make a difference in the world. He knows

I'm a big blabber-mouth but would never do anything to hurt him or his cause. He knows I will do everything I can to help him, and part of that is getting you on board . . . to join in his cause.

"You are young and, according to Skip, just like him when he was your age: idealistic. He knows your happy-go-lucky personality masks a deep and sincere desire to help humanity turn away from the disastrous path it is on. Don't ask me how he knows, but trust me . . . he knows!"

"He certainly behaves that way," said Perfecto. "I never expected to be given such an assignment as I now have—for example, sitting here talking to you. What's that all about? You know? He told me to drive around the city and countryside and do whatever I please; he told me that if anyone asks what I'm doing, I should say that I'm doing God's work."

"Let me tell you something. It may seem odd to you now, but there is a serious purpose behind whatever he asks you to do. And don't ever forget that. Your reward will be in heaven, but there could be some goodies along the way, too," Tyrone said with a smile.

"But what about *your* dream? You said you had a dream about cars, but like Skip . . . Oh, shit! I can't believe I said that! I mean . . . the Holy Father. Oh, my God," Perfecto whispered, putting his hands over his face. Tyrone laughed and slapped the table and said, "You're my man, Perfecto! Are you done? Want some dessert?"

"Sure," Perfecto said. "I'd like some of that chocolate cake I saw in the display cabinet when we came in."

"Okay, good. Waiter? Could you bring us a couple pieces of that chocolate cake?" The waiter nodded.

"You haven't talked much about *your* dream, Tyrone. What exactly was it? You said something about innovation."

"I'm over sixty years old and I'm still working on it—my dream, that is. Maybe I've already accomplished it. I've given up on coming up with a new car design. Today, that's probably impossible for a single person like me with limited resources.

"I'm realistic, if nothing else in this world. I'll settle for something that would be an innovation that would stun the auto design/manufacturing world, even if it isn't an entire car.

"Now, you take the 'Tucker Torpedo,'" Tyrone said, as he forked a piece of cake into his mouth. He chewed as if he couldn't wait to continue. Gesturing with his fork, he said enthusiastically, "A guy by the name of Preston Tucker, after the war, designed a car that was so innovative, and would have been so popular, that it threatened to cut into the Big Three's profits."

"Big Three?"

"You are a young whippersnapper, aren't you? Ford, Chrysler, and General Motors. He was shot out of his sky of dreams like a gas blimp—like that German Hindenburg blimp that crashed and burned in Jersey in '37. Some senator in the pockets of the car-industry big shots launched an investigation into Tucker's policy of selling accessories before production began on the car.

"Even though the charges against Tucker were dropped, the public backed off and his enterprise collapsed. I tell you, I would give anything to come up with a car as revolutionary as that car was at the time."

"What could be so revolutionary about a car? I mean the DeLorean had some innovations, like the gull-wing doors and the stainless steel body and I guess some other features, like being able to fly—even back to the future." Perfecto laughed.

"Actually, you named the latest attempt to take on the establishment and it crashed and burned, too. Yet, almost ten thousand of them were built before the company was forced into bankruptcy.

"The DeLorean did have other innovations that were eventually used. But I'm talking about a different time and a different car. Only fifty-one Tuckers were built. But do you know what? A cherry Tucker Torpedo will sell for around a million bucks today."

"Wow! It must have been some whiz-banger of a car."

"It really was. Studebaker was the first all-new post-war model that looked like it was going backwards while speeding down the road because it had a trunk and rear windshield that looked like the front of any car known to exist at that time.

"Still, the Tucker Torpedo, while looking sleek and classy, imitated profile designs of the 1942 model cars. They were in production, which was halted when the Japanese bombed Pearl Harbor in December 1941.

"Mr. Tucker's design included innovative safety features: a perimeter frame surrounded the car for crash protection. The steering box lay behind the front axle to protect the driver in a head-on collision.

"The car had three headlights, the center one turning in the direction of the steering, for better night visibility. The car had a padded dashboard and an instrument panel on the steering wheel. The engine and transmission were mounted on separate sub-frames. That way, the engine and transmission could be removed and replaced with loaners, while the originals were repaired.

"There were innovative designs that had to be dropped due to financial and production problems. Still, those innovations, such as disc brakes, mag wheels, and direct-drive, torque-converter transmissions were the forerunners of things to come."

"Sounds fascinating! I'd love to see one someday."

"Oh, I'm sure you will," Tyrone said, with a big smile. Want anything else before I pay the bill?"

"Not really. Thank you."

"Now, let's go for a ride. I want to show you my chop-shop . . . where I do my real work . . . my creative work. I really don't need the income from the repair shop, but it provides spending money and I enjoy the interaction with the locals."

As they approached Tyrone's chop-shop on the northwest end town, Perfecto saw a police station in the middle of the block. Next to it was an oblong lot of about four acres. Near the street stood a rectangular Butler Building about the size of three, huge Iowa barns.

When they approached the side entrance—a small walk-in door— Tyrone entered a code into the security box next to the door. He could hear dogs barking inside the building. "That's my security when I'm not here. I leave a couple of them running loose and I have another two Pitbulls in a dog-run behind the building. I use them on special occasions when I'm away from home. They have their own special way of defending the place. Tyrone attached leashes to the dogs' collars. When visitors came he kept the dogs at bay.

"Come on in, young man, and tell me what you see."

"Wow! I wasn't expecting to see this! What? Over a dozen shiny hot-rods, a fancy looking car in the middle and a small airplane at the far end. I had no idea. What are you doing? Collecting cars and . . . that airplane?"

"All of these cars, except the one in the middle, are ones that I created from scrap: shells of old and abandoned cars. The only collector items in here are the car in the middle and the airplane at the end. I'll sell all the others. And even the airplane is not a collector item, as such. It's one I purchased and fly, only for recreation, but it has some special features as well."

"And the one in the middle?"

"Go take a look."

Perfecto walked over to the car, approaching it from the rear, walking around the left side of the car, stopping and looking at the front. *Three headlights?*

"It can't be!" he exclaimed. **"Is this a Tucker Torpedo?"** he blurted out, excitedly. "You said you were sure I'd get to see one someday. I had no idea 'that someday' would be only twenty minutes away. It's a beauty! Where did you get it?"

"In the late 1960's, I walked in on a friend screwing his buddy's wife; he gave me his aging Tucker so I wouldn't rat on him. Today, it's worth over a million dollars. I think I enjoy looking at it almost as much as you do. Except for the fact that it represents to me a dream I had at one time and will not be able to realize. I just let this car be my 'invent-a-new-car' dream."

"And the hot-rods?"

"I keep a few of them on hand for buyers who come by to see my work. Most of my work is done on a contract basis. They tell me what they want and I make it for them, if I can find the frame and body. Occasionally, I advertise the ones I have on hand. I sell them to people all over the world. They are people with more money than they can spend and often turn to collecting cars. I have a guy who buys for the Russian nouveau riche . . . Igor Yavolinski. Quite a guy! I'll introduce you sometime. I'd like for you to meet him.

"You'd be surprised at how many Butler Buildings, filled with cars, are hidden in the orchards owned by California millionaires. Besides the large automobile museums, hundreds of wealthy people, all over the world collect cars, some for investment purposes, but for many, just the pleasure of being able to look at the beautiful creations of their manufacturers. I like looking at the Tucker Torpedo and my own creations."

"Speaking of Butler Buildings with treasures stored in them," said Perfecto, I'm surprised you don't have this place surrounded by a high, steel fence with concertina wire strung along the top. Aren't you afraid someone will bypass your security system, break in and make off with their booty?"

"Perfecto," said Tyrone, "I have a reputation around here for not being stupid. The locals know better than to mess with me, but if—say some outsiders—had occasion to disturb my automobile family, they would face some very unpleasant circumstances—that you can take to the bank."

With that introduction to "Skip's" friend, Perfecto thanked his host for lunch again and expressed his gratitude for showing him his prized collection of hotrods, the airplane and the Tucker Torpedo.

It didn't occur to him until he was back on the road, approaching the Autostrada, to ask about what looked like a small modern car—covered by a black tarp—located to the right of the airplane. On the wall was a draw-down projector screen, but no evidence of a projector. *I wonder what he's hiding.*

Chapter 40

Severino Costa didn't take chances. He didn't go to restaurants that didn't allow him to sit in a corner with his back to the walls—for a reason: A capo knew better than to sit anywhere else. Thus, his choice of restaurants was limited. A short, stout, gray-haired man, with a bulbous nose and beady eyes, Severino walked with the confidence of a bantam rooster.

His favorite restaurant, located a few blocks southeast of the Vatican, was a couple doors up from a Prawdoocty: a Russian convenience store.

Igor Yavolinski paid a clerk for a Russian newspaper and a sack of pastry, walked out the door, turned right, went up the street to Bruno's Ristorante Pesce, and sat at a sidewalk table near the entrance. He read the newspaper, waiting for the restaurant to open.

He watched Severino and a companion, Alejandro "Decap" Ruiz, as they parked their car, walked toward him and entered the restaurant; it was 10:30 p.m. on an unusually warm Christmas Eve. Severino slipped the maître de a one-hundred euro bill and asked for a private room.

Yavolinski peered over his newspaper as O'Reilley entered the restaurant; he was directed to the same room that Severino and his partner had entered.

O'Reilley did not look like a cardinal. He looked like a middle-aged, American tourist, wearing white tennis shoes, blue jeans, a blue-and-white-striped, cotton shirt and a brown leather jacket.

Severino and "Decap," looking like an up-tight guerilla, stood inside the door. When the door closed, Severino spoke. "So . . . ,' wat's up, O'Reilley? You din't sound so good on da tellie," Severino said, in a raspy, Brooklyn accent. "Oh, by da way, dis's a friend of ours, Decap. Decap, Cardinal O'Reilley."

Decap put out his right hand and said nothing; his silence had its intended effect: O'Reilley looked nervous. "I've ordered soma dose fishes—dat swim where we sometimes dump cargo—for dinner. You know, da ones dat still have dare heads on when day show up on da plate? And some coffee and white wine. Is dat okay wit you, Cardinal O'Reilley?"

"Certainly . . . fine with me. Shall we sit? We need to talk."

"Dat's wat you said on the tellie. Wat's goin' on?"

"We've got a problem. The new pope has ordered me to approve over a thousand annulment requests by the end of this month. He has terminated our annulment policy."

Severino leaned back, pulled a cigar from his shirt pocket, lit it, flamboyantly shook the match-stick flame to death as he sat up, looked at O'Reilley and said, "You gotta mouse in your pocket?"

"No. What do you mean, Severino?"

"Well, you said, *'We've* got a problem.' I taut maybe you meant you and a mouse have a problem." After taking a deep draw on his cigar, he removed the cigar from his mouth and blew smoke into O'Reilley's face. Holding the cigar between his stubby right index and middle fingers, he leaned forward, put his arms on the table, stared at O'Reilley and said, "You didn't mean to include me wit da problem, did'ja?"

"Severino, we had a deal. I would provide you with Vatican stationery letterhead which you would use to scam annulment petitioners into paying an extra thousand euros over and above the five hundred they normally pay their own bishops in order to get special attention from my office.

"When you received the money, you'd give me half and you'd keep the rest. We've received hundreds of thousands of euros over the past couple years. The pope twisted the knob on that spigot this morning. No more annulments. No money for either of us. Got it?"

"Cardinal O'Reilley. I got a couple idee'rs. I tink you won't like da first one, but I tink you will like da second one. Da first one is dis. Stand up and strip."

O'Reilley looked at Decap and then stared at Severino. "What?"

"You heard me. Stand up and take all your clothes off."

"Why?"

Decap stood up, walked around the small table and stood glaring down at O'Reilley.

"I've done nothing wrong, Severino. Why are you doing this? We had a deal and now it's over."

Someone knocked on the door.

With his head, Severino motioned Decap to let the waiter in. Parking a serving cart laden with their dinner, the waiter said, motioning to the cart, "Will there be anything else?"

"Not right now," said Severino.

Severino took a puff on his cigar and said, motioning to the fishes gazing at the ceiling with their vacuous eyes, "Do as I say or you will be swimming wit dare relatives," He put the cigar down and started eating.

Cardinal O'Reilley stood up and unbuttoned his shirt and laid it on the chair back. He removed his shoes, unbuckled his belt, pulled his zipper down and removed his blue-jeans. He looked at Severino.

"Go ahead. Take off da skivvies," Severino said, after washing down a big hunk of fish with a gulp of white wine. "Dare aren't any ladies here."

Cardinal O'Reilley lowered his underwear. "Check his butt-crack, Decap. I want to make sure he doesn't have one of dem,"—he waved his right hand over his head—"digital du-dads hidden in dare dat can record wat we are saying. Check his clothes, including his wallet."

Decap did as instructed and found nothing.

"Go ahead and get dressed and join us for dinner. I don't want any more *unpleasantries* here tonight."

Severino and Decap ate in silence until they were nearly finished before Severino spoke. Cardinal O'Reilley hadn't taken a bite. "Now for da second idee'r . . . here's da deal, O'Reilley. Wit dee ever increasing divorces and dose annulments? I figure we done about five hundred annulments at a tousand euros a pop. Right?

"Which means we brought in about 500,000 euros. We split da take evenly as da money came in. I set up an off-shore bank account for you in da Cayman Islands, laundered by the pope's bank. So you should have about $250,000 euros in that account . . . or somewhere else.

"So now," Severino continued—like a compassionate doctor counseling a terminally ill patient—as he pointed his fork at O'Reilley, "what ya need to do is take all dat money and give it to me since dare won't be any more money comin' in. I'm an honorable man, Cardinal O'Reilley.

"I'm fair and decent, but you really screwed up when you promised me we'd each make millions of euros over several years, and now look at me. I'm almost due for da poor house. So you owe me. You shoun't a built up my hopes like dat.

"Decap, here? He needs to be paid whenever I ask him to decapitate someone; so you can imagine, I have *off-wit-da-head* expenses here dat you don't have in your job. It might be a little less," Severino said, lifting his arms, leaning forward over the table and wagging his head, "as if, for example, he strangles da guy and trows him in da river, or someting like dat . . . it's less messy, so he don't charge as much. I'm sure you can sympatize wit dat." Severino stared at O'Reilley nonverbally asking for agreement. He didn't get it.

Cardinal O'Reilley hadn't touched his meal. "Wat? You ain't hungry?" Holding his arms out as if welcoming a long-lost friend, he said, "Wat's da matter? We're, da boat of us, we're just here doing business. Dare's no need for fasting or indigestion."

O'Reilley stared at his antagonist. "Okay. I can see you don't want to discuss what you're gunna do," Severino said, standing up, tossing his linen napkin on the table. "And I understand. I'm sure dis is not very pleasant for you. I expect to see two 250,000 euros, in cash, witin a week or Decap here will have another job to do. Right Decap? You could use a little cash, right?"

"Right, boss. I like the jobs where I make the most money, but whatever you decide, I can do it. All I need is the signal, and it's done."

"All right den. Since you asked us to dinner, Cardinal O'Reilley, you pick up the tab. You need to tip generously for dis private room, which will cost about two hundred euros extra for da privacy. We'll arrange for da pay-off as soon as you have da money. And I want da cash in hund'erds."

Igor Yavolinski watched as Severino and Decap walked out of the restaurant, turned right and walked toward their car about a half-block up the street.

A shiny, black BMW with security windows and three men inside, pulled away from the curb in front of the restaurant and moved slowly toward Severino and Decap. The windows on the right side of the car descended. At a break between cars, the man riding shot-gun and the one in the rear opened fire with sub-machine guns. Severino and Decap fell to the sidewalk . . . dead.

The black sedan merged into the passing traffic. The noise emptied the restaurant as patrons and passers-by stood gawking at what they knew was another gangland killing.

Cardinal O'Reilley walked out of the restaurant past the gawkers and headed home. Yavolinski finished a strawberry gelato, paid the fare and added a generous tip. He stood up, replaced his chair to its original position with the back against the table, turned and walked in the opposite direction from the mafia hit.

Chapter 41

Maria's year of healing and regaining strength had passed quickly. She was ready to search for an answer to her dilemma: what to do about the charge: *"You are God's messenger."* She browsed the internet and religion sections of several bookstores in Minneapolis and St. Paul.

The bewildering array of titles was a barren fruit tree. Having made several trips and getting more frustrated each time, she decided that if she wanted to know more about God, perhaps she should think about attending an institution that *teaches* about God.

Googling seminaries in Minneapolis/St. Paul, she found several seminaries, including those serving Catholics and Lutherans. Although the options were drastically reduced—comparing seminaries with hundreds of books—the same question arose: *Where do I start?*

She examined their curricula and didn't find anything interesting until she noticed that a new Lutheran seminary had opened recently in Minneapolis. Its claim to uniqueness was based on the fact that, while it trained men and women for service in the ministry, it also had a master's-level program in which one—who did not seek a career in the pastoral ministry—could pursue a degree with courses based on personal interest.

The idea behind this innovative approach, according to their website, was that nothing is nobler for academic institutions than the pursuit of truth. For anyone familiar with traditional seminaries, that would seem odd, because the assumption would be that the truth was already known. Thus, "pursuit of truth" would be a waste of time. *We are here to teach the truth to pastors who will pass it on to their flock,* was the idea.

She thought some of the course requirements would help her focus on learning the basics of the Judeo-Christian and other religious traditions; if the seminary did not offer courses of interest, she could attend the University of Minnesota to satisfy her curiosity.

She decided to check it out. She filled out an application online, which included a required statement why she wanted to enroll at Minneapolis Lutheran Seminary. She submitted it electronically and within a week had an email response: *"Please call for an appointment with an admissions counselor to go over your application. Bring supporting documents that cannot be sent via the web."*

Maria's adrenalin was flowing like a river over the rapids when she climbed into her new, silver, Maserati coupe. *Would a Lutheran seminary be a good choice?* The only way to know would be to take steps in the pursuit of her goal and see what happened.

Following the guidance of her GPS mapping system, she pulled into the parking lot of the seminary, reached for her handbag and headed for the entrance.

Inside, seeing an *Admissions Office* sign, she entered.

"Good morning," a cheery, twenty-something voice said from her left. "May I help you?"

"Yes. I'm Maria Luderenko. I came for my admissions interview. I have an appointment at ten."

"Just a moment. Yes, I see. Okay, follow me. I'll take you to our admissions counselor's office. My name is Gloria," she said offering her hand and then twirling and walking down the hall as if she were doing the runway at a high-fashion show.

Maria followed Gloria down the hall. They entered an office on the left. "Angie, this is Maria Luderenko. She has an appointment with you at ten."

Rising and extending her hand over her desk to Maria, Angie said, "Please have a seat. It is a pleasure meeting you. This is my first day on the job, so I haven't seen your application. I was looking it over and hadn't gotten to the end. I've read all the fill-in-the-blank stuff, but was starting on the brief statement of why you want to come and study with us. Excuse me a moment while I finish."

"Certainly." Maria watched Angie as she read.

Angie's face became increasingly stretched into a puzzled look, a knitted brow, as she apparently struggled to understand what she was reading. *A person who is "God's messenger" who doesn't know what the message is? Wow! That's rich!*

Angie looked up. "Excuse me for a moment, Maria. I'll be right back. I'll need a little help on this one. It's a little above my pay grade."

Dr. Sally Holden, a Lutheran and a graduate of Harvard University with a specialty in the Reformation, was sitting in a corner office with a sign on the wall next to the door: *Chair, Graduate Programs.* In her late fifties, she had salt and pepper hair, made up into a modified page-boy style for easy care.

She had spent most of her career earning her degrees and teaching religion at a couple mid-western Lutheran colleges. Medium build, dressed in a gray pantsuit, with low pumps, she was excited about the opportunity to be on the ground floor development of a new and innovative seminary. Happily married for over thirty years, she had two children and four grandchildren.

"Dr. Holden," Angie said, "Will you take a look at this application? It is very unusual compared to the others I've seen this morning. The applicant is in my office. I assume you haven't seen this since our policy in the admissions office is to merely see if the person has the minimum qualifications for admission before inviting them for an admissions interview. Should I have her wait in the lobby?"

"Yes, do. I'll be just a minute."

Dr. Holden looked at the routine sections of the application and went quickly to the essay.

Whoa! What have we here? She arranged for two of the graduate faculty members to come to the small conference room next to her office. They entered and sat on opposite sides of the rectangular conference table, as Dr. Holden took her seat at the head of the table.

Dr. Jenny Fitzsimmons sat to Dr. Holden's left. A professor of comparative religion, she served as the Catholic Church's ecumenical contribution to the new Lutheran seminary. It was not uncommon for protestant and Catholic institutions of higher education to exchange professors in areas where there would not be a lot of controversy over what would be taught in the classroom. She welcomed the opportunity to be a part of this new institution that was, as she occasionally joked, "in enemy territory."

She earned her doctorate at Columbia University in religious studies and had taught at Notre Dame for several years. Up until her temporary job at the Lutheran seminary, she was teaching at a Catholic seminary in Chicago. A brunette, in her late thirties, with straight hair falling slightly below her shoulders, slender, she carried herself with an air of confidence. Dr. Fitzsimmons wore a dark-blue skirt, well-coordinated with a white-colored shirt, and black, high-heeled shoes. She married in her mid-twenties and had two children who were in elementary school.

Dr. William "Willy" Severson sat on the right side of the table, directly across from Dr. Fitzsimmons. A professor of Old and New Testaments, he graduated from the Lutheran seminary in St. Paul, spent some time as a pastor in a small, rural Minnesota farming community west of the Twin Cities and earned his doctorate at Harvard Divinity School.

One of his friends said his namesake was General Patton's dog: *William the Conqueror,* whom Patton renamed "Willy" after he was intimidated by a British woman's miniature poodle. No one attempted to figure out what the connection was, but Willy didn't care; he was amused by the joke.

"Willy," in his late forties—nearly six feet tall—had a full head of graying hair and a beard with hairs wrestling to escape his face. Recently divorced with no children, he spent most of his free time on a local golf course.

He wore a blue blazer, a white shirt with a narrow black tie, black loafers and faded blue-jeans. The clothing mixture mirrored his somewhat "mixed" personality: a combination of a fun-loving guy with serious mission on behalf of God.

Sally thanked Willy and Jenny for their immediate responses to her request for help. "We have an applicant sitting in the waiting room who has applied to enter our alternative master's program. It is quite unusual. Please look over the application before we invite her in."

Having finished reading the application, the two faculty members looked up. "God's messenger? Interesting," said Dr. Fitzsimmons. "Yes, isn't it?" said Holden. Dr. Severson put the application down, leaned back in his chair, smiled and said, "Well, aren't we *all* God's messengers?"

"Perhaps so, but this one could be unique. People don't go around announcing they are 'God's messenger'. I'll bring her in and we'll have a chat. Okay?" asked Dr. Holden, looking at her two professors. They both nodded, *okay.*

"Wait." Said, Jenny, "I wonder if that's the woman I just saw getting out of a flashy, Maserati sports car. She was dressed to the nines and walked like she hung a couple galaxies."

"We'll soon find out, won't we?" Dr. Sally said with a smile, as she walked out of the office.

"Maria, this is Dr. Jenny Fitzsimmons and this is Dr. William Severson. Dr. Fitzsimmons is on loan to us for two years from a Catholic seminary in Chicago; it's a part of the effort between Lutherans and Catholics to get to know each other. Her specialty is comparative religion.

"Dr. Severson is a Lutheran pastor who has taught at a couple mid-west Lutheran colleges and teaches Old and New Testament courses. I'm the Chair of the Graduate Studies Department and my specialty in my doctoral program was the Reformation.

"Please have a seat here at the foot of the table."

"Thank you," said Maria, thinking, *This should be fun!*

"Maria," Sally began, "we don't usually get involved in the application process at this point, but we thought it might be helpful to get to know each other now and perhaps save time, and even annoyances, down the road, if we don't find a match."

"Match?" Maria asked, pleasantly.

"Well, yes. I think you would agree you are not our typical applicant. We don't get a lot of applicants claiming they are 'God's messenger'. I'm sure you can understand our curiosity. Am I correct?"

"Oh, absolutely; I understand," said Maria. "I only wish I understood my mission as clearly as I understand this situation. I was hoping you could help me with the pursuit that I mentioned in my essay."

"Well, we'll do our best, I can assure you. Now, let's start with your name: Maria Martinovna Luderenko. That name sounds familiar, but I can't place it. It's a rather unusual name for around here; nevertheless, there's something familiar about it."

"If it weren't for the 'enko' on the end," Maria replied, "it might not be so unusual, because 'luder' is a German name that was Ukrainianized back when Germans lived in the Ukraine and inter-married with the locals. Whenever you see 'enko' at the end of the name, it is Ukrainian."

"So," said Jenny. "You are Ukrainian."

"No, I'm Russian by birth with Ukrainian ancestry, but I am an American citizen because of my adoption by a farm couple from Sylvan Lake when I was twelve. My earliest years were in Vladivostok, on the Pacific Ocean not far from Japan. I've been an American citizen now for over a decade."

"Hmmm . . . Sylvan Lake," Willy said with a furrowed brow. "Luderenko. Are you the woman who murdered that high school football star from Sylvan Lake? I don't mean, 'murdered'; as I recall, that woman was acquitted."

"Yes, that would be me." Maria answered.

Willy and Jenny looked at each other. Jenny squirmed in her chair; Willy leaned back and pushed his hair back on both sides of his head as he studied this new applicant. Dr. Sally Holden sat still, gazing intently at Maria.

Maria picked up on the gaze, looked at Sally and raised her eyebrows with a non-verbal question: *So?*

"Oh," said Sally, "I was deep in thought. I find your name very interesting. You say the root of Luderenko is 'Luder'. And your middle name is "Martinovna." Does the middle name have some derivation also?"

"Yes, Dr. Holden, it does. In Russia, when names are given at birth, the child takes a middle name based on the father's first name. My father's given name was Martin . . . and because I was female, they attached 'ovna' at the end of Martin: thus, Martinovna. If I had been a boy, they would have made the middle name—or patronymic—Martinovich. Does that explain the complexities of Russian names?" Maria said, pleasantly.

"Yes, very clearly. Thank you. So, if I understood you correctly, if you remove "ovna" from Martin and "enko" from Luder, you would have Martin Luder. That is correct isn't it?"

"Yes, Ma'am, it is."

"Are you aware that Martin Luther's original surname name was 'Luder' and that he changed it to Luther when he was a young man?"

"So his name at birth was 'Martin Luder'?" asked Maria. "That's news to me, but I don't know that much about Martin Luther. I associate his name with the Reformation, but that's about it. I'm wondering . . . is this a big deal to you?"

"Well, I don't know how big a deal it is to me, but you might find it interesting that you, being 'God's messenger', have the same name as the greatest religious reformer of all time: Martin Luther. That's your father's name and your name as well, given the patronymic you just explained.

"Is there some coincidence here, or is this some divine comedy? Perhaps there is some existential revelation we can expect from you—of the same magnitude that Luther brought to humanity?"

Maria laughed, heartily. "You are asking the wrong person. I know so little about religion that I don't have a clue what my dictum 'God's messenger' means. All I know is what I've told you in my essay about my near-death-experience.

"As I wrote in my essay, I've been trying to figure out what a messenger from God does, or is supposed to do. What's worse, I don't have a message. I wasn't getting anywhere by browsing the internet and book stores. There is such a wealth of information I don't know where to begin.

"So I thought I'd start here, in a program with a focus, and see where that leads. Maybe this isn't the place for me. But I'd appreciate a little feedback from you three, if you have the time to discuss my dilemma."

"Yes, we have a little time," said Sally.

"Maria, I'm curious," said Jenny. "Are you really serious about your quest? I mean, couldn't your experience have been just a dream induced by the drugs you were given while you were in a coma for several days?"

"Not really. I experienced the out-of-body experience and encounter with God before I had any drugs in my system."

"Oh," said Severson, "you interpret the experience with the cloud to be an encounter with God?"

"Yes, I do. This was effulgent love. The message came from that very bright, pink-gold cloud of pure light that embraced me. I did not interpret the message as a command. I have a choice in the matter. Yet, the entire experience was so compelling that I haven't been able to release it from my thoughts. I need to find out what this is all about. Maybe I will find nothing."

"The last 'God's messenger' that comes to mind, was Joan of Arc. Are you familiar with her story?" asked Jenny.

"Yes. I saw the movie—with LeeLee Sobieski—on video years ago. I'm not sure why that hasn't surfaced in my memory. Maybe it is because she not only had a message from God, but it came directly to her out of a beam of light and the appearance of saints; her mission was very clear: lead the French Army to victory against the occupying British. Maybe I have some sort of subliminal fear of association here, because she was burned at the stake for daring to defy the Catholic Church."

"Don't you remember that she was murdered by the secular powers of the time?" asked Jenny.

"Yes. A bishop arranged to have her captured by his secular cronies so they could do his dirty-work for him or something like that. Maybe I *should* re-consider my obsession with this 'God's messenger' business. You aren't still burning women at the stake are you?" Maria asked, jokingly.

Willy burst into laughter; Jenny burned a hole through his skull with her angry stare; Sally, coughed, putting her hand over her mouth . . . hiding a smile.

Willy raised his arms, palms toward Jenny and declared, "I'm sorry. I'm sorry! No offense intended." Jenny held her glare.

After she recovered from her spasm, Sally said, "Let's get back to why we are here: to determine if this is a good match." She summarized the discussion thus far, hoping to give Jenny and Willy a little time to re-focus. "Now, you've looked over our curriculum and found our required courses, potential electives and the thesis which is required after the course-work. Do I understand that correctly?"

"Yes," Maria said.

"Well, obviously you are sincere in your quest. I don't see why we wouldn't have a match. Still, I will need to discuss this with Willy and Jenny before we come to a decision." Looking at the two of them, she said, "Do either of you have any more questions for Maria?"

"I do," said Jenny. "Maybe I'm a little more concerned than I should be, but I sense you have some residue of antipathy toward the Catholic Church. I'm wondering if that would interfere with our relationship as professor and student. Since I'll be teaching at least one of your required courses, and maybe some of the electives, do you think that could be a problem?"

"I think you are very perceptive of my feelings, Dr. Fitzsimmons. Yes, I do have some negative thoughts about the Catholic Church. I suppose that's why I didn't seriously consider going to a Catholic university or seminary."

Dr. Severson, who was wondering about the need for this discussion, emerged from his increasing somnolence; he sat up and waited for the discussion to continue because he remembered the Star Tribune's account of the sensational trial about a priest who had molested Maria and her high school friend who was also on trial for murder. *This should be interesting,* he thought.

"So . . . why the anger?" Jenny asked, with an edge of annoyance in her voice.

"Dr. Severson probably remembers the trial. My friend, Sammy and I, who were prosecuted for murder, had been molested by a Sylvan Lake priest prior to the unfortunate death of the Sylvan Lake football player. His name was Bubba. Sammy slit his throat while Bubba was on top of me, attempting to rape me and threatening to kill me. Sammy saved me from being raped and most likely saved my life. It was a heroic act.

"We were acquitted, partly because Sammy is developmentally disabled, and because of that unfortunate burden, the priest targeted him for exploitation.

"Our attorney successfully argued that, because of the severe trauma Sammy had endured from months of sexual assaults by the priest, and his knowledge that that same priest had sexually assaulted me, Sammy transferred his revulsion for the priest and was overcome by anger for what Bubba was doing.

"It turned out that the priest who had sexually assaulted me and Sammy had sexually abused numerous other children over a period of fifteen years. As if that weren't enough of an outrage, the priest was promoted to Bishop and transferred to the Vatican where he would have diplomatic immunity from prosecution; he has since been promoted to cardinal.

"On my flight from Moscow to San Francisco, a man gave me a book he had finished reading about the Catholic Church's sex abuse scandal. It turns out that thousands of priests from numerous countries around the world have been accused of sexual abuse of tens of thousands of children.

"And those numbers are considered minimal because only a small percentage of abuses are reported. Surely you must be aware of this situation, Dr. Fitzsimmons. Perhaps you can understand why I have antipathy relative to the Catholic Church.

"To answer your question, I see no reason why we shouldn't be able to get along in a power relationship of professor and student. You seem to be a fair, decent and honest person. I don't think you would allow your personal feelings to interfere with your professional judgment. I understand if you are annoyed at me for my attempt at humor a few moments ago, but I meant no harm."

"I was annoyed at Dr. Severson for his outburst more than I was your flippant remark," replied Jenny. "And, yes, I am aware that thousands of priests have molested children, but I am also aware that a very high percentage of our priests have not engaged in such outrageous behavior. I know the Church is trying to put these embarrassing revelations behind us. Thank you for your confidence in my professional integrity." Looking at Sally, Jenny said, "That's my only question."

Looking at Dr. Severson, Sally waited for his response.

"I don't have any more questions for Maria."

"Okay, then." said Sally. Looking at Maria, she said, "It will be a month or so before we make a decision about your admission. We have administrative processes that take time, including evaluating all other applicants and the number of spaces we have available. So we'll be in touch by email. Do you have any other questions for us?"

Looking at all three of them, Maria said, "Not really. I appreciate your taking the time to make an initial evaluation of my candidacy. It has been a pleasure talking with you. I am looking forward to coming here. I think we have a good match; I hope you will also."

Three weeks after the admissions interview, Marie received formal notice that she had been admitted to the Minneapolis Lutheran Seminary. Dr. William "Willy" Severson would advise her on her course schedule, the selection and development of her thesis topic, and answer questions.

Chapter 42

Opus Dei, (Work of God) was founded in Spain in 1928 by a Catholic priest: Josemaria Escriva. The organization was given final approval by the Vatican in 1952 and was established as a personal prelature in 1982 by Pope John Paul II. It is one of many such organizations that come under the direct supervision of either the curia or the Congregation of Bishops. It has over 86,000 members in nearly one hundred countries.

About sixty percent of the members live in their private homes, leading normal secular lives, except of course, for their participation in Opus Dei activities. The other forty percent are celibate and the majority of them live in Opus Dei centers. About sixty percent of members reside in Europe and thirty five percent live in North and South America. A large majority of members belong to middle-class and lower levels of society, in terms of social status, income, and education.

Following are several types of membership held by members: *Supernumeraries:* sixty percent-householders; *Numeraries:* twenty percent-celibate men and women who live separately in centers and may become supernumeraries. *Numerary Assistants:* five percent are unmarried celibate females who take care of the domestic needs of the centers.

In smaller percentages - *Associates:* celibate females who have family or job obligations and do not live in centers. *Clergy:* priests who serve under the prelature of Opus Dei, who became priests after a while at lower levels in the organization. *The Priestley Society of the Holy Cross:* priests who come under the prelature and priests who report to a diocese, but are given Opus Dei training. The founder of Opus Dei was made a saint in 2002 by John Paul II.

The cilice (a metal chain about six inches wide, with inwardly-pointing spikes and long enough to wrap around one's thigh) is used to induce pain in the practice of mortification: the voluntary practice of offering up discomfort or pain to God. Members assert that very few actually engage in this practice, although no outsider knows whether the statement is accurate.

Celibate members practice other forms of "self-mortification," such as sleeping without a pillow, sleeping on the floor, fasting, and remaining silent for hours during the day. Escriva's dictum on pain: "Loved be pain. Sanctified be pain. Glorified be pain!" (ODAN-**O**pus **D**ei **A**wareness Network website)

LEGIONARIES OF CHRIST

Opus Dei has a reputation as being one of the two most controversial forces within the Catholic Church: the other being **Legionaries of Christ.** The Legion was founded in the 1950's by a Mexican priest, Father Marcial Maciel, who had been kicked out of two seminaries for reasons that remain obscure. His claim to fame came with the establishment of dozens of seminaries in several countries through which he produced an increasing number of priests each decade.

He was honored by Pope John Paul II for his fund raising skills as the renowned leader of the Legion. He joined the pope on three of his trips abroad, including two trips to Mexico. Allegations of sex abuse by Father Maciel were covered up, even after six priests came forward with irrefutable allegations of sex-abuse against him. Maciel was forced to resign shortly before he died.

Communion and Liberation

A lesser known, but nevertheless powerful, conservative Catholic group joined Opus Dei and the Legionaries of Christ as one of the notorious, scandal-ridden factions within the Vatican orbit in April 2012.

The Communion of Liberation was founded in Italy around the same time as the Legionaries of Christ in the 1950's. It has grown to become a world-wide presence in some eighty countries, including the United States. For them, as Christians, their religious life cannot be separated from sharing responsibility for the social welfare of humanity. But that lofty aspiration was sullied when, in April 2012, some of its most prominent members were investigated for bribery and even charged with embezzlement of millions of dollars from an Italian health institute.

The Communion of Liberation is alleged to be Pope Benedict XVI's favorite among such groups as Opus Dei and the Legionaries of Christ. The pope launched a beatification effort for the founder of Communion and Liberation, the late Father Luigi Giussani, shortly after his death. Giussani's successor, Spanish Father Julian Carron, reportedly confessed consternation that so many people saw Communion and Liberation in terms of money and power, and since that is the case there must be some basis for such opprobrious conduct. (Source: May 2, 2012 NCR Today)

Chapter 43

Political pundits averred that the elections of yet another Italian president and—simultaneously—a new pope, could be a match made in heaven. Mutual interests and similar personalities of the newly elected leaders could trump disparities in the election processes and governance between the two sovereign states.

Thus, when concurrent announcements came from the Italian presidential palace and the Vatican—a month after the two leaders assumed office—that the two newly elected leaders would meet at the Italian Presidential Palace at Palazzo del Quirinale, no one, despite the speculations of the pundits, expected them to break the diplomatic logjam that had existed for decades. The press releases mimicked previous announcements, reinforcing the skepticism of public sentiment.

Yet, the media reported a puzzling disconnect which suggested the pundits might have intuited something the public missed. The leaders' meeting lasted over four hours and well into the evening, whereas previous, initial meetings rarely exceeded the scheduled time allotted: one-half hour. Religious and secular journalists, world-wide, ignited a conflagration of speculation about the meaning of the extended meeting.

They all knew the pope wasted no time in taking charge of the moribund bureaucracy; he issued autocratic decrees and fired cardinals within days— even hours—of taking office. And he sent shock-waves around the globe with his leaked, gloomy assessment of the state of the Church. His actions rivaled that of a monarch.

Yet, the president of Italy does not have the power of a monarch. His position is primarily ceremonial, but he *is* the Commander in Chief of the military. Officially, the person known to the world as the "Prime Minister," also holds the title of "President of the Council of Ministers." Thus, the two "presidents" share powers in the executive branch of government. The legislative, executive and judicial branches' limited powers are embedded in Italy's constitution.

By contrast, the pope's eight titles seem ostentatiously designed to impress upon humanity a redux of the antiquated "Divine Right of Kings," a political and religious doctrine of royal absolutism. The idea is that a monarch is not subject to any temporal authority, deriving his right to rule directly from God.

Reading the pope's eight titles, one wonders if adding one more wouldn't place the pope's authority above God: Supreme Pontiff of the Universal Church, Sovereign of the Vatican City State, Bishop of Rome, Vicar of Christ, Successor of the Prince of the Apostles, Primate of Italy, Archbishop and Metropolitan of the Roman Province, and Servant of the Servants of God.

Clearly, the pope's titles suggest he has powers that exceed even that of a king—serving with divine rights—possesses. The extent to which Pope Immanuel would exercise his "divine rights" worried a lot of people.

Whatever the pope and the president had discussed would remain a matter of intense speculation that generated a blizzard of articles in the mainstream media, the internet, and professional journals. Even before anyone had unassailable facts of what had occurred between the pope and the president at their first summit, books were being written about what actually happened. Still, it would be a matter of years before the public learned what the two leaders had discussed.

At their first meeting, Pope Immanuel and President Alessandro Bianchi kept introductory niceties to a minimum. The pope made the transition bluntly. He said, "Mr. President, as you know, our respective states have been in a deadly, mutually destructive dance with the Devil for decades. The 'smoke of the Devil' has thickened, rather than dissipated in recent years. I would like to discuss what we can do about that."

Raising his eyebrows, President Bianchi asked, "the 'smoke of the Devil?'" .

"Yes. I am referring to the financial scandals that occurred shortly after the middle of the last century when Paul VI believed the Devil had entered the inner sanctum of the Church."

"What do you have in mind?"

"Can you assure me of absolute confidentiality for our discussions today? We have already agreed to exclude translators and other diplomatic aides since we both speak fluent English. I want reassurance that what we discuss today will not be leaked to the press. I would prefer that no notes be taken or official written reports produced.

"What we will be discussing, with your agreement of course, are portentous matters, indeed. They involve life and death matters and I am not excluding the two of us in that warning."

President Bianchi replied, graciously, "I understand your reference to Paul VI's remark. Also, I can assure you of complete confidentiality. Now, I suppose if I had not already known of your integrity and sincerity, I would take offence at your question.

"Yet, I don't, because it appears you have come to me with a profound desire to explore issues of grave importance to both of us and the sovereign states we represent. I want to assure you of my willingness to cooperate in taking our discussion in that direction. As you know, whatever problems you have inherited could not be worse than mine."

The pope laughed. "I appreciate your candor, Mr. President. So, if I may, I'd like to throw a rock into the pond and see how much of a splash it will make. I'm here to discuss organized crime."

"Well, Your Holiness, I'm intrigued. The rock you threw is more like a boulder. You made a big splash with it because it is an event I have dreamed about my entire political career. The criminal families are destroying the political, social, financial, moral and religious fabric of my country. We are doing what we can to fight them, but it has been a losing battle. I have always thought that Italy would never solve its organized crime problems without the cooperation and assistance of the Church.

"Now, *I* want to be frank with *you*; I believe the Vatican Bank holds the key to the door through which my country has marched into the abyss that Dante so eloquently described and Milton less vividly portrayed: Hell."

"Mr. President, I have suspected what you just told me for many years and I vowed that if I ever became pope, I would confront those responsible for the mess we are in. Is there a way for us to work together to find out what is really going on between the Vatican Bank and the crime syndicates?"

"Your Holiness, I think we already know up to a point. The barrier to going further is the stonewalling we get where the money trail ends—usually at the Vatican Bank. As you may know, the modern-day scandals that began during WW II and exploded into public view in the sixties and seventies faded from public awareness. The failure of the new pope to change the Vatican Bank policies, after Paul VI died in 1978, encouraged the criminals. Their activities have reached intolerable heights in my country.

"They became bolder with each successful, illegal transaction that involved the Vatican. The Vatican Bank has become the institution of choice for the criminal families."

"Yes, I agree," said the pope, "not to mention a tax haven for thousands of well-connected, extremely wealthy people in Italy and other countries. Even though I am the owner of the bank, I don't have the facts to back up that belief."

"I want to reassure you," replied the president, "that if you want to take on the criminal elements in Italy, you will have my full support. We already know a lot about your bank's involvement, but it would be a significant break-through if we could get cooperation from your banker."

The pope responded. "When I questioned the President of the Supervi-sory Commission of Cardinals, which has oversight of the bank's operations, he dissembled and refused to be candid with me. I'm quite certain he knows very little of the bank's operations; still, his failure to be open and truthful with me suggests ominous consequences for anyone who probes too deeply into the banks activities.

"Therefore, at this time, I don't want to rock the boat on my side of the cooperative equation we are creating here. I will need all the ammuni-tion I can muster for the war I will start when I take on the manager of the bank.

"I'm sure it sounds strange to you, for me to be talking about my impo-tence relative to knowing what my own bank is doing and my inability to find that out. Still, that is the situation. To be clear, if I were to order my bank manager to come clean and reveal, immediately, everything he knows about his involvement with the Mafiosi, the war would start and I would be killed, and it would be back to business as usual."

With a smile on his face, Pope Immanuel continued. "I'm not quite ready to pass on to my reward yet; I want to handle this situation with some cun-ning—clandestine and strategic thinking—behind what we do to optimize our odds for success."

"Your Holiness, I understand your caution and will honor your willing-ness to join in the fight against organized crime, despite the personal danger involved. Now I want to share with you what my country is planning, which is relevant to what you are thinking.

"As you may know, I was responsible for the District Anti-Mafia Director-ates prior to running for election. Not long ago, the federal government estab-lished an organized crime task force which created zones within Italy in which they set up anti-crime directorates; they were to identify who was involved in criminal activities, what they were doing and how they were functioning. Those phases have been completed.

"The next phase—which is only the beginning—is to look into how the criminals finance their operations. I must say, your timing is exquisite; you couldn't have come to me at a better time.

"Allow me to give you an overview of our strategic thinking and the plans we have yet to implement. We plan to build four prisons to house all the criminals we expect to arrest and detain when we strike with a knockout blow against them. We will build modern, state-of-the-art prisons in Sicily, and in the southern, central and northern regions of my country.

"We anticipate it will take three years to build and test the security systems and then vet and train all the personnel required to administer the prisons. We have already begun training that will involve, among other things, utilization of sophisticated security equipment.

"Here's the kicker. While we need the prisons, we also need evidence to convict the criminals who will occupy these new facilities. It has been a daunting task to get such evidence in the past.

"Many brave law enforcement officers and courageous, loyal patriots have died, including judges and other government personnel, attempting to bring the hoodlums to justice. When investigators ask people for their cooperation, they clam up for fear of reprisals, which usually means death; one can hardly blame our citizens for wanting to save their own lives. I want to remove our citizens' fear.

"We have concluded that, when the government contracts are let to build the prisons, there will be a tsunami of criminal activity occurring: bribery, intimidation—you name it. It will include financial corruption, a subject that interests you and your bank.

"We are preparing a comprehensive monitoring system that will include documentation of everything related to the construction of the prisons: architectural designs, site preparation, building materials, construction equipment, supplies, environmental impact studies, water resources, transportation equipment, highways and bridges leading to the prisons. I think you get the idea.

"Doing that is not something we routinely ignore; we do it with every government building we build. What is unique this time is that we will be monitoring, very carefully—clandestinely, I might add—every transaction that occurs: documenting evidence involving criminal activity from all four regions of the country.

"Because of the tens of millions of euros involved, we think many, if not all the major crime bosses in each region, will be involved and competing for the government largesse which they will view as potential, financial windfalls.

"We are casting a large net when one considers the size of the systems of organized crime in this country. We want to take down the crime bosses and put an end to organized crime in Italy. That is our goal. In cooperation with local authorities, we will be rounding up hundreds of lower-level criminals who will also be detained and prosecuted.

"We are already planning a series of sting operations in each of the four regions: for example sending letters to criminals on the lam, inviting them to come to a specific location to claim some prize they have won which is worth several thousand euros—that kind of thing. That operation will coincide with our nationwide strike.

"As I have indicated, our objective is strategic: to haul in as many 'big fish' as we can with the nets we are casting in the four regions. We'll be doing several things: (1) identifying the financial streams that flow from the fountains of wealth and end up in the hands of criminals and how they dispose of their loot; (2) learning about intimidation tactics, fraudulent transactions etc.; and (3) understanding the intricacies of the social systems used by organized crime syndicates.

"Obviously, there is more to be said here about the strategic plans. But I think you get the idea. Oh, one other thing. Soon we will begin designing and building a huge new headquarters for the national military/police, the Carabinieri, a couple blocks east of the Swiss Guard barracks.

"We contracted with a German construction company to design and build the facility, utilizing only German citizens in the construction phase to prevent implantation of electronic surveillance devices. Because of the proximity of that facility to your Swiss Guard barracks, we have been working with Colonel Isenberg on some clandestine interactive possibilities. You might ask him to keep you posted on the progress we are making."

"I will do that," replied the pope.

"Now, to complete the circle I have been drawing, sometime in late 2008 or early 2009, we will declare martial law and send our military units into every region of the country to support local law enforcement agencies in rounding up the criminals. This will be a drastic and unprecedented action for our country: a dramatic strike at organized crime.

"We have been organizing and training special operation forces units in each branch of our military services, which will be used alongside our conventional forces. Crucial to our success in prosecuting the criminals will be arresting the suspects and gathering evidence in a lawful manner.

"Toward that end, we have organized and are training Carabinieri special operation forces which we call the GIS—or Special Intervention Group.

As you know, the Carabinieri is our national military police force, with civil, military and other police duties, as well as military peacekeeping and war-fighting capabilities. The GIS features some one hundred or so troops trained in counter-terrorism operations and they will be used as needed in highly specialized situations.

"The operation could include, in some limited way, the Special Operations Forces of NATO because of the high likelihood our operations will involve foreign nationals from other NATO countries.

"Nearly all NATO countries, if not all, are plagued by these international crime organizations. We have been talking about Italy, but we now have documentation of just one glaring example of what I'm talking about, and that is toxic waste.

"It is a billion dollar business and a lot of that stuff passes through our Naples ports on its way to Poland. We have our own toxic waste problems in the Naples area. Organized crime controls that industry. I know my peers in other NATO countries want to help bring that travesty to an end.

"Between now and 2008, we will be conducting nation-wide military training operations, simulating the massive strike across the nation. They will be done under the guise of preparations for any natural or man-made disaster that could befall our country. Of course we should be doing such training anyway.

"This gives us the opportunity to train, *covertly* for a deadly blow against organized crime." President Bianchi paused and reached for a cigarette. "I've been trying to quit, he said, but when I get all riled up just thinking about these momentous events, my defenses weaken. Do you mind if I have a few puffs?"

Lighting the cigarette and inhaling, smoke wafted around his face as he said, "we are thinking, as I mentioned, late November three years from now might be a good target date for our strike against the gangsters. Does that sound feasible to you, in terms of coordinating simultaneous moves?"

"Yes, Mr. President. Now, I must say, your timing on these matters coincides quite well with my plans. I, too, have been thinking strategically, especially about the timing of dealing with the Vatican Bank.

"I've had some very radical thoughts about that, which I will share with you in future meetings. If we agree on what I'm thinking, I'll need some military assistance to pull it off. I, also, have been thinking of NATO forces since I have a lot of foreign nationals working and living in the Vatican and they will need protection if things get violent when I make my move.

"I'm looking at Vatican organizational and doctrinal issues in addition to what we've been discussing. There are powerful figures, within the Vatican and amongst ancillary Catholic institutions throughout the world, who will pull out all the stops when they notice their political and religious power, finances, and prestige are threatened.

"So I, like you, am preparing in a way that will not fail when I finally make my move to do what is in the best interests of the Church and humanity. That has been my life-long goal. We'll see where that takes us."

President Bianchi suggested they meet over dinner occasionally to keep each other abreast of developments on an informal basis and have a final meeting when action is imminent.

"Well," said President Bianchi, "we Italians usually dine late in the evening and it is already early evening, and you Americans dine early. So what do you say? Would you like to stay for a light dinner? Our chefs can have something quite tasty ready for us. You do know don't you, that it was the Italians who taught the French how to cook?" the President said with a smile.

"Yes, I've read that. And I'm sure you know nearly every country in the world has taught Americans how to cook—especially Italian pizzas that became popular in the early fifties."

"Touché," said the President, with a smile, as he squashed his barely smoked cigarette in a tray and led the pope to a lounge near his private dining room.

Chapter 44

For Monsignor Lopez—prelate and leader of Opus Dei with his headquarters in New York, and Father Pablo Nunez, the General Director of the Legionaries of Christ in Connecticut—the emerging crisis was not unlike wars of the past: that is, time elapsed between the initiating events and the culminating event: violence.

Both men possessed enough knowledge of history to be able to use it in times of institutional crisis. They were cognizant of a couple examples in recent history that provided perspective for dealing with potential threats to institutional stability.

Adolf Hitler, the "Austrian Corporal," was arrested for the Beer Hall Putsch, a failed attempt to gain power in Germany in 1923. While in prison, he wrote *Mein Kampf (My Struggle)*, in which he outlined plan for the conquest of Europe and the Soviet Union. Ten years later he gained enough political power, through the electoral process, to take supreme dictatorial power in a slick Machiavellian maneuver in Berlin. Another six years passed before he launched the Second World War, implementing his plan.

Vladimir Lenin, the Bolshevik founder of what came to be known as the Soviet Union, started his quest about twenty years before a civil war erupted, which led to his successful overthrow of the Russian Czarist regime.

Failed assassination attempts against Hitler and Lenin allowed them to continue their efforts to launch a coup d'état. With that knowledge, Cardinals Lopez and Nunez were well aware that—if they were patient—others might eliminate the necessity for them to take action to stifle the new pope's initiatives and restore power to one of their own; yet, they also knew that taking brash action could be counter-productive.

They knew that radical changes—though well-intentioned—could get out of control and lead to catastrophe; no one needed to remind them—nor even Cardinal O'Reilley—of the consequences of Gorbachev's *glasnost i perestroika* that occurred during the nineteen-eighties and early nineteen-nineties.

In the interim, they would work with others—mainly the mafia—on ways to deal with, what could turn out to be, a renegade pope.

Chapter 45

Cardinal O'Reilley had had enough. He had read Father Sandusky's leaked white paper on the Church's problems prepared for Pope Immanuel. Somehow, the security of the paper had been compromised; it was sealed in an envelope—stamped "CONFIDENTIAL." He claimed it was on his desk when he arrived at work.

He insisted he didn't know if someone had hacked into Father Sandusky's computer . . . or what. But he didn't care; he had a copy and that was all he needed. The paper provided incontrovertible evidence that the pope was engaged in a conspiracy to destroy the Catholic Church; he had to be stopped.

How? From what Cardinal O'Reilley had seen thus far, pleas for the pope to cease and desist were not an option. Decisive action was the only thing that would work. Well over a year and a half had passed since the new pope was elected; Cardinal O'Reilley's patience was exhausted.

First of all, he needed to know what Father Perfecto was up to. He sought the services of Father Morales, the General Administrator for the Legion of Christ office in Rome.

Morales controlled the secret investigative unit that was formed to check into violations of the five-pronged oath taken by all Legionaries: (1) vows of poverty; (2) chastity; (3) and obedience—taken by all Catholic priests—plus, two more vows required of the Legionaries: (4) vows to never speak ill of the founder: Maciel; and (5) to not seek higher positions of authority in the institution. Cardinal O'Reilley had no interest in the results of the investigations. He had other fish to fry.

He wasn't sure Father Morales and the Legionaries of Christ could be of assistance, but it was worth a try.

O'Reilley made an appointment to speak with Father Morales—General Administrator for the Legionaries of Christ—at his office near the Vatican.

When he arrived at the Legion's headquarters, Father Morales announced that Monsignor Lopez, Prelate of Opus Dei headquarters in New York, and Father Nunez, General Director of the Legion at its headquarters in Connecticut, had just concluded a meeting in the conference room and would like to join the two of them for lunch. As the monsignor and the director emerged from the conference room, Father Morales introduced them to Cardinal O'Reilley. He said, "I have made reservations for lunch at the German restaurant down the street and around the corner."

Sitting at a sidewalk table on a warm Wednesday afternoon, after customary pleasantries, Cardinal O'Reilley spoke. "I am delighted about this unforeseen opportunity to meet with the three of you. I was expecting to meet briefly with Father Morales, hand him the pope's 'White Paper' and discuss a rather minor matter. Since you two have joined us, perhaps we can take up other matters as well."

"Actually, Cardinal O'Reilley," said Monsignor Lopez, Prelate of Opus Dei, "we've been discussing that perhaps it is time we all talk about matters of mutual interest. When Father Morales told us you were coming over this morning, we decided this would be a good time to have a chat. Why don't you go ahead with the matter you wanted to discuss with Father Morales, and we can take it from there."

"Thank you for your gracious offer to meet with me," said Cardinal O'Reilley. Looking at Father Morales, O'Reilley said, "I need help finding out what Father Gonzales, the pope's junior, personal secretary is doing. We know he spends some of his time at his desk in his apartment next to the pope's, and we know he leaves the Vatican in his personal car several times a week and sometimes spends time at Castel Gandolfo. But we don't have a clue what he is up to.

"Is there any way you can help us find out where he goes and what he does after he leaves the Vatican? As I said, we know he goes to Gandolfo, the pope's castle occasionally, but there he stays in his apartment and goes to his office, apparently whenever he feels like it. And he doesn't do much of anything while there . . . reads a few magazines and that's about it.

"He goes other places also, because sometimes he is gone for several days, but does not show up at Gandolfo. I have someone there who keeps me informed of his time spent and his activities there. Is there anything you can do to help?"

"I'm not sure what you're asking me to do."

"Tail him. Stop him on the road to wherever he is going; search his car; ask him questions; let him know someone is watching him."

"How would I do that? I don't have the Carabinieri to do my bidding. I don't have police cars with uniformed men patrolling the streets and highways. My investigation unit is small and deals with vow violations. I'm afraid I can't be of much help."

"I was afraid that might be your answer; since it is, I'll accept what you say. I have other ways of accomplishing what you say you can't do. Still, there's another reason I came." Pulling a manila folder out of his briefcase, he handed it to Father Morales. "I have a copy of the 'White Paper' that Father Sandusky prepared for the pope."

"How did you get a copy of this report? I don't think this is something the pope wants floating around," Father Morales said.

"It appeared on my desk this morning. Obviously, someone in his inner circle is betraying him. Apparently, they don't like what the pope is doing any more than I do. And whoever it is, he knows I'll do something about it. Father Sandusky has been working on it for well over a year."

"What does the White Paper say?" asked Monsignor Lopez.

Looking at Morales, O'Reilley said, "I'm sure you remember, Father Morales, my coming to you right after the pope took over and started shaking the Vatican tree. I warned that your Legion and perhaps Opus Dei needed to do something before it was too late, and you demurred saying you weren't that worried, but if it came to what I was describing, you'd inform your General Director in Connecticut. Well, now it's approaching two years later and the situation is getting critical. I think when you read this you'll be as disturbed as I am."

"You haven't told us what it says," said Father Nunez. "Give us a brief synopsis, if you don't mind. If it's as threatening as you say, it would be interesting to hear why."

The waiter interrupted the conversation and took orders.

"Okay," said O'Reilley, "Father Sandusky starts with the founding of our Church . . . how it took about four centuries to work out the doctrine and organizational problems that plagued the early bishops. He mentions battles with heretics, especially the Gnostics whom St. Irenaeus, the heresiologist, castigates in his five-volume tome: *Against Heresies.*

"Sandusky has a short outline of the problems faced by the Church, including the wars that led to the crusades at the turn of the first millennium and the Reformation.

"He recounts the horrors of the Inquisition and mentions *The Malleus Maleficarum (The Witches Hammer),* which is the 278-page manual for hunting down, torturing and murdering women suspected of dealing in witchcraft. Pope Innocent VIII issued a papal Bull in 1484 authorizing two authors to write the manual which would lie on the benches (for quick reference) and be used by judges for three centuries.

"Finally, he provides a detailed analysis of our current problems, starting with the Vatican Bank scandals of the sixties, seventies and eighties asserting, that if the world knew how disgraceful the Bank's current involvement with the Mafia, secret bank accounts, and money laundering is, there would be hell to pay for what we are doing.

"Doctrinal issues arise because in recent years, there have many revelations coming from a number of sources that contradict Catholic doctrine. The pederasty scandals and the loss tens of thousands of priests that have occurred all over the world—plus drastic declines in church attendance—are also subjects of interest in his White Paper.

"Pope Immanuel apparently believes that previous popes buried their heads in the sand, or more appropriately, floated somewhere above the clouds where the smoke from the fires destroying the Church wouldn't irritate their nostrils; he intends to take a different tack. Where that will lead, no one knows. But I'm not willing to wait and find out. If no one else will act, I will."

"What do you intend to do?" asked Father Morales.

"First, I will try to convince you—looking first at the Legion General Director, Father Nunez, and then at Monsignor Lopez of Opus Dei—to join me and Cardinal Moretti, whom the pope fired, to formulate a strategy to stop the pope in his tracks.

"Saint Serendipity arranged for us to meet today. Perhaps we can take up my concerns now that we are all here. I would have liked to have Cardinal Moretti here as well, but I can pass on to him what we discuss today."

"Cardinal O'Reilley. Now listen to me and listen . . . *carefully*," Monsignor Lopez said. "Impetuous action at this point could have serious consequences in terms of our ability to deal with this developing situation. I can assure you we in Opus Dei are just as concerned, perhaps more so, than you. Father Nunez and I are in constant touch. We are keeping our constituents informed.

"The worst thing you could do is strike out on your own with some kind of slapdash attack on the pope, or whatever else you might be contemplating. I implore you to be careful. We will work with you to do what is necessary to protect our mutual interests. I worry that you are not listening to us and might make it much more difficult to achieve our goals when the time to act arrives.

"So far, we are only in the infant stages of what could come down. We are using whatever time we have to monitor the situation and make plans for several eventualities. Just because he is taking a comprehensive look at our history and exploring all options does not mean he will select the most onerous one and act on it.

"Fundamentally, there is nothing threatening about exploring options to deal with the condition of the Church today. Until we have a firm grip on where the pope is headed, we will not act; when we do, it will be decisive, thoroughly planned and executed to ensure success. We have a massive amount of financial, political, and if necessary, para-military force to achieve our goals.

"We appreciate the efforts you are making in terms of acquiring information that is crucial to our efforts. The most important contribution you can make, and I must say, have already made—considering the acquisition of the pope's white paper—is to find out what you can, given your insider status at the Vatican. Yet, I implore you to restrain yourself; don't let your anxiety drive you into action you might later regret."

Chapter 46

"Perfecto, thank you for coming." The pope greeted Father Gonales half way between his desk and his office door with a hearty handshake and a pat on his left, upper arm. "I've been very busy and haven't had time to meet with you," Pope Immanuel said, as he turned and walked back to his desk.

"Have a seat, please. Tyrone has kept me informed of your progress with the books. I understand that you have finished reading them and are working on a report for me. Is that correct?"

"Yes, Holiness, it is, except that I've also finished the report. I brought it with me this morning," Perfecto said, as he handed it to the pope before he sat in a chair to the left of the pope's desk.

"Well, this is a pleasant surprise. I was going to ask you to finish it as soon as possible because I have an important meeting coming up with the Italian President and I wanted the benefit of what you have discovered before I meet with him. How have you been?" he said, as he opened the report to glance through it. "Fine," Perfecto replied.

Looking up at Perfecto, he asked, "Have you had any trouble with anyone harassing you? Stopping you on the road to search your car? Anything like that?"

"Not really, Holiness. I'm not trained in detecting a sleuth, but I'm sure I have been followed a few times, and when I was, I always took some crazy route only to annoy them, sometimes leading them through long, winding mountain roads to small villages where I would stop for lunch and then let them watch me while I filled up with gas and take them on another long ride on my way back to Gandolfo. I don't think they've learned anything other than that I'm doing what you told me to do 'God's work'," Perfecto said with a big smile.

The pope laughed heartily. "Okay. It's working out the way I hoped it would. Keep them guessing until things get dicey around here and then we'll have some fun with them. You've performed magnificently. Tyrone is impressed as well." Pope Immanuel paused to glance through Perfecto's report.

"Okay, this looks excellent: well organized, concise, and exactly what I needed. What else would I expect from a Berkeley grad?"

"Nothing but the best!" Perfecto grinned.

"Okay, here's the drill," said the Pope. "I'm going to a meeting with the President of Italy soon. Before I do, I want you to do something for me. First, I want you to look over these annual financial statements that our dear friend the banker, Lidano Russo, has been providing, going back five years.

"There's nothing much to look at in terms of learning what the bank is doing, but at least become familiar with the contents. That shouldn't take more than a day. Then go to the bank and tell his secretary that you work directly for me and that you want to see Mr. Russo. If she dissembles, let me know immediately. It's likely he will refuse to even see you, but short of that, he may keep putting you off. Let me know what happens. Okay? Check back with me in a couple days.

"Oh, in case he will see you right away, tell him I want to see the backup, detailed data on the annual reports."

"Yes, Holiness . . . I, uh . . . got that!" he said with a big smile. "Will that be all? I don't want to waste time."

"You're my boy, Perfecto, the pope said, rising and coming around the desk to shake Perfecto's hand. Thanks for all you have done. Now get back to work!"

"Well," the pope said, "How did your meeting with the banker go?"

"I was quite surprised, actually. He summoned his Office Manager, Sister Aurelia Esposito to join us in his office. He said he always has her with him in important meetings to record what was said so that later, if needed, he can refer to what was discussed.

"I told him what you wanted and he said that it would take some time since the banking operation is very large and those kinds of records are not immediately retrievable. He told Sister Esposito to prepare the report, since she is responsible for the daily functioning of the bank. He said she has only fifteen staff assistants so it could take several months to prepare the report since she must keep up on her daily responsibilities.

"He said he wondered why you had not stopped by, or even asked to see him since you became pope a couple years ago. He said he had asked for an appointment to see you a couple times, but was turned away by your secretary."

"I'm sure that is not true—that he was turned away. But yes, I have not wanted to deal with him because I've been told that everything is under control at the bank and that there is nothing to worry about. I'm sure he would recognize that attitude as a continuation of the policies of my predecessors.

"As you know, I've been very busy with other issues; I select my time for controversy and confrontation very carefully. That time is coming for the bank and the banker, but it will be at a time of my choosing, not his.

"Anyway, Perfecto, thanks for taking on that errand for me. We'll see how soon we get the report. When we do, you will have your work cut out for you. I will want a synoptic analysis. In the meantime, I have a suggestion, but first a question: Are you still driving that old beat-up Volkswagen?"

"Yes, Holiness, I am. I love that old car, but it has had its day and it's time I think about getting another one."

"Interesting that you should say that because I was thinking the same thing. I tell you what; go see Tyrone. He has a car there that I think will be of some interest to you. It won't cost you any money and Tyrone will probably be delighted to take your old 'bug' and do something creative with it.

"Things are going to get precarious around here as we approach what I expect to be a major confrontation with the powers in the Church who don't like what I'm doing. That means that you will need some protection that your old VW won't give you. So you go talk to Tyrone. Got it?"

"Yes, Holiness . . . got it!" Perfecto said with his customary smile.

"Now, we aren't done yet. I am arranging for you to go work with the President of Italy at the Quirinale Palace. I want you to go over there and spend the next few months getting acquainted with the President's staff and gathering as much information as you can about gangland activity in Italy: how many gangs there are, what are their names, where are they operating, what industries are affected, what is being done by the State to fight organized crime.

"After you have a good take on the problem, learn as much as you can about how the crime families finance their operations and the extent to which the Vatican Bank is involved in supporting their activities. Keep a low profile.

"I talked with the President on the phone recently, and we agree that it would be better if you take an apartment there, at the Palace, so you don't need to be driving back and forth from here every day. That will make it a lot safer for you. The closer we get to the truth the more dangerous it will become for both of us.

Chapter 47

The TV had been on for more than an hour. The Sunday morning mass from the Vatican had just started. Mario Marino was in the midst of his preferred Sunday morning activity:

romancing his high school sweetheart, Darly, when his cell phone rang.

"Ah shit, now what?"

"Honey, let the phone ring, Darly cooed. It's never anything important . . . *please?*"

"Damn it, Darly. When you're as desperate as I am for work, you *always* answer the phone," he growled as he rolled over and grabbed his cell phone.

"Hello?"

"I have a contract for you. It will set you up for the rest of your life, if you choose to take it," said a raspy voice. "If you are interested, meet me at the dead-end road that veers off toward the sunset at the bottom of the hill in one hour."

"See. What did I tell you, Darly? I've been offered a contract that will set us up for life. Someday I'll control the whole low-boot of Italy: the toes, the instep and heel . . . reaching up to include the ankle: the whole region. Think of that, will you Darly?"

"I've heard it all before, Mario. I'll believe it when I see it. What are you doing?"

"Damn it, Darly. I'm getting dressed. Are you blind? You're like all the rest of 'em. No faith in me. I'll show you and all those bastards who'll be swimming with the fishes when I get done with them."

"Where are you going? Mario?"

"I can't tell you."

Darly watched Mario—in a state of panic—get dressed. He ran to the bed, brushed a quick kiss across her smeared lips and whispered: "You're the best lay in all of Southern Italy," as he reached under his pillow and retrieved his CZ 2075 RAMI pistol and stuffed it behind his belt in front of his left hip.

Darly sat up in bed and said, "You've been all over Italy, Mario. Are there better one's up north?" she whined.

"Forget about it! I gotta' go." He grabbed his New York Yankees baseball cap he stole from a tourist's backpack, set it firmly on his head, and ran out the door.

Mario jumped into his aging, beat-up, gray, two-door Fiat and raced down the narrow, winding road, running a couple cars into the ditch, another coming close to going over a cliff.

As he sped down the hill, Mario thought about his life thus far. At twenty-one, he had already established a reputation with local mobsters . . . stealing cars for the local chop-shops. Petty stuff, to be sure, but while he was stealing cars, he was building up personal capital that would someday be recognized for its value: he had become a master at accuracy with his pistol. He could hit small targets flying through the air in an arc—consistently—an accomplishment few ever achieved.

Mario, a young man with a slender, medium-to-tall build, black hair, with matching black eyes and mustache on a face that anyone in the world would consider movie-star quality, attracted the local girls' attention; they competed for his affection.

So far, Darly was winning that contest, but not because of her looks: getting laid was her passion and Mario was a more than willing partner in satisfying her lust. She wasn't ugly by any measurement, but she was cute in ways that would make beauty contestants envious.

Darly was fascinated with Mario's passion for success; she chose to tag along. She knew the risks one takes on the paths they had chosen, but the alternatives in that area of Italy were meager, indeed; the Mafia seemed to be the only path.

When he reached the side-road, he headed west for about a mile on a gravel road until he came to the dead-end clearing. *Damn it. Nobody here! Ah shit . . . he said to meet here in an hour.* He checked the time; he was a half-hour early. He should be here around ten. He shut his eyes and went to sleep.

Five minutes before the appointed hour, Gianni and Bernardo pulled out of a slight break in the forest—just outside the clearing—and turned left onto the dead-end road. Gianni was driving his 1941, black, four-door, Buick sedan that some American general had left in Italy after the war. A classic antique car, Gianni had owned it since he was a teenager, eager to join the Mafia. He loved the horn. It had a sound that rivaled the bells at the Vatican . . . nothing at all like the horns these days that sound like flimsy, tin cans.

Seeing Mario asleep in his car, they pulled up to the driver's side of the car and nudged the Buick forward until it was about ten feet from the Fiat, perpendicular to the driver's side-door. Gianni nodded to his partner to take his pre-assigned spot. Bernardo reached into the back seat and lifted a Steyr LG 110 high powered rifle—with scope, mounted on the rear. He headed into the woods off to the right of the clearing.

Bernardo took a prone, firing position behind a log. He signaled a thumbs-up to Gianni. Gianni stood beside the Buick, behind his open door watching Mario snore. He put his right foot on the edge of the floorboard, his left hand on the driver's side-door. His right hand rested on the steering-wheel, horn ring.

Gianni looked at his watch. It was four minutes past ten.

As the second hand clicked into 10:05, Gianni leaned on the horn for a couple seconds and placed his right arm on the roof of the car, visible to Bernardo. The blast sent Mario flying out of his seat as though he had been propelled by a giant spring slamming into his butt. "What the fuck!!" He looked to his left, jumped out of his car with his pistol in his right hand. "What the hell do you think you're doing?"

"Drop the pistol!" Gianni yelled.

Mario hesitated. Gianni signaled with his thumb to Bernardo.

"WHACK!"

The sound of a high-powered rifle split the air as Mario's baseball cap spun around his head and flew to the ground—the bill shredded. Before the cap hit the ground, Mario did a one-eighty spin and landed on his belly, his butt twitching from fear.

"The next shot will be to your head. Leave the pistol on the ground and stand up facing me," Gianni said.

Mario complied. "If you're going to work for us, you'll need to pay attention to what we tell you to do. You showed up here a half-hour early and now you didn't drop your pistol," Gianni said sternly, sounding like Marlon Brando in the "Godfather."

"Who are you? What is your name?" Mario said.

"Shut up and do as I say. My friend has his cross-hairs on your head at all times, so don't try any funny stuff. Pick up your pistol. I want to see if you are as good a shot as they say you are. I'm going to pick up some rocks and throw them into the air, one at a time. See if you can hit them. Got that?"

"Yes, sir. I can hit them."

"We'll see," Gianni said, as he sent the first rock into the air.

Mario took aim and shattered the rock with a direct hit. He did it three times out of four; the last one missed.

"We're going to stop while you're ahead. Now, get in your car and get the hell out of here."

"But I thought you wanted to hire me for a big job."

"I didn't say I would hire you for anything. I wanted to see if you can do what you are told to do and if you are as good a shot as your reputation would make us believe. You failed the first part of the test, but you did okay on the second. I'll have to think about whether I want you to work for me. Maybe I'll give you a call and maybe I won't. Now get lost."

Mario put his pistol in his belt, went to his car and drove off. *Bastards! They ruined my baseball cap!*

For a month, for Darly, Sunday mornings following the disappearance of Mario's baseball cap weren't as wonderful as they had been. Yet, they were okay. The fifth Sunday, Mario's performance in bed recalled the good old days.

"Honey," she said, as she recovered from her climax that coincided with that of Beethoven's Ninth Symphony, which extols the sparks of joy that God sends from heaven. Darly heard, and sang the lyrics, in German, in high school, and fell in love with the music and lyrics. She memorized the words that enlivened the melody whenever she heard Beethoven's Ninth.

Freude, schooner Gotterfunken,	**Joy, beautiful sparkle of the gods,**
Tochter aus Elysium!	**Daughter of Elysium!**
Wir betretten feuertrunken,	**We enter, drunk with fire,**
Himmlische, Dein Heiligtum,	**Heavenly one, your sanctuary,**
Deine Zauber bindern wieder,	**Your magic binds again,**
Was die Mode streng geteilt.	**What custom has firmly parted.**
Alle Menschen werden Bruder	**All men become brothers**
Wo Dein sanfter Flugel weilt.	**Where your tender wing lingers.**

"You got the job . . . the big one you wanted, didn't you?"

"How did you know that?" Mario exclaimed, incredulously. "That was supposed to be kept secret. I never told anyone!"

"But Sweetie," she swooned, as she traced a heart on his chest with her index finger, "you just told me something wonderful and I wanted to know what it was, so I took a guess."

"What?" he said, not amused by her vague language. "I didn't *say* anything!"

"Oh, but you did, Sweetheart! There are more ways to communicate than with spoken words. Don't you get it?" Her words were saturated with cunning joy.

"Oh, *THAT!* Well, that's—but you can't say anything about what I've admitted! This could be serious business. I'm supposed to meet someone about that at ten this morning. I don't know what's going to happen. But it could be my big break—a great opportunity for both of us. We could move out of this dump into a mansion. I need to get going. I need to be on time."

"Okay, darling. But be careful. I want you to come back to me so we can do Beethoven again. Okay?"

Mario got dressed, put his pistol in his belt and went out the door.

Darly lay back and dreamed of good times ahead.

When he pulled into the clearing, Bernardo and Gianni were standing next to the Buick. Mario approached.

"I want to see your pistol. It didn't make any noise." Gianni said, with his chin jutted out.

Mario handed the revolver to Gianni; Bernardo glared at Mario as if they were mortal enemies.

"Very interesting," Gianni said, as he opened the cylinder to the reloading position. Instead of the cylinder dropping to the right, the rear of the cylinder pivoted out on a spindle at the front, holding the cylinder at a forty-five degree angle from the side of the pistol. "I don't get it. It has two chambers, but it looks like the bottom chamber is the firing chamber. I've never seen anything like this! Where did you get it?"

"If I told you, I'd have to kill you and your sidekick here," Mario said with a smile as he nodded toward Bernardo. Bernardo's face, already taut, turned red.

"You can't see by merely looking at it the way it is now, but upon opening the cylinder, an automatic ejector partially withdraws the clip that holds the five rounds in place. Nearly all revolvers entail inserting the rounds one at a time. But this one is different from all others I've seen. The silent ammunition is loaded with a five-round clip, which insures faster loading."

"What's this chamber on top of the firing chamber for? Usually that's the chamber you fire from."

"That cylindrical housing contains an integral, laser pointer/sight. The fact that the revolver fires from the lower chamber instead of the top of the pistol axis makes the muzzle-jump minimal."

"Who makes this thing?" Gianni asked.

"It was designed and made in Russia as a special weapon for the successor of the KGB, the FSB. It was designed by a Russian weapons expert: I. Ya. Stechkin."

"So, the laser enhances the accuracy—correct?" Gianni asked.

"Yes. I'm a good shot without the laser, but it does help in some situations."

"You will need to be as good as you are if you are going to kill the pope."

"What? What did you say," Mario asked in amazement.

"That's your assignment—to assassinate the pope. Do you have a problem with that?" Gianni asked.

Bernardo glared at Mario.

"Mario looked at Bernardo and back to Gianni."

Mario straightened up, put his hands on his hips, stuck his chin out, raised his head slightly and, looking down his nose at Gianni said, "That depends on what I will get out of it. What are your terms?" Bernardo wanted to whack the punk then and there but he wasn't calling the shots.

"I give you two thousand euros today. After you kill the pope, you get 100,000 euros."

"How do I know you'll give me the final payoff?" asked Mario, with a slight nuance of insolence, lowering his arms . . . raised palms forward.

"I'll deposit that amount in a secret account that you can access after the hit is successful. There is no way I can guarantee that result. You will need to trust me."

Mario laughed, as he morphed out of his arrogant pose. Bernardo made a slight move toward Mario, but Gianni motioned him to back off.

"Now Mario," Gianni said in a fatherly, raspy voice that never modulated, "if we are going to do business in a respectful way, we can't be talking like you just talked. You are young and you need to learn the manners of our System. We treat others with respect. That's—what's the word . . ."

"Death, if you don't!" Bernardo sputtered, speaking for the first time, sounding like a stupid goon.

"Naw," Gianni said with his head cocked to the right, his brow furrowed, struggling to find the right, sophisticated word appropriate for the occasion. "That's axiomainiacal—I think that's the word I want; which means you're fucked if you don't show it at all times—respect that is."

"Okay. Okay. I meant no disrespect," Mario said, holding his hands up . . . surrendering. "**When?**" I'm tired of being a petty car thief for the chop shops. When do I kill the bastard?"

"It would be better if you didn't use that word. We prefer the term *hit* or *whack* to 'kill'. They don't sound so . . ."

"Bloody!" Bernardo offered.

"Well," said Gianni, "I suppose that's what could work in this instance, but there are other ways of whacking a man—like throwing him in a well, followed by a couple hand grenades, or giving him the piano-wire treatment from the back seat of the car, or poisoning him—you get the idea, don't you Mario?

"I mean there are ways of killing a man without blasting him in the belly with a shotgun, which is really messy—you know . . . bloody," Gianni said, with a twisted grin. "Believe me; I know. So, you've decided you want the job, right?"

"Sure, but first I need to know when. I'll need to figure out how to do it: where and when."

"You won't need to do that. Everything is set. All you have to do is carry out our plan. You'll whack the pope next Wednesday—at his audience in Vatican Square."

"What? Are you crazy!! With two thousand people watching?"

Bernardo's face turned purple.

"Even if I'm able to get into the square with my pistol and . . . uh, *whack* him, how would I escape without being captured or killed?"

"My bosses insist he needs to be killed and this is the only way to get to him when he isn't heavily guarded by his goon squad. There are other ways, such as road mines or bazookas, but he travels in an armored car, so the chances are remote for getting him on a road.

"We can get you into the square with your pistol. You are an excellent shot. You've proven that. He wears a bullet proof vest, so you'll have to hit him in the head. He'll be in one of his popemobiles. He has two. One with a seat and bullet-proof glass all around him; the other is a small pickup where he stands in the cargo section, holding onto a bar.

"He makes a swing down the corridors past the crowds, most of whom are sitting on the inner side of the U-shaped corridor; the remaining people are lined up behind a wooden-fence barrier about four feet high. You'll stand at a specific spot at that barrier and shoot him as he passes in front of you.

"He'll be within thirty feet of where you will be standing. He'll be moving slowly in the pickup truck, so you'll be aiming at a moving target. Do you think you can hit him in the head from that distance under those circumstances? He's been using the pickup instead of the bullet-proof popemobile since he took office."

"Which eye do you want the bullet to enter?"

"Don't get too cocky. There's a lot that needs to be done before you pull the trigger." Looking at Bernardo, Gianni held out his hand, palm up. Bernardo reached into his back pocket and handed Gianni a paper. Gianni unfolded it and laid it on the hood of the Buick. Mario and Bernardo stood on either side of Gianni, staring at the plan.

"Okay. You'll leave here in a few minutes—as soon as you are clear about the plan and you have the money we promised. You'll go to this address." Gianni pointed to the first of three addresses listed on the right side of the paper. "You'll stay in Cosenza tonight until eleven p.m. You'll travel at night only, to avoid traffic jams. Next, you'll stop in Salerno.

"If you leave Cosenza at midnight, you should arrive in Salerno by dawn. Leave Salerno headed for Rome at midnight on Monday and arrive in Rome early Tuesday morning, before rush-hour traffic. If you get held up for any reason, you'll have plenty of time to reach Rome before Wednesday morning.

"So—you stay at this hotel in Rome and go to the Vatican by nine a.m. to make sure you get a spot on the barrier with no one in front of you. The pope makes his circle through the crowd shortly after arriving in the Square. So he should pass by you soon after ten a.m.

"The name of the hotel in Rome is: Alimonde. It's across the street from the Museum entrance on the north side of the Vatican. I have a new driver's license with an assumed name and address for you." Bernardo handed it to Gianni.

"Pay cash at the hotel," Gianni said.

"What if I get stopped by the police? This driver's license won't match my license plate."

"Use the one you have on you now. You do have a license, don't you?"

"Yes."

"Well, use that one until you need the false one to register at the hotel.

"Your contact will be in room 412. Call that room when you arrive. Do you understand so far?"

"Yes."

"Okay. At each of these stops you will be hosted by one of our friends. They will take good care of you. You should get as much rest as you can. You will not be allowed to leave the apartments and the hotel after you arrive except to move on to your next destination. No partying! Got it?"

"Got it."

"Our person at the Rome hotel will provide you with a pair of white tennis shoes, a pair of faded Levi's, a loud Hawaiian shirt and a blue and white LA baseball cap—to make you look like an American tourist. What size shoe do you wear?"

"Ten" Mario answered. "Pants?"

"Thirty two, thirty."

"Small-size shirt, right?"

"Yes."

"Okay, the cap is adjustable so that will fit. We'll have some white socks for you as well.

"Okay. You should have no problem getting into Vatican Square with your pistol. We've been monitoring their security for the last month, and from what we've seen, they've become very careless. They have the same equipment you go through at the airport.

"But at the Square, we've noticed they make enough errors for me to smuggle in one of our Navy/Marine platoons armed with pistols. There is one security station in particular that is weak. It's this one right here." He pointed to a station at the far left, between the Bernini columns. "This is the sixth station counting from the top down on this map. If this one is not manned, choose any of the others and go on through."

"But I can't just walk through with my pistol in my belt. It will set off the alarm!"

"Yes, but so will your cell phone. By the way, give me your cell phone."

Mario handed him his phone.

Gianni took the phone to the edge of the clearing, removed the battery from the phone, placed the phone on a rock, picked up a near-by rock and slammed it into the cell-phone a couple times; he picked it up and threw it and the battery into the woods.

"Why did you do that?" Mario said, angrily.

"You won't need it. I don't want you making any phone calls to anyone. We'll provide you with a non-working phone along with your American clothes. Now. . . to answer your question.

"When the pistol sets off the alarm, you act surprised and pull this cell phone out, smile at the guard at the gate, shrug as though you forgot you had it in your pocket and he'll wave you through. We've seen the guy at the gate I pointed out to you do that several times. He won't know that a pistol also set off the alarm, and will let you through."

"And if he doesn't?"

"Good question. Do you speak English?"

"No. Not at all."

"Okay. Here's what you do. When you enter the square and you are stopped by the security guards, they'll probably assume you are an American from the way you are dressed, and speak to you in English. You want them to think you are an American, so you flip some sign language on them to show them you are deaf and can't speak."

"I don't know sign language."

"Doesn't matter. You pretend you do by holding your hands up and wiggling your fingers very rapidly like the signing people do. If you have a problem, do that and offer them your LA baseball cap. That'll win them over and they'll forget why they stopped you."

"So, you'll walk straight ahead to the barrier and take your place and wait for the pope to pass and you'll whack him and leave before anyone knows what happened. With your silent ammunition and special pistol, the guards won't know where the shot came from. Those around you will, but they won't try to stop you from walking away because you will have a weapon and they won't risk their lives trying to stop you.

"We'll have a black BMW waiting for you. Go through the gate in the barriers that will be up where the circle in front of the basilica leads to Via della Conciliazione. Right here," Gianni said, pointing to a spot on the map. "That's that wide boulevard that takes you into the city.

"That's where your getaway car will be waiting for you. It's the street Mussolini—God rest his soul," Gianni said, crossing himself—"named to commemorate the reconciliation of the Italian State and the Church in the 1929 Lateran Treaty. Did you know that, Mario?"

"Well, thanks for your history lecture; no disrespect intended, but I don't give a damn who named the street. What I want to know is: What if I'm discovered? Say, someone unmasks me at the barrier where I shoot the pope? Then what?"

"Now, Mario, if you're going to enter the big-time business with us, you need to have, uh . . . what's the word? sophistitution . . . or . . ."

"BALLS!" Bernardo shouted into Mario's ear.

"Calm down, Bernardo. Now," Gianni said, with faux sympathy, "to answer your question about what to do if you're uncovered shooting the pope . . . Have you seen any of those American, shoot-em-up movies where the bank robbers leave the bank in a hail-storm of bullets and make their getaway? Or American westerns where the bandits shoot their way out of Dodge and escape? How many Mafiosi movies have you seen?"

"Dozens! All of them."

"So—what's the problem? It's not astronomical physics to figure this out. There won't **be** any bullets coming your way because of the crowd in the square. Those cops will not risk killing or wounding an innocent bystander to whack your skinny ass. They can't shoot straight anyway. So don't worry. Just do what you need to do. If necessary, shoot your way out. That's it. Okay?"

"Yes. Is that it? Where's my two thousand euros you promised me?"

"Not so fast. Let's go over what I just told you to make sure you understand what is expected of you." They did and Mario said he understood, but he had a request.

"I want to go home to tell my girlfriend I'm leaving."

"You dumb bastard. What have I been telling you? You will do no such thing! You'll go directly from here to Cosenza and take it from there. I told you that I don't want you talking to anyone about where you are going, or that you'll even be gone for a while.

"They'll figure that out for themselves when you don't come home. We'll get you back home when the deed is done and it's safe to return home. Don't screw it up. This is an incredibly simple job, considering who's getting whacked. I can't believe it can be so simple. There isn't another world-famous figure that exposes himself like this pope does; soon the world will be shocked by what you have done.

"Here's the money. Good luck. You wait here a half hour before you leave. We are leaving now and will await the news of your success. It will be all over the news Wednesday morning and you'll be a rich man."

Mario counted the euros—nearly all of them in one-hundred-euro denominations; he smiled and said. "It's all here. Thanks. Don't worry; I'll get the job done."

Chapter 48

Perfecto pulled into the repair-shop parking lot and honked his horn at Tyrone, who smiled broadly and waved Perfecto into the shop. "I want to take a good look at this piece of junk," Tyrone said, as Perfecto drove onto the lift rack. "I never trade cars unless I know what I'm getting and in this case, it doesn't look like much."

Perfecto climbed out of his car, stuck out his hand to greet Tyrone, who pulled his hand back and said, "I don't want to spoil your prissy, clean hands with my greasy fingers. How the hell are you?"

Perfecto laughed and said he was fine and was excited about getting a new car. "I don't have any money to pay for it, but the pope said yours was as much a piece of junk as mine so you'd probably make a trade without much fuss."

"That's Skip for you. Always ready to have some fun with us poor bastards who have to work for a living. I don't include you in that 'us' by the way."

"All I do is have fun," said Perfecto. "Why don't you become a priest and join the party."

"I'd rather join the Communist Party," Tyrone said with a smile. "Their party isn't quite as terrifying as yours; only kidding my friend. Now, let's take a look at what I'm getting here. Ah yes, do you see the beauty that I see?"

"Beauty? All I see is a broken-down, old Volkswagen that is ready for the junk yard."

"But given a little creativity, a few new parts, and a lot of tender, loving care, she'll be a beauty. Had lunch yet?"

"No, I was hoping I'd get here before you ate, because I love that little pizzaria."

They ordered their pizzas and beer sitting at a small round table.

"How are things going?" asked Tyrone.

"I'm not sure. But I think we are headed toward what could be an apocalyptic showdown with the cardinals and the Mafia."

"I tell you this, Perfecto, Skip has serious stuff on his mind and you are playing an important role in wherever it all leads."

"So far," said Perfecto, "it's been interesting and fun, but I realize this might not last—that things could get nasty. But I'm ready to do what I can to help.

I've learned a lot about what has him upset—enough to take drastic reform measures."

Tyrone entered the security code at the entrance to his private museum. "So . . . Skip told you I'd have a new car for you, right?"

"Right. But he didn't give me any reason why I needed a new car other than that mine has one wheel in the grave and that things might get a little dicey for me as he proceeds with his reforms. I have assumed that it probably has something to do with my driving aimlessly around the countryside for the past couple years."

"Skip is always thinking light years ahead of everyone else. Everything he has told you to do and asked you to help him with has a purpose that supports what he's up to. Trust me: He is no fool and those who oppose him don't have a clue what they are up against. What is coming down will be more dramatic and astounding than any Hollywood screenwriter could imagine. And you will be 'on stage' playing an important supporting role. I'm here to provide a major prop and a few costumes for the drama. Are you ready for this?"

"I'm an Eagle Scout, Tyrone, ready for anything at any time. Let's see where it leads."

They walked over to the shrouded car next to the airplane. Perfecto was thinking: *Now I'm going to find out what's under this mysterious cape.*

"Ta-Da!" Tyrone shouted, as he swept the canvas off the car. Perfecto immediately recognized it as a four-door Fiat Panda. Described as "cuddly" by its promoters, it did seem like a teddy-bear when compared with the behemoths that fit in the same class as a Ford Expedition.

Tyrone climbed into the car, rolled down the driver's-side-window, started the engine, drove it in a semi-circle and pointed it toward a seven-foot high, and five-foot wide projection screen on the wall.

"Okay. Now turn around and lift up the screen." As the screen disappeared into its roll at the top, Perfecto found himself staring into a mirror the same size as the screen.

"Now, Perfecto, come and sit in the passenger seat . . . What color is this car?"

"Red."

"Close your eyes."

"Okay, they are closed."

"Open your eyes and look at the mirror." Perfecto complied.

"What? That's impossible! The car has turned yellow!"

"Close your eyes." Perfecto closed his eyes. "Open your eyes."

"What's going on? The car is blue."

"Next the car will be purple. The car has four possible colors. I told you I like the adventure of designing cars, but this car was designed by someone else who doesn't have as much imagination as I have for innovation. Did you notice the license plate numbers change every time the color changes?"

"No, I didn't notice that."

"Okay, I'll change the color to purple and you watch the license plate." It changed simultaneously with the change of color.

"Awesome, man! Just Awesome!"

Climbing out of the driver's seat, Tyrone asked Perfecto to take his place, walked around the front of the car and sat in the passenger seat.

"Now, Perfecto, reach under the steering wheel and locate the buttons that are lined up in a row underneath the dashboard. Do you feel them?"

"Yes."

"How many are there?"

"Let's see—there are seven, but there is a 'bar' between numbers six and seven."

"That's correct. Watch the mirror and press the button on the far left—button one. What did you see?"

"The car turned from purple to red."

"Now, count buttons from the left, and press the fourth button from the left. Watch the mirror." Perfecto did as requested. The car turned back to purple.

"Look at the back seat and press button five."

The rear seat-backs were already folded forward, lying flat to create more cargo space. As Perfecto pressed button number five, the right, seat-back panel flipped open, secured at the bottom by a continuous hinge that held it in place. Flattened against the top of the panel was a row of three baseball caps—orange, purple and black—fastened with metal clips. Below the caps, two men's hairpieces and one woman's blonde wig with long flowing curls were attached with clips and a net that kept them flattened and in place.

"Okay, put your finger on number six and press. What happened?"

"All the windows turned dark, including the windshield. I can see out, but I assume no one can see through the windows from the outside. Is that right?"

"Yes," answered Tyrone. "The only time you would use this one is if you're in some kind emergency situation and you don't want someone to see you in the car from the front if they are shooting at you. Don't use it in any other situation. Now. . . number seven: What do you notice here?"

"It is larger than the others in diameter and thickness; and it includes a cap to flip open, in order to use this button."

"Good. Leave it alone. This button should be used only in emergency situations when you are being chased and want to lose your pursuer. You can use this as a last resort. It will not work on a dirt or gravel road.

"This button can be used only three times. You press it once for the first application, twice for the second application and three times for the third application. The cap over this button is a safety device to prevent the button from being pressed inadvertently.

'The purpose of button number seven is to activate a spraying mechanism under the rear bumper which dispenses a substance onto the pavement which will send the pursuing car into a slide.

"The substance is designed to lose its slippery quality within a few seconds after hitting the pavement so that cars following the pursuing vehicle will not slide. A car hitting the spot within seven seconds will spin out, but that is the limit. So practice estimating the distance a car travels within that time frame at given speeds.

"Do you see a 'thumb print' at the bottom of the dash board, right outside the button locations?"

"Yes."

"Put your left thumb on that print and see if that helps you locate the first four buttons."

"Yes, it does."

"Do you notice that it has a tiny raised peak in the center of the print?"

"Yes."

"Good, because you will need to be able to locate those buttons while driving on curves and won't be able to take your eyes off the road to place your thumb in the correct spot to quickly reach the buttons. It's like placing your thumb on 'Middle-C' so you can find your way around on a piano keyboard.

"We don't have time today, but come back and we'll practice your being able to locate the buttons quickly, blindfolded, so that in a tight situation, you will be able to operate the buttons without distraction."

"I understand the possibility of the slippery-fluid dispensing mechanism, but the color changes on the car's surface? I wouldn't believe that's possible if I hadn't seen it."

Chapter 49

Mario arrived at the Cosenza apartment Sunday evening, had dinner, took a nap and left for Salerno as planned—at midnight. The highway was not crowded the evening before, but Mario was expecting more traffic closer to Rome. The trip from Cosenza to Salerno was uneventful, arriving before dawn Monday. He left Salerno at midnight Monday—next stop: Rome.

An hour north of Salerno, lightning and thunder preceded a shower, then blowing rain that reduced visibility for a while, but that passed and the sky was clear again.

Mario was dreaming of Darly when he noticed a tailgater. He wasn't speeding. It most likely meant a highway patrolman checking the license plate number on his computer to see if the car was stolen. Of course it wasn't, but there could be another problem.

Mario had had a series of brushes with the law a few years back. Thus, a warrant for arrest could still be active; or it could be a patrolman on a grave-yard shift getting bored and deciding to pull someone over. Mario saw the lights on the patrol car flashing. *I could do without this shit. Damn!* He pulled over.

The patrolman aimed his spotlight at Mario, blinding him. Cautiously, the patrolman approached Mario's car, walked along the passenger side and motioned Mario to lower the passenger window.

"Good morning. Do you know why I stopped you?"

"No, sir."

"One of your tail lights is out. Please hand me your driver's license and registration."

Mario removed his wallet from his back pocket and handed his driver's license to the officer. He reached into the glove compartment and removed the automobile registration paper and handed it to the patrolman. The officer glanced at the documents and then at Mario to make sure he looked like the picture on the driver's license. He did.

"Wait here. I'm going back to my car to make out the warning ticket. I'll be back in a moment."

In his car, the patrolman had a hunch. His subject hailed from an area notorious for its drug trafficking. He checked his computer for a record.

Nothing. *Well, this guy could be transporting drugs. I need to check that when I get back to the car,* he thought. Approaching Mario's car on the driver-side, taking care to avoid a passing car, the patrolman handed the license and registration to Mario.

"Mr. Marino. Please step out of the car. I need to check for illicit drugs."

"I don't have illegal drugs, either on me on in my car. I don't do drugs, nor do I transport them."

"Nevertheless, I need to do the check. I need to do a body check and take a look at the car. If you are clean, you'll be on your way in no time."

"Officer. I'm not doing drugs or transporting them . . ."

"I'm asking you to get out and put your hands on the roof of your car. Do as I say or I will arrest you for disobeying a law enforcement officer."

The two-thousand euros in his back pocket would be hard to explain to an officer who was suspicious of drug dealing. Worse, he did not have a license to carry his highly sophisticated pistol. The officer could verify the illegal weapon on his computer. He knew he would be arrested on the spot and hauled in for questioning if he got out of the car. He wanted to avoid a confrontation if at all possible. He knew he could not outrun the patrolman, but he could try to escape long enough to figure something out.

If he started the car and took off, the patrolman would not try to stop him by shooting him, but would call for reinforcements and they would eventually box him in. Then he would have five or six officers to deal with. All of these considerations raced through his mind as he desperately searched for a way out of this predicament without a confrontation. One hundred thousand euros were at stake and he wasn't going to let this cop stop him . . . come what may.

"Okay, officer. I'll do as you say." He grabbed the door handle with his left hand, as he reached for his pistol under his shirt—just below his navel—with his right hand. The patrolman reached for his pistol.

Before he could take aim, he was dead—shot in the head. He fell to the pavement. Mario grabbed his feet and dragged him to the passenger side of the patrol car, dropped his legs, opened the passenger door, pumped a few rounds into the radio, and was on his way toward Rome in a matter of seconds.

I have less than a half hour to find another car; after that, half of the Italian highway patrolmen will be looking for my ass. He saw a sign pointing toward Fomia heading west toward the sea. Entering Formia, on the southeast side of town, he turned off SS 213 and headed north alongside Vindicio Beach, and turned right onto SS 7, the old Via Appia highway.

Frantically searching for a place to steal a car, without being caught in the act, he spotted an entrance to a hospital and said to himself: *Perfect! Middle of the graveyard shift. Plenty of cars to choose from. It'll be several hours before anyone comes for the car.*

He was in and out of the parking lot in a couple minutes. The first car didn't have much gas, but the second had over a half tank, so he chose that one and was on his way.

In a couple hours he was parking the car at a remote section of Fumiciano airport outside Rome. He walked slowly toward the train station across the street from the airport terminal and purchased a train ticket.

He boarded the train headed for the Vaticani Stazione, a ten minute walk from his hotel where he checked in and went to his room. After taking a shower, he dialed the room number he was given: 412.

"This is Angelica," a sleepy, lilting voice answered.

Puzzled, Mario hung up the phone. Maybe he dialed the wrong number. His contact could wait; he'd try again a little later. It was six a.m. Tuesday morning.

Chapter 50

Almost two years after Maria was admitted to the seminary she sent an email notice to the committee with her thesis attached for the committee's review

THE MICHELANGELO DECEPTION
A Thesis
Prepared in Partial Fulfillment
of the
Requirements for a

MASTER'S IN THEOLOGY
Minneapolis Lutheran Seminary
Minneapolis, Minnesota
by
Maria Martinova Luderenko

INTRODUCTION

Who was Michelangelo di Lodovico Buonarroti Simoni?

Michelangelo Buonarotti was born in Caprese, Tuscany, Italy, on March 6, 1475 and died in Rome on February 18, 1564. He was 89 years old.

He was born of a wealthy Florentine family, his father a Resident Magistrate in Caprese. He was reared in Florence and was placed in the care of a sculptor and his wife in Settignano, where his father owned a small farm and marble quarry.

In 1484—age nine—his parents enrolled him in a Latin School. His teacher: Francesco di Urbino. Years later, Michelangelo hired Urbino to help with the mundane aspects of his artistic endeavors.

During a brief apprenticeship that began when he was thirteen, under an artist named Domenico Ghirlandajo, the young man encountered age-peers from varying social strata while training as a designer and painter; he gained experience in panel and fresco painting. He was an inveterate sketcher, drawing buildings, landscapes, animals and human figures.

Michelangelo's precocious works attracted the attention of Lorenzo "Il Manifico" Medici, whose family was involved in fine arts, finance, letters and politics. In his early teens, Michelangelo was invited by Lorenzo to live at the Medici Palace where he was exposed to a circle of leading writers and scholars: including two Jews who taught Michelangelo what they knew about Jewish mysticism: Kabbalism.

While at the Medici Palace, he turned to sculpturing and produced a faun from a piece of scrap stone, which attracted the attention of Lorenzo. Later, he produced two reliefs: *Battle of the Centaurs* and *Madonna of the Steps*. Lorenzo died in 1492, leaving Michelangelo adrift at the age of seventeen.

He returned to Florence in 1495 (age 20) whereupon, Cardinal San Giorgio of the Vatican, bought his marble *Cupid* and summoned him to Rome in 1496. There, influenced by Greek and Roman antiquity, he produced the *Bacchus* and the *Pieta,* which marked the beginning of his association with the Catholic Church.

Four years later, he returned to Florence where he produced his marble *David*. He also painted the *Holy Family of the Tribune* and the *Madonna*.

In 1503 the new pope, Julius II, summoned Michelangelo (age 28) to Rome. He commissioned him to construct the pope's tomb, which he worked on for 40 years. But it was not completed because of demands made by various popes.

Pope Julius II commissioned him to paint the ceiling of the Sistine Chapel in 1508 (age 33). He agreed to abandon the sarcophagus project, but under fierce protest; he loved sculpturing and was not fond of painting, in spite of his hefty talent. Michelangelo completed the ceiling fresco in 1512 at the age of thirty- seven.

Fifteen thirteen to 1537—nearly a quarter of a century—is known to be a period of minimal artistic accomplishments. At age sixty one, in 1536 he was commissioned by Clement VII to paint the *Last Judgment* and began painting in 1537. He completed the project in 1541.

In 1547 he was appointed Architect of St. Peter's basilica to which he devoted himself until his death at the age of eighty nine. He is considered one of the greatest (some say *the* greatest) artists of all time.

Scholars agree that his homoerotic tendencies cannot be successfully contested; whether or not he engaged in homosexual acts is not known. At the age of 57, he fell in love with Tommaso dei Cavelieri, a handsome, twenty three year-old courtier who shared Michelangelo's passion for the fine arts.

Numerous homoerotic poems about his ardor for this young man have survived. That he was even a lover of young boys is asserted in that in his late sixties he met a fifteen-year-old named Bracci. Bracci died in 1544, at age 16. Michelangelo, mourning the boys passing, wrote about fifty poems expressing his feelings for this boy.

Some of the most famous sculpture, painting and architecture in the world, was created by Michelangelo Bounarotti.

Michelangelo was hot-tempered. Another sculptor flattened his nose in a fight. He seldom washed, slept in his studio alongside his work, and though he became wealthy, he ate and dressed like a pauper.

Of course, volumes have been written about Michelangelo. No attempt will be made to summarize what his critics and apologists have averred; nevertheless, we refer to some of them to make a case for Michelangelo's deceptions in this presentation.

So there you have it: a very brief and incomplete account of the artist's tumultuous life. We will learn more about him as we discuss his deceptions.

MICHELANGELO'S DECEPTIONS

The preponderance of Michelangelo's trickery is found in the Sistine Chapel, the most famous chapel within the Vatican walls, and arguably, the most famous Christian chapel in the world.

The original Sistine Chapel was constructed on the site where the Cappella Maggiore (Greater Chapel) was known to exist in 1368 for the use of the papacy. By 1473, it had deteriorated to the point where the walls were leaning. Under the orders of pope Sixtus IV, the chapel was demolished to make way for a new chapel, which would eventually require buttresses to hold its walls in place. It was named the "Sistine Chapel" after pope Sixtus IV. Dates of its construction vary somewhat, but it is generally known to have been built sometime between 1473 and 1481, with the dimensions of Solomon's Temple in Jerusalem. Several tapestries, frescoes of the Life of Christ, Moses and some popes were finished in 1482. The first mass was held in 1483. Since then, the chapel has been used for various religious activities. When a pope dies, Cardinals meet there, in conclave, to select new popes.

In 1508, a little over a quarter of a century after the chapel was built, Pope Julius II ordered Michelangelo to paint the deteriorating Sistine ceiling, portraying the papal family and Jesus and Mary surrounded by the Apostles. But he ignored the pope's banality and substituted his own subject matter. Why?

By then, age 33, his erudition in the fine arts surpassed any of the popes. A talented sculptor and painter, he couldn't tolerate inanity, especially when it was forced upon him by powerful people, including popes, who wanted to exploit his outsized skills in sculpturing and painting to satiate their lusts for power, prestige, fame and fortune.

When Michelangelo refused to paint the Sistine Chapel ceiling according to Pope Julius's facile instructions, a furious encounter ended when the ailing pope, ravaged by syphilis, relented. Instead of painting hackneyed stories about Jesus, Mary, Moses and the apostles, the artist's brush strokes followed Michelangelo's inner drumbeat.

Hyperbole, generated by Catholic scholars, journalists, and authors with dubious agendas, reaches ludicrous heights when it spins the artist's portrayals on the ceiling of the Sistine Chapel. Catholic apologists don't—and cannot—exaggerate Michelangelo's artistic achievement. Still, the Sistine frescoes, allegedly glorifying Christian orthodoxy, are mockeries of Catholic doctrine accompanied by outrageous and personal insults to the popes who commissioned the paintings.

Rabbi Benjamin Blech and Roy Doliner, a reputable scholar of the humanities, an occasional docent in the Sistine Chapel and advisor to scholars in Rome and the Vatican, have published a recent book, *Sistine Secrets*, exposing what Michelangelo was really up to well over four hundred years ago when he painted the Sistine Chapel ceiling and The *Last Judgment* on the wall behind the altar. The central point of their book is that Michelangelo's concealments in the Sistine frescoes advocate universal tolerance: reconciliation between reason and faith, between the Jewish Bible and the New Testament and between Jew and Christian.

According to Blech and Doliner, one thing is certain: the artist was not glorifying Christianity in the most sacred Chapel of Christendom when he painted the Sistine ceiling. In fact there is not a single Christian figure in the ceiling.

After expressing the Vatican's point of view—or spin, as it were—about the artist's ceiling fresco, Blech and Doliner quote a poem Michelangelo wrote after finishing the ceiling. The poem describes how Chalices and crucifixes are melted down and made into helmets, swords, lances and shields, while the blood of Christ is sold indiscriminately.

Yet, Christ's patience seems inexhaustible, says the artist in his poem, and implores Christ not to come to Rome for his blood pressure would rise to the stratosphere and beyond because now his flesh and blood are being sold, and virtuous behavior has disappeared.

This poem foretells the frustration and anger Michelangelo still felt toward the popes—and the Church they created—when he painted the *Last Judgment* twenty-five years later.

Blech and Doliner assert that the artist embedded secret messages in the Sistine ceiling, the surrounding spandrels and lunettes, and in The *Last Judgment*. The messages include, but are not limited to: **(1)** advocating a revolutionary change in Christianity's relationship to Judaism; **(2)** condemning the Church's failure to acknowledge its debt to Jewish origins; **(3)** emphasizing the universality of God, beginning with the Creation story, not the birth of Jesus; **(4)** stressing tolerance of all faiths, including that of the persecuted and reviled Jews of his time; **(5)** hiding antipapal messages consistent with his own universalist propensity; **(6)** concealing Kabbalistic truths more important than the images within which they were embedded.

These are major themes, but there is more: a book full of embedded secrets which, if discovered during Michelangelo's lifetime, likely would have resulted in his untimely death.

For example, some of the most provocative "secrets" include two instances of putti making obscene gestures ("flashing the finger" or "the fig"); the most notorious example is a putto "giving the finger" to Pope Julius II.

Even more shocking, is the lunette portraying an angry God, creating the sun, moon and stars; included in the scene is God's bare buttocks, "mooning"—as Blech and Doliner assert—Pope Julius II, "sticking out the Divine backside over the papal ceremonial area:" the altar of the Sistine Chapel.

Now, the research for and writing done for this paper go beyond the thesis and findings of Blech and Doliner, while giving the two authors due respect for their stunning discoveries. While Blech and Doliner were making their discoveries from a Jewish perspective, and publishing the results of their research, we were finalizing our analysis of the artist's deceptions from a Christian perspective, unaware of what Blech and Doliner had achieved. We had made our discoveries *before* we learned of their work done from a Jewish perspective.

Michelangelo's deceptions beg the question: What motivated him to embed secrets and create deceptions in the Sistine Chapel frescoes?

When Michelangelo parachuted from the spiritual world onto Planet Earth in the late fifteenth century, he landed in a world of hurt, as it were. A description of this world serves as an introduction to understanding the artist's motivations for poking his thumb in the eye—and spear in the heart—of the Roman Catholic Church. His antipathy for the popes—to be sure—was provoked by papal treachery and personal insults; however, there was more than these aggravations motivating his deceptions.

William Miller, Visiting Lecturer in American History at the Yale Graduate School—writing in his *A New History of the United States,* (1963, Revised)—devotes the first chapter of his book to "The Four Worlds of the Fifteenth Century", which provides a context for understanding the founding of the United States of America. Among the four worlds he describes is the "The Troubled World of Christendom."

Miller, suggesting that the world of Christendom in the middle of the twentieth century isn't any better off than it was in the fifteenth and sixteenth centuries, gives us a concise and illuminating description of the world of Christendom into which Michelangelo was born and lived for 89 years:

Miller's account goes into considerable detail about the fourteenth century: the century before Michelangelo was born. The Bubonic Plague and Black Death epidemics had wiped out a third of the Western European population. Almost continuous wars decimated families and destroyed property and production capacity to the point that what remained of the population was ravaged by starvation. The wealthy were not spared in this chaos.

Wavering trade infrastructures that collapsed added to the tragedies and many individuals were driven to insanity or became "beggars, scavengers, thieves and convicts." But that was not all: The loss of hope and lack of opportunity for a decent life disappeared and human behavior deteriorated into—as one historian put it—"brutes devoid of sense and reason." The downtrodden turned against the aristocracy—and businessmen struggling to survive—with a vengeance.

And where was the Church in all of this? Miller states that the people could not find solace in religion. In the century before the century just described, the Church had achieved its greatest power because it owned most of the land and had the greatest income in all of Europe. Whatever spiritual charm the Church may have enjoyed amongst the populations of Europe, it declined as the Church continued its evil ways, characterized by the crusades and increasing secularization of the preceding two centuries: Secularism had crept into the sacred corridors of the Church as profligate popes and their minions were consumed by political, economic and financial matters. The sacred charm of the Church deteriorated, denying the faithful of the solace they sought from a God the Church was supposed to represent.

As corruption proliferated, the Church's wealth declined forcing it to take extreme measures to maintain its political power over the masses. Church offices, including the papacy, were auctioned off to the highest bidder; sins were forgiven for a price and the selling of relics boomed. Such profligacy did not escape the notice of the more sophisticated observers, but the gullible people remained terrified by the power of the Church over their lives while, humble souls were deeply disturbed by the Church's offenses to Christ.

The invention of the printing press in 1440 opened up the Bible in ways theretofore unheard of; disgruntled clerics took advantage of that pivotal event. [Martin Luther, recognizing the power of the Word, translated the Bible into German—and . . . as the saying goes—the rest is history.]

The same popes who patronized the most famous artists [including Michel-angelo] engaged in personal excesses that rivaled that of the most decadent kings. While so engaged, they re-instated—ten years after Michelangelo was born—their official sanction of burning women at the stake for their alleged witchery. Murders committed in the name of the Church soared.

It seems impossible to imagine a more dissolute epoch in the history of organized religion, but according to Miller and numerous other, more contemporary authors—for example, Williams' *The Vatican Exposed: Money, Murder and the Mafia (2003)*—significant evidence of such profligacy remains associated with the Catholic Church today. The world-wide, clerical, pederasty scandal has served to remind us that the Catholic Church's detractors are not engaged in a vicious smear, but that there is a raging fire underneath the dark cloud hanging over the Church today. Therefore, recounting of the era in which Michelangelo lived is helpful in our attempt to understand why he had such contempt for the corrupt popes and the depths of degradation they had foisted upon their people.

Moreover, knowing that the great artist painted secrets and deceptions—exposing the Church and its leaders for what they were—in the most famous chapel in Christendom, gives us a link to a past era when squalor sullied the image of the Church. Michelangelo had his paint brushes and a single chapel to express his outrage. Today, we have world-wide print, video and internet media that is exposing the Church's current folly; in that sense, we are partners with Michelangelo, linked by a bridge with a span of almost 500 years.

While Michelangelo's motivation for the secrets and deceptions that he painted into the Sistine Chapel ceiling involves personal insults he felt from the popes, his disgust with the corrupt popes he served and what they were doing to humanity, intensified and had reached its apex by the time he began painting the *Last Judgment*—twenty five years after he completed the ceiling.

Despite Pope Julius's initial admiration for Michelangelo, they did not hit it off from the beginning . . . and there is a story that illuminates that sketchy fact. As we have already mentioned, Pope Julius II commissioned Michelangelo to sculpt a tomb that would be worthy of any Caesar.

The artist agreed, but his obsession with perfection drove him to seek stone which was not available in the immediate vicinity of Rome. For eight months he searched for the ideal stone. . . and found it.

Upon his return to Rome, he learned of Julius's plans for a monumental, new basilica—*a perfect home for the tomb* . . . he thought. Thus, happily, he went to work on the tomb at his studio located near the Castel Sant'Angelo, a quarter of a mile east of the Vatican on what is now the Via della Conciliazione.

Michelangelo paid for the stone that would be the pope's tomb out of his own pocket and worked for months without—agreed upon—remuneration for his labor. He went to the Vatican several times to present the bills to Julius and receive reimbursement. Each time, he was rebuffed; Julius was too busy with the construction of the new basilica see him.

After months of planning the blueprints that would guide the construction of the basilica, the cornerstone was ready to be installed. Hours before the cornerstone-laying ceremony was to begin, Michelangelo was informed by the guard that Julius had ordered him banned from the Vatican. Why? Julius had spent his treasure on the basilica. The Vatican was broke. Michelangelo would not be paid, and the pope did not want to be bothered.

Outraged, Michelangelo rented a horse and took off for Florence at full-gallop with Julius's henchmen in hot pursuit. As he rode, he seethed with suspicion that Julius's new "golden boy," the brilliant Bramante (who had been Michelangelo's close friend) of treachery . . . convincing Julius to sideline Michelangelo. After acquiring fresh horses along the way, he reached Florence late that night.

He left a note behind for Julius that if he wanted his services, he would first have to find him. Julius tracked him down and ordered him to sculpt a bronze statue depicting the pope as a conquering hero of rebellious Papal States, restoring the Church's rightful place as the dominant authority in the region. He moved to Bologna and a little more than a year later completed the huge bronze statue; afterwards he returned to Florence.

At Julius's beckoning, he returned from a two-year absence to Rome still angry with Julius and the conniving Bramante. He assumed he would resume work on the sarcophagus, but Julius ordered him to paint the ceiling of the Sistine Chapel.

He was furious and told Julius to get someone else to do it, maybe one of his golden boys: perhaps Raphael. When the two colliding super-egos ceased bickering, Michelangelo began work, but only after rebuilding the scaffold that Bramante had built for the job; he suspected Bramante of building a flaw into the scaffold that would send his rival plunging sixty feet to his death.

Michelangelo believed Pope Julius's offensive behavior gave him ample reason to get revenge: on the ceiling; he would paint frescoes embedded with "secrets," some of which were shocking insults and others that had very little—if anything—to do with Christian doctrine. The artist's frustration and anger—inspiring fresh deceptions—reached new heights when he painted the *Last Judgment* thirty years later. While Blech and Doliner's assertion that the artist's fundamental message is one of reconciliation, we believe that premise is the source of their missing the central message in Michelangelo's *Last Judgment*.

As we shall now see, when Michelangelo commenced painting the *Last Judgment*—at the age of sixty two—the depraved state of Christendom had not abated, but intensified under successive popes; he saw his commission to paint the *Last Judgment* as a rare opportunity express his anger—for the benefit of his contemporary world and future generations—over what the Church had done to humanity. We don't see a lot of tolerance or attempts at reconciliation exhibited, if any, in the artist's *Last Judgment*.

During his visit to Rome in 1510—when Michelangelo had painted about half of the Sistine ceiling—Martin Luther became, like Michelangelo, outraged.

Both men were angry at the licentiousness of the popes and their priests, and vowed to do something about it. Seven years later, on October 31, 1517, Dr. Luther posted his "Ninety-five Theses" on a church door in Wittenberg, Germany, igniting the religious conflagration that would give an era in history a name: *The Reformation.* He was excommunicated in 1521. Sixteen years later Michelangelo would start painting the *Last Judgment.* A prominent, dark cloud hangs over the *Last Judgment;* it permeates the patina and penetrates to the core of the *Last Judgment's* message.

Michelangelo could not have imagined that nearly five hundred years would pass before someone would discover his deceptions. By contrast, Martin Luther's rebellion was open, blatant, and ignited a massive schism in the Roman Catholic Church during the lifetimes of both men.

Chapter 51

At six a.m. on that same Tuesday morning—in a hotel not far from where Mario had been greeted by a mysterious "Angelica" when he dialled room 412—Anna Berhoff lay awake savouring what would be her last two days in Rome . . . on this trip. She would be back for her tenth trip in a couple years—*God willing*—*she* always said to herself, when she talked about her future. God's willingness might be vanishing, due to her rapidly advancing age.

At eighty-nine, she knew her years were numbered, probably on one hand; she was determined to make them the best years of her life. Most people looking at her would think she was the archetype of an over-the-hill, little, old, white-haired lady. Still, she was not "over-the-hill." She was neither little in heart . . . nor old in her thoughts; she had a big heart and a young, inquisitive, and idealistic mind.

Anna did not belong to any church, but she thought the Vatican museums, and especially the Basilica, were monuments to the glory and wonder of God. Never mind that most of the brilliant artwork in the museums were of "pagan" origin and some of the more sophisticated observers considered the Basilica to be a monument to popes with outsized egos and little appreciation for the fine arts.

The Chair of Peter, for example, seemed to be a grotesque caricature of a myth that stood on shifting sand. Michelangelo's dream for the interior of the Basilica was that it should mirror the simple purity of divine nature, and emulate his poems that expressed his longing for the quietude that accompanied his transcendental experiences.

Instead, his detractors succeeded in creating a raucous, discordant mishmash that disturbs more than it edifies the human soul. Yet, Michelangelo's *Pieta* stands—near the entrance—inside the basilica as a powerful testimonial to what might have been . . . had Michelangelo had his way.

Anna Berhoff had visited the Vatican dozens of times over the years and always brought along her binoculars. She liked to examine the architecture—soaring in the clouds—up close and personal: It was a ritual she had established over the years—one that never lost its patina.

The binoculars were a curious sight for young people who had never seen such monstrosities. Large and black, it had cylinders holding the mirrors and magnifying lenses that required more space than the modern glasses—thus, larger and much heavier.

She had to stop and rest her arms frequently, but she didn't mind. She could look at the same things from a different perspective without the magnification. She would do the Vatican Gardens tour today, Tuesday, and then attend the pope's Wednesday audience in Vatican Square tomorrow.

That event came quickly, like time compressing at light-speed, much like the rest of her life these days. She could not figure out how time could pass so rapidly from New Year's Day to the following Christmas. Yet, she was not complaining; the alternative was too uncertain to contemplate.

She had grown up in a small town in eastern Pennsylvania and lived there all her life—alone, except the four years she attended a small liberal arts college nearby. She went back home and started as a clerk in the local library and quickly rose to become the manager. Under her guidance, the library had been expanded three times during her forty-year tenure. The community had rewarded her with an appreciation that no award dinner could match—their patronage.

Now, once again, she was standing at the barrier that would put her close to the pope as he made his short trip, greeting and blessing the adoring crowd in his small popemobile. She wore a blue bonnet that resembled one of those throwback-in-time religious hats that some women wear. She wore a florid shirt that hung over a dark-blue, cotton skirt; white walking shoes over white socks—that reached half-way to her knees—completed her sartorial ensemble.

She had come early, because during the tourist season, thousands gathered in the square and jostled for a view up front—at the barrier.

She took her favorite place: facing the Apostolic Palace where—on special occasions—the pope lectured the audiences from his apartment window.

She marveled once again at the statues of the apostles and the Bernini Columns; she never became weary of trying to imagine what life must be like living in the Apostolic Palace with its opulent apartments. All she could see were the windows on the wall facing the square.

Her fondest dream would be realized if she could somehow get a tour inside that palace. Yet, she was realistic enough to know that would never happen; all she could do is look at rare pictures of the apartments in coffee-table books; she had a dozen of them at home.

The size of the crowd increased rapidly as the ten o'clock hour approached. A young man, who seemed be an Italian-American, had taken the spot to her left behind the barrier. He wore a loud Hawaiian shirt, blue-jeans and white walking shoes.

His black hair fluttered gently in the mild breeze. He seemed a little nervous; he would look to either side and to his rear and then place his right hand on his belly, as if checking something.

Chapter 52

OUR ASSESSMENT OF THE *LAST JUDGMENT*

A close look at the *Last Judgment* reveals substantial deceptions in a painting which appears to be what Michelangelo was commissioned to paint.

The *Last Judgment* is not what modern Catholic apologists have exulted: for example, that the painting reasserted the supremacy and/or the authority of the Catholic Church over all other religions. Michelangelo would have had a good, private laugh at such descriptions, had they been written during his lifetime.

One of the artist's poems—in *The Poetry of Michelangelo,* (Clements, p. 295)—is a good place to start our analysis:

> Rend thou the veil, O Lord, break down this wall,
> Which by its hardness keeps retarding so
> Thy holy sunshine, in the world gone out
> Oh, send the light so long foretold for all,
> To thy fair bride, that so my soul may glow,
> And feel thee inwardly, and never doubt!
> **Michelangelo – 1525** (John S. Dwight, trans.)

Here we have the core of Michelangelo's conflicted soul as it relates to the Catholic religion . . . and the key that opens the door to the deceptions he imbedded in The *Last Judgment.* This poem reveals the artist's awareness of God as "holy sunshine."

That awareness had its origins in his conviction that his creative impulses came from God. In fact, they were so powerful and insistent that he could not resist materializing what the impulses demanded.

He drove himself mercilessly, furiously chipping away at stone to find stunning beauty within, and gracefully transforming a puddle of paint into the greatest works of art ever created.

Yet, he yearned, as did Mother Teresa, for "the light so long foretold for all"; he wanted to experience—*within*—the light of God's saving grace and compassionate love, for that would remove all doubt about his fate after death.

Still, like Mother Teresa, he was denied the reassurance that he (and she) sought—*within*. Mother Teresa's letters convey the same idea that the artist was expressing, but, for her, the intensity of emotional loss and spiritual depravation reaches stratospheric levels.

Michelangelo and Mother Teresa are two poster celebrities who took their religion to the extremes of logical conclusion . . . with disappointing results. Yet the contrasting experiences could hardly be more striking. At one point in her life, Mother Teresa wrote in a letter that she had been told that God loves her; and yet she felt an emptiness, coldness and darkness. Nothing touched her soul. It was so bad that she also stated in another letter that if there is a hell, living in this world must be it.

Mother Teresa, a beautiful spirit, following the dictates of her religion, dedicated her life to helping the homeless, sick and downtrodden people of the world. She wanted to be reassured that, upon her death, she would be greeted by a loving Jesus, impressed by her charitable accomplishments, and not a judgmental Jesus who might condemn her to hell.

Instead of the reassurance she craved, we read—repeatedly—of a woman living a life of inner darkness, terror and despair: Her prayers for consolation unanswered, she lived with a loss of faith: a devastating blow to what she believed should have been a glorious life in service of her Lord. Her terror lasted nearly a half-century—unabated.

Unlike Mother Teresa—who only suspected the existence of a divine light within, which would reassure her that her eternal fate was guaranteed—Michelangelo experienced the divine glow that flowed out of his sculpturing chisel and his paint brushes. Yet, he too, longed for the comfort of *experiencing* that divine glow *within.*

While fear and terror might not reign in the experience of a lot of Christians—after all, there are over 1,200 Christian denominations and sects—Christianity, as it is known today, has inherent elements of fear and terror by virtue of the sin, redemption, resurrection, salvation and damnation elements embedded in its belief system. Even the Christian sects and denominations that are the most distant from the Catholic Church—doctrinally—make no apologies for declaring that those who do not believe as they do will not be saved from an eternity in hell.

The deceptions, embedded in the *Last Judgment,* reject this doctrine in a painting that was supposed to have been a portrayal of ecstatic faces rising to eternal bliss in heaven and terrified and despondent faces getting what's coming to them: descent into an eternal torment in hell.

Chapter 53

Anna Berhoff was known to be something of a psychic to her closest friends. She never told anyone else about her very limited experiences finding objects, and other types of eerie events.

Anna had had occasional para-normal experiences later in life, but the most bizarre of all was an "out of body" event, which had occurred in her late fifties: she had never mentioned it to anyone . . . until now. . . to Jane, a close friend, who had called about another matter, needing help.

Anna had been thinking about telling Jane the story that follows for years, but had demurred in favor of protecting her highly valued reputation as a relatively sane person.

On that long-ago night . . . about thirty years ago . . . she had an out of body experience; she found herself sitting in the front row of a classroom, when a man walked in and went to the whiteboard. He pointed to a large, shimmering, vibrating "E," written in cursive, on the whiteboard. At that moment, a thought from the man came to Anna: "This symbol represents the reconciliation of time, space and matter." The next moment, she felt her-Self return to her body, with a mild jolt, which woke her up. She had no insight into the meaning of this strange message.

Jane, who lived several hundred miles away, received this new (to her) revelation as though she had just heard Anna describe her morning doing the laundry. She wasn't interested in discussing Anna's inter-galactic travels because it was well beyond her ken; she had more important things on her mind; she had lost her keys, and had called Anna to see if she could use her psychic powers to find them.

Anna, not one to take her unusual powers too seriously, laughed at the prospect, but, *what the hell*, she thought (she never spoke like that out loud), *why not give it a try.* "What were you doing when you lost your keys?" Anna asked. Jane remembered visiting a friend a couple doors down the street the day she lost her keys.

Anna said she would see what she could do and would get back to her . . . if she came up with anything.

The next day Anna called Jane and told her she had only two clues: the keys are located near a couch . . . not your couch, because your living room had no couch; and airplanes have something to do with where they are located: That was it. Again, they laughed at such vague nonsense.

Jane thanked Anna and said she would check at her neighbor's house. She had checked there when she realized they were lost, being careful to check around the couch where she sat during the visit, but found nothing.

Let's see, Jane said to herself, as she entered her neighbor's house, apologizing for the interruption, *it's a couch and has something to do with airplanes.* She went to the couch and went to the end where she had been sitting. She saw a coffee-table book about airplanes lying on the end table. *Maybe this is it!* She got down on her hands and knees, swiped her arm under the couch and pulled out her keys.

Another bizarre event was not an "out-of-body" experience; nevertheless, it was compelling.

On September 10, 2001, Anna went to bed her usual time around nine p.m. She glanced at the clock which showed 9:11. The moment she looked at it, a shiver went down her spine and she felt an overwhelming wave of horror coursing through her body. *What is going on?* She thought. *Am I having a silent heart attack, a stroke or some other potentially fatal episode? Should I call 911?*

It seemed to Anna that the 9:11 on the clock was stuck on that time element forever. It didn't seem to go away and the longer it stayed, the worse she felt. At long last, the clock changed to 9:12; she relaxed and fell asleep. The next day, she went out for her habitual walk up the street and back. She had walked about three blocks when she saw an elderly man pacing back and forth in his front yard. The front door to his house was open and she could see the TV was on from her position on the sidewalk.

As she approached the man in the yard, he said: "Have you been watching TV?" Anna replied that she had not. The man, with a slight quiver in his voice, told her about the airplanes flying into the twin towers and things weren't looking good at that point.

Anna thanked him for informing her. She did not immediately make a connection between what he had said and her "9:11 experience" the night before. The rest of the story she would soon learn; the connection between the two events never left her thoughts. What did it all mean? She didn't have a clue, except, perhaps, that she had experienced some premonition of things to come.

Chapter 54

Art historians employ four methodologies in their research into the qualities, nature and history of objects: (1) formal analysis; (2) stylistic analysis; (3) iconographical analysis; and finally, (4) theory, to frame their inquiries into artistic objects. We will not use any of these methodologies, because our purpose is not the same as art historians: to locate the qualities, nature and history of objects. Our purpose is to expose Michelangelo's deceptions for contemporary and future generations.

Still, a few interpretations, taken from *Sistine Secrets and* various art critics, put our assessment of the *Last Judgment* within the context of previous analysts' work. *Sistine Secrets* is the best contextual framework within which we place our analysis, because it is a comprehensive study done from the perspective of "hidden secrets"; our study is closely related, but done from the perspective of "deceptions." Of course, overlap between the two perspectives occurs, and that will become evident as our analysis progresses.

The authors of *Sistine Secrets* do not **quarrel** with traditional interpretations of the *Last Judgment* with respect to its façade: a painting of the second coming of Christ. *We do.*

Yet, their invaluable—and chief contribution—lies in exposing Michelangelo's personal beliefs relative to Jewish mysticism (in the ceiling fresco) and the Church's attitude toward Jews in general; for example, in the *Last Judgment,* Michelangelo adds a new twist: Jews and homosexuals are included amongst those who are already in, or destined for heaven; this is in direct opposition to what the Church leaders thought about the Jews at that time.

In one section of the painting, several nude males are seen embracing, kissing and gazing into one another's eyes. Here, a close examination clearly reveals gay men enjoying the prospect of entering heaven with their lovers; a ridicule of the Church's attitude toward Jews.

Had these "secrets" been discovered and acted upon during Michelangelo's lifetime, it is likely the painting would have been "modified," just as it was when blatant nudity in the fresco became a major problem. This observation suggests that the secrets about Jews, women and homosexuals in the *Last Judgment* went unnoticed until Blech and Doliner exposed them in their recent book.

Christ, according to Blech and Doliner, instead of sitting on his throne of glory, is perched on a pedestal, in the act of rising to pronounce his severe and final judgment, separating the sheep from the goats. Their analysis agrees with traditional interpretations; ours does not, which we shall see in a moment.

For Blech and Doliner and traditional critics, "Mary" sits to Christ's right, looking away, seemingly not wanting to witness Christ's final blow condemning the damned to hell. We think otherwise.

"Mary," according to Blech and Doliner, is also turning away from Christ as a symbol for Michelangelo's turning away from Catholicism. We agree that the artist rejected Catholicism, probably as a teenager, became enamored with Kabbalism, and then veered toward Protestantism later in life. Therefore, he adopted a mixture of both Kabbalism and Protestantism and finally transcendentalism before he died. Consequently, we think that both the traditional as well as Blech and Doliner's interpretations of "Mary's" pose are inaccurate. A brief explanation is in order here.

According to Blech and Doliner, "Mary's" gaze is directed at Colonna to draw the viewer's attention to her and her place of honor in the fresco. We think that stretches the band of credulity, because, clearly, this woman is looking directly at her bare, lower torso, including her buttocks, which the "Breeches Makers" eventually covered with a green cloth.

Art critics claim that Michelangelo included an experimental art form—a technique called *pointillism*—when he painted the face of "Mary" with tiny dots. The index finger on her left hand points to her face to draw attention to the new method.

We think the finger-pointing is suggesting something far more important than some obscure art form: the finger is suggesting—*Look at **me! All of me!*** The "pointillism" theory is a red-herring to draw attention away from the artist's most powerful deception in the fresco: that the figure everyone assumes is Mary the mother of Jesus, is **none other than Mary Magdalene.**

Chapter 55

The young man with black curly hair standing next to Anna Berhoff at the Vatican Square barrier seemed to be up to no good. She couldn't figure out what was going on with that, because he appeared to be a clean-cut, young American; yet, there was something about him that worried her—put her on guard, intuitively. There was no rational thought involved.

While Anna was scanning the crowd with her binoculars, the ten o'clock Vatican bells rang, indicating that the pope was due at any moment. But there was not the usual stir that preceded his arrival at the platform set up on the steps of the basilica for the pope's address to the audiences. The pope would be late.

The enormous, sonorous, Vatican bells always set-off a tune in her mind: *The Bells of St. Mary's*. And then, as always, she started to hum the tune, with Bing Crosby's mellow voice wafting through her mind:

The bells of St. Mary's
Ah, hear they are calling
The young loves, the true loves,
Who come from the sea.
And so my beloved,
When red leaves are falling,
The love bells will ring out, ring out
For you and me.

The young man with the curly hair turned to look at her. He knew she was there, but hadn't paid much attention to her because it didn't occur to him that she could be a problem—but now she was: she was humming a tune that Darly hummed every time she felt romantic and wanted to get laid.

She never said: *I want to get laid*. She started humming one of Bing Crosby's most famous renditions of all his songs: *The Bells of St. Mary's,* from the movie with the same title. It was one of Darly's favorites of all the old-time American movies she loved to watch.

And now this old woman next to him was humming Darly's tune, *wanting to get laid*—**Huh?** . . . *Maybe not **every** woman who hums this tune wants to get laid.*

He wanted to tell her to *Shut the fuck up!* Before he had a chance to determine if that was a wise move, he heard the distant sound of a helicopter coming from the southeast.

As it rose, like an anxious sun rising over the Roman horizon, Anna focused on it with her binoculars and had an interesting thought: *If I get him to look at the helicopter with my binoculars, maybe I can see what's under the shirt that is loose and flapping in the breeze.*

She lowered the binoculars and tapped the stranger on his right shoulder and asked him—in English—if he wanted to take a look at the helicopter with her binoculars. He looked at her in surprise and remembered Gianni's advice to use sign language in awkward situations.

He pointed to his ears and mouth and made some wiggles with his fingers and gave an arms-out-palms-up gesture of "What do you want?" She handed him the binoculars and pointed to the helicopter and said, "Take a look! Il Papa," echoing what some in the crowd were shouting.

He understood, forgot why he was standing there, and grabbed the binoculars to take a look. Anna feigned a stumble and fell into him, giving him a slight jolt, while she was pulling up his shirt, confirming her worst fears: *He has a gun!* Mario seemed fascinated with the magnified helicopter as it raced toward its destination: the helicopter pad on the west side of the Vatican fortress.

The pope would be here soon and that's when Mario realized he may have made a stupid mistake. Anna apologized for bumping into him, although he hadn't understood a word. Yet, he knew what she was conveying. He checked to make sure his pistol was still in place with his left hand as he handed the binoculars back to Anna.

Anna took the binoculars and followed the helicopter as it disappeared behind the Apostolic Palace. She swung her glasses to her right, toward Via della Conciliazione, the street leading into the center of Rome, then slowly brought them back over the crowd until she had made a full half-circle. It was as if she hadn't seen a thing—as if she were blind.

Her mind was on: *What next?* She was convinced that the man in the Hawaiian shirt next to her was about to shoot the pope. *But what to do?* The long half-circle sweep with the binoculars drew a blank.

The "Hawaiian shirt" seemed to be getting more agitated by the moment. *Should I attack him with my binoculars to create a scene to get the attention of the guards before the pope arrives? That could be very dangerous for everyone around me.*

There will be at least a half dozen more guards near here when the pope arrives; as it is now, I see only five; one is standing near our railing about twenty yards to my right. Two others are on the other side of the corridor: one about thirty yards to my left and the other about thirty yards to my right.

If I wait, there will be several more guards when the pope arrives in our zone. That increases the odds of having some success in thwarting an assassination of the pope. If I do **anything**, *my life is in grave danger. I could be shot by this guy, or take a stray bullet from one of the guards.*

Anna was pretending to look at the crowd, the basilica and the apostolic palace while she continued her desperate search for an answer. *I could retreat and get the hell out of here.*

Leaving seemed to make the most sense on some level, but she knew she would take such cowardice with her to the grave—and beyond; it was the "beyond" that troubled her.

She wasn't a religious person, but she was a deeply spiritual person and she intuitively knew right from wrong. She had never needed some church authoritarian to tell her what to think and do. And now the pope had arrived in the Square through a door to the left of the main basilica entrance.

As always, there was a stir up there that she couldn't make sense of, even with her powerful binoculars. But she knew the drill and within minutes he would be riding in the cargo bay of the white pickup truck, reconfigured into a popemobile with a hand-bar across the bay for the pope to grab if necessary.

She brought her binoculars down, wrapped the straps around her right wrist and dropped her right arm to her side and waited. She would wing it. *Here he comes!*

As the popemobile closed, Mario kept his right hand near his pistol—his right-hand thumb hooked into the watch-pocket of his blue-jeans, making sure part of his hand was under his shirt. Anna noticed that, unlike the year before, the pope had a plain-clothes cop standing behind him in the bed of the popemobile.

The pope's routine in the popemobile was similar to that of previous popes—lifting his arms, blessing the enthusiastic fans. Of all the celebrities in the world, he had millions, even hundreds of millions of fans—more than sports heroes, presidents, movie stars, warriors, writers, musicians—you name them.

Anna couldn't make up her mind: hit the assassin on the head, the arm, or his shoulder with her binoculars, or simply plow into him with her body as if someone had given her a hefty shove. Perhaps she could knock him out if she hit him hard enough on the head with her binoculars. Any one of those options would deflect the bullet away from its intended target.

Still, she wasn't absolutely convinced he intended to assassinate the pope, but if, in a betting situation she had a choice, she'd give ninety to one odds he was about to do just that.

The moment of decision was pressing her like a hot, steaming iron on a wrinkled shirt. She wouldn't panic and do nothing. All of her options, except panic, were still on the table. She would know, when the moment of decision had passed, which alternative she had chosen.

Mario did a 360 scan of the happy throng—after the helicopter arrived at the Vatican—looking for anyone who could pass as a plain-clothes cop. He saw none. The only man that caught his attention was the man standing next to him on his left—not because he suspected he was an undercover agent, to be sure.

However, he was under cover—under the cover of a Stetson hat—the Texan icon of the spirit of the early western United States. Mario had seen the bold hats in movies, always vowing, at the end of each movie, that he would purchase one, put it on and go to the States to see the OK Corral at Tombstone, Arizona, where, in 1881 the sheriff Wyatt Earp—his two brothers, Morgan and Virgil—and Doc Holliday shot it out with notorious outlaws: the Clantons, McLaurys and Billy Clairborne.

That pleasant thought invaded his consciousness at an awkward moment, piled on top of his annoyance with the fact that the huge hat obstructed his view of the approaching pope.

He desperately wanted to poke the cow-poker and tell him to remove the hat so he'd have a better shot at the pope, but that would be tantamount to rousing a sleeping cheetah protecting her cubs secured under her right front leg.

Anna—tense now—awaited her fateful moment. Mario's right hand moved toward his pistol.

Chapter 56

"Perfecto, it's the old adage: *You don't need to know how a clock is made to tell time.* But I will give you some mumbo-jumbo explanation of how the car-colors change; that might satisfy your curiosity.

"A *diode* is a two-terminal device between which signals may flow and some are used as adjustable capacitors.

"A light-emitting diode—formed from a direct, band-gap semiconductor—has carriers that cross the junction and emit photons that recombine with the majority carrier on the other side. Depending on the wavelengths, colors are produced. The first light-emitting diodes were red and yellow and higher-frequency diodes have been developed over time. I took the modern light-emitting diode technology and applied it to a highly versatile micro-thin, silicone sheet.

"The best way to describe it in laymen's terms is this: A micro-thin sheet embedded with multiple, micro-thin threads attached to fluctuating diodes, connects to flux capacitors that generate varying wavelengths of light: red, yellow, blue and purple, depending on which button you push under the dashboard.

"Then I create a pattern of the automobile's surface and cut the sheets to conform to the pattern, as a seamstress would use a pattern to cut the sections of a dress . . ."

"That part I understand," Perfecto interjected excitedly. "Now I'm getting it."

Tyrone smiled and said, "Well, finally! I was beginning to worry that I'd lost you somewhere along the way, but I can see you are a fast learner after all! Anyway, that's about it.

"How I apply it to the surface of a car is a trade secret that is going to make me even richer than I am now. People will be able to change the color of their cars to fit their moods, just like they change clothes. Now, one more thing. Underneath that dazzling surface is a bullet-proof body with a bullet-proof, rear window. How about that, young man?"

Perfecto looked at Tyrone as he if he were a higher-level being than a pope—almost as if he were the God that made the pope, instead of the pope being the guy that made God. He didn't ask about the other windows. "Where do you work? I mean here? I don't see any kind of laboratory or workshop."

"Like the innovations I have made for cars, my lab location is a secret. It's located on these premises, but I would challenge anyone to find it. But before we go further on that subject, I want tell you one more thing about this car. Go stand behind the car and take a look and tell me what you see."

"Uh . . . a car with a rear window?"

Tyrone roared with laughter. "You see, young man, that's why you're an intellectual and a priest, and I'm merely an old car-junkie. Take a look at the wheels; notice anything unusual?"

"Well," said Perfecto, "they stick out a little. Is that what you mean?"

"Gimme five!" yelled Tyrone. "You're a genius after all! I modified the engine, the wheel-base, and lowered the center of gravity so you could hold your own in a race with a much larger and more maneuverable car. You can take this car around curves faster and more safely than any luxury Mercedes. So when you get the car, take it out and get a little training on curving mountain roads. By now you know where they are, so get used to this little wonder-of-wonders."

As that explanation ended, Perfecto felt a sinking feeling—sinking, that is, as in descending beneath the surface of the ocean. The difference in this case was that he was sinking beneath the surface of a concrete floor. Concrete is not a fluid that makes sinking beneath its surface possible—unless a slab of concrete is perched on a large, round, hydraulic post that eases the platform down to the floor below: and that's what was happening; Perfecto was descending into Tyrone's secret domain, his high-tech shop and office. Tyrone had punched a key on his remote while they were talking and down they went.

Perfecto's eyes widened as he slowly comprehended what he was seeing. He saw three cars in various states of renovation and redesign, benches with tools, and high-tech instruments, and a couple pin-up girls in WW II vintage posters.

"You're really something. You know that?" asked Perfecto. "Any other secrets?"

"Only one, but I save that one for anyone who tries to open the front door. You haven't seen my dog-run behind the building, but that's where I keep a couple Pitbulls. They are part of my security system.

"Now you know everything, and normally I kill people, who get this far into my secret world, but I won't kill you because I know Skip would be pissed, and I *don't* want to get on the wrong side of that man; I feel sorry for anyone who does. Got that, Pal? I'm not going to kill you," Tyrone said with a smile.

"Well, thank you for small favors, you big oaf! How about a 'high-five' on that?" Perfecto said, as he raised his hand, which Tyrone immediately slapped and said, "You're my man, Perfecto, you're my man!"

"Now, one more question. What about the airplane?"

Tyrone smiled and said, "Come on, get in the car and we'll go topside and I'll show you."

Back in the showroom, Tyrone pulled out his remote and pressed a key. A huge, roll-up door, nearly the size of the back end of the building began rising, revealing a grass field leading from the door out to the end of the huge lot, a runway long enough to accommodate a small plane. "Want to go for a ride?"

"Are you a pilot, too?"

"Yes, but you'd be risking your life in going for a ride with me because I haven't been trained as well as I should be to reduce the risk of accidents to an acceptable level. So I don't give people rides merely for pleasure. If the situation arises that I need to use the plane, I will use it and take passengers: but only in an emergency."

"Does it have special features like the Panda?" Perfecto inquired. "It seems to me you mentioned it does. Maybe you'll take me for a ride and show me those as well?"

"Man, you *do* have a death wish don't you? If you look carefully at it, you will see an aerodynamic hump on the top that holds a secret I won't reveal, even to you, because I *do* value your life as much as Skip does. I've trained myself to use that feature in an emergency."

"How many passenger seats does it have?"

"There are two seats for the pilots and three for passengers. But since I fly alone, I have room for four people.

"Let's go back to the auto shop. I want to take a good look at your junk-heap to make sure it will run until you can leave it here with me and take the Panda with you. You will need to come back two or three times until I am satisfied that you can operate those buttons automatically, blindfolded. Then the car will be yours."

As they passed through the showroom heading toward the small door on the other end, Perfecto stopped with a puzzled look and said, "There's something missing and I can't place it."

"There's more than *something* missing," Tyrone said with mischievous look on his face.

"Ah!" Perfecto shouted. "It's the Tucker! That's what's missing. What happened?"

"I thought you'd never notice. But to give you a little slack, it disappeared after your last visit. I sold it to a Russian billionaire. It was purchased by his agent, my Russian friend. Remember I told you about him? He has purchased other cars from me for his clients in Moscow. The agent gave me an offer I couldn't refuse.

"I think I told you that the Tucker's current market value is about one million euros. I didn't really want to sell it, so I told the agent my asking price was two million. He looked at me and said, 'Would you take three million in cash?' I said: What? I just told you two million and you're saying three million? Why?

"He said, 'You see, the billionaires are fierce competitors for prestige. The more they pay for a car, the greater their prestige amongst the car collectors. They can say they paid two million, I take a million for my work; everybody is happy. Been doing it for years. No problem. Do you want to sell or not?' the guy (his name is Igor) asked . . . with a grin. So . . . I said, 'YES.'"

Chapter 57

As Mario's hand reached the lethal weapon, Anna's right arm was rising from her side, carving out a line in space that would arch over her head and crash into Mario's skull.

Mario's arm stiffened into firing position. Anna's binoculars were about to crash into his head, when she felt a hand grab her right arm from behind. The hand belonged to Angelica Greco, whose voice Mario had heard when he dialed room number 412 the previous morning.

Angelica and Mario had spent most of that day and last night in bed, in room 412 of the Alimonde Hotel. After breakfast in the room—steak and eggs, coffee and pastries—Angelica handed him new underwear, socks, the LA cap, Hawaiian shirt, blue-jeans and white walking shoes. Mario dressed. Angelica kissed him goodbye and sent him off to assassinate the pope.

As she edged her way toward Mario, Angelica noticed—as the popemobile moved slowly toward Mario—that he wasn't wearing the cap she had given him; she assumed it was the same cap she had seen lying on top of one of the security guard's surveillance machines.

Angelica had followed him at a distance to the Square to make sure his feet did not turn to mush, steering him away from his target, and absconding with the two thousand euros. She moved slowly and politely as she brushed past eager onlookers . . . positioning herself behind Mario just before the pope approached Mario's place at the barrier.

She, an unlikely enforcer for the mob, would do her duty—as with all enforcers—for a price. Sometimes her "duties" went beyond the range of activity associated with male enforcers, but she didn't mind so long as her partners in sexual encounters weren't disgusting pigs with bad breath.

Angelica did not anticipate Anna's move to prevent Mario from assassinating the pope, because she concentrated on Mario, monitoring his moves and contemplating her responses to whatever happened after he shot the pope.

When Anna raised her right hand in a high arch over her head, Angelica, surprised by Anna's move, reached with her left arm to stop the momentum of the binoculars toward Mario's head. Underestimating the force of the heavy binoculars, she grabbed Anna's wrist within inches of Mario's head.

But her impulsive act put her off balance, so that the force of the soaring binoculars was transferred to her teetering body, throwing her into Mario a split-second before he pulled the trigger. The bullet whizzed by the head of the plain-clothed Swiss Guard standing in the popemobile. Before Mario could aim again, the pope was safely hidden in the bed of the bullet-proof pickup truck—under his bodyguard.

The commotion created by Angelica's move against Anna and her crashing into Mario, alerted the guards walking alongside the popemobile. The agents could see Mario attempting to aim another shot, but it was too late, so he lowered his pistol, stuffed it under his belt, and turned to flee. He turned to his right and crashed into his most recent lover: Angelica.

She watched the expression on Mario's face turn from surprise to horror as she raised her right hand and slit his throat with a single-edged, long-handle razor blade. The shock turned to grimace, and then a vacant stare, as he fell to the ground, mortally wounded.

Four undercover agents leaped over the barrier as Mario fell. They converged on the bloody scene as Angelica screamed that she had prevented the bastard from killing the pope as she charged into the crowd and vanished.

The plain-clothes Swiss Guards could not have known that Angelica's most crucial part of her mission was to do exactly as she had done: to slit Mario's throat *whether or not,* he killed the pope. Gianni did not want Mario to survive the assassination *or attempt,* whichever it turned out to be.

He did not want Mario singing like a yellow canary about who had put him up to the dastardly deed. If Mario had managed to survive Angelica's attack, he would have encountered an empty space where his getaway car was supposed to be waiting; if he had escaped despite that treachery, he would have discovered his two thousand euros were counterfeit.

Gianni, fared better: he had received up-front money: one hundred thousand euros in legal tender from a cleric's intermediary whom he trusted, but whose name he would never know; his name wasn't important—the good money was.

Anna survived the shock of her last visit to the Vatican. In the commotion that followed Mario's death, she disappeared into the crowd.

As she lay dying in the modest Eastern Pennsylvania home the following holiday season, she was thankful for a long and satisfying life. Although she had had a dreadful experience during her final visit to her beloved Vatican, she was pleased with her part in preventing the assassination of the pope.

Chapter 58

"**Cardinal O'Reilley, you really** screwed-up this time!" said Monsignor Lopez. I thought we made it *very* clear that you were to back off and not do anything drastic about the pope. Now you've made things infinitely more difficult for the rest of us who are trying to deal with this situation; you don't seem to understand the gravity of what you did."

"Monsignor, I have no idea what you are talking about—my 'screwing-up,' as you call it. Who the hell do you think you are talking to me like that?"

"I'll talk to you any way I choose. You have no standing with the pope and less with your colleagues. The only reason you are a cardinal is that the previous pope was protecting you from prosecution for molesting children. He kicked you up the stairway to nowhere—more accurately, where you could do the least harm. But you have chosen to act like a buffoon ever since you arrived at the Vatican and now you tried to kill Pope Immanuel despite the fact that I told you . . ."

"What the fuck are you talking about?" Cardinal O'Reilley interrupted angrily. "Monsignor Lopez, I've never killed anyone, not to mention the most powerful religious leader in the world."

"On that we can agree; you've probably never personally killed anyone. You didn't listen to what I said—that you *tried* to kill the pope. There is little doubt in our minds you were behind the attempted assassination. If you had any brains you would know that saying the things you have said to us is tantamount to announcing your intentions to put the pope out of his misery.

"We have reliable information that you were behind the gangster killing of the two mobsters near the restaurant where you dined with them. What were you doing dining with gangsters? Can you explain that?"

"I'm not obligated to explain anything to you. How is it that you have knowledge that only gangsters would know?"

"I'm not going to argue anymore. We have more important things to discuss today. We invited you here to express our displeasure. We've done that. Now you can leave."

Cardinal O'Reilley stood staring at Monsignor Lopez.

"If you aren't gone in ten seconds, Father Morales will call the police and have you thrown out. Wouldn't *that* make a good headline in tomorrow's paper?"

"You are the ones who don't know what you're doing. Some day you will find out!" O'Reilley shouted, as he turned to leave the Legion headquarters. When he reached the door, he turned and said, "I came with this. He tossed a brown, nine-by-twelve envelope on the lamp table next to the door. "Read this and you will know how serious this business is getting."

Monsignor Lopez walked to the table, retrieved the envelope and returned to his seat. "I guess this is yours, Father Morales. What's in it that is so threatening?"

"We'll find out soon enough." Father Morales said, as he opened the envelope.

Glancing through the report, Morales looked up at the monsignor and said, "Another report for the pope prepared by our friend, the elusive Father Perfecto. It looks like a summary of several books that are critical of the Vatican in general and how it operates in particular.

"From what I can see, there are several journalists, priests and even bishops who have weighed in on the sins of the papacy, not unlike the report that Sandusky prepared in that sense, but more along the lines of financial, authority and power issues at the Vatican. While there is one book that specifically deals with the financial scandals during Paul VI's papacy, I don't see anything directly dealing with current Vatican Bank operations."

"When that happens, let me know immediately," said Monsignor Lopez. "If Pope Immanuel starts tinkering with the banking operations, or worse, puts in his own man to clean up the corruption that we know exists, it will be time to prepare for action, because our constituents will not tolerate a pope who threatens the financial empire that the Vatican Bank controls and exists to serve our most wealthy supporters; in addition to that, we know the bank receives billions of dollars in fees for laundering gangsters' ill-begotten wealth."

"I agree with you, wholeheartedly," said Father Nunez. "There will be drama around here that will rock the world if this pope takes such foolhardy steps. Let's hope he is creating a loaded, ersatz deck to intimidate the cardinals who will oppose his reforms: *Do it my way, or else!*"

"That could be what he is doing and I hope it is," said Monsignor Lopez. "We can deal with that and defeat him at his own game, if that's what he's up to. We have been wise to wait him out before we act. The problem in these situations is that unforeseen events have a way of interjecting themselves into the mix which creates a lot of uncertainty.

"That's why I asked you to let me know immediately if it appears the Vatican Bank is becoming a serious issue; if it does, that will be our signal to gather our executive board for a meeting to let them know what's coming. I have already begun planning for that eventuality.

"It takes months of planning and some training for an effective execution of our plans. My people have been making plans since the Sandusky report came out, but I've kept them close to my chest. Now this report justifies what I have done.

"Make a copy of this report for me. I want them to be thinking about the possibility of taking drastic measures, which could include mustering and training a paramilitary force to back up our actions at the Vatican, if that becomes necessary."

"Okay," said Father Nunez, "and let me know as soon as you can if I can assist in any way."

"Will do. Make a copy. I need to catch my plane. I'll read it during the flight."

Chapter 59

Sister Aurelia Esposito joined a half-dozen Vatican employees in accepting an invitation by the pope to attend his daily morning mass in his personal chapel only a few feet from his apartment. About that many outsiders were invited also.

The small chapel ceiling and some of the side walls are replete with gaudy, lighted panels depicting gospel scenes. Two three-candle candelabras rest on either side of the altar, which is draped in a white, laced-silk panel; the candelabras are flanked by fresh-cut yellow flowers.

A red, concave, backdrop panel provides high relief for a near-life-sized bronze crucifix. A coordinating, beige concave wall behind the red panel depicts two scenes: to the left of the crucifix is the upside-down crucifixion of Peter—on the right, the beheading of John the Baptist.

Flanking the altar are two larger bouquets of flowers, which are accompanied by floor-standing candles. *The effect of the three murderous scenes complementing the free-standing altar is one of horror,* thought Sister Aurelia, *hardly a welcoming effect for one coming to worship a loving God.*

In the center of the chapel is a convex, bronze-backed chair for the pope's comfort during extended periods of prayer and contemplation. The chair stands on a brown oblong carpet which covers almost one third of the width of the chapel, which, to Aurelia appeared to be about twelve feet wide.

Along the side walls, about a dozen padded stools provide some relief for those who choose, or need to sit during the mass. The floor, with its faux, splintered birch-wood design, seemed to be designed to enhance the general ugliness of the chapel.

Aurelia wondered why anyone would want to come to such a place. But this was her opportunity to meet the pope, a chance that had kept her waiting for nearly four decades and it couldn't have been more serendipitous if God had arranged it Himself. The mission she was on this morning far exceeded an opportunity to meet the pope.

The pope was praying, kneeling at the altar when his guests entered the chapel. At precisely seven a.m., ushered in by the Vatican bell tower, the pope rose and the mass began.

When it was over, he greeted each attendee personally. Sister Aurelia held back to make sure she was the last one he would see.

She introduced herself and asked if she could meet with him privately, hastening to add that she was the office manager at the Vatican bank and that she had a gift for him and a personal confession that involved the salvation of her soul. She stared at him, giving him a non-verbal message that said: *Don't be a fool and turn me down!*

The pope paused, staring back at her, slowly absorbing what he had just heard. "Why, yes . . . of course," he said, "please come with me." Father Sandusky was standing at the pope's apartment door waiting to speak with the pope, but Pope Immanuel waved him off as he escorted Sister Aurelia into his apartment.

He motioned for her to sit across from him; a coffee table stood between two love seats. Aurelia crossed herself, unzipped her habit from her chin to her waist and pulled out a brown legal-sized envelope that bulged with compact disks and hardcopy documents.

She handed them to the pope and said, "I thought you might need these for whatever it is you plan to do about the bank. I've been working there for nearly forty years, working my way up to office manager. I've held that position for thirty years. I know everything that has gone on in the bank and my gift to you this morning is proof of that fact. The documents I'm giving you have details of the illegitimate operations of the bank. They do not include legitimate operations, which will be available to you if you need them.

"I know I am in grave danger by coming to talk to you and that is why I want to confess my sins this morning and ask for your personal absolution. Will you grant me that favor?"

Pope Immanuel accepted the envelope and asked if he could look at the documents before they continued.

"Certainly, take all the time you need."

The pope opened the envelope and thumbed through the documents, taking enough time to see that he was holding a treasure he had wanted to see since the day he took office. The hard copy documents contained an index file of the CD's so the pope could see—at a glance—the contents.

He was surprised that it came to him in this manner. The initial delight he felt melted into shock as he realized what this brave woman was doing. He put the documents on the coffee table and—looking compassionately at Sister Aurelia—asked if she wanted to proceed with her confession.

"Yes, Your Holiness, I do. I know your reputation well enough to know that I do not need to go into detail about crimes that I have committed over the past forty years. Until you came along and started acting with integrity, I was convinced that I was doing nothing wrong by just doing my job at the bank, even though I knew that most of our major transactions would be illegal in the secular world. I rationalized my behavior by saying to myself that if *this* pope approves, who am I to worry about issues that are a zillion ranks above my pay-grade.

"But now,"—she began to cry—"I know that my entire life has been an appalling failure—for deep down I knew I needed to get out of this mess and lead an honorable life: perhaps even taking off my habit and going secular. But I couldn't bring myself to do it."

Pope Immanuel's eyes filled with tears as she continued. He reached for a tissue for himself and handed one to her. She wiped the tears from her eyes and cheeks and, looking down noticed her habit was still unzipped, reached down and zipped it to her chin, exclaiming, "Oh, my goodness! You know, you try to live a life of holiness and then you encounter so many things that run counter to that grain, sort of like the zig-zag lines I saw in the floor of your chapel this morning. My boss—Mr. Russo—is terrified. He knows you are a man of integrity honor and since you sent Father Perfecto to talk to him, he has not been the same.

"He knows what's coming down and is waiting for the other shoe to fall; he knows that when it does, it will not be pretty for him, no matter which way it falls. He's Opus Dei and they will crucify him if he betrays them. But if he remains loyal to them, and you succeed in your efforts to clean up the mess around here, he will be in trouble with you.

"So, part of my confession to you is that I pray that you will give him an opportunity to help you, in spite of what he has been doing all these years. I understand what he is going through. I've made my choice this morning. I am hoping that, with your granting me forgiveness for my sins, God will forgive me and that I will dwell with him for eternity despite what I've done with my life. That's my confession and my request for Mr. Russo. Basically, he's a good man."

"Sister Aurelia, as you can see, I am touched by your bravery and confession and your request on behalf of Mr. Russo. Give me your hand."

Pope Immanuel leaned forward, took her right hand in his left hand and placed his right hand over her head and said, solemnly, ***"God the Father of*** *mercies, through the death and resurrection of his Son, has reconciled the world to himself and sent the Holy Spirit among us for the forgiveness of sins; through the ministry of the Church, may God give you pardon and peace, and I absolve you from your sins in the name of the Father, and of the Son, and of the Holy Spirit. May God bless you my dear Sister."*

"Thank you, Holiness. Now I can go in peace. May God bless you and give you the wisdom and courage to do what is in the best interests of humanity. That is my parting prayer for you this morning."

"My dear child, you cannot just walk out of here. As you said, you are in grave danger from what you have done this morning and I agree with you. As you know, we are talking about people with huge financial stakes in what you have done and what I may do. This involves powerful organized crime syndicates around the world. They will not tolerate anyone, including you and me, messing with their cherished, fraudulent banking operations. I have protections that you don't have and I want to provide you the protection you will need, now that you have come to me in this way."

"Your Holiness—believe me—I appreciate what you are saying, but I cannot and will not accept your offer. I do not want to live the rest of my life like a terrified, cornered rat. With your forgiveness and blessing this morning, I am at peace and will live whatever life I have left that way. I will go down to the bank and inform Mr. Russo that I am resigning my position.

"Then I will go home, take off my habit and go grocery shopping. I will take in a movie that I have been wanting to see. I will go home, eat dinner and go to bed, thanking God for you and praying that he will bless your efforts for faithfully and earnestly serving Him. Goodbye and God bless you."

Pope Immanuel escorted her to the door, opened it and said goodbye. Father Sandusky was standing in the corridor talking with "Fingers," one of the janitors and nodded to the pope as he closed the door. *I guess he didn't want to talk to me after all,* mused the pope.

"Fingers" Morticelli was a transplant from the Bronx and described his profession, proudly, if anyone asked what he did for a living, as "a sanitation engineer at the Vatican".

That impressed most, if not all people, but they wondered about the latex gloves on his hands: They had never seen him without them. Indeed, he rarely took them off, except to bathe and sleep; he never revealed why he wore them. Most people thought he was a germ-freak.

The pope went back to the table between the love seats. He picked up the envelope, replaced the documents and took it to the small, self-standing safe he had behind his desk where he kept his personal "Top Secret" documents and papers. He twirled the dial back and forth until it released the lock. He opened the safe door and placed only a few of the more innocuous hardcopy documents on top of Sandusky's white paper and Perfecto's report, closed the door and twirled the dial to reset the lock. He placed the CD's and remaining hardcopies in the envelope, went to his bedroom, and shoved it to an unnoticeable point under his mattress.

Chapter 60

On a chilly summer evening, at an abandoned campsite in the rolling foothills of the Blue Ridge Mountains of North Carolina, Colonel "Bull" Masterson shouted greetings to para-military recruits. Seated in a semi-circle on camp stools, one hundred men gazed at their new leader with awe and respect.

An American hero of the Gulf War and the war in Iraq, Masterson acquired his name as a child when people still gave nicknames (that stuck) to children based on their appearance: names like "Sky" (for an unusually tall child; "Pug" (for a nose that is somewhat flattened and turned up at the end); and "Twiggy" (for an extremely slender person). The list goes on.

Paul "Bull" Masterson got his nickname as a child because he looked like . . . well, a bull, with a sloping forehead and a chin with a permanent jut that seemed to suggest: *don't mess with me!* But those who knew him in the Marine Corps thought he got it because he was as stubborn as a bull in a ring that refuses to charge the muleta.

At age of 52, he ran three miles a day, did fifty sit-ups and could out-perform anyone in whatever physical test military men are required to perform. He had been chosen by his peers to lead them in a noble cause, which to him rivaled his service to his country. The cause: take down the new pope by whatever means his employers chose. He had been recommended to Monsignor Lopez by a Legionarie, Navy chaplain assigned to the Marine Corps who had served with the "Bull."

Monsignor Lopez contacted Masterson three months after his retirement. A member of Opus Dei, Colonel Masterson was well aware of the organization's mission and how that related to the Roman Catholic Church.

He believed that Opus Dei would someday *be* the Church and he worked toward that end. If he played his cards wisely, he could end up in a prestigious, post-retirement position in the Church. The prospect of achieving such status amongst the religions of the world in the foreseeable future energized Masterson to a point of fanaticism.

The Vatican Ship of State, with the pope's hand at the helm, sailing on a collision course with conservative elements within the Church—and its ancillary organizations associated with the Catholic Church—presented Opus Dei and the Legionaries with an opportunity they couldn't ignore:

to take over the Vatican, re-install one of their own, and save it from the approaching shipwreck.

Monsignor Lopez had briefed him on the potential need for a para-military force to deal with a developing situation at the Vatican. All Masterson knew was that events at the Vatican could spin out of control; he wanted to help prevent that from happening.

Col. Masterson was charged with raising and training a force of about one hundred men for that mission. He put out a call to all Opus Dei organizations in several countries asking for former members of military organizations to volunteer to come to North Carolina for one week, every other month, for training: three hundred responded.

He selected one hundred of the most experienced men with a variety of military specialties, including infantry, intelligence, special forces, and communications. He told them to arrive in camouflaged utility uniforms, sleeping bags, their own rations and cooking utensils sufficient to last a week. An abandoned Summer Bible Camp site—where small cabins could protect them from the elements—would be their training facility. The camp included a dining hall and meeting rooms.

"Bull" Masterson's new recruits' age-range: from twenty-five to the late forties. Most of them were from North America and Europe . . . with a few from Australia, African and Asian countries. Fluency in English was a requirement.

"Gentlemen!" Masterson shouted, interrupting their excited chatter. His men were seated in a semi-circle in a clearing outside the dining hall. A full moon provided illumination for the meeting. "You know why you are here. I will give you as many details as possible about our training regimen as that relates to our mission when we arrive at the Vatican to remove the pope.

"I have chosen you because you fit a profile established to flesh out two platoons of forty-five men each. Each platoon will have three squads of thirteen infantry, three medics, two communications specialists, a platoon sergeant and a lieutenant as platoon commander. Lt. Col. Paducca, here," he said, "will serve as my executive officer and Sgt. Major McKenna over here will be our top non-commissioned officer. Both of you please stand." They stood and faced the crowd. "I have chosen six extra men in case of attrition."

"We do not expect any action for several months—it could be a year or two—so we will meet here for one week every two months for physical conditioning, bonding with the units to which you are assigned, and practicing tactical maneuvers which will be used within the confines of the Vatican City State.

"How many of you have visited inside the Vatican walls? I don't mean only Vatican Square and the basilica. I mean have been inside the walls?" About half of the men raised their hands. "Good! We'll be studying the topography, the layout of the buildings, and cover and concealment available in the gardens: all the standard requirements before setting out on a mission to take a military objective.

"All of you have professional military training so I don't need to go into training details. You know that tactical maneuvers involve various types of communication, movements, barriers and deceptions: the list goes on.

"You have been assigned positions and ranks in each of the platoons. We will observe standard military protocol in terms of respect for authority and obedience. Training will begin at 0600 tomorrow with loosening up exercises: then breakfast and introductory classes for the rest of the day. Classes will be taught by me and the platoon commanders. Questions?"

"Yes sir! In the back over here," Col. Masterson said, pointing to a man who stood for identification.

"Sir, my name is Sergeant Jim Collins, from California. Colonel, what kind of weapons will we be carrying when we take over the Vatican?"

"Good question. That is an issue that we have considered carefully and have a simple solution to the problem. As you know, we can't take weapons on flights to Rome and we can't conduct operations within the State of Italy.

"The only place we can legally operate is within the Vatican City State, which is a sovereign country with diplomatic relations with well over a hundred countries."

"Yes, over here," pointing to a man standing in the front row.

"Colonel Masterson. The Vatican and the pope are protected by over one hundred, highly trained Swiss Guards and all that implies. How can we expect to capture the Vatican under such conditions?"

"Let me be clear. Opus Dei and I, of all people, would not seriously consider this mission if we did not believe we have an excellent chance of succeeding without casualties.

"There are strategic plans that have already been worked out which will be revealed to you before the operation begins. Keep in mind; we have sympathetic friends in Italy and in the Vatican who will be assisting us. That's all I will say on this subject."

"And what happens if we fail in our mission?" someone shouted from the center rear, without standing.

"Would the gentleman please stand and identify himself?" He stood.

"Captain Walter Fitzgerald. Australian Special Forces, sir!"

"Captain Fitzgerald, you can pack your bags and go back to Australia. Anyone talking failure doesn't belong here. Since there are no more questions, this meeting is adjourned."

Chapter 61

She couldn't hear the desperate scream launched from the depths of her being. She struggled. But the huge, gloved, left hand crushing her face did not budge. In his right hand, the assassin held a small-bore pistol—with silencer—an inch from her forehead—and fired.

The day following the early-morning murder, Italy's leading daily newspaper, *Il Repubblica,* reported the death of Sister Aurelia Esposito, an employee at the Vatican Bank. She was found in her bed with a bullet wound in her forehead and a rock in her mouth—a Mafia hit . . . and a warning.

Chapter 62

Father Perfecto returned to Tyrone's showroom for training; he needed it before he would be allowed to take the car off the premises. Within a couple days, Perfecto had passed his tests.

"How's the pope faring after the assassination attempt?" Tyrone asked.

"It's as though it never happened," replied Perfecto. "He doesn't want to talk about it. He has more important things on his mind, but I will say it convinced him he needs to use the bullet-proof, glass enclosed popemobile during his audiences in the Square."

"I tried to tell him that. I told him that perimeter security wasn't doing its job, but he wouldn't listen," said Tyrone.

"Did they find out who did it?" asked, Perfecto.

"Yes. Skip said it was a car thief from Southern Italy who had loose mob connections and a reputation for unusual accuracy with a pistol. The would-have-been assassin was the one who killed a Carabinieri patrolman on duty a couple nights before the attempt. Skip suspects one of the Cardinals was behind it, but has no evidence."

"Well, he warned me things could get dicey, but I'm not worried. Anyway, thanks for all you are doing to help me and Pope Immanuel," said Perfecto.

Chapter 63

Father Perfecto Gonzales stood at the head of the polished-oak table in the ornately decorated Quirinale Palace conference room waiting for Pope Immanuel and President Allesandro Bianchi to finish their chat so he could begin his presentation. They were discussing Sister Aurelia's bravery, her unfortunate death and what the pope's enemies might do next.

Perfecto was proud of his PowerPoint presentation—a work of art with its bells, whistles, colored graphs and charts—and he was ready to dazzle his audience of two. The president was telling the pope how impressed he had been with this young priest: his professionalism, knowledge of accounting and finance, and his interpersonal skills. "So," said the President, "are you ready to impress your boss with your brilliant mind, Father Gonzales?"

"Yes sir, I am Mr. President." And so it began: a presentation that lasted a little less than one-half-hour and covered details about the extent to which the organized crime virus had infected almost every aspect of Italian civil society: economic, political, social, financial, and even religious institutions.

Perfecto's sources for his presentation included studies that had been done by the presidential bureaucracy which included journalists' and professors' articles and books, and copies of the reports and documents that Pope Immanuel had provided: the cardinals' analyses, Father Sandusky's report, Father Gonzales' report, and Sister Aurelia's bank documents.

The documents that Sister Aurelia gave the pope were by far the most explosive of all Perfecto's sources and would play a crucial role in the plans the pope and the president would develop.

The purpose of the briefing was to provide a catalyst that could be used as tool for understanding each other's critical, strategic issues. Both leaders understood that their respective responsibilities involved the entire global community. By coordinating their tactical strikes, they might be able to influence the course of history, sort of like the earthquake in the early nineteenth century that changed the course of the mighty Mississippi River.

That lofty aspiration might not seem all that daunting for the most powerful religious leader in the world. But for the president of a small, relatively poor country? How could he have such influence? Father Gonzales' briefing would balance the scale for both men. Italy, indeed, has global influence, not the least of which is its reputation for producing some of the world's most accomplished fine artists and high-style innovators in the garment and automobile industries. Unfortunately, criminality has overshadowed the core of that reality.

Perfecto started his briefing showing a map of Italy, with the football at its toe. With his laser pointer, he circled Sicily, Calabria, Naples and Milan as he explained the major regions (Sicily, southern, central and northern) where gangsters, belonging to separate systems, operate.

"Books and articles, of which President Bianci is aware, provide detailed accounts of how devastating this situation is to normal family life in Italy. In deference to President Bianci's detailed knowledge of gangster activity . . . and not needing recount them in this briefing, I have included a separate summary, in writing, of those accounts for you, Your Holiness.

"Now, shifting gears; Pope Immanuel asked me and Father Sandusky to spend several months researching and writing reports on a wide-ranging list of topics, all related to the history and current state of the Church and how that information conflates with potential reforms. Father Sandusky's area is located in doctrinal areas; my responsibility involves issues surrounding finance, power and scandalous events. Of course, my area also includes organized crime: specifically the Vatican bank and its dealings with the Mafia. So we'll deal with that separately from what I've already discussed.

"Pope Immanuel wanted to know what professors, authors and journalists (Catholic and non-Catholic) are recommending. In a nut-shell, the recommendations vary from fairly minor adjustments (recommendations that came from several cardinals) to simply throwing in the towel and calling it quits. By the latter I mean, dissolving the superstructure of the Catholic Church, thereby giving each diocese the freedom to organize and worship as it best serves its congregants—without Vatican control or interference.

"Admittedly, that idea sounds somewhat bizarre until you realize that that kind of freedom is what happened in the British-American colonies where people were free to worship as they pleased.

"The process of exercising that freedom has not stopped; today over 1,200 Christian sects and denominations thrive around the world. In other words, 'do what serves your spiritual desires and needs—until it doesn't, then try something else.'"

"In America, rented room and store-front congregations appear like mushrooms in the spring, and sometimes disappear almost as rapidly in the fall.

"But a few survive and some become mega-churches with world-wide TV audiences. In the United States, at least one Catholic congregation voted to separate from the Vatican; in one major city over thirty percent of the congregants in several churches indicated the desire to do the same. I found no studies indicating how wide-spread this phenomenon is.

"So, Your Holiness . . ." Perfecto paused for effect, "you have many options at your disposal. Before I finish, you may be asking: 'Where is the towel? I want to give it a toss.'" he said, accompanied by his signature smile.

"Well, Father, before President Bianchi's expectations soar over the moon I want the record to show that I'm not planning anything *that* radical. However, I'm keeping all options open."

"You're my man, Holiness . . . ." Backtracking slightly from what could appear inappropriate familiarity with his boss, Perfecto said, "I'm sorry Holiness, I couldn't resist it."

"Please proceed," said the pope, with an approving smile.

"Okay. My PowerPoint presentation hits the highlights of written reports you have in front of you, so allow me to touch on a few major outcomes of our research into the issues.

"Father Sandusky's research involved founding of the Roman Catholic Church and its history to the present. Hundreds of books have been written on the subject. My presentation can only mention the outcomes of major events, although our reports provide detailed analysis.

"The early Church was founded in a doctrinal, war-like atmosphere. The conflict was primarily with a group of Christians called the Gnostics, who claimed that Jesus came as a teacher of divine wisdom, not to atone for the sins of mankind.

"The winner of the dispute was the Catholic Church, which embedded its doctrine in the myths of the Old Testament, thereby adopting the concept of an angry God and all that that implies in terms of various types of violence. Historians, professors and journalists have documented violent acts ranging from the mythical acts within the First Family to our current pedophiliac scandals.

"The losers of the war, the Gnostics, recorded many of Jesus' sayings which diametrically oppose Catholic doctrine, a fact that is documented in St. Irenaeus's *Against Heresies, which is* a diatribe of falsifications, straw-men, and cherry-picking the most bizarre (to Irenaeus) myths to knock down. gear

"The Gnostics were harassed, driven out of their seminaries and monasteries, and their books destroyed. Fortunately, some of their books were buried in secret places along the Nile River and remained there until they were discovered in the last century.

"We have English translations of the Gospel of Judas and thirteen books in the Nag Hammadi Library. These books belie St. Irenaeus's claims and give us crucial, additional evidence that Jesus is among many teachers (of divine wisdom, including Eastern Masters such as Lord Krishna, Buddha, and Shankara and Moses, in the Middle East) who have had their teachings inverted, leading humanity astray, into an abyss of ignorance.

"The latest revelation of divine wisdom came to us within the last fifteen years in the form of some dialogues, purportedly between 'God' and Neale Donald Walsch, who recorded and published the dialogues in three books, titled *Conversations with God (CwG)*. The three books have been published in one volume, resulting in 744 pages.

"In these books, God observes that current religions have done a very bad job of representing who **He** *really is* and that the consequences have been devastating for humanity and the world, as we know it. The "world as we know it," within the confines of the three monotheistic religions (Judaism, Christianity and Islam), is confined to the planet Earth, insofar as intelligent life is concerned. Yet, that is a blinkered—even blindfolded—view of reality, according to God.

"One could make comparisons between Christian doctrine found in Catholicism and a New Spiritual Paradigm recorded in *Conversations with God;* Father Sandusky has indicated he will get to it when he can.

"Your Holiness and Mr. President, I am taking a 'devil's advocate' approach in this part of my presentation for a reason: Whatever decisions you make, Holiness, these are the types of issues you will face as you analyze the power, authority and respectability of the Church.

"Now, one final issue before I depart and leave you to your private deliberations: the Vatican Bank. This will undoubtedly be the most explosive issue that you will face, Holiness, because it lies at the core of the power of the Church. In other words, 'money talks': even in religion—especially our Church. There will be hell to pay for any pope who dares to tinker with the bank, as John Paul I found out.

"You have all the details you need from Sister Aurelia's documents to prove egregious violations of lawful banking practices that involve 'cut-out banks'. While other countries (including the United States) have criminal elements using such banks for all kinds of fraudulent activity, none of the criminal elements—owning and/or controlling the banks—represent large religious bodies.

"According to an article in the London Daily Telegraph in 2001, 'Top scoring 'cut-out' countries, which make it hard to trace the ill-gotten gains back to the getter, are Mauritius, **Vatican City,** Macao and Nauru followed by Luxembourg and South Africa. According to Paul Williams—author of *Vatican Exposed: Money, Murder and the Mafia*—the criminal activity of the Vatican Bank continued well into the twenty first century.

"So, there you have it: an overview of documented evidence of illegal activity that amounts to billions of dollars over several decades. These activities involve people and banks in other countries, not just Italy. What Your Holiness and President Bianchi should do about it is well above my pay-grade level of advice.

"Are there any questions?" There were no questions, but both thanked Perfecto for his presentation and work in preparing the reports for their review. Father Gonzales gathered his presentation instruments and documents and departed.

The pope and the president took a brief coffee and cookies break and returned to the conference room.

President Bianchi spoke first. "Well, Your Holiness, I have the smoking gun (Sister Aurelia's documents) and Russo's testimony. I need to clinch the evidence we will need to convict dozens of Italian criminals. We can share that evidence with other countries that have people who are directly involved. What you do as the supreme ruler of the Vatican City State and the Holy See is your business. Yet, I want assure you of my full cooperation in assisting in any way possible as you seek to clean up the mess you inherited."

"Mr. President, I welcome your very generous offer and I can assure you I will do everything I can to assist you and your efforts as well. At this point, I really don't know precisely what I will do, because I need to contemplate what is possible and then decide what is appropriate in terms of the moral issues and the interests of humanity.

"You know, President Bianchi, since Father said that one of the options available to me is to 'throw in the towel', I have had thoughts about what that option might involve; they have been only fleeting thoughts. But I'm wondering if we could discuss that issue for a moment before lunch."

"Certainly, Your Holiness, what are you thinking?'

"Allow me to speak extemporaneously for a few moments. First, you should know that my purpose all along has been—and remains—to initiate reforms on a broad front, ranging from doctrinal and procedural issues, to personnel issues, the extremes that may flow from the Vatican Bank documents, and last but by no means the least, the pederasty scandals that could spread to every country where we have priests around the globe. I need a little time to absorb the reports that Sandusky and prepared. Barring some unexpected event that produces further information and/or evidence, I have no intention to "throw in the towel," as Perfecto puts it.

"Nevertheless, I have this nagging feeling that we should prepare for any eventuality, including the 'towel' business.

"I recommend that we begin immediate, joint, strategic, operational planning that will study how we can optimize our resources to strike simultaneously at the core of our problems . . . *should* I decide to simply dissolve the Roman Catholic Church."

"Your Holiness, I'm surprised that you would seriously consider such an option."

"I'm sure you are, and I should say I'm a little surprised to hear myself say it. It is not something I have ever intended to do. But as the evidence mounts, I'm beginning to wonder if significant, life-transforming reforms are even possible.

"Assuming I survive sweeping reforms, which is doubtful . . . soon after I'm gone, the conservative powers inside and outside the Church would mount efforts to undo the reforms and return to the sordid 'business as usual' that we are experiencing today.

"However, if I were to attempt drastic internal reforms instead of the 'towel business' we are discussing, years of chaos –not unlike those that erupted when Gorbachev attempted to reform the Soviet Union—could ensue and end the same way the Soviet Union did."

"But Your Holiness, the Catholic Church is not the Soviet Union."

"Of course, Mr. President, but I didn't start noticing the similarities just now, yesterday or even a few months ago. Ever since that communist empire collapsed—an event that seemed impossible before it happened—I have wondered about the vulnerability of my Church. I don't want to go into the details of comparison here, but suffice it to say, they are numerous and quite alarming. That's a possibility I need to consider when I'm thinking about my options.

"Now, as I think we both have suspected all along, the bank issue is emerging, not only as a hub of our problems, but like a festering boil, it is coming to a head. According to Sister Aurelia—God rest her soul—Mr. Russo, my bank manager, fears for his life. He's been engaging in criminal activities on behalf of the Vatican for decades and now has some options: (1) If he retires, he will be dead before he reaches his office door because of all he knows; (2) he could remain and resist efforts I make for reform, thereby at least saving his life; (3) he could come to me with his confession, resign and ask for protection; (4) he could wait for me to go to him and ask for his cooperation. There may other options, but those come to me at the moment."

"Given what you have said so far, it seems to me the last option is the most viable."

"Why is that Mr. President?"

"Well, because many rewards accumulate from that. First, you would be saving him from his most pressing misery and he might want the opportunity avoid at least some of the unpleasant consequences of criminal prosecution. He would be an invaluable asset to our prosecutors when they haul the criminals into court. You could talk to him and offer him that option. My guess is he'd take you up on your offer, but I see problems in terms of timing." The president paused to think.

"What are you thinking?" asked the pope.

"He's already in grave danger of being murdered for all the obvious reasons. If we wait to act, we might be too late. But now that I think of it, he probably has not communicated his fears to anyone other than Sister Aurelia so our enemies in this game might not know that he is any less loyal to them today than he has been for decades.

To them, it might very well be that the longer he stays on the job, the more secure their assets are. After all, the assassins and their bosses sent him a powerful warning, undoubtedly meant for Mr. Russo, when they killed Sister Aurelia and left a rock in her mouth," said the president.

"So what do you recommend we do?"

"My advice at the moment is to do nothing about Mr. Russo. He's not a stupid man, having been in charge of your bank for decades. My guess is that he will stay where he is until you make a move to upset the bank's apple cart. When you do that, not only will the apples spill, but all hell will break loose and the only thing I will predict is that the consequences will not be pretty. The good news is that we—you and I—have the advantage of controlling when you grab the wheels of the apple cart and give it the heave-ho," said President Bianchi.

"I've been thinking while you were talking that Mr. Russo could be a big help in making plans to transfer the Vatican bank to your control, if that should turn out to be our decision."

"Yes, of course he would, but his being in our midst to do that is not essential to our success. With Perfecto's expertise in accounting and finance, working on your behalf with my financial people, we could get all the necessary paperwork ready for your signature in a few weeks and have it ready when we make our moves."

"Okay, then," said the pope. Thank you for your advice. I'll leave my banker alone for the time being and see what happens. Now, I want to touch briefly on our strategy for the next few months.

"Our moves," the pope continued, "as you have been referring to them, will involve the assistance of your military forces and, as you mentioned, perhaps NATO Special Operations Forces."

"I agree, Your Holiness. We are only a few months if not weeks away from when we will make our nation-wide strike against the organized criminal elements. Our so-called 'national disaster training exercises,' that involved major military movements in every region of my country, have been very successful and they are ready to move anytime I give the order."

"I am pleased to hear that," said the pope. "Let me suggest this: I will brief the commander of the Swiss Guards about our planning and suggest that he contact your top military commander to begin joint planning sessions with their respective subordinates. It is not inconceivable that I may need assistance of your military and the NATO Special Forces to maintain order and the safety of some of us in the Vatican, should things get nasty.

"I will notify you immediately, should I decide to use the proverbial "towel" to solve my problems, but as I have indicated, I want to do everything we can to be ready, should that become an option—an unlikely one at this point, but one never knows."

"Okay, I think my chefs have lunch ready for us. I invited Father to join us for lunch. He's quite a fine young man, he is."

"Yes, I agree. Oh, my goodness! That's as close as I get to swearing, Mr. President," the pope said with a smile. "I don't think I made clear that 'throwing in the towel' included disbanding the entire bureaucratic infrastructure at the Vatican and transferring the entire estate to your country.

"I would, with the stroke of my pen, declare the Vatican City State non-existent as a Catholic entity, and I would transfer to you all the assets that the Vatican owns, not only within the ancient walls of the Vatican, but all the buildings in Rome.

"As you know the Vatican does not own any of world-wide church assets; each diocese owns the churches, rectories and has investments that the Vatican can't touch; so we don't need to concern ourselves with that issue. I would also, at that same moment, dissolve the Holy See.

"We will need to meet again soon to discuss ramifications to set the direction for our subordinates to work together to have all the paperwork done when we make our move in that direction, should that happen."

"In that regard," replied President Bianchi, "I've thought of a name for this nascent operation we've been discussing. What do you think of "OPERATION STRIKE?"

"Sounds good to me," replied the pope.

Chapter 64

(Continuation of Master's Thesis)

Having summarized Blech and Doliner's "secrets" related to our topic and expressed scepticism about some of their interpretations, we can now move on to <u>our</u> understanding of what Michelangelo was up to when he painted the *Last Judgment*—the rest of the story.

Our analysis is more closely associated with Christian doctrine than Judaism, although, as pointed out elsewhere, Judaism and Christianity have a symbiotic relationship.

While our analysis and theirs' involve revealing both secrets and deceptions, in some cases our revelations imply blatant skullduggery.

For example, we think the *Last Judgment* is, by a long shot, far more deceptive than the Sistine ceiling because its title purports to be an authoritative, artistic representation of the Second Coming of Christ, yet is saturated with messages that suggest there is no such event in the works for humanity.

Of course, the ceiling is deceiving as well, because, it was supposed to have been a story about the papal family, Jesus, Mary, the apostles, and possibly John the Baptist. Instead it is a story beginning with Creation and ending with Noah in a drunken stupor and two men posing in a homoerotic act.

We believe Michelangelo embedded "secrets" in the *Last Judgment* that Blech and Doliner missed precisely because they assumed that the fresco behind the altar is, in fact, what the artist intended: a portrayal of the Second Coming of Christ. Ergo, the thrust of our analysis: The overarching theme is fourfold: (1) there will be no "last judgment"; (2) Michelangelo's ridicule of the papacy; (3) derision of the Church's doctrine of fear and terror; and (4) exposure of the misery the Church has foisted on humanity.

We will discuss our interpretation of the evidence that supports our thesis in the context of: (1) the title; (2) lack of joy in the painting; (3) the massive display of naked genitals and buttocks; (4) the absence of children; (5) Michelangelo's portrayal of himself; (6) The Unborn Truth; and (7) A gloomy patina removed by restorers.

1. THE ERSATZ *LAST JUDGMENT*. The first deception of the painting is the title: The fresco is not what the title indicates and what the painting appears to be. The following deceptions support that conclusion.

2. "JOY, THOU BEAUTIOUS SPARK SENT FROM GOD": Where is it?

The expressions on the faces of the four hundred characters are devoid of joy. We challenge anyone to find more than one face replete with joy in this painting. One would expect to find joy on the faces of those moving toward heaven; it is absent. We found one woman in the lower-left quadrant of the fresco in a pose that suggests blissful gratitude for the salvation of her soul. All other facial expressions are somewhere between indifference and down-right hostility. We think the blissful woman is a counter-point—a point of contrast—to all other expressions: *This is ecstasy! Do you see it anywhere else?*

The "spin" some critics and apologists have provided to account for the lack of joy is that the final judgment is yet to be announced. Thus, those who are heading toward heaven are not presupposing salvation, even though—according to Catholic doctrine—they were "saved" or "condemned" imme-diately after death and this is merely a public display of their respective fates.

If a personal judgment granting salvation happened immediately after death, why the lack of joy? And why the rampant hostility—most notably amongst Jesus disciples? Did they first hear shocking news from God Him-self that they are condemned to hell, and now they are demanding a reversal of that decision from the second and last judge—Jesus Christ? If so, one can understand their hostility, because what they are seeing is anything but a sec-ond and "last judgment" in progress; they desperately want one—they want Jesus to reverse God's decision!

They are seeing a blissful Jesus modeled on the pagan god Apollo, and Jesus pregnant lover, Mary Magdalene—unconcerned about the whole scene—sit-ting at Jesus side, staring at her buttocks and swelled belly, drawing the view-er's attention to that area of her body. *Look at me! I am pregnant with our child.*

Jesus' left arm is a barrier protecting him and Mary Magdalene from the angry disciples as if to say: *Go away. I am not the righteous judge you were expect-ing. If you manage to breach this barrier, my right hand will drive you back; there is no judgment going on here.*

The artist created a veil of negativity—evident from the absence of joy—that permeates the entire fresco. For the artist, the hurly-burly of tangled bod-ies, with every expression imaginable on their faces—except joy—creates a depressing view of humanity , , , the result of a corrupt Church and its doctrine of negativity.

When asked, after he had completed the painting, to change it to suit his critics, Michelangelo's reply was that the suitability of the painting was a small matter compared to what the popes had done to their people; when the popes changed their ways, changes in the painting would follow.

We think Michelangelo was not only referring to the nudity, but to the entire painting. He was showing the lack of joy in peoples' lives and the horrors—people condemned to an eternity in hell—which the Church had inflicted on humanity. But, *Guess what! There is hope for those who see what I have done in this fresco because there will be no "last judgment."*

3. A NUDIST COLONY EXPOSE`: The third deception is Michelangelo's famous "excessive" display of male genitals, female breasts, and buttocks of both genders. This deception epitomizes the artist's ridicule of the papacy. He knew how they would react: He was holding up a mirror to their pathological view of human nakedness.

At the unveiling ceremony, Pope Paul VII fell to his knees and reportedly declared: "Lord, charge me not with my sins when thou shalt come on the Day of Judgment." (That was the first reaction, confirming once again, our emphasis on the Church's doctrine having at its core fear and terror.) Then . . . there was laughter amongst the assembled dignitaries invited to the august event.

The amused crowd noticed something very funny. In the lower right corner, Minos—the Judge of the Underworld—is standing with a serpent wrapped around his body; his genitals are in the mouth of the snake. The likeness of "Minos" is none other than the pope's Master of Ceremonies, Biagio da Cesena.

Biagio made the mistake of telling the artist that "it was mostly disgraceful that in so sacred a place there should have been depicted all those nude figures, exposing themselves so shamefully," and that such displays belong in a bordello.

When Cesena complained to the pope about the insult and asked him to make Michelangelo remove it from the fresco, the pope is said to reply that his jurisdiction did not extend to hell; the painting would remain unaltered.

This assault by a serpent on the genitals of the Judge of the Underworld is a clear message that the surrounding scene of the condemned entering hell is a joke: a necessary integral part of a "last judgment" scene—certainly—but a deception because the apparent "last judgment" is an illusion.

Given the Church's attitude toward human sexuality from the beginning to Michelangelo's time, it is not surprising that the *Last Judgment* became an object of derision and a basis for dispute between the artist and the Church hierarchy.

Cardinal Carafa started a movement known as the "Fig-Leaf Campaign" to have the offending nudity removed: The immorality and obscenities of hundreds of naked figures inside the most sacred chapel in Christendom was intolerable.

His campaign was not immediately successful, but twenty-four years later, shortly after the Council of Trent ended in 1563 and the artist's death in 1564, Daniele da Volterra, an Italian painter and sculptor, was commissioned to cover the offending genitals and buttocks in the fresco.

He became known as the "Breeches Maker." Before he completed his commission to cover all the offending bare genitals and buttocks, the pope died. Because they needed the chapel for the pope's funeral, the scaffolding was removed; Volterra's work stopped.

Over the next several centuries, the remaining offending sights were covered. During the restoration of both Sistine frescoes in the latter part of the twentieth century, all of the loin cloths and buttocks drapes were removed except for what Volterra painted.

Volterra did more than cover genitals and buttocks. In the far-right center, of the painting, St. Catherine, in a green and yellow drape, holds a broken wheel; behind her is St. Blaise holding the iron combs of his martyrdom. *This is _not_ what Michelangelo painted.* In the original poses, St. Catherine is bent over having sexual intercourse with St. Blaise, who is standing behind her looking at her bare buttocks.

What does a massive display of nudity and a couple having intercourse have to do with the artist's deceptions? He thought his frescoes would be a perfect place to present the authorities with a mirror image of their absurdities.

Ergo: the hundreds of "obscenities" foisted on the popes and the public. But are "private" body parts obscenities? Michelangelo didn't think so; they are integral parts of the most magnificent of God's creations—the human body.

> Nor does God in his grace show himself to me elsewhere
> More clearly than in a graceful and mortal veil:
> And that alone do I love because in this he is mirrored.

Here it is fitting that I pause and sleep a while,

So that I may return to my terrestrial veil in all its beauty.

So that I may make eternal in stone my terrestrial veil.

(Clements, *The Poetry of Michelangelo,* p. 75)

And . . .

He who made the whole made every part,

And then from the whole chose the most beautiful part,

To exhibit here below his most lofty creations,

As he has now done with his divine art. (Clements, p 63)

Michelangelo wanted to show the human body in all its glory, including its genitals and buttocks. Apparently to him, "in all its glory" meant in a buffed, body-building image, even for female bodies. All naked bodies in the *Last Judgment* are buffed; even "Mary's" right bicep looks like she's been pumping iron to get in shape.

Other female bodies have male torsos with female parts, namely breasts, stuck on chests, looking like falsies. In other paintings, even children and some babies look as though they had started their body-building regimen in the womb.

Historians have speculated about this aspect of the *Last Judgment* and his other works of art where the same phenomenon occurs. Their conclusions are nearly as plentiful as there are critics and historians. Our conclusion is that it is a product of the artist's knowledge of human anatomy and physiology; he is putting on display the musculature potential of the body.

All of which leads us from generalities about the artist's deceptions associated with the exposure of genitals and buttocks to more specific reasons why we think this deception holds a place amongst the other deceptions which illustrate our thesis: this is no "last judgment." Jesus helps us understand what Michelangelo was getting at in the following parable:

In the non-New Testament Gospel of Thomas, Jesus' disciples ask when he would reveal himself to them. Jesus replies that when they take all their clothes off and trample on them like little children; then you will see the son of the living one and you will not be afraid. Scholars have varying opinions about what Jesus said; here's our view.

Jesus doesn't mean that if the disciples take off their clothes and trample on them, he will reveal himself and thereby become visible to them. *No. When your consciousness rises to a level that nakedness is as natural for you as it is for a child running around naked, then you will have achieved the blessed innocence that comes with inner, divine self-realization.*

Make that your goal and your sexual pathology will disappear and your need for a doctrine of fear and terror will dissipate like steam above a pot of boiling water. There will be no "last judgment" because there is nothing to judge.

4. WHERE HAVE ALL THE CHILDREN GONE? The fourth deception is the absence of children in the painting. Where are the billions of God's little ones: children who have died—or are living when Christ returns—represented in this painting? There *is* no representation: a stunning nonappearance of a third of the human race at the "last judgment." Why?

We think this is another major pillar holding high the banner of our thesis: *There will be no "last judgment" because there is no need for one.*

It was incomprehensible to the artist that God would create such magnificence—innocent children who would become magnificent adults—to be condemned to an eternity in hell if they didn't submit to the tyranny of the Church.

How can there be a "final judgment" with one third of humanity not in attendance? Is there an encore in store for obedient children headed for heaven and disobedient children condemned to hell?

We think Michelangelo was suggesting that, if there were no children for the Church to lead astray with their doctrine of an angry and vengeful God, there would be no need for a final judgment because there would be nothing to judge: no original sin, no sins of omission, no sins of commission, no need for redemption and no need for a redeemer.

Jesus is neither a redeemer/condemner, nor a judge. Therefore, in the fresco behind the Sistine altar, there is no judgment in progress; there is only a deceptive appearance of a final judgment of humanity.

5. MICHELANGELO, WHEREFORE ART THOU? Our fifth analysis of the artist's deceptions is Michelangelo's likeness of himself. In the painting, to the right of Jesus left leg, St. Bartholomew sits holding the knife that was used to skin him alive—or, so the spin goes. In his left hand he holds—what traditionalist critics declare—St. Bartholomew's full-body, shriveled skin. But the face is not his: it is Michelangelo's. If anyone doubts that Michelangelo is engaging in deception in this painting, the doubts should be removed with this deception.

The deception of the face was not discovered until 1925, 384 years after the painting was finished. In general, scholars do not think the face has anything to do with the function of the painting, but that critics use this image to provide insights into the artist's psyche.

However, it seems obvious, if you take it out of the context of Catholic doctrine and place it into the context Michelangelo's other deceptions, it becomes, while not necessarily an obvious deception, one of the most important deceptions in the painting.

Here we have Michelangelo telling us that his body will die and shrivel . . . that's it: end of story for the body. What he is telling us is that his body will not be resurrected to ascend into heaven *nor* descend into hell because there will be no "*last judgment*" and thus, no resurrection nor descent for the human body.

His is the only "body" in the painting that isn't "resurrected" with the skin in the process of being expanded with bones and flesh as other characters are, amongst the living and the dead. His body will stay in a shriveled state and eventually turn to dust: but the dust will not be gathered together to form a new body at the "*last judgment*" because no "*last judgment*" will occur.

The preferred view amongst critics is that the skin belongs to St. Bartholomew: that he is holding his own skin in one hand and in the other a knife which was used to skin him alive at his death . . . so the spin goes.

But notice that he is wearing his skin now; if the artist had wanted the shriveled skin to be St. Bartholomew's skin, he would have painted him without his skin, with the subcutaneous musculature showing. Historians know that the artist studied human anatomy in detail and could have painted a skinned Bartholomew as proof that the skin was his.

Nevertheless, some art critics assert that the artist painted his own face on St. Bartholomew's skin: Michelangelo's signature on the painting.

That could be a plausible explanation, except for one thing: Look at the knife St. Bartholomew is holding. It is not what he was holding in the original painting: The saint was holding a sculpturing tool with a knob on the end. When the painting was restored in the late twentieth century, the sculpturing tool was painted over and a knife painted in its place—a shameful attempt on the part of the restorers to deceive viewers; by altering the artist's intentions, the knife in St. Bartholomew's hand supports the spin that the shriveled skin is his own skin, not Michelangelo's.

Michelangelo, by putting a sculpturing tool in St. Bartholomew's hand was suggesting that the skin in the other hand was none other than his own skin attached to his head, the identifier of the skin. *See, I'm not being judged; My body is not going to heaven in this scene, nor is it going to hell; this is not a "last judgment" because none will occur.*

6. THE UNBORN TRUTH: The portrayal of Jesus and "Mary" is our sixth and most explosive evidence of deception in the fresco.

First, we will discuss the two figures' contributions to our thesis separately, debunking traditional assessments of their roles in the painting.

Jesus in not sitting on an elaborate, elevated throne, surrounded by pillars, decorated with plush draperies, flowers, and vines constructed to impress upon his subjects his lofty status—thus, reinforcing his elevated, divine status, emphasizing his apocalyptic decisions.

Instead he seems to be sitting on a rock on his right buttock, the left one hanging over the edge with his left leg propping him up. Some art historians have him rising to pronounce the judgment that has not yet taken place. Yet, there is no such motion, nor is there a judgment about to occur.

This image of a modest and compassionate Jesus is another slap in the papal face and a spear in the heart of orthodox Christian doctrine. Contrast Christ's image here with the image of popes (from ancient times to today) dressed up in fine, expensive, ostentatious gowns, wearing silk shoes and party hats, carrying elongated, gaudy staffs and sitting on huge elevated thrones, surrounded by sycophants.

The image the Jews were expecting to see in their prophesied messiah was a charismatic leader who would restore Israel to its mythical glory days under the reign of Kind David.

Instead, they got an itinerant carpenter/preacher, who, to them, did little more than stir up trouble amongst the masses, spread false doctrine and question their authoritative, male-dominated religion. And now, Michelangelo is reminding the Church leaders of their misguided expectations and the popes of their deplorable stewardship of Jesus' legacy.

What better place to remind the popes of their perfidy than here in the *Last Judgment* where there is no "last judgment" occurring. For Michelangelo, it's a double whammy: *Not only have you substituted Jesus message of love and compassion with your depraved, false doctrine of sin, redemption and condemnation, you have blasphemed his name with your pompous, hollow posturing as His vicar here on earth.*

You have made the lives of your people miserable, which I have demonstrated here with the hurly burly of tangled and troubled bodies dominating the scene.

And you can take this for good measure: If you look at the upper left corner of the fresco, you will see a young man, (directly below the head of the man at the bottom of the cross) who has his right hand on the upper right arm of the woman with a blue truss to hold her yellow hair in place.

Here I am giving you the proverbial "fig," or "finger" (thumb between index and middle finger), as it were, to support those who interpret my painting as I have intended. It is an in-your-face blast at your hypocrisy and a clue to the deceptiveness of this fresco.

Now, we turn to "Mary." You may have noticed we have been placing her name in quotation marks—for good reason: She is not the mother of Jesus; she is Mary Magdalene, one of the three major "Mary" figures in the New Testament—the other two: Mary the mother of Jesus and Mary, the sister of Martha, the busy-body who preferred to scurry around the house, while her sister preferred to sit and listen to Jesus talk.

Blech and Doliner's analysis of the *Last Judgment* assumes that this fresco is a portrayal of the end of the time—the end of life on Earth as we know it: the apocalypse. They point out anomalies similar to those noted by most art critics: for example, the artist's use of the Apollo head to represent Jesus, instead of the bearded ones we usually see. Blech and Doliner see—correctly—numerous references to Jewish mysticism represented symbolically in Kabbalistic doctrine. And Michelangelo points out Jews embracing and headed toward heaven.

Yet we think the authors of *Sistine Secrets* were unable to see the forest for the trees. They failed to see the two "holy ones"—Jesus and Mary Magdalene—occupying a yin and yang pose in a womb, waiting to be born through the birth-canal opening, protected by two saints and the two people Michelangelo loved most: Vittoria Colonna and Tommaso dei Cavalieri. As Blech and Doliner point out, the bottom rung of the grill . . . which Saint Lawrence is holding , , , is the **exact center of the fresco**; the middle of the bottom rung also draws our attention to the opening of the birth canal, emphasizing the profound significance of this deception.

Blech and Doliner also seem to ignore the blatant hostility directed toward the two in the Womb of Truth; we know of no art critics, nor Catholic apologists who satisfactorily explain this phenomenon: the pervasive facial expressions of hostility on both sides of the womb.

Two hostile figures grab our attention: They are precisely the same distance from the target of their glares: Jesus. The tilt of their heads and the expressions on their faces are exactly the same, as though Peter were staring at himself in a mirror. Peter stares from Jesus' left and the other (an unidentified) figure, stares from the right. It is as if the Michelangelo created "two Peter's" to double the intensity of the stare focused on Jesus to maximize the anger Peter feels toward Jesus for what he is doing.

And what is Jesus doing? We'll see in a moment.

To understand that, we need to know who his "twin" is; all art critics have assumed it is his mother.

Is it a womb? We think it is because it has the shape of a womb and a birth canal, and is located beneath what appear to be two, ample, female breasts. The opening of the birth canal is located at the exact center of the fresco—in the center of the bottom rung of St. Lawrence's grill—elevating its importance: it is through this opening that the Truth will emerge.

What is the Truth?

Clearly, Jesus is the dominant figure in the fresco. Located in the upper center of the painting, he sits in a pose that nearly all critics interpret to be one of a judge damning unrepentant sinners to hell: Jesus is ready to strike the final blow with his right arm. The authors of *Sistine Secrets* agree with this interpretation.

Nevertheless, Blech and Doliner also have Jesus pre-occupied with Cavalieri, his dearest love, in an eye-to-eye lock, which is impossible because the "gaze" would need to make a forty-five degree turn in order for their eyes to meet. Gazes don't bend. If Jesus is gazing at anything in particular, it is at the man with yellow hair holding his fist in Jesus' face.

Yet, we think his gaze is only toward the angry crowd to his left. We don't think Jesus gaze—as interpreted by Blech and Doliner—is consistent with the Jesus poised to blast sinners into hell with his right arm . . . an interpretation, we repeat, they assert along with so many others.

Why all the anger coming from Peter, Jesus' disciples and other religious followers on both sides of the womb? We think the source of their anger has something to do with his "twin", the co-occupier of the Womb of Truth: Mary Magdalene.

The "twin" is not Mary the mother of Jesus; clearly the woman Jesus is protecting from the angry mobs around him and his twin is Mary of Magdala: the woman Jesus loved more than anyone else; the woman he kissed on the mouth; the woman who, in this painting is bearing his child. *Mary Magdalene, in this fresco, is pregnant.*

Her left index finger is pointing—saying, *Look at me! Can you see I am pregnant? Do you see the blue drape falling away, exposing my right buttock and my swelled belly? Do you see the red dress I'm wearing?*

The blue drape is a deception to make it look like I'm Jesus' Mother because she is often portrayed in blue. However, as you can see, the blue drape has fallen so far down that it exposes "Mother Mary's" backside: she is exposed for who she really is—a human like all the rest of us, not some divine goddess to be worshipped. "Mother Mary" is not who she appears to be in this fresco.

(The Church altered the painting here as well; it covered "Mother Mary's" backside with a green drape and painted over Mary's exposed leg which shows beneath the blue cloth in the original painting.)

I—Mary Magdalene informs us—on the other hand, am dressed in red, for two reasons: The Church maliciously characterized me as a harlot and their artists dressed me in red-light-district red to emphasize my alleged depravity. They maligned me because they feared that the power of my leadership in **our** *nascent Christian Church—based on love and compassion—would interfere with* **their** *developing "Christian" doctrine based on fear and terror.*

I was the leader of the women who followed and learned from Jesus and remained loyal to him when you, Peter, along with your proud and ignorant comrades denied Jesus and fled when the authorities came to murder him . . . fearing for your lives. I remained with Jesus while he was crucified. I was the first to discover his empty tomb and I was the first to speak to him when he re-constituted himself in human form after his death.

I was one of the few to whom Jesus revealed the secrets of the universe . . . knowledge, which you, Peter, in your ignorance, could not understand. In your unawareness and arrogance, you and your followers established a church based on fear and terror while crushing the movement that was based on the truth revealed to me by Jesus: a truth based on the love of God and love of our neighbors as ourselves.

So now, here you and your cohorts are, outraged that Jesus and I have come together, not to judge, but to bear witness to the truth that you squashed during your triumphant victory over us. When our place in this womb and the truth we bear is discovered (born), you will know that your disgraceful end is imminent.

Jesus' left arm is raised as a barrier to hold off the angry mob to his left—to protect Mary and their unborn child; and to preserve the truth for generations to come. His right arm is raised, poised to strike back, if the mad disciples, led by Peter, breach his first line of defense. The Truth will be protected and descend through the birth canal, past Michelangelo's dearest friends guarding the opening.

That Truth is the same truth that Jesus spoke: it was recorded by his faithful followers. Some of what he said has already been "born"—has come to us in recent revelations liberated from their hiding places in the Middle East: the

Gospel of Judas and the Nag Hammadi Library found along the Nile River south of Cairo in the last century. Other Truth has come to us from teachers of divine wisdom and God's messengers.

The truth in the womb is not frozen there for eternity. It is born every time a soul—discovering what Jesus and other masters teach—become Self-realized; when that happens, Il Spirituali (the spiritual ones)—residing in more highly evolved societies—rejoice.

7. IF IT DOESN'T FIT, TAKE IT OFF: The last deception involves the *Last Judgment's* restorers removing the artist's final touch on the fresco: a gloomy patina.

The removal of the patina created a split amongst art historians and critics. Some of the professionals believed the restorers deliberately removed the patina and replaced it with bright, shining, flashy colors to arouse a feeling of delight in the viewer.

Others were outraged that those employed by the Vatican to restore the painting to its original state had employed a slash and burn strategy: an outrageous act of vandalism to invert what the great artist had intended. The restorer's response was that they had discovered a previously unknown attribute of Michelangelo's genius: "He's a colorist!"

We side with the critics; what they aver is consistent with the deceptions we have discovered and what we believe they were intended to convey to anyone who had eyes to see what he had done: there will be no "last judgment." The murky patina was designed to enhance an already gloomy portrait of what the popes had done to the people they served; they had presented the people with a religion based on fear and terror: *you had better pay attention, because at the end of your life you will be judged. If you don't get it right, you will go to hell.* Michelangelo ridicules this gloomy perception of humanity and tells us there will *be* no last judgment.

CONCLUSION

In this paper, we have used a simple paradigm (noted above and repeated below) through which to analyze *the Last Judgment.* Each of our seven deceptions indicates that the artist's *Last Judgment* is not what it appears to be; each deception is unique in terms of its contribution to our thesis; that is, some deceptions are more compelling than others in terms of their value in supporting our thesis that there will be no "last judgment"; others carry more weight in one of the other three elements of our fourfold paradigm: *(1) No "last judgment" in progress; (2) ridicule of the papacy; (3) derision of the Church's doctrine of fear and terror; and (4) exposure of the misery the Church has foisted on humanity.*

Michelangelo's duplicity (creating a fresco which appears to be something it is not) communicates to us that the religion invented by the founders of the Catholic Church is a fraud. The cynicism that produced such behavior is unfathomable; no attempt is made to investigate it.

Nevertheless, a clue exists. In the Gnostic *Gospel of Mary,* Mary Magdalene has just finished giving the disciples an answer to a question she asked Jesus: whether one sees a vision through the soul or through the spirit. Jesus' answer concerns the evolution of the soul toward enlightenment.

Andrew speaks up and says that these ideas—that Mary claims Jesus said—are strange and he does not believe Jesus said them. Peter responds by wondering whether Jesus really spoke these words to a woman, without their knowledge; and are they to listen to her? Peter says to his fellow disciples:

> **"Did He prefer her to us?"** Then Mary wept and said to Peter, "My brother Peter, what do you think? Do you think I thought this up by myself in my heart, or that I am lying about the Savior?" Levi answered and said to Peter, "Peter, you have always been hot-tempered. Now I see you contending against the woman like the adversaries. But if the Savior made her worthy, who are you indeed to reject her? Surely the Savior knows her very well. That is why he loved her more than us. Rather let us be ashamed and put on the perfect man and acquire him for ourselves as he commanded us, and preach the gospel, not laying down any other rule or law beyond what the Savior said."

Karen L. King, a professor of ecclesiastical history at Harvard Divinity School, and author of *The Gospel of Mary of Magdala,* describes this story and writes that:

> ." . . the controversy is far from resolved. Andrew and Peter at least, and likely the other fearful disciples as well, have not understood the Savior's teaching and are offended by Jesus' apparent preference of a woman over them. Their

limited understanding and false pride make it impossible for them to comprehend the truth of the Savior's teaching. ***The reader must both wonder and worry what kind of gospel such proud and ignorant disciples will preach.*** (Emphasis added.) (King, p. 5)

To us, the wondering and worrying need not continue: We have two thousand years of testimony with which to evaluate the kind of gospel the proud and ignorant disciples preached. Almost five-hundred years have passed since Michelangelo exposed that gospel for what it is. We believe our analysis shows that the artist painted deceptions into his painting in an attempt to shock the Vatican hierarchy into doing something about their proud and ignorant ways. *Now they know what he did. Will they do anything about it?*

Chapter 65

Vans arriving at the gangster boss's estate in the hills above Naples that Monday morning did not carry the cargo they advertised on their side panels: dairy products, vegetables, Coca Cola, bread and other party necessities. Their cargo: Italian gangland bosses representing the Sicilian mafia, the region of Calabria, central Italy, and the boss of the Milano region, plus other distinguished guests who had a stake in the outcome of the impending crisis at the Vatican.

Salvatore Mancini, a short, skinny, balding man, with a pencil thin mustache, and wearing round, gold-framed glasses, greeted his guests as they arrived and directed them to a conference room down the hall on the right. The titular head of numerous independent families acting in concert under his tutelage, he wielded enormous power over gangster activity in central Italy; his colleagues in other regions knew better than to mess with him.

The most lucrative business was the garment industry, but construction was a close second. Large construction-yard complexes dotted the landscape providing easy access to construction sites that needed concrete foundations, roads, buildings with concrete floors, bridges that needed repair—the list goes on.

Cars, trucks (small and large), helicopters and longer-range, fixed wing aircraft were common assets at these sites. Occasionally, blasting their way through rock formations required dynamite and detonators to clear the way.

One of the families owned a construction yard, warehouses and sheds outside the Ciampino Airport near the junction of the Rome beltway Autostrada and the Via Appia Nuova. The airport is about ten miles north of Castel Gandolfo, the pope's alternate residence.

By ten a.m., all invited guests had arrived and were seated around the conference table covered with pool-table-green and fine velour cloth. Each guest had a one-foot-by-two-foot, red writing pad with raised, brown, leather borders on the sides. In the center of the table was a bouquet of red and yellow roses.

Mr. Mancini, who controlled the Central Region, invited the guests to identify themselves: (*) Francesco Lombardi-Sicily (*) "Antonio De Luca–Southern Region;" (*) Nicholas Giordano-Northern Region (*) "Cardinal

O'Reilley, Vatican;" (*) "Monsignor Lopez, Opus Dei;" (*) "Father Morales, General Administrator, Legionaries-Rome;" (*) "Cardinal Moretti – retired;" (*) "Monsignor Nunez, General Director of Legionaries of Christ and Regnum Christi;" (*) "Lidano Russo, Vatican Bank;" (*) "Igor Yavolinski—Russian national—consultant to Mr. Mancini." Yavolinski was an observer and played a neutral role in the decision making process.

Mancini, the boss, opened the meeting. He spoke in English, the lingua franca for such international gatherings. "Gentlemen," he said, slowly, with faux modesty, "I am honored that all—gesturing by raising both arms as if gathering to himself a flock of chickens—*all* of you should come to my humble home to discuss matters of great importance.

"I am especially honored by the presence our Russian guest, Mr. Yavolinski, who has been an invaluable asset to us in our dealings with our friends in Moscow.

"As you all know, we bosses, who represent the saving graces of our beloved country, have had a long and mutually beneficial relationship with the greatest Church on earth. And I am honored by the presence of its representatives here today. I have asked Cardinal O'Reilley to give us a brief statement as to why we found this meeting necessary. Cardinal O'Reilley, the floor is yours."

"Thank you Mr. Mancini. I want to express my deep gratitude for your hospitality. You have, indeed, honored us with your invitation and willingness to work with us in this time of crisis. The seriousness of what we face cannot be overstated. The Church and the organizations represented here today are in danger of divorce . . . of losing our long-time marriage, characterized by mutual respect and common decency. Without one, the other could not exist, each graced by its power, prestige and authority.

"A little over three years ago, our cardinals elected a new pope, whom all knew to be a decent and respectable man, who had a long and distinguished record of sensitivity and responsibility. Little did the electors know that he secretly harbored personal ambitions like that of a brutal dictator, who would go to any length to realize his dreams of power and influence amongst the masses.

"While I was the only one who knew his ambitions from the beginning, others have come to realize, from the realities that have emerged over the last three years, that the time has come to act . . . to prevent this man from destroying our holy alliance. I will mention only a couple of the most critical realities (amongst many), because the crucial ones are the only ones that have brought us together today:

"First, and perhaps the most alarming of all developments, is the potential loss of the benefits that come to both sides through the Vatican Bank operations. I don't need to describe those benefits, nor the consequences of losing them.

"Second—and this one is directly tied to the first—is that the pope has taken a fork in the road that leads, ultimately, to the dissolution of the Roman Catholic Church, not unlike that of the Soviet Union a few years ago. You don't need to be educated on the radioactive fallout that would bury humanity if that were to happen.

"These are the two critical issues that bring us together today. I thank you, Mr. Mancini, for allowing me to state my view of the situation."

"And I thank you for your brief statements. Is there anyone who disagrees with Cardinal O'Reilley's assessment?" No one responded.

"Well, then, I have a question for Mr. Russo. Why didn't you prevent that witch-bitch-of-a-nun from betraying us?"

"If I had known she would betray us, Mr. Mancini, I would have killed her with my own hands,"replied, Mr. Russo."She was a model of efficiency, loyalty and hard work. It will be impossible to replace her. It will take time to get back to the level of efficiency our operations had when she defected to our mortal enemy, the pope."

"You aren't making any . . . what's the word . . . how to say . . . casting asperations about those who killed her, were you?" asked Mr. Mancini.

"That thought did not occur to me. After all, she defected before she was murdered. I have a long and honorable record with this bank and your organizations—pausing to look at each of the bosses—that have benefited enormously by my management of the bank and its assets. I would hope that would buy *some* credibility amongst those present here today."

"My dear friend," Mr. Mancini said, feigning chagrin, "I meant no nugatory implications about your work. Believe me I have nothing but admiration for you and your professionalism. But let's move on. We don't have time for . . . what's the word . . . it has something similar to *criminal* in it . . ."

"Recriminations?" asked Monsignor Lopez.

"Yes. Yes. Thank you Father, uh, what was your name again?"

"Lopez. Monsignor Lopez. Opus Dei."

"Yes. Well, I'm wondering. What's on your minds today? You have come to me with information which I will admit is alarming. But I am merely a humble business man, and while me and my business friends are willing to meet you, we need to know more. What we can do to assist?"

"Mr. Mancini," Father Lopez of Opus Dei replied, "we don't know for certain what the pope will do, but are convinced he is months, if not weeks away from taking some very drastic action because of the stolen bank records; whatever action he takes will certainly involve the bank and, therefore the interests of everyone around this table.

"We are very fortunate that we have been able to attain some of the documents the nun stole from the bank because without knowing that, we might be swimming in the dark, colliding with unseen obstacles leaving a stream of blood in our trail for the sharks to follow, attack, and eat us alive. We think that we got only a fraction of the data that was given to the pope, and if that's the case, we're in big trouble.

"As you know those documents are a paper trail of criminal activity which, if you wanted to walk that path, would take you back fifty or sixty years. And much of that activity involves you, our mutual friends around this table."

"Excuse me, Father Lopez," said Mr. De Luca., who, with a pattern-bald, graying pate, bulging eyes and a body that looked like he could lift a menacing, military tank off a bridge and throw it the river, "did you say 'criminal activity'? What's criminal about friends helping friends when they need each other? I thought that was a central Christian doctrine. I think you should be a little more careful about how you speak about these matters."

The veiled threat was not lost on Father Lopez. "Mr. De Luca, of course I did not mean that we are the criminals; as you say we are friends helping each other, but the corrupt cultures we are forced to live in have their ways of looking at things . . . you know, oppressive laws that limit what honest, hardworking people want to do to improve their lives, and we get caught in the middle. I hope you understand my clarification. I meant no offense."

"What! Now you are insulting my intelligence?" De Luca screamed.

"Now, now gentlemen," interrupted Mr. Mancini, "we need to keep our civility here. We can't be fighting amongst ourselves. What Mr. Lopez said was in no way meant to insult anyone here at this table and he has tried to explain that. So let's drop it there."

"Thank you, Mr. Mancini. Now, as I was saying, we know that the pope is snooping around in the bank vaults . . . the operations of the bank, but we are not sure what he will do. We also know that he is gathering information that will help him decide what to do about the future of the Church in terms of doctrinal and administrative issues.

"In that regard, he has a number of options, which range from minor tinkering with doctrinal matters, to dismantling the Church and destroying two thousand years of a glorious tradition made sacred in the name of Jesus Christ and humanity.

"We in Opus Dei have already begun training a para-military force to storm the Vatican and take over its operation until a new pope can be elected, should that become necessary." Looking at Cardinal Moretti, he said, "Would you like to add to that?"

"Yes, if I may. I was the first Cardinal to be a victim of the pope's depredations. He fired me within a few hours of taking office."

"Pardon my interruption, Cardinal Moretti, but are you suggesting the pope is a queer? I mean, what does that word 'preditations' or whatever you said, mean?' asked Mr. Lombardi of Sicily.

"Oh, I'm sorry; it means bad actions. I warned him he was not only playing with fire, but with a volcano. He ignored me. If we are going to continue as we have for two thousand years, we need to get rid of him."

"Why don't you, then," Lombardi asked, contemptuously. A tall, handsome man, with black curly hair—who could pass for a wanton gigolo—did not tolerate ambiguity in these matters.

"Do you mean murder him? Or have the College of Cardinals throw him out of the office?" asked Lopez.

"Whatever is the easiest and the fastest," bellowed De Luca, of the Southern Region.

Monsignor Lopez stepped in to rescue Moretti. "As you all know," he said, "someone, presumably associated with one of the systems in this room has already tried to assassinate him and failed. Some of us . . ."

"Excuse me," Mr. Giordano, the Milan area representative interrupted, "Are you blaming one of us in this room for that stupid, amateurish act? Only a fool could have had such an idea. To say the least, the timing was way off target and now we are faced with heightened security. Professionals don't fail."

Nicholas Giordano, looked like the wealthy business man he was—albeit criminal entrepreneur—wearing designer, rimless glasses, a three-thousand-euro, pin-striped, blue, business suit, Barker Flex shoes, a white shirt and black silk tie. He could have played a romantic role in a movie fifty years ago, talent or no talent.

Don Mikkelson

"Of course I'm not blaming anyone in this room," said Monsignor Lopez. "As I was saying, some of us have been working on a way to force the pope out of office without violence, that is legally; but the fact is there is no legal way to get rid of him. We can oust him from the Holy See, but not the Vatican City State side of the house."

"Who said anything about legal issues?" hollered De Luca. "You pussies in your fancy garb are just a bunch of ignorant peacocks parading around . . . flaunting your power and authority and the truth of the matter is you don't have any power or authority over anything or anyone, except for your threats of hell and damnation.

"Any fool could figure that out, and many of them have and that's why most of your people have jumped overboard while you are re-arranging the chairs on the deck of a sinking ship. I say, let the Church go to hell; we'll keep the bank and everyone will be happy, except those pretentious asses that would lose their red caps and a shot at the papacy."

"RIGHT ON," shouted Lombardi, why didn't I think of that? That's the solution. Just go in there and gun down those Swiss Guard, pantalooned sons-a-bitches, and anyone else who gets in our way, take over the bank, and Mr. Russo will have tenure for the rest of his life."

"Gentlemen," urged Mr. Mancini, "let's calm down and be reasonable. Fighting amongst ourselves won't help matters any. We need to work together to deal with this unfortunate situation.

"Now, Mr. Lopez,' Mr. Mancini, continued, "you say you are training a para-military force to take over the Vatican. How do you plan to do that since there are over one hundred Swiss Guards there to prevent that?"

"Those of us who have been watching this develop," replied Monsignor Lopez, "thought you might be of some help with the . . . shall we say . . . unconventional tactics that might be necessary. We have a plan that I don't want to discuss right now, but if you are interested in helping, I would be happy to share our intentions and we can take it from there."

"Yes, I think we can help. Give me a call tomorrow and we can arrange to meet privately to coordinate what you want to do. Also, I think it would be a good idea for all of us to meet again to monitor developments as they occur and be able to respond quickly to whatever obstacles arise that could prevent us from achieving our objective of taking control."

"Keep in mind," said Father Nunez, leader of the Legionaries of Christ, that none of what we are discussing may be necessary. The pope has not made any decisions yet and he could merely make some minor changes that involve catechetical issues and not touch the bank, although the latter is extremely unlikely, which, of course is why we are meeting today.

"I think we should assume he will take on the bank when it's most convenient for him, and least convenient for us. We just don't know, but we do have ways of knowing what's going on because someone is stealing his confidential documents out from under his nose. That's how we got the documents we've received thus far. We'll need to be flexible: that means, be prepared for any eventuality and act on what happens, not what we imagine might occur. We'll keep you informed."

"That's good advice, Father Nunez, said Mr. Mancini. "Let's adjourn and have lunch."

As they started to rise from their chairs, Mr. Mancini raised his arms, and with palms down, lowered his arms. "Oh,!" he shouted, "please sit down. I almost forgot! Mr. Russo. I wanted to thank you for your long and dedicated service to the Church, which I am sure benefits all of humanity. Do you have a family?"

"Why, yes of course, Mr. Mancini."

"Well, why don't you tell us about them? Any children . . . uh, grandchildren?" Mancini asked with arms outstretched, palms up. "I have three sons and a daughter. I especially enjoy my grandchildren. I have twelve. Six boys and six girls. What about you?

"I don't have as many children or grandchildren, but I appreciate your telling me about yours."

"Mr. Russo," the boss said, with knitted brow . . . feigning surprise, "why be so modest? We are all family here, and I only wanted them to know a little about the man who has worked so hard on our behalf all these years."

"I really appreciate your interest and praise for my work. I have a son and a daughter and three grandchildren. I love them very much."

"Well, I'm sure you do. I apologize to all of you. I just wanted acknowledge Mr. Russo before the meeting broke up. He is a fine and loyal man. Thank you all for coming."

Chapter 66

Dressed in a white business suit over a black shirt, with plunging neck-line, and coordinating black, spike shoes—all new from an upscale Minneapolis boutique—Maria left the farm house and climbed into her Maserati, sports coupe.

She wore a silver necklace with a Madonna pendant, a gift from an admirer, reminding her of her fondness for the Madonna iconography in the Tretyakov Art Galleria in Moscow. She placed four copies of her thesis on the passenger seat: one for herself and one for each of the thesis-review committee members.

Meeting Sammy in the farm driveway, she waved and smiled as she headed toward Minneapolis. She was thankful for all he had done to assist with keeping her horse fed, bedded and exercised while she was busy with her thesis.

She was excited. This was the day she had been working toward for a couple years: that is, discussing the contents of her thesis with her guidance and evaluation committee. Passing the green corn fields and ripening small-grain fields, she enjoyed the drive to Minneapolis, reminiscing about her first trip down these roads and highways.

Looking over the top rim of her reading glasses, Dr. Holden said, "Welcome back, Maria." Sitting to her left was Dr. Jenny Fitzsimmons, professor of comparative religion. To Dr. Holden's right was Dr. William "Willy" Severson who taught Old and New Testament theology.

Dr. Sally Holden wore a dark-blue skirt, an aqua, V-neck cashmere sweater and a gold necklace with pendant: a cross. Dr. Willy Severson wore his signature, blue blazer, coordinated with khaki, light corduroy trousers, a pink shirt and red and black, plaid tie. Dr. Jenny Fitzsimmons wore an off-the-rack, khaki business suit, over a black, collared shirt. She did not look happy.

Looking at Maria, Sally continued. "Well, it has been some time since we were all together in this room. Has it been two years?"

"It seems much shorter than that," Maria replied, pleasantly, "but yes, I guess it has been that long."

Jenny took a deep breath and stared at a copy of Maria's thesis in front of her as if it were something that required the immediate attention of a bomb-defusing squad. Willy squirmed in his chair, picked up his pen and twirled it between his fingers.

Dr. Holden sighed, and continued. Looking down the table at the candidate for a Master's degree, she said, "So, Maria, our purpose of this meeting is to discuss the thesis you have prepared as partial satisfaction of the requirements for your degree. We have reviewed your academic record and find the course requirements are complete. Your thesis is the final step prior to your degree being conferred.

"We have read your thesis and find it as interesting because of the reason you came to us in the first place—searching for an answer to your conundrum: your role as one of 'God's messengers.'"

Jenny shifted in her chair, crossed her legs and fidgeted with the copy of Maria's thesis in front of her; the twirling pen in Willy's hand accelerated as he stole glances at Maria's chest.

"I'm wondering," continued Sally, in her quintessential, professional voice, "has your experience here been helpful?"

"Oh, absolutely," replied Maria, enthusiastically. "As you know I took classes from each of you and I thought the lectures, course structure, research required, and the interaction in class with other students, was excellent. I could not be more pleased. It has been very helpful and I want to thank all of you from the bottom of my heart. The courses on Judaism and Christianity have been helpful.

"So . . ." Jenny paused, as if she didn't want to hear the answer, "Did you discover what being 'God's messenger' means?"

"I'm getting there. I think I'm close. Still, I'm not quite sure where I'm headed with that. I was hoping that after we've discussed my thesis, the fog, that seems to be blocking a clear view of my path, might lift."

"Frankly, I'm surprised to hear that," said Jenny, with a slight edge to her voice. "My impression, after reading your thesis, was that your role as God's messenger would be to take down the Catholic Church. Apparently, I'm wrong. Is that correct?" She glared at Maria and waited for an answer.

"Yes, I don't think that will be my role as God's messenger. Although, I can certainly see how you would come to that conclusion. Still, the role that is emerging seems to be a much more positive one than you have described. I view the thesis as a first step in my search for the role I am to play."

"Let me jump in here, if I may," said Willy. His demeanor was serious, but not perturbed. "I have a question about the thesis. It doesn't seem to me to be related to the course work you took here at our seminary. None of the work you have cited in support of your thesis was assigned in your classes."

Looking at the other two professors, he said, "If I'm wrong, let me know." They did not respond. He continued. "Where did you get all of these rather bizarre ideas about Michelangelo and the Sistine Chapel frescoes? The last time we talked you were focusing on the history of Christianity."

"Dr. Severson, that is an excellent question, because I think it gets down to the 'nut cutting,' as they say in Wyoming.

"I want to assure you that I was not being disingenuous when I told you that I had received an excellent education on the history of the Judeo-Christian religions; it is directly related to the contents of my thesis. But, I have not limited my search to the education I received here at this institution.

"As background for what I am about to say, you should know that I took a survey of the history of art when I was an undergraduate at the University of Minnesota. I was fascinated by that because I was born in a country which has a rich history of master painters, and museums full of Russian artists' works.

"The *Tretyakov Art Gallery* in Moscow holds dozens of Russian paintings, including an entire floor of Russian icon painting of the Madonna. If you have never visited there, I encourage you to go at your earliest convenience. I visited that museum numerous times when I was living in Moscow.

"After I returned from Russia, I saw the *Da Vinci Code* and then read the book." Jenny rolled her eyes, re-crossed her legs, tightened her lips, and stared at Maria. "Those experiences stimulated further inquiry—beyond what I had in my undergraduate classes—into Renaissance paintings; so I took a class in that period of art at the University of Minnesota.

"I learned that Leonardo and Michelangelo were not only contemporary artists, but both lived in Tuscany, near Florence, at the same time and were friends and competitors. I began to wonder if Michelangelo had embedded coded messages in his paintings as well; or conversely, had Da Vinci followed Michelangelo's lead. That is irrelevant, for our purposes here, but nevertheless, an interesting question."

Jenny's face turned red. As Maria continued with her explanation, Jenny reached down to her purse on the floor and retrieved a high-blood-pressure pill; surreptitiously, she popped it into her mouth, lifted a bottle of water and took a sip.

"I started to examine Michelangelo's most famous paintings in the Sistine Chapel. My first step was to go to the Vatican and take a privately guided tour.

Craning my neck to look at the ceiling was interesting, but hardly enlightening in terms of studying the paintings from the eye of an art critic. For one thing, the ceiling frescoes are sixty feet above the observer standing on the floor. Secondly, the massive display of panels, spandrels, and lunettes amount to a vertiginous, complex tableau.

"Of course, one's neck gets cramped long before one can achieve any clear idea of what's up there. *The Last Judgment,* on the wall behind the altar, is easier to see, but one needs more time than a few minutes on a guided tour that takes you through so many works of art that, by the time you reach the Sistine Chapel, you feel like a saturated sponge that can't be wrung out.

"So you move on, a little dissatisfied with the experience. Yet, for most of the thousands of people who pass through the chapel every day, the value of the experience seems to be: 'I've been there!'"

"In the Vatican museum gift stores, I purchased several books pertaining to the chapel and the artworks in the museums, brought them home and began to study them. Occasionally, I used a magnifying glass because of an intense curiosity about whether I would find any hints of hidden messages in the Sistine Chapel frescoes. As you now know, I was not disappointed with the results.

"Having learned so much about the Judeo-Christian religions in your classes here at the seminary, I had a good background in the history of Judaism and Christianity. As I examined pictures of the *Last Judgment* in the Sistine Chapel, something didn't make sense. There was ambiguity in the artist's painting that didn't seem to correspond to what I had learned about your religions. Certainly, to an uncritical eye, the painting seemed to be about the 'last judgment,' the Second Coming of Christ.

"Nevertheless, my curiosity did not abate, but intensified. I was thinking, *It cannot be! Such blatant, in-your-face messages that do not conform to the Judeo-Christian religions, by an artist who is venerated by the Church . . . and not only that, employed by the Church nearly all of his seventy-five years of adult life.*

"Still, I reminded myself that the reason why I was investigating in the first place was to see if there were, in fact, hidden messages, as Dan Brown averred in his book about secret codes imbedded in Da Vinci's *Last Supper*. I suppose I was stunned by the fact that the painting had been on that wall for well over four hundred years and no one had discovered what I seemed to be uncovering."

"You asked us to provide a screen and projector for our meeting today," Dr. Holden interrupted, "at what point would you like to use it. It seems to me this might be a good time if you had planned to point out some of the deceptions in the *Last Judgment*."

"Thank you for reminding me of that. Yes, that's what I intended to do: show you the deceptions we found in our research."

Becoming more annoyed with each passing second, Jenny broke in with, "You used the first-person plural pronoun in your paper throughout. Why?" she asked, sharply. She was harboring a thought that she might find academic collusion.

"Excellent question!" Maria replied, wholeheartedly. "I can tell you, Dr. Fitzsimmons, I wondered about using the plural form instead of the first-person, singular pronoun. I concluded that I'd use the plural because that ameliorates to some degree the ego that is implied in the 'I'.

"When I was pondering that question, I realized that since I was a child I have used the plural when talking to myself, about something I would do or say. Secondly, in recent years I have sensed a duality in my nature: two selves, if you will. By that I mean, I perceive myself as having a localized self that I associate with my mortal body and an immortal Self that I associate with my spiritual Self.

"You might remember that in my application-for-admission essay, I mentioned having had spiritual experiences when my Russian father died and during my near-death experience. Since then, my awareness of my higher Self has been quite normal for me. So I think of my higher Self as my 'spirit guide', the second part of the 'we' in the plural pronoun. Does that answer your question, Dr. Fitzsimmons?" Maria asked, with a smile.

"Yes. Thank you," said Dr. Fitzsimmons, shooting a skeptical glance at Dr. Holden. Jenny stiffened her back and folded her hands.

Looking at Dr. Holden, Maria asked, "Should I set up the projector now. May I use the pull-down screen behind you?"

"Yes, please do."

"Can I help?" asked Willy. They got the projector hooked up to Maria's laptop and she began her presentation.

"As you saw in my paper, I had seven examples of Michelangelo's deceptions in the *Last Judgment*: (1) the title, itself, is a deception; (2) lack of joy in the painting; (3) the massive display of naked genitals and buttocks; (4) the absence of children; (5) Michelangelo's portrayal of himself; (6) the Unborn Truth and (7) If the gloomy patina doesn't fit what the Vatican wants to see, take it off.

"I pointed out that we would not deal with the ceiling in the Chapel because Blech and Doliner, the authors of *Sistine Secrets,* had recently published their brilliant work on the extent to which Michelangelo embedded secrets in the Sistine Chapel—secrets they were the first to discover. I gave them ample credit for their work, including the "secrets" they discovered in the *Last Judgment.*" Dr. Jenny Fitzsimmons, took a deep breath, stared at the thesis in front of her, shifted her position in her chair and lifted her eyes and stared at the wall behind Dr. "Willy".

"I won't repeat what you've already read in the paper about Blech and Doliner's discoveries and that there is a lot more going on in the *Last Judgment* than they exposed.

"I will use my laser pointer to draw your attention to each of the deceptions we have identified in the painting so that you can see, visually, what I was writing about in my thesis.

"We'll use this slide of the *Last Judgment,* which was cleaned, restored and, to a degree, modified late in the last century We think the title is a major deception because we are convinced the chief, overarching 'hidden message' in the painting is that there will be no "last judgment."

"Excuse me for interrupting, Miss Luderenko, or should I say 'Miss Martina Luther'," Jenny said sarcastically, "but, who do you think you are? You come to us with a rather bizarre request to seek an answer to your conundrum, we indulge your twaddle, offer our assistance graciously, and your expression of gratitude amounts to no less than an arrogant slap in our faces with your snow storm of insults about our religion. I, for one, find your paper repulsive and am having difficulty sitting here while you continue with your presentation."

"Well," Maria began pleasantly, taking Jenny's concerns seriously, "I certainly understand your feelings and thank you for expressing them so eloquently . . .

"Would you **shut up?" I've had it up to my EARS with your saccharine façade,** a Potemkin village for what I think is your underlying contempt for the religion we hold dear to our hearts. How **dare** you come in here with your insults?

"I'd like to remind you that I will have a lot to do with whether or not you are granted your degree. It's true that I am a guest professor, but I have academic responsibility to this seminary, and that will not be compromised merely to accommodate your outrageous behavior, masquerading as scholarship."

"Fine," Maria answered, evenly. "If you will allow me to continue, I would like to address your concerns. May I continue?" Maria looked to Dr. Holden for approval, for which she received a nod.

"I recall that your literature advertises the 'search for truth'. You quote a passage, in your promotional literature, from the Bible: John 8:32—'Ye shall know the truth, and the truth shall make you free.' I took that bait seriously and understood that your institution would honor my search, which I admit was unusual. I chose a seminary which I assumed would be more appropriate for my needs than—let's say, a technological institute that offers degrees in mechanical engineering.

"I'm prepared to leave any moment and never come back—sacrifice the degree I'm working hard to attain—if this institution determines that I have violated its academic integrity policies. Implicit in my thinking all along was that its representatives here in this room would have the professional competence to deal with controversial issues, even if those issues honestly and sincerely questioned the foundations of the religions that are promoted in seminaries, with their blinkered curriculum.

"I don't mean that disrespectfully. I think you would admit that seminaries don't normally bring in students to 'search for the truth'; they are brought in to be indoctrinated *in* 'truth' and then taught how to proselytize the public with their message, and provide spiritual and personal counseling for their parishioners as needed.

"I repeat: If your institution won't live up to its advertised mission, you are quite right—I *don't* belong here. And I can assure you that you do not need to make threats in order to remove me from your presence here at this seminary. Have I made myself clear on this issue, Dr. Fitzsimmons?"

Dr. Severson seemed to be enjoying the cat fight, until Dr. Holden—glancing at the two professors with a look that said, *Don't contradict me!*—placed her reading glasses on her nose. Looking authoritatively over the rim, she said, "We'll adjourn this meeting for today and resume tomorrow. Maria, please come back tomorrow and you may continue with your presentation at ten. This meeting is adjourned."

Chapter 67

Mr. Russo did not sleep well. The not-so-veiled threat concealed behind Mancini's inquiring about his family bothered him, even though he had lied about his family: he didn't have one. A bachelor all his life, he had had affairs with a few women, but his concentration on his work, his long hours, his seeming aloofness, and occasional impotence in bed did not bode well for long-term relationships.

For that he was grateful because, while he was terrified for his own life, he didn't have to deal with worrying about a family that might have been.

Had it not been for Mancini's threat, he might have been able to convince himself that the cordiality shown at the meeting was genuine; after all, the gangsters around the table had hauled in trainloads of money for decades due to his cooperation. But he also knew that would be irrelevant if they had the slightest doubt that he remained loyal to them and the Church.

His attempts to come to some decision that was in his best interests were failing. Yet, he knew that he had to make a decision soon because his fatigue was beginning to show at the bank and that could not be concealed from the mob for long. At four a.m., after another sleepless night, he made his decision.

Chapter 68

The morning after the confrontation between Maria and Dr. Fitzsimmons, Dr. Holden called Maria and said the meeting had been postponed for a couple months due to vacation scheduling problems. They were to meet again in late September.

Three days following the confrontation, Dr. Fitzsimmons called Maria, apologized for her angry flare-up, and invited her to a casual dinner with her family the following Saturday evening. Maria accepted graciously, and said she would be delighted to meet her husband and children.

Dressed in a Carmella Jewell turquoise-over-white layer tank-top, Palazzo wide-leg blue jeans and spiked, leather moccasins, Maria enjoyed the Chinese stir-fry dinner and white wine, with chocolate mousse for dessert. Conversation about and with the children and their activities—in and outside school—dominated the dinner's ambience.

Jenny's husband, a history professor at the University of Minnesota, questioned Maria about her thoughts on the future of her birth-country. Jenny remained quiet throughout most of the meal, except to interject a comment now and then about the children and how wonderful they are.

Previously arranged, Jenny's husband took the children to a movie they had been begging to see so that Jenny and Maria could have some quiet time together.

When the table was cleared and redecorated with a fine, embroidered tablecloth and flowers, Jenny and Maria retired to the living room. They sat facing each other in love seats separated by a coffee table with bowls of nuts, candies and a book that highlighted the beauty of Minnesota lakes.

The conversation started easily with Jenny talking about her background as a child growing up in a Catholic family in a rural farming community in western Minnesota. Her mother was a dentist and her father worked as a trial attorney for a local law firm. She met her husband at the university not far from their current home.

Jenny apologized again for her outburst at the thesis review meeting; Maria brushed it off as something quite normal, considering the situation and expressed the desire to put the issue behind them and move on.

"You know," Jenny said, "I didn't sleep all night that night because I was so confused. I knew what you were saying about our religions—Catholic and Lutheran—had some merit and yet I couldn't control my emotions . . . hearing the truth so eloquently spoken.

"My husband and I have been devout Catholics all our lives and never really spent much time pondering whether or not our faith was somehow flawed. But we have been very conflicted about the birth control and abortion issues, especially. And now the pederasty scandals that have hit the church like a nuclear bomb. 'How could it happen?' the pope asked . . . Indeed!"

"We wanted to rear our children in the Church. We thought that would give them a good moral background for adulthood. But I'm beginning to question even that!" She laughed, nervously.

"You know, Maria, I really admire what you are doing, and that's why I wanted to spend a little time with you. I never really dreamed I'd meet someone who had the inquisitive spirit I see in you; I want to know where all this is headed—I mean, personally, with you. Forget for a moment the academic issues. If you don't want to discuss this, that's fine with me. But . . . "

"Dr. Fitzsimmons, I . . ."

"Please call me Jenny, if you don't mind."

"No not at all. I was starting to apologize for interrupting you, but I guess we are now even." They both laughed, which warmed the atmosphere considerably, given that neither one knew precisely how this conversation would track.

"Well, thank you for your gracious comments," Maria said with a smile. "First, I want to compliment you on creating such a beautiful family. Someday I'd like to find out your secrets for that achievement. And of course the dinner was pleasant . . . sumptuous. Thank you." Jenny nodded acknowledgment.

"You know a little of my personal history, so I won't repeat it, but I want you to know that I grew up in a very loving home in Russia and was fortunate to find an adoptive couple who were and are just as loving. My adoptive dad died a few years ago, but my Mom still lives on our farm outside Sylvan Lake.

"I guess what I want to say, in view of some of the things I'm studying and discovering about religion, is that I admire people who are "church-goers" for the sole reason that they are people who are searching for a way to realize their spiritual selves. It seems so easy for those who, for whatever reasons, don't go to church, to denigrate those who do as naïve, hopelessly deluded individuals.

"I'm discovering that these searching people really didn't have a lot of choices available to them outside the established religious institutions. I suppose there is something of a 'herd-mentality' going on there, also—so to speak: *well, if so many millions are doing it, there must be something to it.* And they grew up, being indoctrinated early on in their respective religions; so what would you expect to see in their adult lives?

"Nevertheless, I don't want to suggest that people who aren't associated with organized religion aren't also searchers. I'm certain many of them are; I'm just as convinced that many who attend church regularly are not serious seekers."

"Why do you say that? It seems you are contradicting yourself. You just said people who attend church are searchers."

"I don't think I am contradicting myself. While there are many who are sincere "church-goers" and genuinely search for ways realize their spiritual longings, there are probably just as many—even sincere, regular attendees—who view the church as a wonderful social organization and/or as a moral training ground for their children and never bother to think—seriously—of about what they are doing. For example, do they reflect on the implications of teaching their children they are sinful beings, incapable of making spiritual decisions on their own?"

Can they, in their heart of hearts, *really* accept the notion that a Divine Being –capable of creating this incomprehensibly vast and beautiful universe with all of its diverse inhabitants—would condemn a high percentage of her divinely created children to an eternity of suffering because they, in their ignorance failed to please?"

I believe that if Mother Teresa—the quintessential 'seeker'—had had the knowledge available in my thesis, she would have had a profoundly different experience from the fear and terror that characterized her spiritual life."

"That makes sense," replied Jenny. "You just described part of *me*. It has never really occurred to me to question my Catholic upbringing. Of course we all have had alternatives: other Christian denominations, other monotheistic religions, Eastern religions, the New Age phenomenon—I studied them all in my master's and doctoral programs.

"But none seemed any more attractive to me than the one I grew up with. But now, I'm beginning to wonder because of what I've read in your thesis. If Michelangelo did, indeed, deceive the Church, as you say, that would be quite a shock to thinking people—Why would Michelangelo, revered by the

Church, do what he did if there weren't some substance underpinning his secrets and deceptions?"

"Well," Maria said, "as you know, I've come to the conclusion there is substance there and that's why I'm pursuing this issue with confidence that I'm on to something. I'm quite certain that before we are done discussing my thesis, you will find a lot more information that will undergird Michelangelo's messages."

"Why do you say that? Now you've really piqued my curiosity?"

"I'm discovering that there have always been alternative spiritual paths that people have taken. Although admittedly, those paths are not well-known, well-defined, nor easily available to most people—homemakers, for example, who need to go to work every day and meet family responsibilities.

"I'm sorry! You asked what time it is and I'm giving you a lecture on how a clock works."

"Oh no, Maria. I'm very interested in what you are saying. Please continue."

"At first, in my research, I found that there seemed to be a very strange phenomenon going on in the history of the human race. According to our current knowledge about the rise and fall of major religious movements, all authentic ones had their origins associated with a master who proclaimed some profound spiritual knowledge and invited people to participate with him in satisfying spiritual needs. Veda Vyasa, Lord Krishna, Lord Buddha, Shankara, Moses, Jesus and Muhammad come to mind.

"In some cases, the movements lasted well over a thousand of years and adhered to the wisdom and knowledge of the masters and then died out as the wisdom and knowledge was distorted and turned on its head, creating a new religion that resembled the initial one, but due to the distortions, caused more harm than good for the societies involved."

"Excuse me for a moment," said Jenny, "please help yourself to the candies and nuts on the table. I was remiss in not asking if you wanted more wine, or coffee after dinner."

"No more wine, thank you, but if you have hot tea, that would be preferable to coffee. I can't drink coffee. It gives me heart palpitations and I don't sleep."

"Okay, I think I'll have some coffee and I'll make some tea as well. Excuse me for a moment."

While Jenny prepared the drinks, Maria munched on some nuts and thumbed through the book on Minnesota lakes. She found Sylvan Lake and recognized some of the points where she had been. She was amazed by the wide variety, shapes, sizes and locations of the lakes. She was putting the book down when Jenny came with the drinks and coasters. "I forgot to ask if you take anything in your tea," Jenny said.

"No I don't, but thanks for asking."

"So where were we?" Jenny asked.

"I was talking about how the ancient master-teachers brought us knowledge about God and his creation and that they all had essentially the same message. Unfortunately, each of them had their messages distorted, which resulted in the religions that are extant today. Judaism and Christianity did not escape that phenomenon.

"This is an area that is so fascinating, because what we learn is that over five thousand years ago, some enlightened seer's cognized the structure of the universe, its origin and how it functions. Eventually, these ideas were written in books called the Vedas, which became the foundations of some of the Eastern religions, especially Hinduism. I might add that Kabbalistic philosophy makes similar claims."

"Cognized the structure of the universe, its origin and how it functions?"

"I know that sounds quite fantastic. But modern scientists, especially theoretical physicists, for decades have been searching for the building blocks of the universe. Some of them have discovered that the origin of the universe corresponds precisely with what the Vedic literature contains and modern scientists are discovering: that consciousness is the basis of all that exists.

"It turns out that "consciousness," pure consciousness, existed prior to the 'big bang' which created the universe as we know it. When the 'big bang' occurred, time, space and matter came into existence creating what we know as "relativity," a new dimension of reality. So that, after the 'big bang', two realities existed: the realm of the 'absolute' and that of relativity. Absolute reality is the source of all that exists in the relative world; it is the home of all the laws of nature.

"Relativity is the world in which we exist; we exist in relationship to every other person, place and thing. Does all this make any sense at all, Jenny?"

"Make any sense? I'm stunned by what you are saying! Yes, it makes sense the way you explain it in such simple, clear terms. Are you saying that God is what you are referring to as 'pure consciousness' and that another name for that is 'the absolute'?"

"Yes."

"But that seems like such an impersonal way to define God. We think of God as a loving father."

"Yes, I know—an angry God, as defined by Judaism and Christianity and adopted by the Muslims."

"But that is an issue I could take up in my paper and deal with in some detail, because it lies at the source of what happened to the divine wisdom that was brought to us by the masters, corrupted and turned on its head by subsequent generations of the masters' followers.

"If you agree," continued Maria, "I'd like to pursue the issue of the 'big bang' and the significance of relativity being created within which we have the honor, privilege—and most importantly—the *opportunity* to live."

"Well, there you go again: insulting all religions. Is that your intention?" Jenny said, not angrily, but nevertheless challengingly.

"I, absolutely, have no intention of insulting religions or anyone in particular. I say what I say as observations, without prejudice or judgment of right or wrong. When I refer to the angry God of the monotheistic religions, that is a fact that is well known, painted into the Sistine Chapel's *Last Judgment* by Michelangelo, not as a deception, but as a mockery of that reality; of which the monotheistic religions seem to be very proud. 'I am a jealous God, visiting iniquity of the fathers upon the third and fourth generation of them that hate me, and showing mercy unto thousands of those who love me and keep my commandments.' Does that sound familiar?"

"Of course that sounds familiar, and I know that God is not only an angry God in the monotheistic religions, but also a merciful one, as you just said. But I will honor your request that we not get hung up on this issue now and move on to the issue of creation and the establishment of a new reality: *relativity*, when the 'big bang' occurred."

"Okay, thanks, Jenny. I appreciate your indulgence. And I know the things I say at first seem very provocative and even insulting, just because they are still outside the contextual field in which they belong. But I am convinced that once you see what I say within the framework of what I could discuss in the paper, you'll know that I have no intention to demean or belittle anyone or anything. So may I continue?"

"Certainly," Jenny said with a smile. "Why is living in a milieu of 'relativity'—meaning, as you said, a 'privilege', when there are days when I feel like I'd like to live on another planet, where having to deal with persons, places and things wouldn't be so unpleasant a lot of the time."

"You just said something so profound, I wish Willy were here to hear it! You have expressed the desire that other planets might exist where life would not be such a challenge as here on earth. And we can discuss that also, but I want to leave that issue for its proper context and if we don't get to it tonight, we'll bring it up in our next discussion in our next meeting. Okay?"

"Well," Jenny replied, "I don't know why what I said is so profound that it would impress Willy, because the only thing that seems to impress him is his low golf scores!" They both laughed because that seemed to be "Willy."

"Okay. It turns out that this planet earth is a very special place for human beings in the context of the universe and what's going on here.

"The best explanation I know of came to us recently in a book titled *Conversations with God.*

"In this book, God declares that the point of all life is that through us He *experiences his own magnificence.* Without us, he could <u>know</u> Who He Is and how magnificent He is, but He couldn't <u>*experience it.*</u> God, existing as pure consciousness, needed a reference point outside Himself from which He could *experience* his magnificence.

"So, He created reference points for both of us. We cannot know who we are if we don't know *who we are not.* You can't experience heat without experiencing cold because without cold, there is nothing to relate heat to.

"In *CwG*, God uses a beautiful metaphor to explain the relationship of our bodies to our souls (Higher Selves) and by extension to God. He says to imagine that we are candles in the sun and want to experience ourselves as beautiful candles. But we can't do that in the brilliant light of the sun, so we must remove ourselves from the sun so we can experience our particularized light.

"Like that, we enter our human bodies at the first heartbeat in the womb and begin our journey of experiencing ourselves in the material world. Like the little candle, we need a system of relativity, a context, wherein we can experience ourselves in relationship to everything else.

"Therefore, during the 'big bang' God created *relativity, forgetfulness, and consciousness.* You know, relativity is what Einstein was talking about, but to put it in simple terms that are relevant for us that you and I can understand," Maria said with a smile, "it's just how we relate to every other person, place or thing in the universe.

"After we are born, we grow in awareness of ourselves and everything around us, but what we don't know is that the scheme is just a trick so that we can't know that we are one with everything that exists.

"And consciousness is _The All_ that exists in the form of vibrations. It is the source of all true knowledge and spirituality because it is <u>That</u> which created and sustains the universe.

"Excuse me, Maria. Are you saying God is a trickster? Can you elaborate on that a little? It sounds very confusing to me. Why would God pull a trick on us?"

Maria laughed. "Good point, Jenny. At first, I was wondering what that means, too. The system of relativity that was created by the Big Bang is a trick in the sense that when we enter this planet it seems that relativity—the phenomenal world that embraces our experiences of the senses, our emotions and the intellect—is all there is to life. We enjoy the experiences that the five senses produce: seeing, touching, tasting, hearing, and smelling.

"Likewise, our experiences created by intellectual stimulation can be fascinating and very satisfying; that is, we exercise our minds to navigate the waters of our lives. Sometimes the waters are calm and pleasant and other times threatening violence and even death. So we get caught up in the dramatic fluctuations of our lives, thinking that this is all there is to life . . . until we don't.

"Like Mother Teresa's expression that her life of desperation was a living hell, Shakespeare's Macbeth expresses a similar, cynical view: 'Life's but a walking shadow, a poor player, That struts and frets his hour upon the stage, And then is heard no more. It is a tale Told by an idiot, full of sound and fury, Signifying nothing.' That's in Macbeth, Act V, Scene V.

"So the saving grace of relativity is that this "trick"—played on us by the phenomenal world—is a blessing in disguise . . . until it is no longer a disguise . . . until we discover an alternative to what the phenomenal world has to offer.

"The good news is that that alternative is available to us while we live in our human bodies. That alternative carries with it the promise of a blissful existence that keeps on giving for eternity as we move on to enjoy life as higher evolved beings in this life—and in the spirit-world beyond—and in other bodies on other planets."

"Okay, thank you. That seems to make sense in light of what you have already said. But you just created a zillion questions. Let's start with this one. Why is submission to total amnesia necessary?" Jenny asked.

"Remember the little candle? It separated and _left behind its knowledge_ of its brilliance in the sun, in order to experience in another venue _what it is not_. It needed a reference point outside the sun from which to observe itself. Carrying remembrance of the brilliance from whence it came would make it impossible to experience the opposite of brilliance because the brilliance of the sun would still be with the little candle.

"For us in relativity—in the material world of the earth—we experience what we are not: life in the phenomenal world—the opposite of bliss—until we don't, and then we experience *who we really are*: indestructible, immortal, blissful beings enjoying higher and higher levels of consciousness until we realize we are one with God. If we carried remembrance of that bliss into this world, we couldn't experience what we are not. That's why *forgetfulness* is necessary."

"Thanks for that explanation, Maria," said Jenny. "Could you elaborate a little on what you made reference to earlier about masters coming to us for the past several thousand years, starting spiritual movements, only to have them die off and turn into something antithetical to what their masters were teaching? You suggested that Christianity has suffered the same fate. Quite naturally, I'm interested in what you have to say about that issue."

"Actually, Jenny, you have raised an excellent point. It occurs to me that my 'God's messenger' role is becoming clearer as we talk. I'm wondering if it might be possible for me to include what you are suggesting in a revision of my thesis. I really felt somewhat unsatisfied with what I had done, because I had not come to a clear understanding of why I came to you, Sally and Willy in the first place.

"The three of you might be able to help me more than you already have. What I am suggesting is that I take up what you have requested when we resume our meeting in September. Do you think that would be possible?"

"Yes. I think it would," replied Jenny. "I tell you what," she continued, "I'll talk with Dr. Holden and Dr. Severson about what you are requesting. You are suggesting a very provocative issue that could shake the foundations of our current religions; by that I mean, that all masters were basically saying the same thing: *go within* to find God. But the religions we have today fundamentally inverted that idea."

"That's well stated. I'm wondering . . . is there any reason we couldn't continue in the kitchen while I help you clean the dishes and put them away?" Maria asked. "We are *women,* after all, the multi-taskers of the universe," Maria said with a smile.

Jenny laughed and said, "Sure, why not? This stuff could get too heavy to lift if we aren't careful."

As Jenny bent over the dishwasher, placing the rinsed dishes in their proper spots, she looked over her shoulder at Maria and asked, "Could you turn on the TV to the weather channel?"

"Sure." She picked up the remote for the small TV on the kitchen counter separating the kitchen from the breakfast nook and pressed the Power button.

The weather report indicated it would be mild and sunny for a few more days, turning to scattered showers later in the week. The report was interrupted when Jenny's husband and their daughters returned

Jenny's husband replaced the remaining dishes in the dishwasher, while Jenny joined Maria and the girls in their chat.

The children calmed down and went to their rooms. Maria thanked Jenny and her husband for the dinner, a pleasant evening . . . and said goodbye.

Chapter 69

Perfecto had been working at the Presidential Palace for a few weeks when one of his colleagues handed him a note: *The pope wants you to come immediately.*

"Where did you get this?" asked Perfecto.

"The president gave it to me. He said it was urgent."

Perfecto went to the parking lot, unlocked his car door, got in, started the engine, put it in reverse, backed out of his parking space and headed toward the exit, turning right onto V. D. Dataria, down Via dell Umilta, a left turn onto Via del Corso, turned right on Via del Plebiscito and went about a mile to the Ponte Vitorio Emanuele and turned left onto Via della Conciliazione which took him toward St. Peter's Plaza, a short distance away.

Approaching the plaza, he turned right up a narrow street to Borgo Pio, and turned left. In two short blocks he entered the Vatican through St. Anne's gate, being waved in by two Swiss Guards who saluted as he passed. After two years of practicing evasive driving and keeping one eye on the road and the other eye on the mirror, he had become 'wall-eyed', splitting his vision, which in time gave him a headache.

No one would believe he could actually do that, but that's the way it seemed to him. As he passed the St. Anne Hotel on his right, a block from the entrance to the Vatican, he noticed, in his rearview mirror, a shady-looking character staring at his license plate and writing something on a pad, presumably the number. He parked and headed to the elevator that would take him to the third level loggia and the pope's office.

As he walked he reflected that, although he had made only a few trips to the Vatican in the two months since he moved to the presidential palace, he had become aware that he was being watched. So far as he knew, he had been followed only once. The 'tail' picked him up as he left the Vatican, so Perfecto took him to Villa Stritch, an apartment complex, built on the side of a hill, in the opposite direction from the Presidential Palace. The villa was named after an American Cardinal, who had it built for visiting American dignitaries, but it was now occupied by high ranking Vatican clerics.

He had pulled into the parking lot, through a large gate, circled around to the left, parked, went in and went to the bathroom, chatted with the security guard, came out and drove to the Presidential Palace. His 'tail' had disappeared and proudly reported to his boss that *we now know where the pope's priest lives and that we need to keep someone posted there also, to follow him whenever he departs.*

Perfecto exited the elevator and walked down the loggia past Raphael's frescoes and entered the pope's office antechamber. A Swiss Guard invited him to enter the pope's office. "The pope is waiting for you," he said. Perfecto was surprised to see Mr. Russo standing and talking with Pope Immanuel.

"Perfecto," said the pope, "thank you for coming on such short notice. Both of you, please have a seat." The pope went around his desk, sat, put his arms up on the desk, folded his hands and looked at his two guests, pausing to gather his thoughts for the right words in this delicate, yet momentous occasion.

"Gentlemen, we are entering a very dangerous period in this game we call life; I mean all three of us. Perfecto, I haven't brought you up to date on what has been happening. Mr. Russo has just informed me that Opus Dei and the Legion—in cahoots with the gangster bosses, Cardinals O'Reilley, and retired Cardinal Moretti and some hoodlum from Russia—are conspiring to get rid of me, one way or the other and take over the Vatican because they fear what I might do.

"The gangster boss has threatened to kill Lidano's phantom family and him, if they suspect he is thinking of defecting to me.

"Mr. Russo has come to me and asked for help, which I have agreed to give. Obviously, he needs protection. I have already talked with President Bianchi, who has agreed to house Mr. Russo at the palace, which would be very convenient because his financial and security people will spend the next few weeks debriefing him on what he knows about the Vatican banking operations.

"I want you to take him to the Presidential Palace. I am confident that you will be able to take him there, even though you will be watched . . . tailed.

"My spies tell me our entrances and exits are being watched twenty-four-seven, so use whatever tactics you have available to avoid confrontation with our adversaries. Some of our employees are keeping an eye on the parking lots to keep the guys watching for you at the gates informed . . . so you can count on being tailed when you leave here today. Are there any questions from either of you?"

"No questions, Your Holiness," said Mr. Russo, "but I want to repeat how grateful I am for your help. I will not let you down. I know enough to put all those bastards in jail for the rest of their lives."

"I'm sure you will do a lot more than that to help after you find out what we are planning. But I don't want to get into that now. In that box over there is a nun's habit and wimpel that you can use as a disguise. Perfecto, put on your business suit; have a wig and cap ready if you need them in your evasive maneuvers."

"Please leave before the rush-hour traffic slows you down. Good luck."

The "business man" and the "nun" climbed into the Panda and fastened their seat belts. Exiting the Vatican through the St. Anne's gate involved passing over a slight rise in the pavement, enough to conceal the small Panda shortly before reaching the crest of the hump in the street. After pulling out of the parking lot and just before the Panda became visible to anyone observing the entrance/exit at St. Anne's Church, Perfecto pressed button number two: yellow.

"I'll explain this to you after we get to the palace," Perfecto said to Lidano Russo, who looked very uncomfortable in the nun's habit and wimpel, which covered most of his head and face. "Don't talk; I need to concentrate on my driving and who might be tailing us."

Colombo sat slumped in his car waiting for the red Panda to exit St. Anne's gate. About an hour after he had seen a yellow Panda leave the Vatican with a man in a business suit driving, and a nun in the passenger seat, he sat up in a violent jerk, as if poked in the butt with a policeman's club, and exclaimed, *Ah shit! I bet that bastard changed cars. I **thought** the man in the business suit looked like that fairy-prince who has always worn an overwrought, black dress topped by a white dog collar. Damn it! Why didn't I think of that then? Fuck! I missed him. And who was that nun? Is he 'doing' nuns these days?*

Chapter 70

On a cool September day, Drs. Holden, Severson, and Fitzsimmons met with Maria to continue the meeting that was interrupted by Jenny's angry outburst.

"Welcome back, all of you," Dr. Holden said. "I understand, Maria that you and Jenny have reconciled any discomfort that may have come from the last meeting and that we can continue with the review of your thesis. Is that correct?"

Jenny nodded that it was.

Dr. Severson helped Maria set up her laptop computer, the projector and screen and took his seat. Maria removed her laser pointer from her hand bag, stood up and clicked on the *Last Judgment* slide and proceeded. "When we discontinued the meeting several weeks ago, I was about to point out . . ."

"Excuse me, Maria, but before we proceed, I have a question," said Dr. Severson."

"Well, thank you for helping me set up. What's your question?" asked Maria, with a smile.

"Actually, it's for Jenny. What is a 'Potemkin village'? You mentioned it as some sort of deception in our last meeting."

Jenny laughed. "Oh, that! Well, in the eighteenth century the Russian Czarina, Catherine the Great, wanted to impress her lover, a statesman, Prince Gegori Aleksandrovich Potemkin, with the modernization of her country, so she took him down a river in one of her boats to show him a magnificent city on the bank of the Volga River.

"However, no city existed; so before they went on their show-and-tell trip, she had a movie-set type village constructed with only the fronts of the buildings showing on the left bank of the river. That's where that expression comes from. It is often used to express deception. As you can see, Michelangelo isn't the only famous, historical figure to engage in deception, right Maria?"

"Right you are, Jenny."

"Oh, okay. Thanks Jenny. Sorry to interrupt, Maria," said Willy.

"No problem, Dr. Severson," said Maria. "Jenny's explanation provides a convenient segue from where we left off last time." Maria reviewed the seven deceptions listed in the thesis pointing to relevant points on the fresco as she spoke. She stated that deception number seven—the removal of the gloomy patina and replacing with bright, gay colors—is consistent with another issue that she had already addressed: that of Mary Magdalene appearing with Jesus.

Maria continued: "We found a photo of the original painting showing her wearing a much brighter red dress than the washed-out pink we see in the restoration. By contrast, the blue drape falling from her waist exposing her buttocks is actually brighter in the restored fresco than it was in the original.

"The blue drape, falling from her waist exposing her right hip was meant to deceive uncritical eyes into thinking this was Mary the Mother of Jesus. *We can't have the public thinking this is someone other than the Holy Mother.* Yet, that is exactly what the artist intended: a crucial deception, which if examined closely will reveal a very pregnant Mary Magdalene as well.

"Notice here," Maria continued—pointing to a green "Breeches Maker" drape painted along the back side of "Mother Mary's" right hip—"the ludicrous length they went to ensure that *no one* would see her 'backside.' The blue drape only *suggests* her backside is bare, but just in case anyone—with an over-active imagination—could "actually see" her bare behind, they would encounter one of the hundreds of drapes used by the 'Breeches Maker'." .

"In summary, all of these deceptions suggest, with varying degrees of intensity, that there will be no 'last judgment'; it's the message the artist wanted to provide for posterity. He was hoping that the deceptions would not be discovered before he died, because if they had been, his life would have been in danger. The most offensive deception in the painting is the figure here, that 'gives the finger' (or 'fig') to no one in particular, but most likely to the pope."

"Are there any questions about the painting or anything else in the paper?"

"I'm curious," said Willy. "I'm thinking your paper is just idle speculation and a waste of time; interesting maybe to some people, but unless you can show something more than what you are showing, all I can say is: 'So what!'

"However, let's assume for the moment that your assessment has some merit; after all, an entire book has been published asserting essentially the same thing you are averring: that Michelangelo embedded secret messages in his Sistine frescoes. But you claim that Blech and Doliner missed the biggest deception in their analysis of the *Last Judgment:* that there will be no 'last judgment.'

"I read their book, by the way, and I found it very impressive, indeed: well documented, well written and very persuasive for their point of view. They had, by virtue of the views they presented about Jewish mysticism, a somewhat positive message, beyond the artist's ridicule of the popes and the way they treat their people. I didn't see that added value in your paper."

"My goodness, Dr. Severson, you do have a good question. You have identified the issue that I believe will lead to my realizing what my 'God's messenger' mission really is. I agree with you; if the deceptions we have identified were all I had to offer they would be interesting stuff . . . but so what?

"They might be explosive revelations—to realize that this great artist painted deceptions and insults into the *Last Judgment*—asserting that there will be no "last judgment" and that we are just now discovering his tricks. But how relevant is that to my purpose in coming to your seminary for assistance?

"Let me put it this way. I'll refer you to the part in my paper where we were discussing Mary's role. Do you remember where I was saying that Blech and Doliner said she was gazing down at Colonna, Michelangelo's platonic lover? Well, first of all, we don't think, as I said, that "Mary" is Jesus mother.

"Secondly, we disagree with where her gaze was going, but that doesn't diminish the importance of Colonna being placed in the painting in the position she's in. She's there because she was the leader of what came to be known as the secret cabal, *Il Spirituali,* in Italian, or *The Spiritual Ones* in English.

"Colonna was a rarity in her time. She was one of the few published, widely followed poets and an intellectual who led a cabal of Church reformers who were fed up with Vatican corruption and deceit. She and her associates— including Michelangelo—met regularly and secretly over dinner to discuss their desire to bring about reform of the Church from within and heal the wounds brought about by the Reformation.

"They wanted to move toward the Protestant doctrine of salvation by faith alone and free access to—and personal interpretation of—scripture. Michelangelo and she found in each other their intellectual equals and exchanged passionate, but platonic letters expressing their love for one another."

Pointing to the center of the painting, Maria said, "Colona is hidden behind the grill upon which Mary's foot rests. This is the artist's way of honoring her in this painting. She could also be there as a protector of the birth canal we mentioned when discussing the womb deception.

"So what does all of this have to do with your question, Dr. Severson? It points out what we," Maria said (with a smile at Willy), "have in common with Blech and Doliner's analysis, and where we differ.

"First of all, they point out that Michelangelo is not the devout Catholic that one could plausibly (but erroneously) infer from the fact that he *is* the artist who painted the Sistine ceiling and the *Last Judgment* in the most famous Catholic Chapel in the world—and then spent the last twenty or so years of his life as the Chief Architect of the Basilica. However, we think that the artist had not become a devout Lutheran either, as Blech and Doliner seem to suggest.

"We agree with the authors of *Sistine Secrets:* they are more prone to put him in with Jewish Kabbalists, than they are any other religion. It might be a matter of degree of perceptions; they wanted to highlight his association with the cabal that had veered toward the reforms of the Reformation to emphasize his rebellious nature one more time.

"Remember . . . he finished the *Last Judgment* thirty-three years after he was commissioned to paint the ceiling so it is not surprising that his religious views evolved over those three decades.

"Now, here's the kicker—in answer to your question. We believe, unlike the authors of *Sistine Secrets,* that there is sufficient evidence to show that Michelangelo was, in fact, a harbinger of a "new spiritual paradigm" that has surfaced within the last twenty years. I hasten to add that this new paradigm—with a central feature being "going within to find God"—is not new, but is embedded in the most ancient of all spiritual movements. So, it's quite likely that's where his spiritual inclinations led to his desire for finding . . . **within,** "the Light so long foretold for all."

"Ancient and at least one modern master, have taught that the Kingdom of God can be found within, an idea that Michelangelo shared—but was unable to realize fully—thereby eliminating all doubt about his fate after death.

"We can show that the core of the paradigm is that which all great, enlightened masters have taught down through the ages. They include, but are not limited to Lord Krishna, Lord Buddha, Shankara, Moses, and Jesus.

"They are the ones who have taught that we are all created with a divine inner Self, which is none other than God in us, and whom we can realize as our own Self without the help—or rather the *burden*—of organized religion."

"Whoa! Now you've said a mouthful, if I ever heard one," said Dr. Severson. "You're saying that Michelangelo's messages in the *Last Judgment*, and I presume elsewhere, at least hint at a new religion that would be a blender full of all religions, both East and West? Is that what you are saying?" asked Dr. Severson.

"Not quite. I didn't say he was the prophet of some new *religion*. And I would say that his *Last Judgment* is more of a desperate plea for something better than Catholicism than it is a hint at a new religion. It is from the 'else-where'—his life and artistry generally, and his poetry more specifically—that we infer a hint of a new spiritual way of dealing with our spiritual longings: *'Rend thou the veil, oh Lord, break down this wall [...] so that I may feel thee inwardly and never doubt.'* I meant to say he was 'implying a new paradigm', not suggesting he is a prophet, seer, or a fortune teller who can predict the future.

"The central issue here is that—for Michelangelo—it is inconceivable that a God of infinite and unconditional love could create a universe in which humans or other beings are created, given laws to obey, and then condemned to an eternity of torture and terror if they disobey.

"That deceitful doctrine made no more sense to Michelangelo than it makes to me or any other person who thinks for her/himself, or more importantly listens to one's intuition and pays attention to one's feelings.

"Our emotion—and intuition—is God speaking to us in the most effective way imaginable. How can we contact that intuition? 'Be still and know that I am God' (Psalm 46:10), says the Psalmist. Quiet your mind long enough to be able to 'hear' what your inner voice is saying, what God is communicating to you.

"That's what Jesus meant when he said, **'Whoever has ears to hear, let him hear. There is light within a man ...'** (Gospel of Thomas # 23). This is what all masters have taught. Most extant religions are derivatives of that truth turned upside down.

"The captivating thing about Michelangelo is that he intuited that inner being, undoubtedly because his divine, artistic inspirations came to him in his painting and sculpturing. It seems that the only time he was truly thrilled to be alive was when he was sculpturing and less so when he was painting.

"However, creating works of art was not enough for him. He very much wanted that Divine Being to reassure him of his eternal fate; his poetry reveals that.

"He felt the presence of God 'outwardly' in the sense that he appreciated the divine beauty he saw in the human body, the human skin, the figures he sculpted, the frescoes he painted, and nature in general. He felt the pleasure of creating from a level of divine inspiration.

"But those are different experiences from that for which he yearned: an **inner** awareness of incontrovertible assurance that he is the indestructible, divine being he suspects he is, but has no *proof* of.

Mother Teresa is the apotheosis of 'faithfulness'. Yet the certainty she hoped for was absent in her life; she had agonizing doubts about her fate after death. She pled (unlike Michelangelo)—desperately—for rock-solid reassurance that her fate be determined before she died. 'When I raise my thoughts to heaven—there is such convicting emptiness . . . those very thoughts return like sharp knives & hurt my very soul.'

"Dr. Severson, does that answer your question?"

"Well, it's been so long since I asked I forgot what it was."

"I apologize. It was such an important question that I wanted to clarify the answer in my own mind as much as respond to your question, which was: Where is the added-value in the content of your thesis comparable to what Blech and Doliner had in their book? Here's my short answer.

"For anyone who has had enough of the phenomenal life of this world, or whose religion has somehow failed to serve their spiritual longings, there is hope. And I have something in mind that justifies that hope. Michelangelo and Mother Teresa remind us of the need to provide for fulfillment of that desire: a spiritual paradigm that does not terrorize us and one that will gently help us to break down the wall that separates us from the Divine Light within."

Willy looked at Maria and said, "I appreciate your lengthy answer; I think I understood about half of what you said, but let's not belabor the issue any more than we have. Please proceed."

"Okay. Thank you for your question and attention to my answer. Now, it occurs to me that, with this committee's permission, I could extend my thesis to include what I referred to a moment ago: the fact that nearly all ancient masters were bringing essentially the same core message to humanity: something that the Eastern religious masters, Moses and Jesus all aver: that the *Kingdom of God is within.*

"A recent book, *Conversations with God,* outlines in some detail a new paradigm that fits perfectly with what all masters have said. I could elaborate on that theme and then, provided I have come to a final conclusion about what my 'God's messenger' mission should be, include that as a part of my thesis as well.

"Dr. Holden, you have been silent through all of this. I really appreciate your attentiveness. And I'm looking forward to your feedback on my paper and what I am now proposing. Do you think my proposal to extend my thesis would be a possibility?"

"Thank you for your kind words, Maria. I'd like to think about that proposal for a while. Frankly, I'm a little concerned that it could get to be too cumbersome for a master's thesis. Perhaps we could assess the thesis as written, and then if you like, I'm sure we could make time to listen to more of your very provocative statements about the current state of world religions and what can be done about it.

"I'm skeptical about your idea that all masters expressed the same core message; maybe the Eastern masters, but Judaism and Christianity? What do you two think?" Sally said, looking at the two professors.

Jenny spoke first. "I'd be delighted to be involved in this next phase." Glancing at Sally and then looking at Willy, Jenny said, "As I told you Sally, Maria and I had a very interesting discussion at my house and she shared some of her thoughts on what the new paradigm might be. I'm sure what she will tell us about the masters' messages and how all that morphed into the religions we have today, would be interesting, if not enlightening. We might become mid-wives in birthing a modern-day *Martina Luther*, after all. Who knows?"

Willy indicated his willingness to go along with whatever the others decided. He was late for his golfing date with his buddies.

"Okay then," said Sally. "Let's adjourn for today. Maria, let us know when you are ready to resume your presentation."

"I think I can be ready in a month or two. I want to thank all of you for your attention and support. It really means a lot to me."

Chapter 71

Sal's face turned purple, suggesting an imminent, mild, apoplectic seizure caused by restricted blood flow to his brain and face. Sitting at the head of the oblong conference table, he shouted, **"First that nun witch-bitch, and now that devil, Russo.** If we don't do something fast, that black bastard, who claims to be the Vicar of Christ, will bring ruin to all of us. Does anyone know where Russo's family lives? We'll feed all of them to the fishes!"

Cardinal Moretti nodded his head in agreement. The Russian, Igor Yavolinski, glanced around the table: Antonio De Luca's eyes nearly popped their sockets with rage; Nicholas Giordano polished his rimless glasses as if cleaning them would help him clear his mind from the anger he felt over Russo's defection; Francesco Lombardi held a small mirror in one hand while straightening his curly, black hair with the other—a twitch to reduce excessive anxiety; Monsignor Lopez and Father Nunez stared at Mancini in silence: their moment was at hand.

"Mr. Mancini," said Monsignor Lopez of Opus Dei, "I understand your anger. But before we start talking about heading down the road of revenge and violence, I want to introduce our guest, a professional warrior with years of combat experience.

"Gentlemen, this is Colonel 'Bull' Masterson. He recently retired from the Marine Corps after a distinguished career as an infantry officer. He earned several medals for bravery and outstanding performance in the Gulf and Iraq wars.

"For nearly a year he has been training a para-military force of one hundred men in the Blue Ridge Mountains of North Carolina. We have brought him here because the Vatican Ship of State is heading toward an iceberg and a Titanic redux."

"Why not just whack that bastard who calls himself the Vicar of Christ— get it over with— forget about all this bullshit?" asked De Luca.

"SMEAC," Col. Masterson shouted.

"What?" De Luca said, "We're speaking English here. Colonel, I suggest you do the same."

"You've mentioned veering into violence before even mentioning the need for a plan of action," said Col. "Bull" Masterson.

"So, what was that you said? A new swear word?" said Giordano.

"No, it's an acronym, a word that is formed from the initial letters of a group of words: **Situation, Mission, Execution, Attack and Consolidation. SMEAC!** It's the five-paragraph order the Marine Corps uses before every attack. It is the rubric used at every level of command, from the commanding general down through regimental, battalion, company, platoon and a squad of thirteen men. That's a disciplined way to prepare for battle. The first step is describing the situation, and then lay out the rest of the battle plan by the numbers. So who can describe the situation that brings us together?"

Monsignor Lopez responded. "The pope has been studying the situation in the Church for three years and has come to the conclusion that reforms are necessary and plans to announce them in the near future; we think within the next month.

1. "We believe he will take the Church down an extremely destructive path and even destroy the Church if he is not stopped.
2. "For decades the Church has had a very lucrative, mutual relationship with these business men sitting around the table; that relationship is threatened by the theft of bank records by one of the bank employees, and the defection of the bank manager to the pope. Those facts, alone, would be destructive enough if the pope is not stopped.
3. "But that's not all. The pope is seriously considering major doctrinal, legal, and administrative changes within the Holy See, the religious arm of the Vatican. He might even be considering declaring the Roman Catholic Church extinct.
4. "According to canon law we can remove him from the Holy See, but there is no legal way to remove him from the Vatican City State position.
5. "The Roman Catholic Code of Canon Law (RCCL) grants the pope supreme power over all things: temporal power within the Vatican City State—a sovereign state among nations—and eternal (or religious) power within the Holy See. All he would need to do is abrogate the 1929 Lateran Treaty we have with Italy to dissolve the Vatican City State. He could—as Supreme Pontiff—declare the Roman Catholic Church extinct before he signs the Lateran Treaty. I won't attempt to explain the catastrophic consequences of such acts.
6. "Of course, there are legal scholars who would insist that pronouncing the Church extinct is impossible because the papacy is an essential element of

the nature of the Church which Jesus Christ Himself instituted and *against* which He declared, *'the gates of Hell will not prevail.'*

7. "However, if the pope were to conclude that Jesus Christ never instituted the Church in the first place, for him the Code of Canon Law wouldn't be worth the price of a roll of toilet paper. Jesus of Nazareth didn't write the Code of Canon Law; men did, long after Jesus died.

"That's the situation. **In a sentence: The pope is threatening to destroy the Church.** Now, what is the next step?"

"Mission," replied Colonel Masterson.

"Okay, then, *MISSION,* continued Monsignor Lopez.

"To prevent Pope Immanuel from leading the Church down a path that will lead to its destruction.' That's the mission in a nutshell, but for our purposes here, I'll explain what I mean by that so that everyone is on the same page regarding what we need to accomplish.

1. "To prevent Pope Immanuel from terminating the relationship of the Church with traditional Vatican Bank customers.

2. "To prevent Pope Immanuel from initiating major doctrinal, legal and administrative changes within the Holy See.

3. "To prevent Pope Immanuel from declaring the Roman Catholic Church defunct and abrogating the 1929 Lateran Treaty.

4. "In order to achieve the multi-faceted nature of the mission, invade the Vatican City State with legally constituted, para-military members of the Roman Catholic Church, and force the pope to resign before he acts.

"Colonel Masterson. Next step?" asked Lopez.

"EXECUTION," said Masterson, "but first I want to point out that your last point does not belong in the *MISSION* phase. It belongs in the next step. So if nothing has changed when I present that phase, it will be our first point in the next phase.

"But I have a question before we proceed. Has anyone tried to talk him out of the course he's on? It seems to me your first step should be negotiation."

Retired Cardinal Moretti spoke: "So far as we know the pope does not know we are reading the papers Father Sandusky and the mysterious priest have prepared. I'm not sure he would care if he knew we were. He seems to be biding his time for the right moment to make his move and I suspect the banking issue will be the catalyst that triggers his move.

"We can't confront him with the papers and demand an explanation and negotiations because we don't want him to know we are aware of what's in the papers. If he finds that out, the source will dry up and we'll be flying blind-folded."

"I want to caution all of you that I, Monsignor Lopez, the Opus Dei leader, in consultation with the Legion and others around the table will make the decision when to move. We will hold out hope that if things start to get nasty, that if the threat of violence is imminent, we might be able to reason with him . . . to enter into negotiations with us to save himself and the Church.

"So Colonel Masterson, you'll need to make plans for several contingencies based on the situation we just outlined and my cautionary words. Now, what is the next phase of your attack plan?"

"Thank you, Cardinal Moretti. *Execution* is the process of planning *how* to execute the attack, which is determined by what the objective of the attack is. For example, the plan of the attack will depend on the terrain and the situation: Is the objective of the attack to rescue hostages, or is it to capture a hill held by the enemy? The *Attack* carries out the plans made in the *Execution* phase. *Consolidation* occurs after the attack is successful to maintain control of the situation. For example, if the objective of the attack is to take a hill from the enemy, after the hill is taken, you would set up a perimeter defense to keep the enemy from taking the hill back in a counter-attack.

"Obviously, we can't do the planning now because the execution phase will require reconnoitering the objective of the attack, which means analyzing the Vatican City complex to determine the best tactical maneuvers to ensure the accomplishment of the mission. The attack and consolidation phases will be decided at a time to be determined after the execution plans are finalized. I suggest we adjourn so I can get to work. I will let you know when I have the *execution* phase completed."

"Not so fast, Colonel," said De Luca. "I repeat, why not whack the fucker and get it over with?"

"Mr. De Luca, I'm not calling those kinds of shots here. The rest of you in this room are, so take up your beefs up with them. I'll do my job. You do yours."

Chapter 72

Dear Dr. Holden,

I have finished the written presentation we agreed upon at our last meeting. It is attached. I am prepared to meet with you again to discuss its contents at your convenience. I am sending hard-copies via snail-mail.

It has been a couple months since we met so I'll summarize where we left off. I had finished my analysis of the *Last Judgment* and we were discussing Michelangelo's intimations of another way to look at our spiritual yearnings and how to deal with them. I suggested that nearly all masters of divine wisdom have taught essentially the same thing that the artist was inferring: that God can be found within, but the monotheistic religions deny this, while Eastern religions have inverted the process of "going within." I begin this continuation of my thesis with that summary in mind, and then move on to weave the major religious threads into my mission as "God's messenger."

Please let me know when it would be convenient to continue our discussion.

Sincerely,

Maria

(C O N T I N U A T I O N)
of the
Master's Degree in Theology Thesis

Michelangelo's deceptions in the *Last Judgment* served as a vanguard in my search for my mission as "God's messenger." Discovery of his deceptions piqued my interest in the history of Christianity.

That history involves a war that was waged by the emerging Catholic Church against *so-called* heretics in the centuries following Jesus' death; it involves two thousand years that read more like the history of a totalitarian state founded on the basis of fear and terror than a religion founded in the name of Jesus who preached love and compassion.

I have included a brief review about some of the masters of divine wisdom: how their wisdom was overturned by their followers and how a similar phenomenon occurred after the death of Jesus. Using a quasi-content analysis model, I'll use selected Gnostic gospels, the Catholic Church's spiritual paradigm and the New Spiritual Paradigm—found in *Conversations with God*—as support for the core of my thesis which is: *There is hope for anyone who seeks an alternative to extant religious or non-religious belief systems.* Finally, I weave a single, brief tapestry from these threads and include Michelangelo's deceptions, his spiritual yearning, and Mother Teresa's anguish.

SPIRITUAL MASTERS ON THE SAME PAGE

Nearly all teachers of divine wisdom have taught us that God consciousness is accessible to every human who seeks that reality. Among the greatest of God's teachers are Lord Krishna, of India, Moses of the Middle East, Lord Buddha of India, Shankara of India, Jesus of Nazareth, and Maharishi Mayhesh Yogi of India (1918-2008).

The latest revelation from God comes to us through three books titled, ***Conversations with God (CwG), (written*** and published by Neil Donald Walsch between 1996 and 2005), in which a <u>New Spiritual Paradigm</u> is offered to humanity as an alternative to extant religions. Adding credence to ***Conversations with God,*** and the assertions that the teachings of Jesus were overturned by the founders of the Catholic Church, is the knowledge contained in the recently discovered **Gnostic Gospels.**

In the Preface of ***On the Bhagavad-Gita: A New Translation and Commentary-Chapters 1-6,*** Maharishi Mahesh Yogi offers a summary explanation of how the teachings of ancient masters of eternal wisdom waxed and waned over thousands of years. Veda Vyasa, an ancient historian, recorded the primordial, oral traditions of Vedic masters.

In India, Veda Vyasa recorded the people's descent into unrighteousness which occurred several thousand years ago. Lord Krishna came to teach essentially the same message of the Vedic masters: that is, the true values of life which can be realized through contact with transcendental Being.

His wisdom came in the form of a book, titled the *Bhagavad-Gita,* attributed to Vyasa. Here Lord Krishna, in a dialogue with a warrior named Arjuna, reveals the secrets of "going within" to contact our divine inner Selves.

Over the next two thousand years, Lord Krishna's teaching became overshadowed by beliefs resulting from the attractions which were glorified by living a life of ignorance—characterized by limiting one's life to the experience of the senses and intellect, constricted by the binding influence of wealth, fame, power and glory—a life separated from the divine, inner self.

About three thousand years ago, Lord Buddha came teaching essentially the same wisdom that Lord Krishna taught, but he included a meditation technique that involved a concept of *Being, thinking and action.* However, because no systematic way of teaching the wisdom and the meditation technique was established, society again deteriorated into ignorance and profligate living.

His teaching ("Yogastah kuru karmani" . . . a Vedic phrase which means, *"Established in Being, perform action."*) was turned upside down. Lord Buddha taught that one uses meditation—not to be mistaken for "right action" or "good works"—to become established in "Being," and then "right action" would follow as a result of "right thinking" which is automatic for those who function from a higher level of "Being."

Yet, eventually, the knowledge that Lord Buddha taught became obscured because teachers began to place the cart before the horse: "Right action" came to be regarded as the means of gaining enlightenment, whereas right action is the direct result of having become established in Being; that is, having become enlightened.

Within three or four hundred years, Lord Buddha's teaching, "Being, thinking and action," was lost to the public and once again society deteriorated into worshiping the relative aspects of life.

Then Shankara, another Indian teacher appeared on the scene and once again restored the proper sequence of establishing oneself in "Being" first . . . and then performing action. Like Lord Buddha, Shankara used the *Bhagavad-Gita* texts as the basis for his teaching. He established training centers throughout India to restore the fullness of life, and was successful for a time, but living eventually became mired in the superficialities of life. His message suffered the same fate of the teachers who had gone before him.

Unfortunately, once again, the statements about the nature of the goal *(Being; Self-Realization or Enlightenment)* had been mistaken for the *path* to Self-realization. Because the teachers are misunderstood by those who do not function on the same level of consciousness, the teachings are corrupted over time and society deteriorates once again.

That happened to Shankara's wisdom because the custodians of his teaching gradually assigned more importance to the goal than assigning equal importance to the path and the goal. In other words, the path to enlightenment, Transcendental Meditation—going within to experience one's divine Self—was ignored in favor of attention on the goal (the state of Being that one achieves as the result of meditation).

Both aspects—simultaneous development of the heart and mind—are important for Self-realization. But Shankara's followers eventually reversed his knowledge by promoting *contemplation* of the goal instead of going within to *experience* the goal.

At the middle of the twentieth century, Maharishi Mahesh Yogi began his sixty-year journey to re-establish what Shankara had done; by the beginning of the twenty-first century, hundreds of Transcendental Meditation Centers had been established around the globe and hundreds of thousands had learned the TM technique for "going within." According to Maharishi, the TM technique is easy to learn and practice: anybody can do it. By contrast, one example (of those who choose to interpret the *Bhagavad-Gita* by distorting the teaching therein) is to claim that contemplation of the goal (as a meditative practice) is a struggle because "the mind is restless . . . it is often turbulent and powerfully obstinate . . . but with steady practice, and non-attachment, it can be controlled. Success in yoga (Self-realization) is extremely difficult if you can not control your mind . . ." (Satchidananda, Sri-Swami (1988) *The Living Gita:The Complete Bhagavad-Gita:A Commentary for Modern Readers* (Integral Yoga Publications,Yogaville,Virginia) (p. 93)

All of the Eastern religious denominations and sects that made this mistake contend that transcendental consciousness is the last step of a devotee's achievement.Yet, Shankara believes that transcendental consciousness is possible from the beginning; the *first step* for Shankara is the *last step* for the religions that turned his knowledge upside down.

The tragedy for Indian culture was that the sects' idea came to be interpreted to be for the recluse alone, thereby establishing the basis of Indian culture in terms of the recluse way of life: renunciation and detachment. Shankara's philosophy of spiritual seeking turned upside down resulted in centuries of Indians being lost in a futile search for God.

Even Patanjali's Yogic eight-fold path was reversed. Instead of starting with transcendental consciousness (as Patanjali taught), the sects started with the secular virtues as a beginning on the path toward Self-realization.

JUDAISM & CHRISTIANITY DISTORT MASTERS' WISDOM

The reversal of masters' wisdom in India is not unlike the tragedy that has occurred in cultures that adopted the monotheistic religious paradigm. One can only wonder what would have happened if what Moses and Jesus really said—and modeled for good living—had not been distorted by the founders of Judaism and the Roman Catholic Church. According to *Conversations with God,* all masters' teachings have been misunderstood and distorted, including those attributed to Moses and Jesus.

And yet, in *Conversations with God,* God insists that commandments are the fictions of religionists and a distortion of what he and Moses discussed. But, it is important to remember that Jewish mysticism—in the form of Kabbalism exists.

Islam is another matter: a far more complex issue than its sister monotheistic religions, for there is no clear demarcation line between what the master intended and what his followers did. Why? Because as one author declares, writing about Muhammad—the founder of Islam—"Violence and gentleness were at war within him . . . seeing the world about to be destroyed by the flames of God and [yet] in a state of divine peace." (Payne, *The History of Islam*, p. 66).

The Quran, according to Payne, reveals the quite astonishing polarity of Muhammad's mind; it goes on exhorting Muhammad's followers to violence against the infidel, while quoting some of the most majestic spiritual passages ever uttered by a human being. Sorting those facts out as a means of determining the extent to which Muhammad's followers distorted his teachings—if at all—is well beyond the parameters of this thesis.

JESUS AND HIS LEGACY

Jesus of Nazareth came to Middle East, was born into a Jewish family and taught a path to "salvation" that involved seeking—*within*—sacred knowledge (gnosis) that would rid oneself of the ignorance which separates

humans from their divine inner selves. He spoke of the same path to "salvation" that the Vedic masters before him had taught: "Go within to find God."
But only a few of his disciples "got" the message. Among the most prominent
that we know about are Philip, James, Levi, Judas Iscariot and Mary Magdalene.

They, as we'll see in the Gnostic gospels, were the ones who understood
and, in some cases (those who were functioning on a level of consciousness that
would make it possible for them to understand what he was saying) received
"secret knowledge" about the mysteries of the universe from Jesus. "Mysteries" can be interpreted to mean knowledge which lower levels of consciousness cannot comprehend.

However, that statement should not be interpreted to be pejorative;
humans live on several levels of consciousness and evolve to higher levels
through experiences attained here on earth and beyond. As we shall see, that
is the purpose of life here on earth: to evolve to higher levels of consciousness.

The chief difference between the development of the Eastern religions
and two of the monotheistic religions (Judaism and Christianity) is that the
Indian masters had considerable successes by "going within"—which lasted up
to several centuries before declining.

For Jesus and his Gnostic followers, their movement—based on Jesus'
words and deeds—was squashed early on by men who, not comprehending
what Jesus was saying, envisioned a power-grabbing opportunity to create an
institution based on fear and terror.

The success of Roman Catholicism's establishment of a church is thoroughly documented by historians. For Jesus, his *Gnostic* teachings were not
only squashed, but his teachings of love and compassion were corrupted by
the founders of what became a religion established in his name: "Christianity."
By the fourth century, the dispute—between the Gnostic Christians and The
RCC—had been decided. The Roman Catholic Church had won.

Similarly, the early Hebrews, ignoring the fact that Adam and Eve represented an uplifting—an awakening into the mysteries of good and evil—
(rather than a fall into original sin)—adopted a creation myth which had as its
source an angry and vengeful God.

In order to explain evil in the world, the founders of the Judaism had
one of God's angels rebelling, resulting in the Devil, who became the source
of all evil. The Devil and God became mortal enemies in battle, the outcome

of which was uncertain. (Those who study Gnostic philosophy will discover that some Gnostic sects fashioned a similar myth to account for the apparent evil and suffering in the world; they believed that the God of the Hebrews, an angry, lesser, "Creator God" was responsible.)

Nevertheless, for the Hebrews, there was a remedy for humans caught up in this drama: obey the laws that God handed down to his "chosen people" and wait for a messiah who would come someday to triumph over all enemies and usher in a new and glorious world.

However, Jesus arrival on the scene created a problem for both the Jews and the would-be founders of a new religion: Roman Catholicism. The hierarchy of the established Hebrew religion rejected Jesus because he did not fit their expectation of the promised messiah.

The Jews were expecting a warrior-type—a glorious, charismatic, powerful messiah (like the legendary David)—who would lead their nation to new heights of conquest and power. Jesus was not only **not** *that,* but was something worse: a rabble-rouser, who rejected the law-laden, rule-bound, and, institutionalized religion of his heritage.

For the emerging founders of a new religion, Jesus appearance on the scene was a little more complex. Although the Jewish religious hierarchy rejected this Jewish rabbi, the incipient "Christians" saw in him a perfect actor for their nefarious purposes: they would adopt him as the promised Jewish messiah—giving him a powerful, lineal legitimacy—dating back to King David, thereby co-opting the God of the Jews—and all that that implied. They would inherit the Jewish Bible all the way back to the Creation myth. Now it was up to them to create their own Bible, but there was a problem.

This Jewish rabbi, Jesus, was saying a lot of things, and some of them just didn't fit neatly with the emerging doctrine of the nascent "Christian" Church.

The proto-orthodox "Christians", as some scholars refer to them, liked the idea that they could distort Jesus' authentic message for their own purposes. They had the perfect ersatz formula: (1) an angry and vengeful God; (2) a savior who—they claimed—preached faith and good works as a path to salvation from original sin (the Adam and Eve drama); (3) the atonement for sins of omission and commission; (4) a penalty for rebellion against this doctrine: eternal damnation to a life of unspeakable suffering; and (5) life as a "one-shot-deal": get it right, because there is only one life in a human body with no re-runs; and (6) *if you manage to overcome your sinful nature and deviant ways by believing in and doing what we teach, an eternity in heaven will be your reward.*

Thus, Jesus' authentic message, extant in the Gnostic gospels (and other Gnostic scriptures), written following Jesus death, became a serious threat to the false religion of the emerging, proto-orthodox Christians, because much of what Jesus was saying was diametrically opposed to the budding doctrine of the new church. And followers were buying the Gnostic message.

Some historians assert that Gnosticism had several sects and denominations, so it is difficult to state, precisely what Gnosticism is. It is unlikely that the Gnostics had as many sects and denominations as modern Christianity—which number in the hundreds. Yet, the Gnostic Christians, like Christianity today, had core ideas that identified them as belonging to the movement that became known as Gnosticism.

Most of what was known about Gnosticism, up until the present day, was what one could glean from St. Irenaeus's *Against Heresies*—*a* five volume diatribe—which cherry-picked, from Gnostic literature, the most esoteric passages (which he used for ridicule) while ignoring what Jesus said. Irenaeus had good reason for such deceptions because what Jesus said was antithetical to the emerging orthodox Christian doctrine, which Irenaeus was promoting and defending.

Today, St. Irenaeus is venerated by the Roman Catholic Church, the Eastern Orthodox Church, the Lutheran Church and the Anglican Communion as a hero—a saint—who played a major role in the founding of Christianity.

It is clear, from two thousand years of recorded Roman Catholic Church history, and recent discoveries of what the Gnostics believed, that a grave injustice was done when the founding fathers of the Catholic Church persecuted the Gnostics and denigrated Gnostic versions of Jesus' legacy. Beginning in the late twelfth century, the Catholic Church launched a crusade followed by an Inquisition against Cathar heretics in the Languedoc area, located in the South of France. The campaigns would last for 112 years. Time magazine, referring to that period, in an article dated April 28, 1961, stated, "Historians estimate the total number of casualties to be a million, but that has never been verified; a more likely number is in the tens of thousands."

That number refers to the massacres that began in earnest at Beziers, Languedoc, when on July 22, 1209, crusaders from France put to the sword twenty-thousand men, women, children and babies. The slaughter lasted for a few days. Few avoided death, but those who did wandered away from the city, their bodies disfigured and their minds tortured. Historians do not dispute the twenty-thousand number. While those who were tortured and killed during the 112 years of the Crusade and Inquisition is unknown, what is known is that a systematic destruction of the Cathars' religious texts and historical records was a major feature that accompanied this holocaust.

Catharism was a religion that emerged in Armenia and Bulgaria, was active in Italy, Flanders, Germany, and England in the eleventh century, but mysteriously appeared in the independent Lanquedoc region in the South of France, where it flourished in the twelfth and thirteenth centuries.

Following a brutal crusade and murderous inquisition which took the lives of tens of thousands of Cathars, the Cathars were all but exterminated when, in a final push to rid themselves of the heretics in France, the Roman Catholic Church burned two hundred men and women, "Cathar heretics," at Montsegur in 1244. But the Cathar sect (a derivative of the Gnostics) was not the only heretical movement persecuted by the Roman Church. Like the Gnostics and the Cathars, several other Christian sects with dualistic ideas appeared in the Eastern Mediterranean area as early as the first century. Some of the more notable ones are the Mandaeans (Iraq), Manichaeans (France, Saxony, Italy), and the Bogomils (Bosnia). The persecutions—against not only heretical Christian sects, but also, notably Jews—began several decades following Jesus death and continued—off and on—until the middle of the nineteenth century . . . the end of yet another holocaust known as the Spanish Inquisition.

There seems to be no disagreement that there are significant differences between the Gnostic belief system and that of the Cathers. The chief differences are twofold: (1) the Gnostics' emphasis on "going within" to experience God directly and thus, salvation while in the human body . . . not the case in Catharism; and (2) asceticism—as practiced in Catharism—is a path to God: be initiated, and then learn, follow and obey the way of the ascetic and you will earn your salvation which is experienced following death. Cathars, who chose to be "followers" rather than becoming "perfected"—thereby joining the ranks of the Perfect ones—would reincarnate after death and, once again, have a chance to be perfected.

However, similarities abound: (1) both religions considered the passion of Christ (his life, death, resurrection and atonement for humanity's sins) nonsense; (2) both religions believed in a doscetic Christ; (3) both believed in reincarnation; (4) both had similar beliefs in Good and Evil; (5) Both believed that humans possessed a divine spark within.

Today, Gnostics worship in a small number of churches that are active in the United States. However, from what we have been able to determine, contemporary Gnosticism bears little resemblance to the Gnostics who were persecuted in the decades following Jesus death. Gnostic worship today, in the United States, resembles the Roman Catholic mass in form and substance; there is little to suggest that "going with" to find one's salvation—as that idea was understood by the earliest Gnostics—is a significant element in modern Gnosticism.

We think the persecution of the Cathars in the Languedoc area of what would later be the South of France, was—at a minimum—a consequence of the nascent Catholic Church's failure to completely wipe out Gnosticism during its battle for supremacy over the sect they considered to be a hotbed of heresy.

The Catholic Church was successful in destroying or driving underground—literally—Gnostic sacred literature, thereby denying future generations the full wisdom of Christ's teaching. The upshot was that the Cathars adopted much of what they knew about the Gnostic teachings and perhaps adopted elements of other similar religions as well.

At least one modern scholar has vindicated Cathar claims to represent a survival of the Earliest Christian Church . . . that is, the Gnostics. (McDonald, J., "The Cathars and Cathar Beliefs in the Languedoc," url:http://www.catharinfo.com, 17 January 2012).

The Crusades, witch persecutions, and inquisitions are three examples of sustained—centuries-long—campaigns against innocent people whose only "crime" was to disagree with Catholic Church doctrine and object to the behavior of Vatican clerics.

Fortunately, today we have access to some of the gospels that the Gnostics wrote and used in their worship of God in the early centuries following the death of Jesus.

The latest treasure trove of lost Gnostic gospels was discovered in 1945 by two brothers—Mohammad Ali and his brother, Khalifah—farmers, who were digging for fertilizer near the banks of the Nile River, about three hundred miles south of Cairo, Egypt. Likewise, in the mid-nineteen seventies, the Gospel of Judas was discovered, again near the Nile River, about one hundred miles south of Cairo.

WHAT DO THE LATEST REVELATIONS SAY?

We have already mentioned three major revelations that have come to us within the last several decades: Transcendental Meditation, *Conversations with God* and the Gnostic gospels. Our discussion thus far has provided ample representation of the Transcendental Meditation movement and *Conversations with God*. However, we have not provided—thus far—sufficient evidence for the claims about Gnostic literature, which includes the most recent revelations that came to us from the Egyptian desert.

`To fill that void, we will start with synoptic summaries of the Gospel of Judas and three of the Gnostic gospels found in the Nag Hammadi Library. We will then provide quasi-content analyses of the Gospel of Thomas and the Gospel of Mary, also in the Nag Hammadi Library; although other books within the Nag Hammadi Library reinforce what we have summarized here.

We will close with the informative contributions of Michelangelo's deceptions and Mother Teresa's agony. All coalesce into a single message—that extant religions have gotten it all wrong; but there is hope for those who seek a better way.

GOSPEL OF JUDAS: The traditional spin regarding Judas Iscariot characterized him as the most villifiable, historical figure in Christendom. He was accused of betraying Jesus to the Roman authorities with a kiss. Over the centuries after Jesus death, he was portrayed as the most despicable human being that ever lived. According to one Biblical account the Devil entered him before he betrayed Jesus. As the twisted account goes, he suffered horribly from guilt which drove him to suicide.

Another account has him buying a piece of land with the 30 pieces of silver he was supposedly paid to betray Jesus to the authorities. When he went to the land, he fell headfirst and his bowels spilled out of his broken body.

St. Irenaeus, the notorious, heretic specialist of the emerging Catholic Church, condemned the Gospel of Judas as heresy in 180 AD because it was considered a grave threat to the Church's survival.

The **Gospel of Judas** discovered in the mid-nineteen seventies in Egypt, tells another story: that Jesus asked him to kiss him so the Roman authorities would arrest the right man. Judas is one of the apostles who understands who Jesus really is and understands what he is saying when he talks of so-called "secret knowledge." Instead of being the most heinous traitor that ever lived, he turns out to be a heroic figure . . . a model for anyone choosing to follow Jesus' teachings.

GOSPEL OF TRUTH: This gospel is a difficult read because of esoteric references to various ideas. Nevertheless, it contains a concept central amongst Gnostic ideas: that inner knowledge of the Kingdom of God obliterates one's ignorance and ushers in a state of blissfulness when contrasted with the suffering of those who have not become enlightened with "gnosis": knowledge.

GOSPEL OF PHILIP: This gospel does not follow the life-story-of-Jesus pattern found in the New Testament gospels, but it has some sayings attributed to Jesus, some of which are found in the Christian Bible. Like the Gospel of Truth, it discusses the need to experience "resurrection" while on this earth. (Discovering your inner and higher Self)

GOSPEL OF THE EGYPTIANS: This is another work that is not easily understood because it describes the spiritual realm which emanated from the Great Invisible Spirit and discusses the origin, preservation and salvation of the race of Seth. He appears as one of the first heavenly beings born into the spiritual realm and then "puts on Jesus as a garment" and comes to earth to perform his salvitic work.

GOSPEL OF THOMAS: This gospel is highly readable because it consists of 114 sayings attributed to Jesus, over half of which make direct references to Gnostic ideas: **seek and find your salvation within**—10 *sayings*; **solitude is a key to saving yourself**—four; **going within to experience God directly**—12; **secret sayings revealed only to a few**—seven; **immortality in a spiritual realm**—five; **kingdom is both inside and outside oneself**—three; **self-realization as salvation of one's Self**—17; **one dwells in poverty if not self-realized**—five; **everything will become known**—two.

The other sayings are mostly parables, some similar to those found in the New Testament gospels, but many of them have some indirect reference to gnostic notions.

GOSPEL OF MARY: Like Judas, the legacy of Mary Magdalene was considered to be a serious threat to the Church's campaign to destroy all vestiges of what Jesus really said and did. What better way to discredit the person Jesus loved most than to portray her as a harlot. It was well-known that Mary of Magdala was Jesus' favorite disciple for it is recorded that he even kissed her on the mouth. She was a loyal and fearless leader of a group of woman who followed Jesus on some of his journeys. She had become a threat to the male-dominated emerging Church and had to be neutralized.

The **Gospel of Mary**—recovered from the Egyptian desert in 1945 along with 47 other gospels, tractates, sentences and fragments—is short and fragmented. It contains a conversation between the risen Jesus and his disciples about the nature of sin and matter. He says—in so many words—that sin is not a moral category but a cosmological one in which all human actions will be resolved in accordance with the laws of the universe.

Secondly, it contains the conversation we have already discussed in which Peter questions Mary about what Jesus told her and wonders if Jesus preferred her, a woman, to him and his fellow disciples. "Did he really speak with a woman without our knowledge and not openly?" Mary asks Peter if he thinks she would lie about her conversation with their Lord.

CONCLUSION

Think about it. Here we have two poster icons closely associated with the Roman Catholic Church: (1) a deeply spiritual, man who is one of the greatest fine-artists of all time—Michelangelo Buonarotti; and (2) Mother Teresa, a deeply religious woman, who dedicated her life to God, while strictly, passionately, and even fanatically obeying the dictates of the Roman Catholic Church.

Michelangelo's talents—not limited to sculpturing and painting—wrote a deeply personal, poetic prayer imploring God to tear apart the veil that separated him from the divine light from above so that he would not have doubts about his fate after death.

While seeking personal alternatives to the oppressive doctrine of the Church that employed him, he used his access to the Church's very core (the Sistine Chapel) to expose its betrayal of its most sacred trust: the legacy of Jesus of Nazareth.

In his teenage years he, Michelangelo, was attracted to Jewish mysticism—Kabbalism—and, over the next several decades, embraced Protestantism. And yet he yearned for an incontrovertible experience of *God-within*—a concept that is anathema to Protestantism—so that he would never doubt his eternal fate.

As we have seen, Mother Teresa fanatically searched for God within by reciting perfunctory prayers and pleading desperately for some sign that Jesus was listening . . . but all she got was a terrifying silence that tortured her soul.

Judaism, a religion that was a distortion of Moses' legacy, became the foundation of the Christian religion.

Nearly all of the apostles—and those who followed—ignored Jesus' teachings. They created a religion with hundreds of laws, rules and regulations.

Had that not happened, the billions of people who lived on this earth for the past two thousand years would have had a God-given alternative to the religions that were available to them; and, perhaps Mother Teresa—and others like her and Michelangelo—would have found what they were seeking.

Finally, we are blessed with the scriptures of the Nag Hammadi Library, the Gospel of Judas, Transcendental Meditation, and *Conversations with God,* reinforcing our belief that nearly all religions have inverted the messages of their masters, creating disastrous consequences for the spiritual welfare of human beings and their earthly environment.

But all is not lost. In *Conversations with God,* we are reassured that a rise in global consciousness has—indeed—begun; it is up to us to ensure that the ascent will continue. As Einstein allegedly said, **"The problems of the world cannot be solved on the same level of consciousness that created them."** We have the tools to raise personal, group, national, and global consciousness. Why not use them?

Chapter 73

Saturday, 25 October: 2 a.m.

Pope Immanuel, not prone to sleepless nights, pondered his options in the wee hours of the morning as "Operation Strike"—with all its portentous implications—approached.

The restless pope rose, went to his computer and composed a list of proposed reforms.

1. *Initiate* an affirmative action program to bring women into the priesthood and other leadership positions traditionally held by men.
2. *Abolish* the celibacy requirement for priests.
3. *Veneration* of relics will cease.
4. *Laity* in local congregations will select priests.
5. *Laity* in local congregations will control funds.
6. *The* creation of saints will stop.
7. *Laity* will select bishops and archbishops.
8. *Sacraments* will be reduced to two: Baptism and Eucharist.
9. *All* people will be admitted to the Eucharist.
10. *All* ancillary Catholic organizations, such as Opus Dei and the Legionaries of Christ and Regnum Christi, will be cut off from their ties to the Roman Catholic Church.
11. *The* policy of excommunication will remain a relic of the past.
12. *Harassment,* intimidation and persecution of clerics and professors who criticize the Church (otherwise known as an Inquisition) will cease.
13. *All* clerics will cooperate with local legal authorities in prosecuting clerics accused of violations of local, state and federal statutes. All documents relating to accusations of sexual abuse of minors will be released to local police and legal authorities.
14. *All* illegal transactions at the Vatican Bank will cease.
15. The pope typed up one more reform, **Number 15,** adding it to the list of fourteen reforms; he printed out the list of fifteen reforms and placed it in the safe behind his desk: ***Abolish the College of Cardinals*:** Reason: *because it has become a poster-child for all that was abhorrent about the Church's image: old men parading in fine robes in a display of power and authority over the masses and other religions. Whatever administrative functions they performed world-wide, would be done by non-clerics, including women.*

Next, Pope Immanuel made several critical moves:

1. He sent an email—with the **fourteen** proposed reforms attached—to Father's Sandusky, and Perfecto all one-hundred-twenty cardinal electors—except Cardinal O'Reilley—worldwide and invited them to respond to Father Sandusky with brief comments via email (not to exceed 500 words) stating support or objections by **Thursday, 30 October**.

2. He summoned, via email, all cardinals employed at the Vatican to a meeting on **Tuesday 5 November,** to discuss his proposed reforms: the results to be published and sent to all cardinals world-wide.

3. Via email, he called a consistory (a meeting of all 120 cardinal electors world-wide) to begin at the Vatican on **Sunday, 10 November** to discuss reforms. Presentations and discussions would last for a week.

Chapter 74

Under her Marc Jacobs, black, wool trench-coat—with matching gloves—Maria wore a personally tailored, dark-blue business suit over a white shirt. She shook the snow from her Goya-suede, ankle boots before climbing into her Maserati, placed four copies of her revised Master's Degree thesis in the passenger seat and waved goodbye to Pat.

Passing the fields covered with several layers of early winter snow, she was pleased that the farmers would have a good layer of moisture in the soil to nurture their winter crops. In the spring, farmers would emerge from their winter hibernations to crawl across the fields planting the seeds for their summer crops that would provide an abundant harvest in the late summer and fall.

Drs. Sally Holden, Willy Severson, and Jenny Fitzsimmons took their respective places at the conference table: Sally at the head of the table was dressed in a tan, wool pantsuit over a dark brown shirt. Willy wore his blue blazer over a pink shirt accented by a red and black, plaid tie. He wore tan, corduroy trousers. Maria sat opposite Sally.

The professors had copies of Maria's thesis. Jenny had a copy of *Conversations with God* in front of her. Sitting across from "Willy," she wore a black, V-neck, Kashmir sweater over a white collared shirt, with gray wool slacks and black pumps.

"Well, Maria" said Sally, cordially, "I see you have been busy since our last meeting."

"Yes, I think that is an accurate observation," replied Maria, with a smile.

"As you indicated in your note," Sally continued, "we agreed that you would do some work on how nearly all masters of divine wisdom have had fundamentally the same messages and that each of the messages had been used as some sort of basis for the religions we have today. You also indicated that you wanted to explore how a new book, titled *Conversations with God,* might be of some value to you in your search for your mission as God's Messenger. Is that correct?"

"Yes it is," Maria replied. "And you raised some doubts about whether or not the masters of divine wisdom were really that similar in their ideas and the outcomes of those ideas. You also suggested that we could decide at this meeting whether or not this additional work should be included as a continuation of my thesis."

"Yes, I remember. That provides a segue into why we are here today: to evaluate our candidate's thesis, based partly on her responses to our questions about its organization and content. It is important that we all agree on where this meeting is headed. Do you both agree?" asked Sally,   glancing from Willy to Jenny. They both nodded agreement.

"Do either of you have any questions?" Sally asked. Willy spoke first.

"It looks like Jennifer is on the hot-seat here today," said Willy with a smile, as he sat up straight and thumbed through Maria's paper."

"How so?" Jenny asked.

"Well, the way I read this continuation of Maria's paper; it is a significantly more severe indictment of your Church than the first presentation when you went ballistic. I have been looking forward, with some pleasure I might add, to your response to this continuation."

"So, you see this meeting as some sort of inane entertainment hour, like a **Reality** show on TV, is that it Willy?" Jenny asked, in a friendly voice.

"I wouldn't go that far. I'm sure you understand that academic discourse can, at times, be entertaining, especially when controversial issues arise. Wouldn't you agree?"

"Yes, I agree with your proposition, but I'm curious as to why you think Maria's paper puts me on the 'hot seat', as you put it."

"As I said, we have here in front of us a paper that calls into question the very foundation of the Church you represent and comes up just short of rec-ommending that it simply close and lock the Vatican doors . . . then go away. If I were a Catholic professor of theology, as you are, I would be a little con-cerned about the implications of this paper. I find a lot of what is discussed to be somewhat plausible, don't you, Jenny?"

"Have you read *Conversations with God,* Willy? All three books?"

"I did get a copy, started and got through a few chapters, but our annual golf tournament sabotaged those good intentions."

"I see. Let me see if I can find the part in Walsch's book that pertains to **your** Church." Jenny picked up the book which had a snow storm of sliced, colored "post-its" protruding from the pages with brief notes on each one. She found the one with "Lutheran doctrine" on it. Let me see if I can paraphrase what God says with regard to your church.

"We are *born* in sin and we will *die* that way because sin is our nature. One of your religions even teaches that you can do nothing about this. Our attempts—if we ever decide to do anything about what I just said—are irrelevant and meaningless. In this religion, it is arrogant to even think any action of ours can get us to heaven . . . to be 'saved.' We will be saved only by the grace of God.

"Does that sound familiar, Willy?" Jenny said with a smile.

"Yes, of course, it's the core of Lutheran doctrine, but he doesn't mention the Lutheran Church."

"Of course he doesn't. If you ever get around to reading the book you will notice that anyone, with a limited knowledge of doctrines associated with various churches, would recognize the ones he is referring to throughout the book.

"So, while I will admit that Maria has singled out the Catholic Church in her comparisons of its doctrine with that of the *New Spiritual Paradigm,* she has done that for a very appropriate reason: The Roman Catholic Church *was* the 'Christian' church that won the war against the Gnostics and all other 'Christian' denominations and sects are derived from her. The most prominent of all derived 'Christian' Churches is the Lutheran Church. From what I have read in Walsch's book, Lutheran doctrine receives the most severe criticism of the denominations and sects mentioned. And that would include the doctrine of my Church. So, welcome to the hot seats, Willy," Jenny said with a smile.

Willy looked to Sally for a response. *After all, she is the Chair of a department at this Lutheran seminary,* he thought.

Maria's thoughts were a little more interesting: *This is better entertainment than anything I have ever seen on TV.*

"I don't think we are here to play 'gotcha games,' said Sally. "Willy," she asked, "Do you have any other observations you want to share?"

"I'll defer to Jenny on the bit about the masters' ideas coalescing into a single dominant theme, since that is her specialty. As for other matters, I think Maria has done a credible job in expressing herself. The organization of her paper is excellent. She supports her assertions with reasonable documentation. Her composition skills are of the first order. So far as I'm concerned, Sally, I can go to the indoor driving range any time you are ready to give Maria our approval."

"Not so fast, Willy. Your golfing-practice will have to wait until we are done here today. I'm not sure how long this will last, but we'll be here as long as it takes to satisfy this committee that we have done a fair and complete evaluation of Maria's paper and her responses to our questions."

Turning to Maria, Sally said, "I found your work on Michelangelo convincing. Also, I am impressed with your presentation of the masters and how they all had fundamentally the same message, at least those who were the sources of the Eastern religions. I wasn't so sure how Moses, Jesus and Mohammad fit into that mold.

"However, I got very interested in the part on the Gnostic gospels—what Jesus allegedly said, and how that relates to the founding of the Catholic Church. So I read the gospels you take quotations from and some of the other scriptures in the Nag Hammadi Library. Then I read some of the books by scholars who have analyzed these works, which I will admit had some influence on my impression of your attempt to locate Jesus' teaching within the rubric of the Eastern masters.

"As you probably know, analyses of the Gnostic Gospels vary: They range from extremely biased assertions that the gospels are vicious attacks on the Catholic Church to sophisticated commentary by thoroughly trained exegetes, who understand the importance of unbiased, thoroughly researched biblical scholarship. I can see from your paper that you are convinced of the authenticity of the Gnostic Gospels. What is your opinion of the scholarly criticism of those scriptures?"

"My goodness, Dr. Holden, I'm impressed. You must be a speed-reader."

"The month-long delay of our meeting today gave me the time I needed to prepare for this meeting."

"Well then, to answer your question, Dr. Holden—yes, I am convinced of the authenticity of the Gnostic Gospels. The chief reason is that they fit perfectly with the cogs in the wheels that synchronize the wisdom of ancient Indian masters, Moses' original revelations, Jesus' words in the Gnostic Gospels, *Conversations with God,* and in significant ways, with the words and deeds of Michelangelo and Mother Teresa.

"If you will permit me to expand on why I am convinced that Jesus' words should be taken seriously with reference to how they relate to the Vedic masters in India, I will integrate that issue with our consideration of the Gnostic gospels and the scholarly criticism that followed."

"Please proceed," responded Dr. Holden. Jenny was listening with intense interest. Willy had pulled himself up to the table and was hunched over Maria' thesis, staring down at it, doodling on the cover.

"First," Maria said, "as for the criticism of these gospels, I agree with your statements about biased criticism contrasting with sophisticated exegesis.

"Now, I think it is important to recognize that *knowledge is structured in consciousness.* By that I mean, the level of one's consciousness will determine how clearly one can understand new knowledge that doesn't quite fit one's dearly held perspectives of reality. And that fact influences critical thinking.

"Einstein said something similar when he stated that, 'Problems cannot be solved on the same level of consciousness that created them.' That suggests that a higher level of consciousness grants one better insights into knowledge, especially knowledge that requires a higher level of sophistication to be understood and appreciated; higher levels of consciousness provide that benefit. To repeat: *Knowledge is structured in consciousness.*

"Referring to the scholarly criticism you mentioned, it is apparent that some of the critics don't understand the knowledge presented to them—I'm referring to the Gnostic Gospels. For example, some critics insist that Gnostics believed that this world is an evil place, a cosmic disaster of suffering and pain from which one must escape.

"Other critics insist that the Gnostic Gospels demonstrate that Jesus came to give humans his knowledge of their divine inner selves, which they can discover for themselves by going within, thereby achieving salvation.

"*Conversations with God,* also indicates that this world is a blessing—not a curse, or some cosmic disaster—where humans have the opportunity to discover their divine, inner selves, and doing so, find their "salvation" here on earth; there is no need to escape this world. In fact, according to *CwG,* this world is a highly desirable place to live because it provides the context within which humans can accelerate their evolution to a greater degree than if they remained in the so-called 'spirit-world.' Humans have freely chosen to come here for that purpose."

"How is that possible?" Sally asked.

"Do you mean how do they find their salvation within?

"Yes."

"It has to do with the experience of the inner life that comes to those who seek and find God within. What do they find when they find God within? Their first experiences, such as expanded awareness, can be terrifying, as Jesus says in one of the Gnostic Gospels. But as they realize what is happening, they come to accept it as merely evidence of their evolving consciousness and when that realization occurs, 'They'll rule over all'."

"What do you mean by 'expanded awareness'?" Sally asked.

"I'll give you one example of my own experience. As a child, I had what I thought was a terrifying dream, but now know it was not a dream at all. It usually happened at night when I was in bed; sometimes when I was extremely tired. I would feel my body shrinking until it was a tiny speck in the corner of my bedroom; simultaneously, I experienced myself as the space in the room.

"I was both a tiny speck and as big as the room. My awareness of my self as being in two places at the same time—one of those places being extremely expanded and the other being extremely diminished—I now know was nothing more nor less than an experience of 'expanded awareness'."

"So," Willy interjected, without looking up or stopping his doodling. "Over whom do you now rule?"

"I think Jesus was speaking metaphorically and didn't mean anyone would be ruling over anyone. Nothing in all the gospels indicates he held such an idea about humans. What I think he meant is that, once one becomes Self-realized—saved—one feels invincible, indestructible, immortal, all-powerful to control one's own destiny, which would be an experience of "ruling over all" in the sense that there is no desire to rule over anyone, since the realized experience to rule over oneSelf is all there is to be desired at that point in one's evolution."

"I have no idea what you just said, but go ahead," Willy said; again without looking up or stopping his doodling.

"Dr. Severson, I will do as you request, and thank you for your question. Besides expanded awareness, early experiences can be seeing visions of divine perfection: (1) lattices of pure gold, in perfect, three-dimensional angles; (2) luminescent, unadulterated, indestructible, colored, fine jewels; (3) divinely constructed black objects that have the quality of absolute solidity.

"These experiences are absolute values that one—who goes within—associates with divine reality and perceives it to be her own divine reality as well. I want to emphasize, very emphatically, that these are merely some of the experiences I've had, but are not necessarily the experiences others have or anyone should expect. Others' experiences might take a different form, but would, nevertheless, have the same absolute qualities I experienced.

"Put another way, one gradually comes to the realization that experiencing absolute values *is experiencing* one's divine Self—one's divine inner, immortal, indestructible Self. This is the 'salvation' Jesus promised when he said that your salvation is not to be expected in some future apocalyptic event, but that it has *already happened:* one's salvation is assured; it is only a matter for us to come to that 'Self-realization' and that can be done while in a human body; that means, we will gradually experience a life of bliss until we experience bliss 24/7."

Jenny was becoming more uncomfortable by the minute and was reaching into her handbag on the floor as if to make sure something she might need was still there. Sally sat back in her swivel chair, looking intently at Maria as she continued to answer the question.

"People—who begin to experience the early stages of Self-realization— feel their lives are turned upside down because, when they go to bed at night, they are *also* 'awake' on another consciousness level than the level of consciousness we call sleep; it's called cosmic consciousness. Most of us are aware of our waking, sleeping and dreaming levels of consciousness. But as our level of consciousness rises, new experiences occur.

"So, for those whose level of consciousness is rising, their nights in bed become more charming than their experiences during the day. Their dreams are dreams of perfection: perfect people, perfect places, perfect things, and perfect relationships. At first, when they have these experiences, they have the impression they have been awake all night long. Of course, they have been asleep because they have been dreaming, but in a very real sense they have been **awake** all night long also, because their cosmic awareness has been awake: they have been 'awake' while their bodies are asleep.

"When they wake up in the morning, they lie there in a state of bliss, thanking God for the wonderful experiences they had while at rest. But they don't just stay in bed enjoying their bliss. They get out of bed and go to work along with the rest of us, enjoying every aspect of life.

"Their inner experiences are so charming, that escaping from this world is unthinkable. This is the life that Jesus and all the other masters spoke of when they encouraged people to 'go within' to find their salvation.

"These initial higher levels of consciousness—some call *cosmic conscious-ness*—*we* have all experienced, even during our activities during the day at some time in our lives, but didn't recognize what it was. Have you ever been doing something and it seemed as though you were watching yourself do it?"

Sally and Jenny nodded in the affirmative. Willy continued to doodle.

"Well, that experience is your cosmic Self, your inner divine Self, revealing itself. You are witnessing yourself from outside yourself, from your 'other Self' that you don't usually experience.

"It usually happens during the waking stages of activity: playing table tennis, soccer, writing a paper—usually when you are concentrating very intently on some activity. But as I mentioned earlier, when this level of consciousness becomes permanently established, you experience it in sleep as well. During the day, when not 'witnessing yourself,' cosmic consciousness can be experienced as just a subtle awareness that all is well . . . not unlike the experience of a contented child who knows that 'mother is at home'"

Jenny's eyes were pools of tears, overreaching their banks and forming rivers, flowing down her cheeks. She pulled tissues from her handbag, and dabbed her eyes and wiped her cheeks. Maria noticed her tears and paused.

"I'm sorry," Jenny said, after gaining her composure, "it's just that ever since my earliest memories as a child I thought that life should be wonderful. And it many ways it has been. I had wonderful parents, a good life as a child and teenager, and it became more wonderful when I went to college and met Jack and even better when our two daughters showed up in our lives."

Jenny paused to regain her composure, clearing her eyes and blowing her nose.

"But somehow, that has not been enough. In a flash, all the things I love in life could be taken from me. Everything is so temporary, *final*. I remember my mother saying something when I was a child. Someone in the family had died and she said. 'Death is so *final.*'

"Nothing lasts forever, least of all sentient life. We live once and then it's all over.

"If we are unfortunate to die a slow death, we agonize over our fates after death, terrified that we might not measure up to the standards set by men who call themselves God's agents on earth. And all too often what we see in them is anything but God's presence in them, not so much our local priests and pastors, but their leaders in the Vatican.

"How could anyone who knows the history of our Church not wonder what life is all about under these circumstances if they are exposed to what you are revealing to us in this paper and expanding on today? What you have just described is what I longed for as a child: that life should be as beautiful and wonderful as you have been describing. But that longing faded as the attractions of our phenomenal world took over my life.

"After reading and even studying carefully *Conversations with God,* and hearing you describe what the life of a person whose life is becoming enlightened is like . . . well, both have touched my heart so deeply I couldn't control my emotions. Finally, I've found an understanding of God and the universe he created that makes sense—one I can accept with confidence and without fear.

"We don't live on this earth only once. We come here to evolve more rapidly than in the so-called spirit-world somewhere else in our beautiful universe; understood this way, life never ends! There are no tragedies for us to worry about. No death to fear. No judgment after life to dread. I'm sorry for rambling on, Maria. Go ahead and continue."

"That is so beautifully and clearly stated, Jenny, you almost had me in tears as well." They both laughed. Willy looked morose. Sally asked Maria if she had anything more to say in answer to the question she had asked about the Gnostic Gospels and the academic criticism that followed.

"Just a couple more things," said Maria. "I am concerned about critics who portray Gnosticism as some crazy fantasy: that Gnostic cosmologies are bizarre and express views that the world is some kind of oppressive prison from which one needs to escape to end one's suffering.

"When the soul enters the body at its first heartbeat, its vibrations have been forced to throttle down to what the soul considers a very low level from what it was experiencing in the spirit-world where, with its high vibrations, it could move freely anywhere in the universe it wanted to go, just by having the thought.

"Now it is confined to a human body and we all know what that means: we can crawl, walk, run, jump, ride an animal or a bicycle, take a car, an airplane, and even take a spaceship to the moon. We are limited by the restrictions of our own bodies and the machines we have created to transport us at a faster pace than we can otherwise move.

"So, in a sense, so confined and limited in our abilities to move around, we do feel—vaguely—as though we are in prison of sorts. But if we understand the *New Spiritual Paradigm* as it is explained in *Conversations with God,* we know that there is a purpose for this 'imprisonment'. We freely accepted it—and feely subjected ourselves to forgetfulness of our divine freedom—when we chose our new parents and entered our mother's womb to begin our journey in our latest human body.

"As I explained, when we go within, we soon have experiences of divine reality—which is referred to as God Consciousness—so that when we look at a gorgeous flower, a fantastically beautiful sunset, or charming, billowing, summer clouds, we associate what we experience within with those outer realities and become aware that we *ARE* both—both the inner and outer realities of our experience. Does that answer your question, Dr. Holden?"

"Yes, I believe so in terms of the doctrinal issues involved. Now I think we can conclude our review of your thesis with this question: Did you receive what you sought when you came to our seminary in search of your divinely inspired mission—being 'God's messenger'?"

"Yes, Dr. Holden, I did. I want to thank all three of you for your patience with my unorthodox quest and the results of my research. I understand that for some people—my conclusions—will be offensive. Yet, I cannot—nor do I want to—control how people react to their life-events.

"I repeat: My view is that people should do what serves them and not worry about anything else; if they choose any religion in the world as their passion and source of comfort and reassurance, then fine. I don't condemn them or their choice. I honor all people—spiritual or otherwise—regardless of their life preferences.

"My message and mission for the rest of my life is to spread the word: (1) that nearly all masters' core message was to go within to find your salvation; (2) *Conversations with God* gives us a new spiritual paradigm which we can use individually to enhance our search for God within; and (3) that Transcendental Meditation provides an efficient meditation technique for *going within.*

"If people—church-goers, spiritualists, agnostics, atheists, whatever—conclude that their chosen path no longer serves them, here is an alternative that might be of interest to them." Maria paused, and then said, "Is it possible to decide now, whether to include my 'continuation' into my final thesis?"

Dr. Holden spoke. "Maria, we haven't told you that we met before this meeting and concluded that, yes, you can integrate this latter part of your thesis into the first and make it one thesis. Just make the necessary adjustments to the format."

"That's wonderful news and I want to thank all three of you for your indulgence, professionalism and assistance." Maria smiled and looked at each of the professors.

They looked at each other for a moment—in silence. Then Willy spoke. "You say you are going to spread the word . . . as you just described it. How do you plan to do that? Are you going to mimic Martin Luther and post your thesis on the Catholic Church door in Sylvan Lake?" Maria laughed while Jenny and Sally smiled. Willy was not smiling. "Well, I suppose there are many options that don't include posting it on a local church door.

"For example, I could attempt to get the entire thesis published in some peer-reviewed journal or I could create a website and post it there, open a blog and watch the fireworks fly from my computer. That could provide endless entertainment for a lot of people and hopefully a few might get my message from all that. Perhaps I will find a way for the pope to see it. It could be as simple as sending it to him."

"Okay," Sally said, "if there are no more questions, we can adjourn and Willy can go to the driving range."

"I have a final question for Maria," said Willy.

"Willy, I'm surprised; don't you know that people prolong meetings by asking questions? I thought you were in a hurry to leave," Jenny said with a smile.

Willy glared at Jenny and then turned to Maria and said, "Don't you think you come in here a little over-dressed in your designer clothes? You look like you just stepped out of an advertisement page in *Vogue*."

"Well thank you, Willy, for the complement and the question. Yes, I suppose I do look a little over-dressed. Have you ever been to Russia?"

"No," said Willy, "but what does that have to do with my question?"

"Actually, it has a lot to do with your question. If you had been to Russia—and I say that only to make a relevant point, not in any way to denigrate your question—you would know that people dress up when they go out in public.

"Maybe in the last few years—since the Russians have learned about Western clothing customs—some have changed their dressing practices, but most still maintain what is essentially a 'dress-up-when-you-go-out' rule.

"This isn't Russia," said Willy.

"Yes," said Maria, "I know. I wear the clothes I have. Nearly all of them happen to be the clothes I wore on the job in Moscow. Because of their high quality they maintain their usability. I see no reason why I shouldn't wear them when the situation calls for a professional appearance. I consider coming to an interview with you distinguished professors a professional situation."

"Willy," said Jenny, "I have noticed that Maria dresses professionally, and probably more upscale than we are accustomed to around here where some professors—who shall remain unnamed—occasionally come to work in their blue-jeans or sweats."

Willy turned red in the face, shoved his chair back, rose and stomped out of the room.

Maria rose from her chair and went to where Willy had been sitting. She found the most exquisite drawings—the finest strokes she had ever seen—creating a variety of animals with various expressions of emotion on their faces. Most of them looked sad in varying degrees. She picked them up and showed them to Sally and Jenny. "Have you noticed these?" she asked.

They both acknowledged they had. Jenny said, "He always doodles in meetings. In a way I feel sorry for him in spite of our occasional spats because, when he was in college, he wanted to major in art, but the main art professor at the small Lutheran College he attended insulted him several times, which led him to conclude he had no potential for—what he believed as young man—was his passion.

"Now, I'm sure he thinks it's too late and he is wasting his life away, earning a living doing something he doesn't really enjoy.

"I've had the impression since you came into our lives that he envies your following your passion so successfully and joyfully—something he has been unable to do," Jenny concluded.

"Is it okay with you two," Maria responded, "if I take his drawings and leave a note with them in his mailbox and suggest he keep his drawings and publish them? If he chooses to ignore what I suggest and I don't hear from him, I'll write to him and ask if he would give them to me as a gift so that I can frame them and someday decorate my home along with other art works I have collected.? Do you think that would be okay?"

"Why don't you try it and see what happens?" said Sally.

"If there is nothing else . . . it has been a pleasure working with you, Maria and I'm sure I speak for all of us when I say we wish you the best in fulfilling your mission as 'God's messenger'."

The following morning Maria made two reservations: World Airways – Rome; Vatican tour

Wednesday, 29 October: 9:30 a.m.—Rome

After breakfast, Maria dialed a number on her hotel phone. "Colonel Isenberg, this is Maria. I met you on our flight from Moscow to the States about three years ago. You offered to share some legumes and gave me a book to read. Do you remember?"

"Why, yes, of course I remember. A man never forgets a beautiful, young woman who isn't too absorbed in herself to talk to an old man like me. My name is Fritz, by the way. Where are you?"

"I'm in Rome at a hotel. Now I'll really test your memory. Do you remember suggesting that if I ever came to Rome, I should give you a call and we'd go to dinner?"

"Yes, of course I remember. I hope you aren't calling to tell me that won't be possible."

"No. It won't have romantic implications, but you seemed like a man I would enjoy spending an evening with. And I do have a favor I will ask of you when we are at dinner. It's not really that big a deal, but I want you to know that this is one of the reasons I called. I would have called without this reason, but now you know. Does this evening work for you?"

"No problem. I'll come to your hotel. Is 10:30 okay? What's your last name?

"Luderenko. I'm at the Excedra: Ten thirty is fine. I'll be in the lobby."

Friday, 31 October: Vatican - 3:30 p.m.

Late in the afternoon, after her tour guide released her group amongst the mass of humanity crowded into the Sistine Chapel, Maria spotted a half dozen college girls and walked toward them, weaving her way through the crowd. She heard them speaking Russian.

Pausing, she followed them as they departed through the narrow door at the rear of the chapel and climbed a short flight of stairs, emerging into a small hall, around a corner to the descending Grand Stairway and colonnaded corridor that led to the famous Bronze Doors: the entrance to the Apostolic Palace, the pope's quarters and offices.

Maria mingled amongst the girls, chatting in Russian with a couple of them. They were from the Russian Far East, attending a Model United Nations Conference and were eagerly anticipating having their pictures taken with the colorful Swiss Guards standing just inside the Bronze Doors.

The Bronze Doors, 24 feet high and 13 feet wide have a steel core between the interior, decorated wood and the outer, bronze panel; they weigh over six tons. They were taken from ancient Roman temples and placed by Bernini, the architect of the colonnade surrounding St. Peter's Square. When open, they leave a space between the inside of the door and the wall—big enough for a person to disappear from the view of the guards.

While the guards were having their pictures taken with the students, Maria slipped behind the doors, pulled a brown envelope out of her backpack and taped it to the door.

TO: POPE IMMANUEL—FOR HIS EYES ONLY

Maria came from behind the doors, inspected the bronze panels on the front of the door, walked to the street curb and hailed a taxi: "Excedra, please."

At the end of the day, two Swiss security guards closed the Bronze doors. One of them retrieved the brown envelope. The colonel's instructions were for them to deliver the envelope to him immediately. Colonel Isenberg thanked the guards for their assistance. He dismissed them and delivered the envelope to Pope Immanuel.

Chapter 75

Tuesday, 4 November: 10 a.m.—Vatican

Pope Immanuel introduced Maria to his ten, high-powered cardinals in the library. Instead of sitting around a conference table the cardinals sat in a semi-circle facing the pope and Ms. Luderenko. The purpose of the arrangement was to generate a more relaxed ambience, thereby encouraging the cardinals to speak their minds. The pope knew they were as angry as a beehive-cone shaken from a tree branch by foolish boys. Anything he could do to reduce the tension was worth a try.

"Gentlemen," the pope said, "this is Maria Martinovna Luderenko. She posted her Master's Thesis on the Bronze Doors last Friday. I have read it and discussed it with her and considered it along with the White Papers that you and others submitted for my consideration shortly after I took office. Some of what she has done is similar to proposals made by a few of your colleagues, but a lot of her work is radically different, even from what I was proposing.

"I was shocked by her analysis of Michelangelo's *Last Judgment*. Yet, I am intrigued by her assertions that nearly all religions were born illegitimately, from inverted divine knowledge. I am also profoundly impressed by the New Spiritual Paradigm that you read about in her thesis, which I posted on my website.

"I have received numerous email responses from cardinals around the world, most of them angry questions and some of them menacing threats. I wanted to meet with you to ask for your assistance in finding ways to open a dialogue at the consistory that I've scheduled to begin in a week.

"I haven't received any emails from any of you. Do any of you have anything to say?"

Silence. The cardinals stared at the pope.

"Well, maybe this will get us started. One of your colleagues apparently leaked the fourteen proposals that I sent out Saturday, 25 October . . ."

"Excuse me, Holiness," interrupted Cardinal O'Reilley. "Did you mean *fourteen proposals*? My copy has fifteen proposals."

"What does the fifteenth proposal say?" asked the pope.

"Well, you wrote it; it says you intend to abolish the College of Cardinals."

"Did you receive that proposal as an email attachment?" asked the pope.

"Just like the others," answered the Cardinal.

"Do any of you have a copy my proposals, which has a fifteenth proposal?" asked the pope?

None of the cardinals responded.

"It is interesting, Cardinal O'Reilley, that you, only, received a copy with fifteen proposals, because I made just one copy and placed it in my safe. None of the other Cardinals received that copy. How is it that you ended up with a copy that was secured in my safe behind my desk?"

"I printed it out on my computer like the rest of them. There must be some mistake." replied the cardinal.

"Yes," said the pope, "and I think the mistake is yours. Papers that I have placed in my safe have been flying out of there as if a breeze came along and liberated them. And I suspect they ended up in your hands. Did they?" asked the pope.

Cardinal O'Reilley, sitting in the center of the semi-circle, began to squirm. His colleagues watched as his face turned red. "I don't know what you are talking about!" he blurted out.

"Well, said the pope," I think you know exactly what I'm talking about. Your friend, "Fingers," the janitor, has been opening my safe almost every night for the past two years. He's been laying documents on your desk when he went to the Roman Rota building to finish his janitorial work each evening."

"That's impossible, shouted Cardinal O'Reilley, unless you gave him the combination to the lock."

"I didn't have to. 'Fingers' is a closet safe-cracker, who retired from the jewelry-theft business years ago and was recruited by one of our clerics to gain access to my safe; using the _manipulation_ method instead of the _drilling_ method, which leaves a mess and an inoperable dial on the safe door, 'Fingers' had access to my safe every night."

"What are you talking about? No one can open your safe, which is a modern one, even with a stethoscope, because the sound of the gates falling into the fence doesn't exist anymore," replied Cardinal O'Reilley.

Maria stared at Cardinal O'Reilley, wondering why he would have such knowledge of safe-cracking.

"That's true, unless they can _feel them drop,_" said the pope. "Fingers wears latex gloves all the time to keep his fingers sensitive enough to feel the gates fall into the fence. He uses a fine sandpaper to keep the nerves on his fingers close to the thinnest layer of skin feasible, which makes it possible for him to open my safe. Now, Cardinal O'Reilley, is there anything you would like to confess?"

Cardinal O'Reilley shifted in his chair, looked at the cardinals, back at the pope and said, "I resent your accusing me, an honorable man, of such treachery, Holiness. Don't you realize you are committing a grave sin with such an outrage?"

Maria looked at the pope and said, "Perhaps I could sing a song that would help Cardinal O'Reilley calm down. The atmosphere in here is getting a little dense, don't you think?"

Pope Immanuel looked at Maria and said, "What do you have in mind?"

"'Ave Maria'; it's one I sang when I was in high school in Minnesota about ten years ago. I sang Schubert's lyrics. I sang in German. Or would you rather hear one of the Latin versions?"

"I'd prefer Latin," said the pope. "Please stand and sing. It might remind all of us why we are here—settle us down so we can have the courage to speak up and discuss the problems facing our Church. Gentlemen, may I present Maria Martinovna Luderenko."

As Maria stood, Cardinal O'Reilley arose and shouted, "This woman is an imposter. Her name is not Luderenko; it's McCarty. I was in her parents' home. What is she doing in this sacred house of God, anyway?"

"Father O'Reilley . . . excuse me," Maria said. "I mean Cardinal O'Reilley. Apparently you never knew I did not take my adoptive parents' last name. When you were at our home, you didn't seem to know I was adopted, because you told my adoptive mom that you thought I looked like her.

"Now . . . I thought if I sang one of the most beautiful melodies that has been popularized by the Catholic Church, you would calm down. I have long-since forgiven you for what you did to me and Sammy and others in our small community.

"If you will sit down and listen, perhaps what I sing will come through to your soul and you will find peace."

Cardinal O'Reilley, not wanting to continue the confrontation, sat down and stared at Maria as she sang:

Ave Maria, Gratia plena,
Maria, Gratia plena, Maria, Gratia plena,
Ave Dominum, Ave Dominus tecum
Benedictu in muliaribus

Et benedictus
Et benedictus fructus ventris
Ventris tui, Jesus
Ave Maria
Mater Dei
Sancta Maria
Ora pro nobis peccatoribus
Nunc et in hora mortis nostrae
Ave Maria

Silence . . . it continued for several seconds. Cardinal O'Reilley, unable to control the turmoil in his mind and body, stood up, charged toward Maria and shouted, "She's a murderer and a witch!"

Pope Immanuel rose and tackled him at the waist, driving his shoulder into Cardinal O'Reilley's abdomen, shoving him onto his back.

The pope rose and stood over him. As O'Reilley tried to rise, he clutched his chest; his face frozen in agony, he was unable to breath. He fell onto his back. The cardinals stood around him, as one of them administered last rites.

Chapter 76

Wednesday, 5 Nov., 6:00 a.m. (CST USA) Wed. 5 Nov., 3:00 p.m. Rome

Sammy Youngstad kicked the snow off his boots. Entering the enclosed porch, he put his woolen gloves in his coat pocket, removed his coat and cap, heaved a sigh of relief and entered the kitchen.

"How is Bog doing?" Pat asked. She had awakened Sammy at 5:30 a.m. to check on Bog who had an infected wound on his leg from a fall on the ice a week earlier. She was preparing breakfast.

"Oh, I think he's okay. But I think he misses Maria. When is she coming home?"

"As you know, when she left, she said she wasn't sure how long she'd be gone, but not to worry about her. I received a text message this morning that said she had arrived safely and is staying in a nice hotel in Rome. Sit down. Have some hot chocolate while I fix your breakfast. Do you want the usual: bacon, eggs and toast?" Sammy said yes, and took a sip of hot chocolate.

The small TV on the counter between the working and dining areas of the kitchen was on. A CNN anchor, Jack Colson, was introducing the Station Chief for CNN in Rome. "Karl Rover is in Rome covering a budding crisis at the Vatican.

"What's the latest, Karl? Is this turning into a catastrophe, or is this just another group of disenchanted fringe-element making a lot of noise?"

"Negative. As you know, when the new pope came into office three years ago, he started shaking things up the first day in office. Apparently, there has been a lot more turmoil going on in the Vatican than anyone in the outside world suspected. The biggest splash he made in the tranquil pond we know the Vatican to be, was his abolishment of the marriage annulment policy only days after he took office.

"According to our sources, he has been considering radical reforms in every area of the Church for at least a couple years. Pope Immanuel is not a capricious old man. He has a reputation for being affable, compassionate, and respectful, but not someone you want to cross swords with.

"We know that about a week ago he sent out emails to the cardinals—worldwide—attaching over a dozen radical reforms. Someone—we presume one of the angry cardinals—leaked them to the media, apparently assuming the outrageous reforms would ignite a conflagration of protest that would force him to relent, or even resign.

"Demonstrations were immediate and surprisingly large, but not for the reasons the cardinals were expecting. Eighty-five percent of the demonstrators are the pope's supporters; they want the reforms he has published. The other fifteen percent are angry counter-demonstrators, horrified by what the pope is contemplating.

"The demonstrations have been limited to just a few in Vatican Square. Is that correct, Karl?" asked Jack.

"They were until today. But by early evening, the demonstrators filled the entire Square, even extending down that wide boulevard—that leads into the Square—to the Castel San Angelo and even across the bridge."

"Why the surge?"

"You won't believe me when I say this Jack, but there is a modern-day Martin Luther who is the reason behind 'the surge,' as you call it. Our sources tell us that she is a beautiful, twenty-something Russian-American woman who posted her Master's in Theology thesis on the famous Bronze Doors at the entrance to the Vatican. This brazen act occurred last Friday, October 31st, the same date that Martin Luther posted his Ninety-five Theses on a church door in Wittenberg, Germany in 1517."

"A female, latter-day Martin Luther? Are you serious?"

"This is not a Halloween trick-or-treat prank, Jack. Yes, I'm serious. What's even more bizarre—and I can't go into a detailed explanation how this happened—but her name is even, indeed, 'Martin Luther' . . . an Ukrainianized, female patronymic version. The pope created a website that has her Master's Thesis: It's at www.thepope.tpx

"Our sources tell us the pope invited her to his office over the weekend, discussed her Master's Thesis and decided to publish it to the world."

"We're running out of time, Karl. Where is this headed?"

"This story will turn out to be the most momentous story of this century. I make that prediction at this point, even before the first decade has become history. This is a major crisis, Jack."

"That's interesting, Karl. We are getting reports that demonstrations—like those there in Rome—are occurring all over the United States and other countries. Thanks, and keep up the good work, Karl."

"Mrs. McCarty, you look worried. You've been watching TV. Is there something wrong? I heard Maria's name."

"Oh, my goodness, I hope not, Sammy," Pat said, turning the TV off. "Nothing to worry about. Let's eat breakfast."

Chapter 77

Thursday, 6 November: 10:10 a.m.—Naples: Salvatore Mancini's mansion

Mancini looked around the table. Two were missing: Cardinal O'Reilley, who died of a heart attack on Tuesday, and Igor Yavolinski. The chatting ceased when someone noticed Mancini about to explode in anger; they all looked at their host. He had his mouth open ready to damn Yavolinski for being late when he walked in as calm as a lion basking in the noonday sun.

"I'm not accustomed to having my employees show up late for a meeting, Mr. Yavolinski. Where the hell were you?" he said, ominously.

Yavolinski took his time finding his place at the table, sat down, looked at Mancini, and said, "How much do you want me to reveal about what I was doing for you this morning?" Mancini glared at him, knowing he had been outwitted.

De Luca—knowing what Yavolinski was referring to—spoke up, rescuing Mancini from his embarrassment. "Mr. Mancini, I can vouch for Mr. Yavolinski. I know him to be a responsible and loyal friend; a prick, but you know how those Russians are sometimes." Everyone burst into laughter, including Yavolinski; the tension in the room dissipated.

"Okay," Mancini said, looking at Lopez, "you called this meeting. You said something about a crisis that is erupting like a volcano over at the Vatican. I've watched some of it on TV. I hope Col. Masterson has done his homework."

"He has, Mr. Mancini," Monsignor Lopez replied. "The pope sent out a list of fourteen proposed reforms to all cardinals; that would be ominous enough to make a move, but the situation has deteriorated seriously since an American woman posted her Master's in Theology on the Bronze doors at the Vatican. The pope studied her thesis and then invited the re-incarnated Martin Luther to the Vatican. After some discussion, the pope posted her thesis on a new papal website. Demonstrations began almost immediately in Vatican Square: they extend down the street as far as the San Angelo Bridge. The demonstrations are in support of the pope and the American woman, not against his proposed reforms.

"If he isn't stopped in his tracks, life as we have known it in the Church and in our dealings with all of you will end. It appears he is planning a Reformation redux.

"What?" asked De Luca, angrily. What do *ducks* have to do with this crisis?"

"Never mind, Tony, he's just pulling words out of his ass to help you stay awake," said Mancini. "Let the man continue."

Lopez continued. "Yet, the kicker is that Russo has defected to the pope and we believe he is holed up in the Presidential Palace singing songs like a yellow canary—tunes Italian anti-crime busters thought they would never hear. With all the documents that Sister Aurelia provided and Lidano Russo's testimony, they will have a good case to prosecute everyone in this room."

"From what I've seen, there aren't that many documents that could hurt us," Mancini said. "But I wouldn't bet that that's all the documents they have. I would assume they have compact disks loaded with incriminating data and that those are being used to analyze what's been going on for the past several years. Either way, we can't afford to make any blind assumptions at this point, other than to believe the worst and operate accordingly. Do you all agree?"

All nodded in the affirmative.

"Okay, then. We will need to move soon because the situation is deteriorating rapidly. World-wide television networks are broadcasting very ominous developments and speculating about dire consequences. If that continues, only God knows what will happen. We must control the events in this crisis, or we will be ruined.

"Col. Masterson is here to explain the remaining phases of his attack plan which he calls: **SMEAC**—Situation, Mission, Execution, Attack and Consolidation. You remember we went through the first two phases at our last meeting. I have asked him to include in his presentation the earliest he could gather his troops from around the world and have them ready for an attack. Col. Masterson, the floor is yours."

"Bull" Masterson reached, with his right arm, down to the right, lifted his leather backpack and laid it on the table. He unzipped the cover, reached inside and pulled out a pistol and placed it on the table.

In unison, as though they had been practicing all morning for this provocation, all four gangster bosses pulled their pistols out of their belts and pointed them at Col. Masterson.

De Luca spoke first. "What the fuck!"

Mancini spoke next. "What kind of a crazy bastard are you? Coming in here and pulling out a pistol? How did you get it in here? I'll have the guard who fucked-up shot! You're lucky we didn't all unload our clips and make you look like a riddled target on a rifle range."

Col. Masterson replied calmly. "You can put your heat away. What you see lying here in front of me is made of plastic. Whoever the jerk was who tried to kill the pope has made it impossible to get weapons into Vatican Square or inside the fortress."

"So, you're going to scare the Swiss Guards with a toy pistol, is that the idea, Colonel? No wonder you didn't make general, if you're that stupid," De Luca said, as he replaced his pistol in his belt.

"If you know anything about the history of warfare, or at least seen a few war movies, you will know that deceptive tactics, such as parachuting dummies into enemy territory to mislead the enemy, is commonplace," replied Col. Masterson. "You will know in due time the purpose of the plastic pistols."

Igor Yavolinski's phone vibrated indicating a text message. He looked at his Blackberry, signaled to Mancini that he needed to talk with him in private. Mancini said, "Col. Masterson, please hold a second, I need to talk to Yavolinski in private." They went into the hallway. "What's going on?" asked Mancini.

"That remodeled car with the cocaine and boatload of cash hidden in it? It didn't get past the dock inspectors; it was discovered by a police dog. I need to get down to the docks immediately. I should be able to take care of the problem and be back before you adjourn."

"Go ahead and take care of it." Mancini returned to his seat and said, "Okay, Colonel."

Before the meeting, Col. Masterson had set up a flip chart, with a topographical map of the Vatican, showing buildings, trees, bushes, roads, and a railroad tunnel; the Apostolic Palace, railroad station and the Swiss Guard barracks were highlighted. His computer and projector were connected and aligned with the screen. He projected the Situation and Mission phases as an introduction to the Execution phase that would lay out the plans for the attack.

"Gentlemen, in the Old Corps we had a saying when planning an attack: *Everything depends on the situation, mission and the terrain.* We have discussed the situation, mission and now you see the terrain we will encounter in our attack. The situation is deteriorating rapidly, requiring serious consideration be given to our mission."

"I still think we should just whack the prick," said De Luca.

"You're sounding like a broken record, Tony," said Mr. Mancini. "Let the Colonel continue."

"Now, here's the deal. In the **Execution Phase**, we take into account several factors; not all of them necessarily apply to every situation: number of personnel; weapons/ammunition; equipment; transportation; communication; medical personnel and supplies; rations; intelligence (information about the enemy), to mention only a few.

1. "In order to achieve the multi-faceted nature of the mission, invade the Vatican City State with legally constituted, para-military members of the Roman Catholic Church, and force the pope to resign before he acts.
2. "I have trained one hundred personnel, organized into two platoons.
3. "We have rented a vacant middle school a mile north of the Vatican and will house our troops there until we move out to take the Vatican tour, which will begin at 1700 hours—5 p.m. for you non-veterans—and will include the entire Vatican fortress and end at the railroad station.
4. "We'll use our cell phones for communication—primarily texting—but can use voice if necessary. You will gather here on the night of the attack to monitor our progress and assist with any command decisions that require your authorization beyond the authority given to me.
5. "Equipment:
6. 'Each para-military will wear cammies with floppy hats. No body armor. Uniforms will be sent to the Vatican, processed and held at the railroad station by an Opus Dei loyalist.
7. 'The Swiss Guards recently acquired new rifles and pistols. They are just starting to preserve and package the old ones at the railroad station; the ammo is boxed, identified and ready to be shipped. We'll have all the weapons and ammo we need.
8. "Each will use make-up to darken faces and hands.
9. "Transportation to the Vatican will be via bus.
10. "Our plan is to infiltrate the walls of the Vatican through the tourist visitor center. Some people arrange for private, after-hours tours to avoid the hordes that pass through there like cattle going to a slaughter house.
11. "We will be the last tour of the day—after hours—for railroad station aficionados wearing caps and jackets with logos representing their local club chapter. My men will split into two groups and will be led by two Opus Dei members. We will enter the railroad station and remain there

until the attack occurs. If we encounter any problems along the way, we can use our fake pistols to keep anyone at bay until we get to the railroad station.

"That's the end of the **Execution Phase.** Before I begin the next phase, we need to give a title to our para-military force. For purposes of telecommunication, we'll call our para-military group a 'Task Force'. Using quasi-military radio communications terminology, my call-sign will be 'Task Force Six', my executive officer, Lt. Col. Paducca's call-sign will be 'Task Force Five' and Sgt. Major Mc Kennan's will be 'Task Force Four'. The two platoon commanders will be "Task Force Three and Two" respectively.

"Now for the **Attack Phase:**

"The attack will begin with the kidnapping of Col. Isenberg, the commander of the Swiss Guards. He goes for a walk along this path regularly, every evening at 11:30 p.m. after dinner."

Masterson, using his laser pointer, traced a path roughly along the perimeter from the commander's apartment near the Guard barracks, going to the right and circling around the north end of the fortress, on to the west side past the heliport, continuing to the south side passing by the railroad station and then heading back to his apartment behind the basilica.

"A guard shack is located in this area," pointing to a side of a hill overlooking the slope toward the basilica. "Buildings and trees prevent the guard from observing activity around the train station. When Colonel Isenberg passes by the railroad station, we will capture him and take him into the train station and hold him hostage for our demands. The capture should occur around midnight.

"Our demands? Order all your guards back to the barracks. After we capture Col. Isenberg and he has issued his orders, we will confiscate his radio. Our men will deploy throughout the Vatican and take into custody anyone they see. After we are certain all the guards have returned to the barracks, a few of my men will surround the barracks to make certain no one leaves.

"We expect this part of the attack to last less than a half-hour. When my men have reported in assuring me that the grounds are clear and that they have taken their posts, they are to arrest anyone who wanders out in the middle of the night. After that, I will order the commander to send a message to his command center in the basement of the Swiss Guard Barracks.

"His instructions will be: (1) to inform his command center that the Vatican has been captured by a force of one hundred men who are armed with ammunition and the old rifles being preserved and packaged in the railroad station; (2) that he is being held hostage at an undisclosed location within the Vatican fortress; (3) that the command center is to inform the pope to proceed by himself to the railroad station; (4) that the commander of the invading force wants to avoid the violence that could occur if his men are forced to enter the papal apartment in order to bring the pope into custody; (5) that the purpose of this action is to convince the pope to sign papers that terminate his tenure as pope; (6) that if he refuses to agree to the demands being made, a bomb will explode, leveling the Swiss Guard barracks, killing everyone inside.

"One squad will be assigned to evacuate anyone living in apartments near the barracks to the Palace of the Governatorate located here.

"That's the end of the **Attack Phase**.

"Now for the final phase: **Consolidation:**

"To help you understand the purpose of this phase, I will describe a typical attack that a company of about a hundred sixty Marines would make on a hill held by the enemy. After the enemy have been killed, captured or driven off the hill, the attacking force consolidates the situation so that the hill will be held and secured from counter attack.

"A perimeter defense is set up, fields of fire assigned, coordination with air/ground assault support is maintained, the wounded and dead are properly attended to . . . that kind of thing and then the unit awaits further orders.

"When our attack is successful, we will do something similar, although the situation is radically different from attacking and taking a hill. After the pope resigns, we will call a press conference to announce to the world that the pope has voluntarily resigned due to circumstances that were brought about by his malfeasance in office and that Opus Dei and the Legionaries of Christ have taken control of the Vatican, which will be administered by the current Camerlengo, Cardinal Petrelli, until a new pope is selected.

"Legally, the Camerlengo of the Roman Catholic Church is the acting head of the Vatican City State between the pope's death or resignation and the new pope's election. The College of Cardinals supervises the Holy See until the new pope is installed. We will maintain a legally constituted para-military force to protect the Vatican against a counter-attack and restoration of Pope Immanuel to power.

"Due to the increasing demonstrations in Rome and around the world, Monsignor Lopez ordered me to bring my troops to Rome immediately. They will arrive Saturday afternoon and get settled in the middle school where we are having cots and other accommodations being set up for their arrival.

"Gentlemen, are there any questions?"

"Colonel Masterson, this is the first time I've heard your last three phases of your Five Paragraph Order," said Monsignor Lopez. "I do not approve of your plan to blow up the Swiss Guard Barracks if that becomes necessary to accomplish our objective. All Swiss Guards are Catholics. Even if they weren't, there must be a better alternative than mass murder. We've had enough of that in our Church history."

"Monsignor Lopez, I understand your concern. I remind you that what you refer to would not be 'mass murder'; we are in a civil war with the Vatican City State—which has all the international rights and privileges of any other country. Therefore, war-time rules apply here just as they did during any war any country has fought. I work for you. It all depends on how serious you are in terms of stopping this pope from decimating the Catholic Church and severing its long-standing relationships with the businessmen at this table."

"I am very serious about what we are doing, or I wouldn't have hired you in the first place," replied Lopez. "I understand that it could take such a threat to get this pope to relent. However, I, after consultation with my colleagues at this table, without their objections, will reserve the right to make the decision whether to use a bomb. Do I make myself clear, Colonel?"

"Yes sir."

"How do you plan to get the bomb inside the Vatican territory to bomb the barracks?" Father Lopez asked.

"Our friends around this table have taken care of that problem; how it will be done will be known only after it happens. We cannot reveal that information to everyone here; I thought it was important, however, that everyone should know of that contingency. Are there any other questions?" Silence.

Igor Yavolinski returned to the meeting, winked at Mancini, indicating everything would be okay.

"Okay, then. I have a question for you. When do you want us to attack?"

"Without objection from you Mr. Mancini, and your friends around this table, Monday, 10 November," said Monsignor Lopez.

"Okay, one more question for you Mr. Mancini and Mr. Lopez. I understand you will be monitoring our reporting on the progress of the attack and consolidation phases, and that will be done from your home here . . . outside Naples? Is that correct?" asked Bull Masterson.

"Yes," said Mr. Mancini. "We have a lot at stake here and we want to be in on any changes in plans as the attack occurs so we can make any necessary adjustments. I have a command and control center in the basement of my home.

"I can monitor the movement of all of my vehicles through the use of the Global Positioning System; there are other features of the system that don't need to be discussed now. If you don't object, we can supply each of your commandos with a GPS device so that we can see what's going on in real time in terms of where they are located in the Vatican."

"I do object," said Masterson. "Military operations get complicated enough without someone micromanaging from afar. I will compromise. Give me one. That will be enough."

"Okay. My word is my honor. I said, 'Unless you object.' You objected. So be it. Now, I have a question for you, Colonel Masterson. What if the pope isn't at the Vatican . . . as you seem to expect? Do you have a contingency plan to deal with that possibility?"

"Yes, of course. I didn't spend thirty five years in the Marine Corps and come out stupid. It'll be the same plan. *Show up or we'll bomb the barracks with all the Swiss Guards in it.* I think that will force him into our hands.

"Do you, Mr. Mancini, have plans to monitor his movements the day of the attack? There is nothing sacred about the Vatican, in terms of capturing him and forcing him to sign his resignation. That could be done in the restroom of a pizzaria."

"Yes," replied Mr. Mancini, "I'll put surveillance on all the Vatican gates starting early Sunday Morning. If he tries to leave, we will kidnap him."

"Just like that? That's it?" I don't think you've thought this through very thoroughly. How are you going to kidnap the pope in a convoy of limos and luxury cars loaded with Swiss Guards armed with sub-machine guns?" asked Colonel Masterson.

"The same way we'll do it if he's in the Vatican. I have enough men and vehicles at my disposal to stop the convoy and demand—through our communication systems—that the pope be turned over; if they don't, we'll bomb the Swiss barracks. It doesn't make any difference what day or hour that is; there are always at least half of the Guards in the barracks at any one time." Mancini looked to "Bull" Masterson for a response.

"And if they turn him over? Then what? How will you transport him and where to?"

"I'll have my private helicopter located at the Ciampino Airport for that eventuality. Wherever we capture him, we'll take him here and keep him until he meets our demands. Does that satisfy your curiosity about my abilities, Colonel?" asked Mr. Mancini, with a bit of an edge in his voice.

"Yes. I'm only trying to cover all our bases . . . that's all."

"If there are no more questions, we'll adjourn. Mr. Yavolinski, please stay a moment so we can chat. Can you do that?"

"Of course, Mr. Mancini."

"I'll see you in the kitchen."

Chapter 78

Mancini entered the kitchen. "Have a seat. Have you had lunch?"

"No."

"Good. I had the maître d' prepare something for us because I wanted to talk with you about something important. But first, I want to thank you for your help with the hit on those two assholes who betrayed me—for your being there to observe and make sure the job got done. O'Reilley is being blamed for the hit and that's good because it takes the attention away from me."

"What did they do to betray you?"

"Severino and Decap? They were moonlighting. In our system, you belong to the system; every penny you earn—*you* get some and your *bosses* get some of the take. They had a deal with the cardinal. When I found out, they were walking dead. This is a good lesson for you to learn without doing it the hard way.

"Now, I have another job for you. I'm sure you understand that since you are only a 'friend of mine,' and not 'a friend of ours', you have no obligation to take part in what I am proposing.

"But it could be an opportunity to become a 'friend of ours' if you pull the trigger. I will let you decide what to do. You've only been working for us for a short time, but I see that you have great potential and could move up the ranks very rapidly if you choose that path.

"What do you have in mind?"

"Those dummies sitting around our table think the pope is the biggest threat to our businesses. He is a threat, don't get me wrong, but one way or the other he will be gone. The biggest threat to our interests is that broad who is getting her moment of fame at the Church's expense and ours. You know who I mean?"

"I rarely watch TV, but I got some glimpses from what was going on with her; I saw the back of her head on TV in a bar last night. When she returned to the hotel, she was surrounded with paparazzi so I didn't get a good look at her. I understand she has created quite stir."

"To put it mildly," Mancini replied. We need to whack her. If she lives, the pope's threat will be like that of a mouse compared with the mountain-lion-of-a-threat *she* poses. In less than a week she has become an international heroine and who knows where that will lead. But wherever it could, she ain't going there and that's where you come in.

"Here's the deal. You know that idiot who screwed up trying to kill the pope? Well, I ordered a couple of my men, Gianni and Bernardo to recruit someone they thought could do the job. My thinking was that if we could kill the pope, we could avoid this war we are about to wage at the Vatican. It smells like rotting dead bodies at the bottom of a well to me. Too many things can go wrong, but I'm participating because we don't have any other options.

"I had Bernardo whack Gianni for fucking up the job. Now, what I want you to do is hook up with Bernardo to whack the broad. It should be easy. Bernardo is like a horse. Do you know anything about horses?"

"No, why?"

"Because if you did, I wouldn't waste my breath telling you about horses and Bernardo. Like horses, Bernardo needs a master—someone to lead him around like you do a horse. He's good at what he does—whacking people— but that's it. He'll do exactly what he's told to do, so be careful with what you tell him to do. If you tell him to shoot you on a drunken, foolhardy dare, you'll die. He doesn't have any discriminating skills like the rest of us—if you know what I mean."

"I know what you mean. Thanks for the warning."

"I'll have someone call her at her hotel Monday night about nine p.m. and tell her the pope is sending a priest to pick her up and take her to his office in the Vatican. You go with the 'priest'—Bernardo dressed in priest's garb—to pick up Miss Celebrity at her hotel.

"You take her to the Naples dock. You drive. She sits in the passenger seat. Bernardo sits behind her in the back seat. Bernardo plugs her in the back of the head before she gets out of the car. You put her in a cotton body bag, attach some cinder blocks and hand her over to one of my men who will be waiting at the wharf to dump her in the bay with the fishes."

"She'll know she's not going to the Vatican," said Igor.

"Sure. That's when you tell her what's coming down. She can wait until you get to Naples, or you can plug her before you get there. Let it be her choice. She might want a little time to say her prayers. I'm a devout Catholic, so my preference is that you give her a little slack—time to say her prayers.

"Apparently, she's a very religious person, so I don't want to get too far on the outs with the Guy Upstairs—if you know what I mean. And I don't want you to fuck her before you kill her. I understand she's quite a hot number and there could be some temptations there."

"Okay. Since we are friends, I will help you out on this one. When and where do I meet Bernardo?"

"There's a bar—American owned, called the 'Barbaria'—near the hotel: some freak getting cute with mixing English and Italian with the name to attract attention. Bernardo doesn't talk much. He'll know his job. All you have to do is introduce yourself and then drive to the hotel.

"Use the back entrance, because there are these reporters and paparazzi harassing her every time she leaves the hotel. You might need to shake them, but don't pull a Diana on me. That would be very embarrassing, if you get my meaning. I'll provide you with the car. Any questions?"

"What does he look like?"

"Tall and skinny, with some of the characteristics of a hollowed out vulture. He is slightly bent, with long, boney fingers and a face that looks like he could be a candidate for anorexic therapy. At fifty years of age, what he has left of his hair is gray and closely cropped. Any more questions?"

"No. You've explained it quite well. But where and when do I pick up the car."

"Bernardo will have it parked outside the bar."

Chapter 79

Friday, 7 November: 2:00 p.m.—Presidential Palace

The hour of decision had arrived—unannounced. It was like a mountain lion sneaking up on a sleeping deer. Although, the President of Italy and the pope of a world-wide religious institution were not asleep, it seemed like the time to act had arrived suddenly, not following years of planning with a pre-determined date for the attack.

The date for the onslaught of climactic events that would rock the world had been set by a cabal of gangsters, a couple recalcitrant clerics and two leaders of Catholic religious organizations.

Fortunately, the pope and the president had not ignored their decision to meet over lunch several times during the past several months to keep abreast of developments and make adjustments to their respective plans as situations dictated. When they saw the crisis developing, they moved quickly.

"Your Holiness," President Bianchi said, after they exchanged their usual pleasantries, "based on my intelligence briefings, which include information we have been receiving from our mole we planted amongst the gangsters, we can expect an attack on the Vatican on Monday, 10 November. We don't know much more than that—except what I've already told you in our luncheons—that a retired United States Marine Corps colonel and about 100 other ex-military men plan to take over the Vatican and force you to resign.

"Based on that and your description of what's going on at the Vatican, I ordered our military forces to conduct another 'training exercise'. In the last moments before the army and police units move out, they will be told that this is not a drill—that it is the real thing and what that 'thing' is.

"My top military commanders have been in constant touch with your Commandant of the Swiss Guards. They are prepared for any contingency imaginable. Colonel Isenberg, as I'm sure you know, has been involved in the training of the NATO Special Operations Forces, should they be needed to assist at the Vatican when the crisis erupts.

"I alerted the NATO command headquarters on Wednesday that the crisis was near and that the USS Lincoln needed to be in place, off the coast of Italy by the end of the week—ready for action."

"Thank you for this information and the *heads-up* on the impending attack," said the pope.

For the pope, his plans were contingency-laden: he was determined to initiate reforms—come what may—but always kept his most radical option open and shared it with the president. At one point, early-on in their luncheon discussions, he told the president that they should prepare for his decision to do the unthinkable: abrogate the 1929 Lateran Treaty between Italy and the Vatican City State that granted the Catholic Church independent national sovereignty, creating the Vatican City State, within which the Holy See—the religious arm of the Catholic Church—functions. The Lateran Treaty can be abrogated by mutual agreement between the two sovereign powers.

The 1929 Lateran Treaty is a thirty-three page concordat with dozens of articles articulating the legalities that—among dozens of other issues—governs the transfer of the properties of the Italian State to the Church, with all rights and privileges appertaining thereto.

The Supreme Pontiff of the Roman Catholic Church has absolute, unimpeachable power, and could, with the stroke of a pen, dissolve the Holy See, thereby declaring the Roman Catholic Church extinct. Legally, the Church would cease to exist before the ink dried.

As a practical matter, declaring the Roman Catholic Church extinct and the 1929 Lateran Treaty dissolved would remove the oppressive Vatican yoke from the necks of the Catholic churches and their parishioners world-wide: their dioceses would be free to operate freely, self-govern, disband . . . do whatever served the people of the congregations.

As a secular matter, all the real estate, chattels (property other than land or buildings owned by the Vatican) and the Vatican Bank and its assets, would be transferred to the Sovereign State of Italy in a legal document signed by the pope, President Bianchi and the Prime Minister of Italy prior to Pope Immanuel's resignation.

The pope had encouraged the president to use Father Perfecto's expertise in finance and accounting to act as a liaison between Italy and the Vatican in preparing for the dissolution of the Roman Catholic Church. "Father Perfecto told me recently that he and your legal staff were working on the document or documents that would need to be created and signed to declare the Roman Catholic Church defunct and transfer all its assets to your country. I'm wondering if you know if the documents are ready for signature."

"The documents have been ready for about a week," said President Bian- chi, "and I heard from the Prime Minister yesterday that he had received the necessary political support for this action; we can sign them any time. My advice is that we do it immediately, before you leave, because of the danger you face. The date we received—Monday, could be a trick—that they will actually attack tonight, Saturday or Sunday night.

"Of course, that's possible, but I understand the information you received about the date of the attack is from a highly reliable source. Is that correct?"

"Yes it is, but I want to be sure you understand the possibilities in these matters. After all, I've been in this business for a long time: you, on the other hand—you have been in a business where trusting other people and putting the best construction on what they say and do is de rigueur."

"I appreciate your persistence and believe me, I thank you from the bot- tom of my heart. However, I'm afraid you might underestimate the treachery I've witnessed in my profession. I will leave it at that.

"There are some things I need to do Monday, acting as the pope, and if I resign today, I won't be able to do them. I need to continue to show my face right up to a reasonable time before they attack, so that they will not be tipped off that we know what they are up to. I'm assuming we don't know enough about their plans to make a pre-emptive strike."

"Yes, your assumption is correct," replied the president.

The pope continued, "I have enough confidence in your intelligence reports—and the preparations we have made to deal with any attack—that I will not be in serious danger and that we will be able to capture the invaders and bring them to justice. I don't want to do anything to sabotage that opportunity. I will let you know when I can return for the signing of the documents; it will be before sunset on Monday. Is there anything else we need to deal with?

"Oh, I nearly forgot," said the pope. "When I heard about the attack date, I thought it might be a good idea to do what you mentioned our enemies might do: pull a ruse. I'm thinking of announcing that I will give an address to the world through the world TV and radio media networks next Tuesday. I can reach nearly every country in the world through Radio Vaticano, and CNN is here covering the demonstrations and clamoring to get a scoop on the devel- opments at the Vatican.

"The ruse will be that our enemies will assume I'll still be pope and want to defend my actions. What do you think about that as a way to hold off the attack dogs at least until Monday night?"

"All we know at this point, Your Holiness, is that they plan to attack '*Monday*'. We have been assuming that would mean sometime Monday after dark: that they would attack at night. Actually, Monday begins Sunday night—one second after midnight.

"For all we know, they could be planning to attack at midnight, just before dawn, noon, or sometime later on Monday, but before midnight; But, I repeat, our information, which is highly reliable is that the attack will come sometime Monday. You could still put out an announcement that you plan an address on Tuesday. I think that's a good idea. You might have something to say to the world as Dr. Marcus J. Madsen," the President said with a smile.

"I like your sense of humor, Mr. President. We can discuss where the address will take place if things turn out in our favor. I'll see you sometime late Monday afternoon to sign the documents."

Chapter 80

Saturday, 8 November: 8: 30 p.m.—Mancini': Operations Control Room

In the OCR, located in the basement of his mansion, Mr. Mancini picked up the phone and dialed Monsignor Lopez's encrypted cell phone number.

"Lopez here."

"Monsignor Lopez, I wanted to make sure that O'Reilley died as the newspaper said he did and that he didn't confess anything about our attack plans. Were you there when he died?"

"No, obviously not. I'm not a cardinal, but I have a couple close friends who were there and I can assure you O'Reilley died as reported."

"Okay then. We can depend on you, Father Nunez, and Cardinal Moretti to be here by late Monday afternoon?"

"Yes. We'll be there and I should let you know in advance that we will bring with us one of the Pope's closest associates who is betting on our success. He will have information of the pope's location when he left the Vatican.

"Now, I have a question of how we will be monitoring the progress of the attack. You didn't explain that in our meetings."

"Never mind my not telling you before this. I don't discuss my secrets in open forum, but I am confident I can trust you. I have an operations control room in my bomb shelter in the basement from where my men monitor all of our activities, including the movement of our cars and trucks and in some cases individuals.

"I have the latest Global Positioning System (GPS) technology. I have computer systems with large screens to project all the maps within which our people operate. That area includes western Russia, all of eastern and western Europe and the areas around the Mediterranean Sea. We can even monitor ships that come within those parameters. I can assure you, Monsignor Lopez, we'll know what's going on during the attack."

Monday, 10 November: 1:30 p.m.—Rome

Perfecto left the presidential palace in his red Panda and drove to the Vatican, entering through the Sant' Anna Gate.

Mancini's goon squads were in place at each of the gates on the lookout for any evidence that the pope was entering or leaving the Vatican. The guerilla, sitting in his black, Ford luxury car near the Sant' Anna gate noticed, from a distance, a Red Panda entering along with a string of other cars streaming from Via Borgo Pia. *If a Panda comes out, I don't care what color it is, I'm on his tail like a dog chasing a noisy motorcycle,* the gangster thought.

Pope Immanuel greeted Father Perfecto in front of his desk in an ebullient mood. "I have plans for you. The events in the next twenty four hours will be crucial to our success. You will play a central and critical role. Are you ready for this?"

"Well, Holiness, I guess that depends on what the meaning of 'this' is," Perfecto said with a big smile. The pope laughed and briefed Perfecto about the details of his plan.

Monday, 10 November: 2 p.m.—Vacated Middle School, Rome

"ATTEN-HUT!" shouted Sergeant Major Mc Kennan.

Colonel Masterson's para-military force stood *at attention* as he entered the middle school lunch room.

"Be seated Gentlemen. Our historic opportunity is now. I'll not waste time; I will issue the five-paragraph order now.

"SITUATION: Pope Immanuel has created a crisis in the Church and must be stopped before it's too late.

"MISSION: Our mission is to capture the Vatican Fortress, locate the pope and force him to resign.

"EXECUTION: Busses will transport us to the Vatican for a private, after-hours tour of the Vatican Gardens. We will be met by two Opus Dei tour-guides at the entrance to the museums at 5 p.m. and led through the security and ticketing lines. We will tour the gardens and end up at the railroad station at approximately 6 p.m. We will change into our uniforms, apply camouflage to our faces, and issue the assault rifles and ammunition.

"ATTACK: The attack will begin with the capture of the Swiss Guards Commandant. We anticipate that will be between 2300 and 2330 hours (11 & 11:30 p.m.). The Commandant will be informed of the situation and forced to withdraw his troops to the barracks. We will take up our assigned positions and await further orders.

"Open fire on any perceived threat. It's kill or be killed.

"CONSOLIDATION: Monsignor Lopez of Opus Dei and Father Nunez of the Legionaries of Christ and Regnum Christi will hold a press conference at the Vatican following the pope's resignation. They'll announce that the camerlengo is preparing for the election of a new pope.

"We leave for the Vatican at 1630 hours. May God bless our cause."

Chapter 81

Monday, 10 November: 4 p.m.—Mancini Operations Control Room (OCR)

In the OCR, Mancini, De Luca, Lombardi, Giordano, Lopez, Nunez, retired Cardinal Moretti and Father Sandusky prepared for a long night. Each had cushioned seats situated in a semi-circle facing several of Mancini's operations officers whose primary duty was to keep track of the systems' vehicle traffic, and occasionally, personnel. At that moment, the big screen displayed a map of Rome and the surrounding area, extending as far north as Florence and south to Naples.

One ops officer had responsibility to keep track of ten luxury cars assigned to monitor vehicle traffic into and out of the Vatican. The purpose of the surveillance was keep track of the pope's movements. "The pope was in his office when I left to come down here this morning," Sandusky reassured Mancini.

Using special secure radio communications equipment compatible with cars and the OCR, the ops officer was able to communicate freely with the surveillance crew at the Vatican.

At 4:30 p.m., cars six and seven watching the north-wall gate reported that a Carabinieri policeman opened the heavy, steel gates revealing the gold-metal plaque—on the curved wall inside the gate—with POPE IMMANUEL inscribed in large, bold, black letters.

Ten minutes later the papal caravan emerged from the fortress gate. The pope's black limousine, with the Vatican City State flag on the left and his personal flag on the right, was preceded by two Carabinieri motorcycle policemen—lights flashing—and three luxury sedans. Following the pope's limo were three more luxury sedans; each of them carried four Swiss Guards—with firearms—in black business suits

The motorcycles turned left and led the convoy north on V. Lione IV, right to Via del Italico, left onto V. Salaria which took them to the entrance to the southeast-bound beltway. Tailing the caravan, at a discrete distance were four Mancini Mercedes carrying twelve gangsters. One of Mancini's men notified the OCR that they were on the pope's tail.

In the OCR, Mancini ordered the ops man to contact a construction yard adjacent to the Ciampino Airport near the Autostrada and Via Appia junction. "Get a semi-truck in place at the railroad overpass on Via Appia Nuova, leading to Castel Gandolfo, in case that's where the pope is headed. If the pope's caravan heads south toward the castle, make sure the truck blocks traffic at the overpass at the southern edge of the Ciampino Airport," Mancini said.

"We might not need a truck from the construction yard Mr. Mancini," said one of the ops men. "I noticed a moment ago that we have truck number twelve heading north out of Gandolfo. He will get there well before the caravan."

"Good work, Alfredo. To be safe, have two of our cars pass the convoy and head toward Gandolfo and take up positions with the truck on that overpass. Make sure they have our two men in police uniforms on either side of the convoy to halt traffic at the bridge.

"Tell the others remaining behind the convoy to let us know, immediately, if the pope does not turn south on Via Appia Nuova, or if he does. Either way; let us know immediately. He's out and about. This would simplify things a lot. Now, one more thing; we don't have time to wire the railroad overpass with dynamite, but a bluff might work.

"Tell the cars that arrive there first and are getting the truck in place to try to bluff their way into capturing the pope. After the caravan has stopped on the overpass, they should order the pope to surrender to them or they will blow the bridge and his car sky-high if he doesn't cooperate."

Looking at the assembled cabal, Mancini asked, "What's with this unusual route the caravan is taking? Any ideas? It's going way out of the way if it's headed toward Gandolfo."

"It's merely a maneuver to annoy anyone who is on his tail," said Father Sandusky. "They know a crisis is looming and they want to create as many problems as they can."

As the pope's limo approached the overpass, the gangsters' truck pulled the trailer across the road at the southern end of the overpass, blocking the caravan's forward movement. After the caravan stopped on the overpass, Mancini's men emerged from their two cars and appeared at either side of the truck with sub-machine guns, one with a bull-horn.

At the rear of the convoy, the other six men emerged from their cars, and took up blocking positions at the north end of the overpass to prevent traffic from interfering and prevent the convoy vehicles from moving out of the blockade. The two gangsters, dressed in Carabinieri uniforms, took positions at the rear and front of the convoy to stop traffic twenty-five yards from the railroad overpass.

Colonel Isenberg emerged from the front car and stood facing the truck and the attackers.

The gangster with a bullhorn shouted, "The overpass is wired with explosives. Turn the pope over to us or you all die."

"The pope is not in the limousine," Col. Isenberg shouted. "We were on our way to Gandolfo to pick him up."

Chapter 82

Monday, 10 November: 5 p.m. –Rome

Modernizing their crime-busting clout, Italy's magnificent, stylistic ways have muscled their way into the Carabinieri (State Police) transportation system: The Lamborghini Gallardo LP 560, endows the Carabinieri with an ostentatious display of law enforcement chutzpa.

It started with a proto-type, customized Lamborghini, capable of 203 miles per hour due to the 560 horsepower engine. It isn't just a muscle bound anomaly. It's smart, equipped with high-tech support systems that might dazzle a moon-traveling astronaut.

An automatic license plate number recognition system can track and send plate data in real-time to the central control rooms, while a forward-looking camera is capable of data-logging GPS information to the video transmitting device providing live-feed to offices in real-time. The camera can record what is happening on the scene, transmit it real-time to the nearest police station and record the transmission for further use in a prosecutorial setting.

The GPS system can calculate the distance, direction and speed the car being pursued and the time lapse before interception. Using the radio-data transmission system, the video system transfers images in real-time to the relevant police department while storing the data to be used for automatic retrieval of plate identity and identification of stolen vehicles. Incriminating data can be retrieved to show that the violator has infractions.

The luggage compartment in front is equipped with a specialized refrigeration system for safe transportation of donor organs. It also has a defillibrator to restore abnormal heart functioning.

Tyrone attracted the attention of the Carabinieri brass with an invention that he wanted tested. Mounted on the dash boards of the two Lamborghini's designated for the Roma beltway patrol, the Laser Activated Electrical System Disabling Device (LAESDD) was designed to reduce the hazards associated with car-chases. LAESDD's would not eliminate pursuing cars because the system did not work unless the pursuer was within thirty yards of the target.

As if it were not enough to impress the world with its artistic achievements, even in what would appear to be an otherwise mundane matter, you could find movie-star-quality women in Carabinieri uniforms sidling up to your car and poking a Beretta 92 in your face.

Ricci Valentino, a crusty veteran of some thirty years of service, was not a beautiful young woman; Carmela Conti was: In a form-fitting, multi-colored blue uniform, she could act deceptively incompetent in dealing with the most hardened criminals. But the word got around: "*Don't mess with her!*"The combo of Valentino and Conti earned *respect*.

They were enjoying one of their occasional trysts in a grove just off the autostrada, when they heard a radio transmission to all Carabinieri units, including their Special Forces, located in the vicinity of the Ciampino Airport. "The pope's caravan is under attack at the railroad overpass at the southern edge of the Ciampino airport. Proceed with caution."

"Damn!" grunted Ricci. He rolled over, pulled up his pants and headed for his car. "Follow me," he screamed, as he pulled out of the alcove. She passed him on the way to the bridge.

Approaching the scene, they heard helicopters heading in the same direction. As they approached the overpass, they saw lines of cars backed up north and south of the overpass.

Four transport and two attack helicopters flew in circles—surveying the situation—considering their options.

Arriving at the scene first, Conti noticed something that didn't compute; the Carabinieri officer holding up traffic at the north end of the overpass was not wearing standard uniform shoes and she didn't see any police cars in the vicinity.

As quietly as a leopard, she walked up behind him. He felt cold, round steel pressing against his neck. "Drop your weapon, or you're dead," Carmela said quietly. He whirled around, his elbow flying toward her head. She ducked. The bullet entered the side of his neck and exited the thug's left eye. He dropped dead.

A nearby gangster raised his sub-machine gun and pointed it at Carmela. Before he could get a round off, Ricci, aiming his rifle resting on the window frame of his door, dropped him with a bullet through the heart.

Forty paratroopers were demanding the surrender of the attackers before they hit the ground. The overwhelming forces falling from the sky, the shots fired at the rear of the convoy killing two of the attackers and one man shot and wounded by a falling paratrooper, convinced the remaining attackers to throw their arms down and their hands up.

The Swiss Guards emerged from their cars and took the criminals into custody . . . all but one. When he saw the paratroopers falling from the sky he took refuge in one of the Mercedes parked south of the truck. He carefully observed the Carabinieri's capture of his comrades. Seeing his chance to escape, he slid into the driver's seat, started the engine, did a U'ie and headed south past a dozen cars stalled by the blockade.

With the Swiss Guards busy detaining the attackers until arresting Carabinieri vans arrived to arrest and transport the criminals to prison, the Lambo twins were the first to react: the second—an attack-helicopter. Maneuvering around the Caravan, the twins were eager to use their superior horse power and technological advantages to overtake the Mercedes.

Yet it would be a challenge because the Mercedes had a half-mile lead by the time the twins realized what was happening. The gangster, heading south, had turned right onto a side road that went through Tyrone's town and then headed north toward the Autostrada. He hoped to make it to Rome and lose his pursuers, if any, in the congested city.

The twin Lambo's had already passed the turn-off when the helicopter overhead spotted the Mercedes speeding west into town. The helicopter pilot informed the Lambo's. With the help of the helicopter with minute-by-minute guidance, the Lambo's were able to close in on the Mercedes as it entered the Autostrada heading west toward the Leonardo Da Vinci Airport.

He had not spotted his pursuers and thought he might have escaped, when the helicopter descended, flying above his car. The traffic on the autostrada would make pursuit more difficult than on rural roads, but the twins were up to the challenge. The first one to get within thirty yards would have the opportunity activate Tyrone's Laser Electronic Deactivating System.

In the Operations Control Room, Mancini screamed at his operations man to find out what was happening at the bridge. He could see on the monitoring screen only one car—number three—moving away from the bridge. The others remained stationary.

"Car three doesn't respond to my inquiries," replied the ops control man.

"See if you can raise anyone else there at the bridge," Mancini demanded.

"No response, sir."

"Shit!" Mancini screamed.

He hit the power button on the TV. A station helicopter had its camera focused on a black Mercedes being pursued by a helicopter and two Carabinieri Lamborghinis passing the Via Aurelia exit north of the Da Vinci airport. Another TV station helicopter focused on the drama at the bridge.

"Damn!" exclaimed the gangster. Having missed the Via Aurelia exit, he pulled into the first exit that looked promising as an escape route. A construction zone—with numerous barriers narrowing the path to a little more than the width of a car—slowed him to a snail's pace.

Winding around in the traffic maze, he spotted a carwash with a huge parking lot embraced on the left and far sides by a recreational park with shrubs and trees—*perhaps a place to escape*. He pulled into the lot—running a red light—knowing the closest Lambo was unable to maneuver past the car behind him. Despite the Lambo's siren, flashing lights and frustrated horn blasts to get the driver to move out of the way, the car—stopped at the red light—did not move until the light turned green.

The few seconds that elapsed before the light turned green gave the escapee time to drive to the far end of the carwash lot, exit the car and disappear into the park. The trees and bushes gave him the concealment he needed from the helicopters following his movements. Conti and Valentino searched the park without success. They impounded the car and had it towed away.

In the OCR, Mancini and his cabal were suffering from their first defeat of the day. Since their man who escaped the caravan debacle did not have a tracking device on him, it was apparent from the GPS monitor that their escaping comrade had been cornered by the police. But the TV reporters were indicating the man in the Mercedes had escaped and his car was being towed to a police, impound lot.

Back at the caravan scene, TV reporters indicated that two of the gangsters had been killed, one wounded and the others captured. Three cars and a truck had been impounded.

"Let me know when you hear anything from or about that coward who fled the scene at the bridge," Mancini told one of his ops men.

"Where is Col. Masterson?" asked Mancini.

"His blip on the screen shows he's in the Railroad Station. He reported that his troops have made a successful entry into the Vatican without incident, are about to enter the railroad station and begin breaking out the rifles and ammunition," replied the Ops man.

"Okay. Good news." said Mancini. Looking at the cabal, he said, "Let's go to dinner now and be ready to follow this thing when the action starts tonight."

Chapter 83

Monday, 10 Nov. 10 a.m. (CST USA) Monday, 10 Nov. 6 p.m. Rome

Pat went to the living room and turned on the TV. She was concerned. She had received text messages from Maria each day reassuring her that she was okay and not to worry. Still, she worried. What she could not know was that in the Operations Control Room Mancini and his cabal were watching the same broadcast.

She had heard late the night before that CNN would have a special report at 10 a.m. on the worsening crisis at the Vatican. The program started with a brief summary of Pope Immanuel's biographical history, followed by an account of the stir he had caused at the Vatican with his radical proposals for Church reform. Then the anchor, Tammy Mical said, "The crisis is worsening."

They showed footage of Maria entering and leaving the Excedra hotel at the Piazza della Republica, surrounded by paparazzi and numerous television correspondents vying for an interview or a statement. She had become the newest, world-wide celebrity.

Karl was among the correspondents. "I can tell you, Tammy, that this woman has been cajoled, threatened, coaxed and even bribed these last few days. Some people hate her for her outrageous thesis—its contents and what she did with it. It seems to have had a profound opposite influence on the pope. How far he will go with his reforms remains to be seen. Yet, from what I've seen here in Rome and from my contacts around this country, the people are going wild over the possibility that the Church may be collapsing the same way the Soviet Union did in 1991."

"What does it look like in terms of when the turmoil will end?" asked Tammy.

"Of course, no one knows for certain, but today the pope announced he would address the Italian people and the rest of the world on Tuesday morning. We'll have to wait and see what he says. But there may be more to this story than just these demonstrations and an eventual peaceful outcome after the reforms are announced and things get back to normal.

"My sources say that major violence could erupt if the pope does not relent—give up on his dream of radical reforms. Remember, there are powerful religious Catholic organizations that raise a lot of money for the Church and have an enormous influence on who gets red hats and therefore, who is elected to the papacy. Nearly all of the cardinals are fiercely opposed to Pope Immanuel's reforms.

"The most explosive issue is related to the Vatican Bank. It is known to be one of the most notorious money laundering banks in the world, processing billions of dollars to off-shore, tax-sheltering banks and taking a substantial cut of the funds for their services.

"We know that Sister Aurelia Esposito was murdered mafia style shortly after providing a boatload of bank documents to the pope. The manager of the bank for the past several decades, Lidano Russo, sought refuge in the pope's office when he was threatened by Italian gangsters.

"The pope, by Vatican statutes, personally owns the bank and is the only person who can do anything about the corruption that has lasted for decades. It is not hard to imagine that thousands of people around the world—besides the gangsters who use the bank—are worried that their piggy-banks will spill into the open, revealing their thievery of tax dollars that belong to Italy and other countries where citizens use the bank to avoid paying taxes."

"Thanks. Stay in touch. It looks like a volcano is about to erupt." The program segued into round-the-world snapshots of massive demonstrations in major cities where Catholics reside in large numbers.

The vignettes began in Boston, spread across the United States, then to several European countries where only a small percentage of baptized Catholics attend church regularly. Additionally, the program producers chose representations of what was happening all over the world. Not all the demonstrations were pro-reform, but assessments were that 75 to 90 percent of demonstrators supported the pope.

After the global glimpses, Tammy said, "Our producers here at CNN have been monitoring the blogging on the pope's website. People from all over the world are in a feeding frenzy.

"Millions of hits and hundreds of thousands of bloggers are choking the digital pipeline of the pope's new website, offering their opinions on Luderenko's thesis, what she did with it and the dangers and blessings it could bring to the Church and humanity. Two new blogging website links were added to the pope's website today to accommodate the overwhelming responses to the Vatican crisis . . ."

"We interrupt this broadcast to bring you the following **BREAKING NEWS** from our sources in Italy that the pope's caravan was stopped at a railroad overpass just north of his summer palace at Castel Gandolfo.

"The information at this point is sketchy, but we do know that there were at least two gangsters killed in an attempt by someone to kidnap the pope from his limousine, protected by about a dozen Swiss Guards as it was traveling from the Vatican to the pope's summer palace at Castel Gandolfo a few miles south of Rome. Apparently the pope was not in his limousine at the time."

"Back to you, Karl. Sorry about the interruption. Anything else?"

"The question is: Where is the pope? No one seems to know where he is."

"Keep us posted, Karl. This is turning into one of the most alarming and portentous crises in the history of the Catholic Church."

Pat turned the TV off as Sammy came into the kitchen.

Chapter 84

Monday, 10 November: 6:30 p.m.—Vatican

Dressed in mufti, Perfecto placed his cassock in a traveling bag in the rear seat of his red Panda and slid into the driver's seat. He headed out the Sant' Anna Gate. He noticed a black BMW pull out, tailing him as he proceeded down Via della Conciliazione. *It's not as though I drive the only Panda in Rome,* he thought, *so let's see what I can do this time to have some fun with this lost soul.*

He turned right and crossed over the Tiber River on the Ponte Sant' Angelo and disappeared into a street maze designed to confuse more than help. *That's a **good** thing,* he thought, with a smile on his face. He placed his thumb on the print and pressed button five, reached back and pulled out a wig, placed it on his head and pressed number three and watched his car turn blue with a new license plate number.

He drove in the direction of the Presidential Palace, frustrated at times with wanting to turn left when the street was one-way to the right. Eventually, he pulled into the Piazza del Quirinale, and through the back gate, into the palace courtyard.

Five minutes after he pulled out of the Vatican, a dark gray, yet to be painted, old—apparently restored Volkswagen bug—joined a long line of Vatican employees in stop-and-go traffic heading home after a long day at work. It took a similar path to the Presidential Palace and entered the courtyard. Pope Immanuel, in mufti, struggled out of the Beetle. "Golly, Holiness," said Perfecto, "I've never seen you in a business suit. You're jumping the gun, aren't you?"

"I can't imagine what you are talking about, Perfecto," the pope said with a mischievous grin.

President Bianchi, Prime Minister De Stefano, the ministers of defence and foreign affairs greeted their guests, and introductions were made. They proceeded to a conference room across the hall from the president's office.

Father Perfecto and the Italian Ministers of Defence and Foreign Affairs would serve as witnesses to this historic event, which would be video-taped. Pope Immanuel excused himself while he changed from his business suit to his papal cassock and white cap.

THE QUIRINALE PALACE CONCORDAT

Whereas the Supreme Pontiff of the Universal Church, Sovereign of the Vatican City State, Bishop of Rome, Vicar of Christ, Successor of the Prince of the Apostles, Primate of Italy, Archbishop and Metropolitan of the Roman Province, Servant of the Servants of God has unimpeachable authority over all rights, privileges and responsibilities appertaining to the Holy See and the Vatican City State, granted by the Code of Canon Law of the Roman Catholic Church, as recognized in the 1929 Lateran Treaty by the Sovereign State of Italy;

And whereas the two high parties of the 1929 Lateran Treaty solemnly agreed in Section Three, Article 44. of said treaty, that: *"If any difficulty shall arise in the future concerning the interpretation of the present Concordat, the Holy See and Italy shall proceed by a common examination to a friendly solution.";*

And whereas, the current two high parties of the 1929 Concordat have concluded that the only solution to the crises plaguing their respective sovereignties is to declare the Holy See (and therefore the Roman Catholic Church) extinct, by abrogating the 1929 Lateran Treaty. The effective time and date for the dissolution of the Holy See and the abrogation of the Lateran Treaty is 12:01 a.m., 11 November 2008

In preparation for the execution of the present Concordat, the two high parties have agreed after the signing thereof, that all real estate and chattels, including the Vatican Bank and its assets, currently owned by the Vatican City State and the Holy See, shall become the sole property of the Sovereign State of Italy. On and at the effective date and time of said Concordat, the Sovereign State of Italy shall occupy the Vatican City State fortress, the basilica and all other property owned by the Roman Catholic Church for the purpose of protecting assets and personnel located and residing therein.

Rome, tenth November, two thousand and eight: 7 p.m.

Pope Immanuel   Allesandro Bianchi   Giovanni De Stefano

Supreme Pontiff   **President**   **Prime Minister**

WITNESSES:

Perfecto Gonzales   Vittore Passagero   Agosto De Laurentiis
Priest   **Minister of Defence**   **Minister of Foreign Affairs**

President Bianchi hosted dinner for the signatories, celebrating the historic occasion.

Pope Immanuel thanked the Italian officials for sending their forces to come to the aid of the papal caravan. The afternoon attack signaled the beginning of a long night. The president had ordered the Italian armed forces—including the Carabinieri police—to stand by for the strike against the gangsters, with the assault on the Mancini mansion cabal at midnight.

A company of the Italian San Marco Marine Regiment was standing by at a remote area of the Leonardo Da Vinci Airport to relieve NATO Special Operations Forces assigned to secure the Vatican if an attack occurred and was repulsed.

Pope Immanuel informed the gathering that he, as Dr. Marcus Madsen, planned to make a television address to the world; he would announce the reasons for his papal decision to declare the Church extinct at an appropriate time the following day. With a wry smile, he had asked the president for permission to use the former papal office for the address and afterwards greet the teaming crowd in Vatican Square. The president, picking up on the rich irony of the request, with a broad smile, said he'd think about it.

Following dinner, all shook hands as Perfecto departed in his purple Panda, followed by Marcus in the Volkswagen as they drove to Tyrone's showroom, arriving around 8:30 p.m. They wanted to share the rest of the day with him, but whatever was left would have to wait until they had downed a couple beers.

Chapter 85

Monday, 10 November 8:30 p.m.—Rome

Igor Yavolinski, dressed in black alligator shoes, black, fine-wool pants, a purple shirt and black, leather, blazer jacket, entered the bar. He wore a modest, gold chain around his neck. He walked up to the only priest in the bar who looked like Mancini's description and said, "I'm Igor Yavolinski; you must be Bernardo."

"That's me. Let's get this thing over. I can't stand this straightjacket."

"Not so fast. We have plenty of time. Mr. Mancini tells me you like beer, so let's have a few before we go pick up the lady—get to know each other. I don't like doing jobs with someone I don't know. I'm told you are a real professional. I'm new at this game, as you know, so maybe you can help me get acclimated a little."

"What kind of shit-talk is that? Aktimated—I have no idea what you said.

The telephone in the lounge of her hotel suite rang. "This is Maria."

"Miss Luderenko, this is Sister Angela," sounding like an older, loving and compassionate woman. "I work in the Vatican. The pope has asked me to invite you to come for dinner this evening. He's dining at 10:30. Would it be possible for you to come? I'm sure the pope would enjoy your company."

"Yes, of course, Sister Angela. Tell the pope I'd be happy to join him. But I'm not sure when I can get there. The media are keeping a close watch on the hotel doors; sometimes it's hard to get past them."

"Oh, don't worry about that. I'm sending a priest and his driver to pick you up. They will take good care of you. They'll be there in about an hour. Is that okay with you? The pope wanted to have a cocktail and chat with you a bit before you have dinner."

"Yes, of course. I'll be ready."

An hour later the front desk called Maria to inform her that her escorts were in the lobby.

Maria, wearing black pants, black spikes, a white, V-neck, cashmere sweater under a red leather, form-fitting jacket, went to the front desk to turn in her key and retrieve her passport that she had forgotten to pick up earlier in the week after checking in.

As she walked through the lobby going to the front desk, she noticed the backs of a priest and a man in mufti sitting in the lounge. Leaving the front desk, she placed her passport in her handbag while walking to where the priest and his companion were sitting.

"Hello," she said with a smile, looking at the "priest." "You must be my transportation to the Vatican this evening. I'm Maria Martinovna Luderenko."

Bernardo didn't respond. Igor rose, and said to himself . . . *the colonel's daughter!*

Before Maria could say any more, Igor said in Russian, "I'm Igor Yavolinski, the bartender who saved you from that moron in a Moscow hotel a few years ago." Maria's jaw dropped. "I'm working as an undercover agent for the Italian Secret Service. This prick has come to murder you. I have come to save you. He thinks I'm one of the Mafia bosses' men. Play along with me on this. Your life depends on it."

"What are you doing, Yavolinski?" Bernardo said, as he rose and stood beside Igor. "Didn't you just hear her speak English?" trying to sound like a sensitive priest. "How do you expect her to know what you are saying? You should treat a woman with more respect."

"Father Bernardo. She understands everything I said. She speaks Russian. I told her, speaking from one Russian to another, how pleased I am to meet a fellow countryman and that it is an honor to meet such a beautiful woman who is so famous and even friends with the pope."

"But how did you know . . ."

Igor interrupted Bernardo and—looking at Maria—said in English, "I'm sorry you must witness such boorish behavior from a fine priest like Father Bernardo. He's had a few too many beers tonight. Well . . .," Igor said, smiling at both of them, "shall we go?"

"I have to take a piss," said Bernardo.

"What? What did you say?" asked Igor, angrily. "First of all, you are in the presence of a lady. You reminded me of that fact, but it wasn't because I was being a fool. Secondly, look at your watch. What time is it?"

"It's 9:30 p.m."

"Nine thirty p.m. That means that if you go to the men's room, this lady will be late for her appointment with the pope. You will have to wait. Let's go."

"But . . ."

"I said, let's go! We don't have time to argue about it."

At the back entrance to the hotel, Maria took the passenger seat; Bernardo sat behind her. Igor headed toward the Vatican, but instead of driving to the Porta Sant' Anna gate, he swung around to Via Gregorio VII, hung a left on Via Aurelia out to the beltway where he headed south past the Leonardo Da Vinci Airport and east toward Autostrada A1 leading to Naples.

Maria, feigning a worried look, turned and said to Bernardo, "I thought the Sister who called telling me about dinner with the pope meant I would be going to the Vatican. We passed the Vatican way back there. Why? What's going on?"

"Miss Luderenko," Igor interrupted in English, "the pope has two 'Vaticans': one in Rome and one just down the road at Gandolfo. There's nothing to worry about. We'll be off the freeway and there in a few minutes." Switching to Russian, he said, "Did I hear you correctly: that your name is Maria Martinovna Luderenko?"

"Da," Maria replied.

"That means that your father's name is Martin Luderenko. Was he an officer in the Army? A tank Commander stationed in Dresden?"

"Da."

"Then . . ." Igor, paused. You were that little girl who told that general what you thought of him outside the base that night we were sent back to Russia?"

"Da," Maria replied, as they continued in Russian. "But how would you know that?"

"Maria, I was standing in the ranks that night and enjoyed every minute of your brazen behavior. I vowed that someday I would tell you what I thought of your bravery. It was not unlike what we had experienced in Afghanistan: A little less dangerous, of course, but maybe not, if it hadn't been for Major Sidorov and a couple of his captains. I was one of the captains who rescued you from that idiot."

Maria stared at him.

"I need to PISS!"

Switching to English, Igor said, "we can't stop on the Autostrada; I'll get a ticket. I'll take the next exit onto a side road and then I'll stop. You'll have to wait."

"Well, **hurry up!**"

Igor took the Laurentina exit, drove to an isolated stretch in the road and stopped on a gravel shoulder. "Hurry up, Bernardo, we're already running late."

Bernardo jumped out of the car. Igor, using the reverse lights, watched Bernardo in the rearview mirror. When he was sure Bernardo had unzipped the cassock and had begun to relieve himself, he shifted to drive, and stomped on the accelerator.

The car lurched forward. The rear door slammed shut. Creating a cloud of dust in his wake, Igor twirled the stirring wheel counter-clockwise and headed back toward the Autostrada, passing Bernardo who was peeing all over himself trying to retrieve his pistol, buried somewhere in the tangled cassock.

Approaching the Laurentina entrance to the Autostrada, Igor slowed and eased into the east-bound Autostrada traffic. He pulled his cell from his jacket and pressed a speed-dial button.

"Tyrone"

"Tyrone, this is Igor. I have Maria Luderenko in the car and just left a rat in the dust. We need a nest; the vultures will be upon us soon. Is Perfecto there?"

"Yes, he just brought in the ex-pope. What can I do for you?"

"We're being tracked by a GPS system. Tell Perfecto to come to the entrance of the Ciampino Airport to pick us up. We'll be sitting in a black Mercedes with the hazard lights flashing."

Igor and Maria squeezed into the Panda, Maria in back and Igor in the passenger seat. The Panda roared south on Via Appia toward Castel Gandolfo. They met a speeding, shiny, black BMW, which, immediately after passing, skidded to a stop, did a Uie, and burned rubber to catch up to the Panda speeding south.

"What the hell are you doing?" said the man in the passenger seat of the BMW to the driver.

"That's the priest who has been evading me too many times and this time he won't get away. I'll get the bastard if it's the last thing I do!" Perfecto saw it all in his rearview mirror.

The BMW had nearly overtaken the Panda, when Perfecto placed his left thumb on the dash imprint. He flipped the cap on button number seven and pressed the slippery-slime button just before making a well-practiced, heavy-breaking maneuver onto the side road leading to Tyrone's shop. The BMW skidded into the ditch. Perfecto kept one eye on the rear view mirror as he accelerated, checking to see if the BMW recovered. The answer came quickly.

The BMW's headlights were closing in on the Panda—again, too close for comfort with pistols blazing and bullets bouncing off the Panda as it slowed before Perfecto made another quick turn, while pressing button number seven twice, sending the BMW careening past the entrance to Tyrone's Butler Building showroom.

The BMW crashed into a truck parked alongside the road, crushing the right-front wheel.

Perfecto raced around to the rear of the Butler Building, entered the "hanger" and stopped beside the airplane. Tyrone had the plane's engine idling and Madsen sitting in the co-pilot's seat when Igor, Perfecto and Maria scrambled aboard and fastened their seat belts. The plane began its exit from the showroom, and accelerated toward liftoff as the massive BB door closed.

The thugs scrambled out of the car and ran toward the Butler Building. They stood and watched as the plane rose gracefully into the sparkling, night sky.

Thinking there might be something worth stealing inside the building— like say . . . Perfecto's illusive car—they walked around to the side-entrance door and jerked violently on the handle. It didn't budge. One of them pointed his pistol and fired his last bullet at the door lock.

Their slide down a ten-foot trapdoor into the faces of two, angry, Pit Bull Terriers—whose sleep had been rudely disturbed—did not resemble a casual walk in the park on a warm Sunday afternoon. If the abrupt loss of solid footing was a shock to the criminals, to the dogs, it was a Declaration of War.

As they scrambled to free themselves from the dogs, the trapdoor returned to its original position, giving the two thugs enough room to out-distance the length of the chains that held the dogs at bay. The slower thug lost the seat of his pants to the jaws of one of the Terriers; she spit the cloth to the floor as she bared her teeth with another menacing move.

Captain Ferguson watched as a small private plane made a pass over the USS Lincoln and listened as his Officer of the Deck (OOD) communicated with Tyrone, giving him instructions for landing. It was 9:58 p.m., Monday, 10 November.

Tyrone eased the small plane onto the massive deck, flipped a switch above his head and prayed the parachute would open. Captain Ferguson, watching the landing, muttered a prayer, joining Igor, Madsen, Maria and Perfecto in their silent solicitations. The Almighty must have been listening—sympathetically—because the parachute opened and performed magnificently, bringing the plane to an easy stop next to the conning tower.

Chapter 86

Monday, 10 November: 10 p.m.—Vatican Railroad Station
The night janitor, a loyal Opus Dei member, entered the railroad station
to begin his nightly routine. Today his task was anything but routine; he had to
clean up the messes made by the preservation and packaging teams that were
preparing the Swiss Guard rifles and ammunition for shipment.

Having never spent time in the military and fascinated by the camouflage
preparations the troops had made, he was, nevertheless, frustrated by their
removal of the packaging that had already been done on the rifles, creating a
bigger mess which meant more work for him.

But there was a silver lining: only half of the rifles and ammunition had
already been prepared for shipment and sealed in the wooden, shipping boxes.
His frustration did not turn him into a traitor. He was a devout believer, and
anything the Opus Dei leaders were doing, must be okay. So, he sighed and
went to work.

Masterson's plan to infiltrate the Vatican with his 100 para-military force
was succeeding without a hitch. Both platoons had changed into cammies and
blackened their faces. Each had received a rifle.

Masterson appeared before them in the lobby of the train station to repeat
the salient points of the five paragraph order he had issued at the middle
school. "Remember," he said, "we do nothing until Colonel Isenberg makes his
rounds. But we need to be prepared for anything, because our informants tell
us the Guard is on very high alert; they have tripled the number of guards at
the gates and at strategic points throughout the fortress.

"The most likely reason for that is that the pope's caravan was attacked
north of Gandolfo, the pope's summer palace, late this afternoon, and was
rescued by Italian Special Forces teams. Two of our comrades were killed and
one wounded. We will stay with our five paragraph order.

"After we capture the Guard commandant, we'll demand that all Swiss
Guards return to their barracks. After the guards are in the barracks we will
move to our assigned posts throughout the Vatican fortress to await the arrival
of the pope.

"I have assigned the First Platoon to remove any occupants of buildings in
the immediate vicinity of the barracks should it become necessary to bomb the

barracks. If they don't produce the pope, we'll blow up the Swiss barracks. We are assuming the threat of killing the entire Swiss Guard contingent will bring the desired results."

Sergeant Major Buster Mc Kennan and the Executive Officer, Lt. Col. Roger Paducca looked at each other—stunned. They did not like what they were hearing about the follow-up plan. They assumed all along that the "higher ups" had sufficient intelligence information to assure that the pope would be in his Vatican office that night, and that he would submit to the demands presented to him, including his resignation. Now, should that not happen, there was a real possibility that 130 fellow Catholics would die.

Chapter 87

Monday, 10 November: 10:50 p.m.—Vatican
Colonel Fritz Isenberg, Commandant of the Swiss Guards, sat at his kitchen table . . . waiting for something to happen. His intelligence sources said the Vatican would be attacked today. The day would end in less than two hours. If an attack was coming as expected, it wouldn't be long before he would know the who, what, when, where and how of it all.

He had done everything he could do . . . except one thing: He could make his routine round of inspections of his guards on duty within the fortress. He would do it now.

With that in mind, he shut and locked the door to his apartment. He decided to reverse his path and start where he usually left off: walking past the Basilica after passing the Railroad Station.

Passing the left side and the rear of the Basilica, something bothered him. Something didn't add up.

Maybe it was the fact that, in all of his years visiting his troops before retiring for the night, he was seeing the same things, but from a different angle. He quickly dismissed the idea as absurd; yet, there was something wrong— something bothered him that couldn't be explained with his reasoning power.

He came to the Mosaic School and a new underground parking garage. *Could an attack force be hiding out in an underground parking garage? But how would they get in?* Knowing that thought would bug him if he didn't check it out, he walked in . . . looked around: nothing.

As he left the garage, he realized what was bothering him: a strange odor that he hadn't smelled since his college days in Switzerland: **pot.** His inner, high-alert meter went over the top just before he felt a sharp poke in his right, upper rib cage, followed by a powerful left hand covering his mouth . . . and a hiss: "Do as instructed or you are dead! Hand over your pistol."

As Colonel Isenberg was retrieving his pistol, the intruder threw his plastic pistol into a near-by bush and reached for his cell phone.

"Thank you, sir," he whispered, "now, I will remove my hand from your mouth if you will assure me that you will not make a noise as I walk with you to the train station. Nod once if you agree to comply with my request." Colonel Eisenberg nodded compliance.

Walking to the train station, former Green Beret Sergeant Casper "Barmy" Blackwood sent a text message to Colonel Masterson to meet him at the front door of the train station in two minutes.

"Barmy" earned his nickname in Vietnam because of his irregular behavior. The moniker was a term of endearment and profound admiration for a man who could break conventional rules with impunity, appeared at times to be a bit wacky, while making certain to harm no one, unless "necessary." Due to his exceptional bravery and unconventional functioning, combined with an uncanny immunity to flying bullets and shrapnel, the army awarded him the Medal of Honor.

In the 1970's and 1980's, having your "colors" and your "personality type" *done,* gained popularity in a small segment of American culture. *Spring, summer, fall and winter,* for color-typing, was used to make matching clothing ensembles easier. "Colors typing" had its corollary for personality typing based on the physical appearance of an individual: *Classic, Romantic, Dramatic and Gentle.* One wag suggested *Gentle* should be changed to *Wimp.*

"Barmy" 'typed-out' with *fall "colors"* and a *Dramatic* personality appearance. He was built with fireplug legs, a barrel torso, and a square head, with long curly, graying-blond hair that formed a backdrop for his bushy beard. His steel-blue eyes suggested a mind as sharp as a medieval, warrior's sword; yet, his eyes also exuded a compassionate heart.

His personal preferences were not compatible with conventional living; he had experimented living in several milieus, but the result was always the same: He needed an adventurous environment where his talents meshed with society's. He even did a stint with the CIA; yet, he ran into a buzz-saw even there during its period of angst that coincided with the 1970's era of malaise.

Thus, when he heard about the possibility of another adventure that did not require the same agility, ability and endurance his earlier exploits exacted from him, he volunteered. He had never heard of Opus Dei.

When Barmy and Colonel Isenberg reached the railroad station front door, Masterson opened the door and stepped onto the front stoop. Before he could speak, Sergeant Blackwood was introducing his guest, as though they were at a cocktail party at the officer's club: "Colonel Masterson, this is Colonel Isenberg, the Commandant of the Swiss Guards. Colonel Isenberg, Colonel Masterson."

Neither colonel raised a hand for a cordial handshake. "C'mon, gentlemen," Blackwood said, "you are both members of the officer class: act that way.

When General Lee, after surrendering to General Grant at Appomattox asked if they and their opposing officers (all graduates of West Point) could meet in a near-by house for a cordial—*for-the-sake-of-the-Long-Gray-Line*—drink, to celebrate the end of the war, Lee's wish was '*Granted*.' Now, don't you think you two could behave like that in this regrettable situation?"

Both colonels stared at Blackwood . . . silently. "Okay . . . well, may I suggest, gentlemen, that we retire to the second floor of this mansion and see if we can negotiate our way out of this unfortunate state of affairs, so that we won't spill anyone's blood on such a beautiful evening?" asked Barmy, sounding like a concierge at a five-star hotel in Paris. "Colonel Masterson, you take the lead. I will fall in behind Colonel Isenberg."

It was a suggestion the colonels could not dismiss because it was the only step that made any sense to either of them. Barmy followed the two colonels through a path separating the two para-military platoons sprawled on the floor of the station lobby, and proceeded up the stairs.

Colonel Masterson ordered Sergeant Blackwood to stay with the colonel at all times. "Don't let him out of your site. Now, frisk the colonel." Blackwood found a Motorola Tetra, two-way radio, the standard communication devices used to communicate with the Swiss Guard Command Center in the basement of the barracks and with all personnel on duty. He handed it to Colonel Masterson.

"Colonel Isenberg," Colonel Masterson said, "order your troops to withdraw to the barracks, immediately." He handed the radio to Isenberg.

Colonel Isenberg complied. "Vaticano Two this is Vaticano One. Code X-2. Over."

"Vaticano One, this is Vaticano Two. Ten-four. Out."

"That's it?" asked Colonel Masterson.

"That's what you ordered me to do. My soldiers will comply immediately. If you wonder about that, take a look out the window."

Colonel Masterson stared at his prisoner. "How do I know that code doesn't contain some other instructions in addition to the one I ordered you to convey, Colonel Isenberg?"

"You don't."

Colonel Masterson ordered Colonel Isenberg to sit across from him at a kitchen-sized, wooden table. "Sergeant Blackwood, since you brought our prisoner to me, I repeat . . . you are assigned to stay with him at all times—even visiting the restroom—unless I relieve you of your duties. We can talk about what you were doing out there without my permission later."

Turning to Colonel Isenberg, Masterson said, "Our purpose is to ask the pope to willingly submit his resignation to us in writing." Looking at his watch, Masterson said, "It's now 2306 hours; we need to have him in our presence, here at the Railroad Station—slipping into his 'civilian time mode'—by 11:40 p.m. That's 34 minutes from now. If he does not come and sign his resignation papers, we will bomb your barracks."

"Needless to say, the latter is not a preferable option for resolving this crisis, but the powers who hired me have given me authorization to carry out my orders. Where is the pope?"

"You are demanding the impossible. I don't know for certain where he is. But I assume he is in his bed asleep. He hasn't had time to travel to the moon so I'm confident he is not there."

"The janitor who cleans this place," said Masterson, ignoring Isenberg's sarcasm, "also cleans his office. I'll send one of my men with him to find out immediately. Sergeant Blackwood, ask Sgt. Major Mc Kennan to come up here."

Blackwood went to the stairwell and shouted, **"Sergeant Major Mc Kennan . . . the boss wants to see you on-the-double."**

"Sergeant Major Mc Kennan, get the janitor down there—his name is 'Fingers'—and have him take you to the pope's apartment to see if he is in. Notify me immediately, one way or the other, and if he is there, bring him here immediately.

"In the meantime, Colonel Isenberg, I suggest you get on that radio and start looking. I don't make threats that I don't keep. I thought it was your job to protect him. How can you protect him if you don't know where he is?"

"Excellent question. Since you don't know the man well enough to know he wouldn't sign such a document under pressure, I'm not surprised you don't know that he is capable of going places without my protection, thereby leaving me without any knowledge of where he is.

"Furthermore, your sponsors—I assume they include clerics, including a cardinal or two—should know that a pope's signature signed under duress isn't worth the paper it's written on: that's according to the Church's Code of Canon Law. I'm certain the pope knows that. So where does that put you in this situation? You've been duped into thinking something that isn't even possible, Colonel Masterson."

Ignoring Colonel Isenberg's answer, Colonel Masterson said, "I repeat; locate the pope and get him over here before the deadline I have set, or your men will die in their barracks."

"I'll do as you request. I'll contact my Executive Officer. 'Vaticano Two. Code X-3, over.'"

"Ten-four. Out." replied Lt. Colonel Acklin.

"There you go again. Talking in codes. What does 'Code X-3' mean?" asked Masterson.

"Locate the pope and have him contact me."

"How do I know that's what your code means?"

"You don't. You'll have to trust me."

Monday 10 November: 11:10 p.m.—Railroad Station

Texting: "*For Col Masterson. Sgt. Major, here. Unable to locate pope. Returning to Headquarters.*"

Monday 10 November: 11:10 p.m.—Construction Yard, Ciampino Airport

At a construction yard adjacent to the Ciampino Airport runway, Carlo climbed into his aging, three-quarter-ton, flatbed truck and headed out the gate toward the San Giovanni dei Florentini Church in Rome, less than a quarter mile from the Vatican; his cargo: a diamond-shaped, steel container about the size of an average, American refrigerator.

The container carried dynamite. It was mounted on a steel frame, lying on its side, with a collapsible, V-shaped arm, attached to four hooks on the body of the container. A delayed detonator would activate the dynamite after falling through the roof of the barracks. That design would keep ninety percent of the blast within the barracks' thick, stone walls; the softer, wood roof would send the blast into the air. The bomb was designed to reduce damage to nearby buildings and their treasures.

Carlo reached for his cell; he hadn't forgotten it.

Chapter 88

Monday, 10 November: 11:10 p.m.—USS Abraham Lincoln
Officer of the Deck: "ATTENTION ALL HANDS! COMMENCE OPERA-
TION *SAFEGUARD!*

"Safeguard, this is Safeguard Six. Commence Operation.

Five troop-carrying and two attack helicopters stood in lift-off formation
on the massive carrier flight deck.

Fourteen helicopter pilots and co-pilots climbed into their helicopters
and began their routine inspections and cross-checking all systems.

Below the flight deck, one hundred members of the NATO Special
Operations Forces Teams commenced a final check of their arms, ammunition and communication equipment; checks completed, they fell into their
five SOF team formations for their Five-Paragraph orders. The NATO SOF
commander stood before them. German-Army Lt. Col. Stephan Becker
spoke:

"SITUATION: Less than an hour ago, a renegade, para-military force of 100
combat veterans—invaded and immobilized the Swiss Guard army unit protecting the pope and the Vatican City State.

"The Swiss Guards are being held prisoner in their barracks. The invaders
are armed with Swiss SIG SC 550 assault rifles.
"MISSION: Capture and disarm the intruders. Protect residents of Vatican
until relieved.
"EXECUTION: We will be transported to the objective on four United
States Marine Corps CH-46 Sea Knight troop transport helicopters.

"Transport helicopters and assault troops will be protected by two U. S.
Marine Corps AH-1Z Super Cobra assault helicopters.

"We parachute into the Vatican Fortress, eliminate resistance, secure
respective pre-assigned team objectives, including fortress-wall gates.

"Do not allow anyone to enter or leave the fortress. Take prisoners.

"Call signs for this operation are as previously assigned and used in our
training exercises. My call-sign is *Safeguard Six:* for the four transport heli-

copters: *Safeguard-five, four, three, two,* and *one,* respectively: for two assault helicopters: *Safeguard nine and ten.*

"ATTACK: Commence firing when fired upon. Occupy and secure pre-assigned objectives within the fortress walls.

"CONSOLIDATION: Hold fortress until relieved by the Italian San Marco Marine company. Helicopters coordinate with ground elements for landing at the Vatican helicopter pad; upon relief, return to the USS Lincoln.

"Are there any questions?" None. "Then, carry out your mission. We will proceed to our objective upon departure authorization from USS Lincoln Officer of the Deck. Dismissed!"

The teams walked calmly to the elevator that would lift them to the flight deck. In team formations, they walked to pre-assigned helicopters. One-by-one they climbed into their pre-designated seats; they sat silently, awaiting the sound of the engines signaling an imminent lift to their objective: the Vatican.

Monday, 10 November: 11:15 p.m.—Mancini Mansion

"Mr. Mancini," his ops man said, "I have a message from Col. Masterson. It reads as follows:

> *Have Commandant in custody. His troops have withdrawn to the bar-racks—break—evacuating apartments and occupied offices near barracks to the Government Palace—break—have ordered Com-mandant to produce pope by 11:40 p.m. —Break—Our troops have captured the Vatican City State without resistance.*

The ops man continued, "Carlo is on his way to the Church. I estimate his arrival time to be 11:20."

"Has our helicopter left the yard yet?" asked Mancini.

"He's on his way now. I estimate his arrival at the Villa Stritch parking lot to be 11:30. I'm transferring their control over to Colonel Masterson."

"Good. Thank you. Now," Mancini continued, "has Masterson reported anything more about the pope?"

"As I said, he's ordered Colonel Isenberg to have the pope at the railroad station by 11:40 or he'll bomb the barracks. He says the commandant doesn't know where the pope is; he's ordered him to find him, or else."

"Or else what?" asked Monsignor Lopez.

"Or else he'll bomb the barracks."

"You remind Colonel Masterson that that decision is still open and that I reserved the right to decide that issue if it arises. Pass that along to Colonel Masterson."

"Will do," replied the ops man."

Monday, 10 November: 11:20 p.m.—Railroad Station

"Sergeant Blackwood, have our executive officer come up here," ordered Colonel Masterson.

Barmy went to the stairwell and shouted, **"Lt. Colonel Paducca, the boss wants to see you."**

"Reporting as ordered, sir," said Paducca.

"You and the Sergeant Major come up here when he gets back. I want you in on my decision on whether to bomb the barracks. We are running out of time, so come up immediately. You are dismissed."

The Sergeant Major was coming up the steps when Paducca reached the stairwell. They stood-by waiting for Colonel Masterson to speak.

"If you are going to bomb the barracks," said Colonel Isenberg, "I request permission to be released to return to the barracks to be with my troops when they die."

Colonel Masterson stared at his prisoner in disbelief.

"Permission denied. That will be your punishment for failing to produce the pope as requested. I suspect the pope is holed up in one of the millions of hiding places of this fortress, and you know exactly where he is. You have less than twenty minutes to produce him, or I'll blow the barracks."

"I need to use the restroom," replied Col. Isenberg.

"What?" Colonel Masterson asked.

"I **said** . . . I need to use the restroom. Where is it?"

"It's downstairs. We don't have time for that now."

"Colonel, I have to **piss!** Do you want me to do it on the floor, or can I go to the restroom?"

"Go to the restroom, but hurry! I want you back here in three minutes. Sgt. Blackwood, go with the colonel. I'll have you shot if you return without him. Do you understand?"

"Loud and clear, sir! Better than you can imagine." Motioning to Col. Isenberg with his head, he said, "Come with me colonel."

Waiting for their return, Colonel Masterson pulled his cell from his right front pocked under the table and sent a text message to the helicopter at Villa Stritch and Carlos the truck driver with the bomb on his truck. Using his thumb he entered a coded command: *Bomb the barracks!*

The helicopter, standing in the Villa Stritch parking lot, lifted off and headed for the Principi Bridge.

Monday November: 11:25 p.m.—Rome

Sitting on a side-street around the corner from the Florentini church, less than a quarter mile from the Vatican, Carlo pocketed his cell. He started the engine and pulled onto the Principi Bridge and stopped. He mounted the flat bed and lifted the V-shaped arm that turned into an A-shaped appendage rising from the diamond-shaped, steel container. He locked it in place and pulled the bolts from the struts that held the container in place during transport.

Carlo reached into the cab and pulled the hood latch, went to the front and lifted the hood. He bent over the engine and fondled some wires.

He heard a car door slam shut. As he pulled the oil dip-stick and wiped it on his trousers, he noticed red and blue, police-car lights flashing. A Carabinieri officer walked up to him and ordered him to move the truck off the bridge.

Monday, 10 November: 11:26 p.m.—USS Lincoln
NATO Special Operations Forces depart deck of USS Lincoln, maneuver into flight formation and fly east toward the Vatican.

Monday, 10 November: 11:27 p.m.—Railroad Station
"You called us, Colonel Masterson?" asked Lt. Colonel Paducca., as Colonel Isenberg and Sgt. Blackwood returned from the restroom.

"Yes. You know the reasons we are here. Colonel Isenberg has not produced the pope and his time is running out. As I've told everyone, if he or someone else doesn't produce the pope, we'll blow the barracks."

"I beg your pardon, sir, but you didn't tell us until today. We've been training together for over a year and you never said a word about blowing up a barracks and killing over a hundred young men who have been serving the Church honorably. Who the hell do you think you are?

"The only reason the Sergeant Major and I have gone along with this plan, after learning about your diabolical scheme, is that we thought we might pull off this stunt and save the Church from, what we all agree, is a disastrous course. Now it looks like the pope won't show up and you want to blow the barracks. Is that it? I thought Monsignor Lopez was calling the shots."

"You're way out of line, Colonel. I'm not accustomed to insubordination and I'm not about to start accommodating your bullshit now."

"There's one thing you're forgetting Colonel," replied Paducca. "We are not a legally constituted organization and you have no statutory authority over me or the rest of the troops. We are gathered together through common consent and mutual interests, sort of like a service club that helps other people improve their lives. We've been playing your military career redux to achieve the ends we all want.

"There isn't a single man below your rank who will support blowing a barracks housing over a hundred young, Catholic men. If you attempt to give the order to bomb the barracks, I'll stop you."

"You wouldn't dare. If you try, there will be a target on your back for the rest of your life. I know the people who hired me and they would not rest until they took revenge for your thwarting their attempts to save our Church from impending disaster."

Chapter 89

Monday, 10 November: 11:30 p.m.—Principi Bridge

"I'm ordering you to get this truck off the bridge. What's in that container?" the policeman asked.

"It's an emergency-backup, sewer tank for the Vatican. I was on my way over there when the truck stalled," Carlo said, as he replaced the dip stick. I'll try to start it again, but the battery is dying, so I don't have many more tries left." He mounted the truck. The starter squawked. Nothing.

"If you don't get this truck off this bridge in one minute, I'm calling a tow-truck to take it off."

"I'll do my best," said Carlo.

Monday 10 November: 11: 32 p.m.—Railroad Station

Sergeant Casper "Barmy" Blackwood, pulling Isenberg's pistol out of his belt and pointing it at Colonel Masterson, said, "I'll save our XO from your threats."

"Ha! Have you forgotten we were issued toy pistols, Sergeant?" Sergeant Blackwood pointed Isenberg's pistol at the ceiling. **"BAM!!!"** With the next shot you will buy the farm!!

"Sergeant Major, pick up that duct tape and tie this bastard up and take his cell phone. Massacring Swiss Guards is not what I volunteered to do. You are a disgrace to the brave men and women who have ever earned the title *United States Marine.* "Here," Blackwood said to Lt. Col. Paducca, handing him Isenberg's pistol, "I won't need this anymore.

"Colonel Isenberg and I are going over to the barracks to see if we can evacuate his troops before it's too late. Put the Colonel over by the window. Open it. I want him to hear the crickets when they come out. Colonel Paducca, order our troops away from the barracks and tell them we're coming through and not to bother us. Let's go, Colonel Isenberg."

Monday 10 November: 11:36 p.m.—NATO SOF Helicopters
"Safeguard Six to Safeguard. We are closing on our objective. ETA 2340 hours. Out."

Monday 10 November: 11:38 p.m.—Principe Bridge
While the starter was grinding, the policeman heard a helicopter approaching from the southwest. It slowed as it came toward the bridge, lowered and hovered over the truck with a hook dangling from its belly. The policeman grabbed his radio to call for assistance. Carlo jumped out of the truck, guided the helicopter to the hook and gave the pilot a "thumbs up."

Monday 10 November: 11:39 p.m.—Swiss Guard Barracks
Sergeant Blackwood and Colonel Isenberg entered the Swiss Barracks.

Monday 10 November: 11:39:45 p.m.—NATO SOF Helicopters
Fifteen seconds away from their objective, the helicopter pilots observed a massive explosion—like a volcano—erupting on the eastern side of the Vatican. They circled the fortress to reassess the situation. The Swiss Barracks lay in rubble. Some buildings around it were damaged and on fire. "*Safeguard*, this is *Safeguard Six, Assault!*"

Monday 10 November: 11:40—Railroad Station

Colonel Masterson, bound to his chair watching the debris fall—and the paratroopers descending into the fortress—yelled into his cell through the open window, **"Open fire, you bastards!"**

That's when the "crickets" started. His highly trained para-military troops were aiming their rifles at the paratroopers and pulling triggers, but all they were getting was a *Click*. To Colonel Masterson, it sounded like crickets had started a nocturnal chorus to mock his expectations of seeing tracer bullets flying up to greet the descending paratroopers.

Sonofabitch! Those bastards! They removed the firing pins before they started preserving and packaging the rifles.

Seeing a hundred Special Operations Forces paratroopers descending like a swarm of locusts into a cornfield, the invaders dropped their rifles and lifted their arms—like devotees at a Billy Graham crusade welcoming God into their lives.

Monday 10 November: Leonardo Da Vinci Airport 11:41 p.m.

A contingent of the San Marco Marine Regiment, traveling in a convoy, having departed a remote area of the Leonardo Da Vinci Airport, entered the Autostrada heading north, took the exit to V. Aurelia and turned onto V. Gregorio VII that took them to the Vatican.

NATO forces welcomed them as they passed through the Petriano entrance on the south side of the Basilica. After being briefed by the NATO forces commander, the Italian regiment took control of Vatican Fortress and stationed troops in St. Peter's Basilica. Confident that they had control of the situation at the Vatican, they relieved the NATO paratroopers, who returned to the USS Lincoln. They began interrogating the para-military force being held prisoner at the railroad station.

C h a p t e r   9 0

Monday, 10 November: Mancini Mansion 11:53 p.m.

"**God damn it, what's** going on?" Mancini yelled at his ops man. Masterson was supposed to keep us informed."

"We have not communicated since I turned control of the helicopter pilot and Carlo over to him. I've been sending text messages asking for updates and gotten no responses. He could be very busy and doesn't have time to respond."

Mancini grabbed a remote and turned on the TV. A "BREAKING NEWS" broadcast—interrupting CNN programming all over the world—was in progress. . . . not clear what happened. All we know is that an explosion in the vicinity of the Swiss barracks occurred just moments ago," said Monica Travorlini, an Italian reporter from a CNN affiliate in Rome.

"That bastard," Mancini screamed, "I'll have Masterson for breakfast . . ."

Lopez, Nunez, Moretti, De Lucca, Lombardi, Giordano and Sandusky heard a faint—and rising—roar . . . over Mancini's desperate rant.

"**Fuck! Helicopters!**" shouted De Luca. "Let's get the hell out of here," doing a 'voice-over' of the ops man who was shouting, "three helicopters circling over us . . . security guards on the perimeter report paratroopers descending around and into mansion grounds . . . . Perimeter guard has message from a paratrooper. . . . . . *Come out of the house with your hands up! You have five minutes. The mansion will be destroyed with rockets by our assault helicopter at midnight. Repeat . . . Come out of the house with your hands up and surrender to paratroops on the perimeter. Anyone remaining in the house will die."*

Tuesday, 11 November: 12:15 a.m. St. George Roma Hotel

The only time Karl Rorer came close to losing control of his diabolical impulses was when the phone rang at ungodly hours. When the phone rang at 12:15 a.m. two hours after he had retreated to his bed, desperately long-ing for at least six hours of sleep, his urge to rip the phone from the wall and throw it through the window flared like a sunburst when the sun is having a really bad day.

Such impulses were nearly uncontrollable when the reasons for the disturbance were routine and could be dealt with when normal people wake up and go to work. But, being a foreign correspondent is neither routine nor normal so far as work hours are concerned.

The caller's message doused the sunburst. It is not every day that a foreign correspondent has an opportunity to cover a bombing inside the Vatican followed by an address by the pope in the middle of the night. *I'd better get moving!*

Tuesday, 11 November: 12:30 a.m.—USS Lincoln

Disembarking from the helicopters, the NATO troops walked slowly to the elevator that took them to a lower deck. The NATO SOF commander, while in transit from the Vatican, had received instructions from Captain Ferguson that Dr. Madsen, Maria, Igor, Perfecto, Tyrone, Barmy, and the NATO forces commander would need a flight back to the Vatican, leaving as soon as the NATO forces had disembarked from the helicopters.

Dr. Madsen was scheduled to give a major television and radio address to the world at 1 a.m.

Monday, 10 Nov.: Sylvan Lake 3:50 p.m. Tues. 11 Nov.: 12:50 a.m. Rome

Pat McCarty sat watching Tammy Mical's hour-long coverage of the failed attempt by Italian Mafiosi to kidnap the Pope from his caravan, when the program was interrupted with Karl Rorer reporting on a bomb leveling the Swiss barracks at the Vatican as a run-up to the pope's imminent address to the world.

The airwaves were quivering—with speculation—as wildly as out-of-control power lines over a massive earth-quake; *Why the bombing? Why is the pope addressing the world at 1 a.m., Rome time?*

Pat rose from the living room couch and went to the kitchen. She took the cookie dough, covered it with stretch-plastic food-wrap and placed it in the refrigerator. She returned to the couch. It was 3:30 p.m. The cookies could wait until tomorrow.

"This is a Special Edition of The World Now. Tammy Mical here, with the latest from Rome. Karl Rorer is reporting. Karl, what's going on? This is highly unusual, is it not?"

"Yes, Tammy, it is. It has not happened before. For months I've been reporting on Pope Immanuel's reforms and speculation about what he would do next. Yesterday, the attempted kidnapping of the pope from his caravan is the first attempt to get rid of the pope since the attempted assassination in Vatican Square last summer.

"The announcement, Tammy, that the 'pope' would be speaking, has us scratching our heads. Here is how it reads. 'Last week Pope Immanuel announced he would be making an address to the world at 8 a.m. this morning. Due to the events that occurred yesterday, have occurred tonight, and are continuing at this moment, that address has been moved to 1 a.m.'

"It's the last phrase that is puzzling—'continuing at the moment'. It's as if blowing the Swiss Guard Barracks is not enough for one night. What else could be happening? No one knows, Tammy. Maybe we'll find out now."

Chapter 91

Dr. Marcus J. Madsen—Address to the World

My dear citizens of the world:

Last fall an assassin attempted to kill me. Yesterday, my caravan was ambushed by Mafiosi in an attempt to kidnap me and force my resignation. Last night a force of one hundred para-military men—hired by Opus Dei and the Legionaries of Christ—invaded the Vatican, ordered the Swiss Guards into their barracks and then bombed the barracks—another attempt to force me to resign.

The fears of the cabal—which includes Mafiosi—trying to force me out of office are well-founded because they know what happened to the Soviet Union when President Gorbachev attempted to reform a country that could not be reformed.

The fundamental principles underlying Soviet governance—fear and terror—**guaranteed** its self-destruction. The fundamental principles underpinning the Roman Catholic Church—fear and terror—**guaranteed** its demise. Illuminating the reasons for the demise of the Soviet Union reinforces the argument that the Catholic Church suffered the same fate for identical reasons—insofar as fundamental principles are concerned.

1. Lenin, founder of the USSR, declared the Communist Party was entitled to use terror to perpetuate its power and expand its control to all countries in the world; *the founders of the Catholic Church substituted Christ's message of love and compassion with fear and terror, which constitutes the foundation of Roman Catholic doctrine.*

2. Meticulous researchers estimate that nearly one hundred million people were murdered by communist and other totalitarian regimes: China-65m; USSR-20m (some assert the number is much higher); Cambodia-2m; North Korea-2m; Africa-1.7m; Afghanistan-1.5m; Vietnam-1m; Eastern Europe-1m; and Latin America-150,000; *tens of thousands of people have been slaughtered in the name of Jesus.*

3. Dictatorships characterized the USSR and its puppet regimes; **a papal dictatorship characterizes Vatican governance.**

4. The Chairman of the Communist Party was the supreme authority in the USSR; *the pope is the supreme authority at the Vatican.*

5. An independent judicial branch of government did not exist in the USSR; *the Vatican has no independent judicial authority.*

6. Legislative bodies were rubber stamps for the decisions of the Communist Party apparatus; *the pope has supreme authority over the Vatican Curia and the code of canon law which guides the pope's decisions.*

7. Competing political parties were outlawed in the USSR; *the Vatican has a "one-party" governing body (the Curia) which disallows competition.*

8. Free elections by the people to select political leaders in the USSR, did not exist; *free elections, allowing Catholic parishioners to select clerical leaders, do not exist.*

9. Elite communist party and government officials in the USSR enjoyed special privileges, ranging from upscale domicile accommodations to restricted shopping oases; *the same holds true for all Vatican employees.*

10. Censorship of the press and various works of art in the USSR was commonplace; *censorship of various works of art, especially written criticism of the papacy and Catholic doctrine, started in the early Church, and continued until I took office.*

11. In the USSR, rampant corruption infected every level of Soviet society throughout its seventy-four year history; *rampant corruption has been a major problem in the Catholic Church from the beginning to modern times.*

12. President Gorbachev tried to restructure the Soviet political and economic systems and failed; *the Catholic Church has failed twice in its attempts to reform: (1) following Martin Luther's revolt in the sixteenth century, which led to the Reformation, and (2) the Second Vatican Council opened by Pope John XXIII in 1962, which led to limited reforms that were squashed by the pope's conservative successors.*

The parallel, inherent contradictions, embedded in Soviet and Catholic ideological and theological underpinnings, resulted in a disconnect between thought and actions in both institutions.

Still, Catholic historians and others are fond of declaring that the Roman Catholic Church is the only institution that has survived for two millennia and that its influence on all of humanity is unprecedented; I agree with both assertions. Unfortunately, as just stated, the influence was negative in the extreme.

In recent decades, hundreds of books and articles critical of the Catholic Church have been written by Catholic clerics, Catholic and non-Catholic authors. Here is an incomplete list of the most recent titles: *Sistine Secrets: Michelangelo's Forbidden Messages in the Heart of the Sistine Chapel* **(2008)** Blech/Doliner; *Confronting Power and Sex in the Catholic Church* **(2008)** Bishop Robinson; *Failing America's Faithful* **(2007)** Townsend; *Sacrilege: Sexual Abuse in the Catholic Church* **(2007)** Podles; *Sex, Priests, and Secret Codes: The Catholic Church's 2,000-Year Paper Trail of Sexual Abuse* **(2006)** Doyle, Sipes and Wall; *Vows of Silence: The Abuse of Power in the Papacy of John Paul II* **(2006)** Berry and Renner; *A People Adrift: The Crisis of the Roman Catholic Church in America* **(2003)** Steinfels.

About the same time Martin Luther was at war with Church authorities, Michelangelo Buonarotti clashed with the pope and other popes during his long life. Books have been written about this legendary figure who painted the ceiling and then the wall behind the altar in the Sistine Chapel. Only recently have we learned that he embedded secrets and deceptions in those famous frescoes which offer an alternative in the ceiling to Catholicism—Kabbalism—and denigrating the very foundation of Catholic theology in the *Last Judgment*. That was over four hundred fifty years ago.

God intervenes by sending teachers and messengers to assist humanity when humans have created potentially disastrous situations that threaten to destroy world civilizations. The latest messenger is Maria Martinovna Luderenko, on whom the camera is focusing as I speak. She is here with me.

Recently, on 31 October, she posted her Masters in Theology thesis on the Bronze Doors of the Vatican, expressing in detail what I have told you tonight. Her academic work has had a profound effect on me and my most recent decisions that involve my duty, integrity, sense of honor and dignity. It reassured me that the actions I have already taken were timely, appropriate and necessary.

The decisions were made with an overwhelming feeling of shame for the pederasty scandal that has rocked the Church in recent years and appears to become more appalling with each flood of fresh allegations of assaults on children and subsequent cover-ups by our Church authorities.

I have before me a copy of a document declaring the Roman Catholic Church extinct. As pope, I had the authority to take whatever action I considered to be in the best interests of our parishioners and humanity in general.

I came to the conclusion that the Roman Catholic Church will never be reformed, just as it was impossible for the Soviet Union to be reformed . . . and for the same reasons; both were founded on principles that are contrary to the Laws of Nature created when the universe exploded into existence, establishing time, space and matter.

Before I declared the Roman Catholic Church extinct, I took legal steps to ensure a smooth transition of the Church from its status as a sovereign state to a failed, state/religion status. A Concordat, abrogating the Lateran Treaty of 1929—in which the Sovereign State of Italy granted the Roman Catholic Church sovereign-state status—was signed yesterday afternoon by me, the president and the prime minister of the Sovereign State Italy. I will quote a paragraph from that **"Quirinale Palace Concordat"**:

> In preparation for the execution of the present Concordat, the two high parties have agreed—after the signing thereof (effective 12:01, 11 November, 2008, Rome time)—that all real estate and chattels, including the Vatican Bank and its assets, currently owned by the Vatican City State and the Holy See, shall become the sole property of the Sovereign State of Italy. On and at the effective date and time of said Concordat, the Sovereign State of Italy shall occupy the Vatican fortress, the basilica and all other property owned by the Vatican City State for the purpose of protecting assets and personnel located and residing therein.

Now that the Catholic Church no longer exists, everyone is free to join any church one chooses; many will want to continue as "Catholics." That is their choice. All Catholics are free to do whatever serves them.

All clerics and religious—who reside the Vatican and Castel Gandolfo—will be ordered to leave. The Vatican City State, St. Peter's Basilica and Castel Gandolfo (south of Rome) will be transformed into museums.

Businesses, maintenance facilities, the post office, tourist related functions, and all other existing entities necessary to maintain the Vatican complex come under the umbrella of the Italian State and are closed until further notice. The Vatican Bank will reopen in one month, owned by the State of Italy.

All existing pensions and related benefits will continue uninterrupted, administered by or under the direction of the Italian State. All properties, owned by dioceses world-wide, will remain under the respective fiduciary responsibility of each diocese.

All residents of the Vatican will be ordered to leave within one month from today. All employees will be given the opportunity to remain in any non-church related personnel positions. All church-related positions at the Vatican no longer exist.

I have asked the Italian government to take responsibility for an orderly transition of Vatican facilities from Vatican State to Italian State control. I have signed all necessary legal documents to accomplish those ends. I have spoken to you directly, honestly and from my heart. What I am doing is not vindictive, nor is it done out of fear; it is done out of love for God, for you, and for all humanity.

May God bless you. Goodnight.

Chapter 92

"Well, there you have it, Tammy. What can I say at a moment like this, except to say—in the vernacular—it ain't over yet. While Dr. Madsen was speaking, I received word that President Bianchi will address the Italian people at 7 a.m. Rome time.

"It is my understanding that, while mentioning the momentous events that have occurred at the Vatican, he will be addressing equally momentous events that are occurring at this moment throughout Italy.

"Because of the sensitivity of those events, we have not been told what's happening, but my intuition tells me President Bianchi will discuss historic occurrences as well."

Tuesday 11 November: 7 a.m.–Quirinale Presidential Palace, Rome
My fellow Italians:
When Prime Minister De Stefano and I came to power three years ago, we made a pledge to you that we would take down organized crime. For the past three years, that has been our main focus. At the time, we shared the frustrations of our brave citizens who had worked hard fighting organized crime, but with unsatisfactory results. A major factor inhibiting our progress was the Vatican Bank because that's where money-laundering trails ended; we had no recourse because the bank refused to cooperate with us.

Thus, I was heartened during our first meeting when the new pope, His Holiness Pope Immanuel, proposed we cooperate in dealing with our respective as well as mutual problems. I immediately welcomed that initiative. Over the past three years, we made joint strategic and tactical plans to maximize our power to overcome the grave threat that organized crime has posed for our country and the Church.

My purpose in speaking with you this morning is to explain what we have been doing during the last twelve hours and ask for your understanding and cooperation from this point forward. We cannot succeed without your assistance.

You know that we have been conducting terrorist response training exercises throughout the country for the past three years. The training and experience gained during those exercises were transferable to our projected operations to stop organized crime—operations that commenced at midnight last night and are continuing as I speak.

Before the operation is over, we will have arrested over a thousand organized crime suspects, including four regional bosses, a retired cardinal, a priest employed at the Vatican, and the two top executives of the Opus Dei and the Legionaries of Christ/Regnum Christi. This cabal will be charged with numerous crimes in connection with the events of the last several years and tonight.

The suspects are being held in the four new regional prison facilities that were completed six months ago; since that time we have recruited and trained hundreds of prison guards.

I asked for, and received from the Prime Minister De Stefano, authorization to declare Martial Law effective midnight last night in order to use all the military and police powers we possess in this mop-up operation against the criminals that suck blood from our civil society and gangster-infected institutions. However, our efforts to eliminate this scourge—now and for all time—are just beginning.

Our military and police units will occupy the major activity hubs of the crime families' businesses, such as the Naples port facilities and the garment manufacturing industry zone. One purpose of this occupation is to maintain law and order while we gather more evidence to convict the suspects. The chief purpose is to recruit and protect witnesses to testify against those suspected of criminal activity. We are in this for the long haul and seek your cooperation and assistance.

Finally, with regard to our cooperation with Pope Immanuel, you already know that he declared the Vatican City State and Holy See extinct, transferring their real estate holdings and chattels to the Sovereign State of Italy.

You may not know how it was possible for the Swiss Guards to enter the barracks just before it was bombed and escape death. Three years ago, I told the pope we were building a new Carabinieri headquarters about two blocks from the barracks and asked if he could think of any way we might enter into a joint project to enhance our mutual interests during the construction of the our new police headquarters.

Pope Immanuel suggested building a tunnel from the barracks to our police headquarters. We agreed and finished the tunnel earlier this year. Last night it saved the lives of our beloved Swiss Guards. In just a few minutes, they will lead a triumphant parade from Castel Sant' Angelo to Vatican Square. Other participants, besides senior Italian officials, are the former pope, Maria Luderenko—the modern "Martin Luther"—and others. You are invited to watch this spectacular event from the sidelines or on television; it will be broadcast worldwide.

May God bless you and our Country.

"Well Tammy, these two great leaders have pulled off the most secretive, stunning, political, religious, and military triumph in my memory. I'll let you take it from here. I need to move to the parade route. We'll have live coverage for you, even if I'm not available for comments."

Pat woke Sammy and told him to come and watch a parade: "Maria is in it."

Marcus, Maria, Igor, Perfecto, Barmy and Tyrone were invited to join the parade—led by the Swiss Guards Band—from Castel Sant' Angelo to Vatican Square. Behind the band, Colonel Isenberg—with Medal of Honor Winner, Sergeant Casper "Barmy" Blackwood at his side—led his Swiss Guards, dressed in their formal uniforms.

Officials representing the Italian government followed: leading units representing the Italian Army, Air Force, Navy and Marines, the NATO paratroopers and helicopter pilots, and a contingent of the USS Lincoln led by Captain Ferguson.

Thousands of Italians and tourists who had come into the streets for the two historic announcements, which were carried on the giant video screens in Vatican Square, jammed the Square and the streets surrounding it.

Carabinieri police in their dress uniforms, lined a corridor on Via della Conciliazione (the Avenue of Reconciliation) running from the Castel Sant' Angelo to the Square—providing security for the parade participants.

Honored dignitaries mounted the papal, canopy-covered platform in front of St. Peter's basilica and waved to the roars of appreciation from the crowds.

Following the parade, a NATO helicopter transported Tyrone and Perfecto back to the USS Lincoln. Then, they flew off the deck and headed southeast to the showroom to rescue their prisoners. Carabinieri officers took the gangsters to a nearby prison. After thanking and feeding the dogs, Tyrone and Perfecto drove back to Rome for dinner at the Presidential Palace.

Chapter 93

After the parade, President Bianchi invited Marcus, Maria, Igor, Perfecto, Tyrone and Barmy to dinner that evening with him, his wife, the Prime Minister and his wife, the Ministers of Defence and Foreign Affairs and their wives.

Following a cocktail party that preceded the dinner in the Presidential Palace that evening, everyone was seated, engaged in animated conversation about the events of the last thirty-six hours.

President Bianchi proposed a toast: "Ladies and Gentlemen," he said, "it is my honor to propose a toast to Colonel Fritz Isenberg and another of our guests tonight. But before I make the toast, I want to make an announcement.

"In consultations with the Swiss government, the Italian government has made arrangements for the Swiss Guards to continue their guard duties . . . including getting their pictures taken with admiring high school and college girls."

The dinner guests laughed and then applauded.

"Now, for Colonel Isenberg: It was he who suggested to the pope that we build a tunnel from the operations room in the basement of his Swiss Guard Barracks to our new Carabinieri Headquarters building a couple blocks east of the Vatican. That suggestion saved his life, Sergeant Blackwood's life and the lives of the Swiss Guards last night.

"Of course the gangsters didn't know about the tunnel, nor did they know they did us a favor by destroying the barracks. The barracks had been emptied of its treasures, the command center moved, and the personal belongings of the guards removed in preparation for demolition. The only things left in the barracks were the beds on which the guards slept.

"They are lodged in a nearby hotel until the new building is ready for occupancy. Here's to Colonel Isenberg and to Sergeant Casper "Barmy" Blackwood, Medal of Honor Winner, who saved Colonel Isenberg from the invaders last night.

"Now, a toast to my dear friend Dr. Marcus J. Madsen, the most principled and courageous man I have known in my long life. I will let his actions speak for me tonight, because there are no words in any language—not even in Italian—he said in English, as his guests laughed.

"We cooperated over a period of three years to bring about the results we have seen in the last twenty-four hours. What else can I say?"

Dr. Madsen returned the compliment in a toast to President Bianchi. Other toasts honoring other heroes were made during the dinner. Following dinner, Tyrone went home. Perfecto, employed by the Italian State as the new Vatican/Italian Bank President, retired to his apartment at the palace. Lidano Russo entered a witness protection program and would play a major role in prosecuting the criminals. Maria, Marcus and Igor returned to Excedra Hotel. Barmy decided to stay in Italy for a while to see if he might find something to satisfy his insatiable appetite for adventure.

Chapter 94

Marcus, Igor, and Maria rode in a limousine to the Leonardo De Vinci Airport, boarded Igor's private Lear Executive Jet—with Igor in the pilot's seat—for their flight to San Francisco where they dined that evening in Dr. Madsen's favorite Italian restaurant: The Gold Mirror. They stayed at the Fairmont Hotel that night. At the dinner table, before retiring to their separate rooms, Maria presented a gift to Dr. Madsen. "Shall I open it now, or later," he asked.

"Now," Maria replied.

A composite of the night sky—with a representation of the 'big bang," swirling galaxies, billions of stars and the earth seen from the surface of the moon—Maria thought would be a capsule of the message she brought to the world.

"It can be a daily reminder," she said, "that the earth is part of a system of millions of observable galaxies, with billions of suns and orbiting planets—not unlike ours—that have thousands of evolving societies, not the least of which is ours here on earth."

Dr. Madsen thanked Maria for the gift and assured her he would place it in a prominent place in his home as a reminder of her message and its influence on his decisions.

The next morning, they parted. Dr. Madsen stayed in the San Francisco/ Oakland area to relax and visit friends and family before flying to Santa Barbara to interview for a job in the Religious Studies Department at the University of California, Santa Barbara.

Maria invited Igor to accompany her to Sylvan Lake. Igor accepted.

Pat arranged for Maria's Maserati to be waiting for her at the Minneapolis/St. Paul Airport.

That night, Maria was eager to sleep with Bog in the barn. She couldn't wait . . . reminiscing about Dana coming out to greet her the night she died. She knew that—somehow—Dana would know she was sleeping in the pen with her colt.

She had nearly fallen asleep, when she heard the squeaking barn door open. Igor made his way to Bog's pen. Maria looked up. He stood there in his pajamas, under his Russian-Mink overcoat and black UGG boots.

"Well, Igor, do you want to join us?" Maria said, with an inviting smile. "I brought an extra comforter and pillow just in case you couldn't sleep in that cold, hard bed in my room. The straw is soft and comfy here and I don't think Bog would mind having another friend in his pen."

"Don't mind if I do."

EPILOGUE

For most of my adult life, I have wondered why Jesus of Nazareth went willingly to his death at such an early age—in his early thirties. Why did he not remain here until his enemies ambushed and killed him? Could he have lived-out his sacred mission several more decades if, for example, he had crossed the Mediterranean to some other country when events became too dangerous for him to live in Israeli territory? Answers to that conundrum are not as elusive as I imagined.

There are commonly known references to Jesus return to earth as a reincarnated Spirit from the realm to which he returned following his bodily death on the cross. He is said to have spent some limited time with some of his disciples in varying bodily forms to pass on post-crucifixion wisdom; what is not commonly known is that he spent *eleven years* with his disciples doing just that. The source for that assertion lies within at least one of several ancient Gnostic documents recovered from Upper Egypt in the eighteenth and nineteenth centuries: that source being the Askew Codex (A.K.A *Pistis Sofia or A Portion, or Portions of the Books of the Savior*). This find consists of 356 pages roughly the size of a modern 9 x 6 inch, paperback book; only eight leaves are missing. It was purchased by the "British Museum" in 1775 from a Dr. Anthony Askew: thus, the title of the codex. The history of this book prior to Dr. Askew's sale is not known. The text contains Gnostic teachings of the "risen" Jesus to, primarily, Mary Magdalene, his mother Mary, and Martha. Another book, the Bruce Codex, containing Coptic and Ethiopic manuscripts, was found in Upper Egypt by a Scottish traveler, James Bruce about 1769. These are ancient Gnostic writings in the form of three books: one titled, *The (2) Books Jeu* and the third titled, *The Untitled Text*. Again, herein lie what have become common characteristics of Jesus post resurrection teachings of Gnosticism: the origins of the divine spark within each human being, the purpose of life on earth and the journey of the soul in the afterlife following the shedding of the body. "The door to God is through 'gnosis,' or knowledge of one's higher Self."

The point is that there is the pre-crucifixion of Jesus and the doscetic, post-crucifixion of Jesus with wildly differing, yet complementary teachings, some of which scholars are questioning in terms of what Jesus really said; the reason is that some of the teachings in the Bible and those esoteric revelations in the *Pistis Sofia* genre seem contradictory if not implausible. But a cautionary note is in order: As these Gnostic books point out, one man's ignorance is another's wisdom, depending on the respective levels of consciousness of each observer. Plumbing that mystery is as remote from our purposes here as the farthest galaxy is from planet earth.

The issues dealt with in this novel are pre-crucifixion in terms of Christian, Gnostic, Cathar and other divine revelations that have come to us within the last century. Numerous ancient documents recovered from Northern Egypt provide clear evidence that Jesus' Gnostic followers ended up in some European countries, crossed the sea and settled in Egypt, where they were persecuted, harassed, and driven underground by the nascent Catholic Church. According to some recent findings by early Christian historians, Gnosticism morphed into a sect known as Catharism, which has some Gnostic characteristics, but lacks the core of Gnosticism: "going within to find ones salvation."

With that backdrop in mind, I now return to the question I asked earlier. Why did Jesus willingly go to his death at such an early age? The short answer to that question might very well be the only relevant answer, which is: He knew he would be coming back shortly after his bodily death to spend eleven years in his doscetic, reincarnated body to share more fully his esoteric knowledge of the spiritual realm and how it relates to life after death. Nevertheless, I will let him speak for himself as part of the long answer to that question, and then suggest some inferences that might be helpful for us to draw our own conclusions about the conundrum. Listen to what Jesus says in the Gnostic *Gospel of Thomas:*

"I took my place in the midst of the world, and I appeared to them in flesh. I found all of them intoxicated; I found none of them thirsty. And my soul became afflicted for the sons of men, because they are blind in their hearts and do not have sight; for empty they came into the world, and empty too they seek to leave the world." He says elsewhere that he is astounded that the divine spirit has made its home in such poverty.

Now, look at this line, also from the *Gospel of Thomas:* ". . . the Kingdom is inside of you, and it is outside of you. When you come to know yourselves, then you will become known, and you will realize that it is you who are the sons of the living father. If you will not know yourselves, you dwell in poverty and it is you who are that poverty." But what does it mean to "know yourself" and just how, exactly, do you do that?

We see in the *Discourse of the Eighth and ninth*—a book in the Nag Hammadi Library—an account that provides a specific technique for "going within" to know yourself" and thereby achieve salvation: Salvation from what? Not knowing who you really are; in other words, not knowing that you are a human being with an internal, divine, indestructible, higher Self which will evolve into full Self-realization . . . an idea that Jesus mentions dozens of times in the Gnostic gospels and which all masters of divine wisdom have taught. The technique for "going within" is meditative and consists of sacred words and long vowels: **"Zoxathazo a oo ee ooo eee oooo ee oooooooooooo uuuuuu ooooooooooooo ooo Zozazoth"** Other wisdom texts provide similar techniques, but do not always provide the mantras that can be used in the meditative state.

The Nag Hammadi Library and other Gnostic texts provide direct—as well as unrevealed (that is secret) ways to take oneself within. Two of the texts in the NHL reveal the experiences of Zorstrianos and Allogenes who achieve ecstasy by "going within" . . . to find their salvation. Thus, Jesus had a technique he could have taught humanity (and probably did teach to a select few who were ready for such seeking within, such as Mary Magdalene, Judas Iscariot, and a very few others). But, in his wisdom, he knew the futility of attempting to teach this wisdom to anyone who *wasn't* seeking it. As pointed out above, there were no seekers to be found; humanity had not evolved to a point where it was ready to—not only accept—but thirst for such wisdom that could be found within.

So, he spoke of the way of love and compassion—often in parables—to help people understand at least that much. And that would have to do until the day would come when humanity had had enough of life in ignorance and suffering and was thirsty for a drink of their divine, inner Selves.

It would be two-thousand years before the time would come when humanity was ready to receive the divine wisdom that Jesus had intended to give to humanity. At the beginning of the 1964 fall semester at the University of California at Berkeley, students—who had been to the Deep South that summer learning how to gain their political ends through non-violence—rebelled against an oppressive administration and won a campus war to exercise their political rights on campus. Their rebellion was called *The Free Speech Movement*.

The movement became more than a matter of free speech. The students, dissatisfied with the status quo in society, were ready to accept alternative ways of feeling better and some were ready to seek new ways to satisfy their spiritual longing by going within, as Jesus had suggested and Maharishi was now advocating. The time for a modern-day student revolution had arrived on planet earth.

The student revolution—young people seeking a better world—would spread around the globe and spawn a bevy of young people who were eager to listen to and learn from a young Indian guru: Maharishi Mahesh Yogi. He, like Jesus, came to launch a Spiritual Regeneration Movement (SRM), to wake people up to their inner, spiritual, higher Selves through the use of a simple relaxation technique. But he, like that young man from Nazareth, found humanity still in a state of spiritual poverty.

Momentarily, the Indian guru considered the situation hopeless, but quickly realized his meditation technique was an exquisite answer to humanity's dilemma —a desperate need to sleep better and reduce daily stresses. *If that's why one comes to meditation . . . well, that is not a game-changer in terms of the ultimate purpose of meditating: to gain spiritual renewal; it is an important first step toward a more pleasant and productive life, with a potential for unexpected spiritual renewal. Less afflicted seekers could leap-frog into a spiritual whirlwind.*

Maharishi attracted young people, taught them to meditate and encouraged them to become teachers of Transcendental Meditation: "going within". By 1971, he had completed 13 world tours and visited dozens of countries. Over the next several decades, thousands of people responded. Today, nearly sixty years on, hundreds of thousands of people have been taught the TM technique and are "going within"—thereby raising the level of global consciousness: turning a corner away from spiritual poverty and heading toward a global peace that Jesus and other masters before him sought.

Perhaps we can infer from these facts that Jesus fulfilled his mission after all, as limited—according to his own words—as it was. It appears that he was very clear in his own mind that he had accomplished what he could do—considering the depth and breadth of ignorance he found here on earth. At the age of thirty-three, he chose to return to the heavenly realm from which he came.

That part of his life was meant to suffice for a planet wallowing in ignorance: blindness to its own spiritual heritage. But then he returned with stupendous revelations that he and scholars have suggested were not meant for the unworthy: that is, those incapable of comprehending what he was saying. Scholars are just beginning to sort all of that out. Thus, these are exciting times, indeed, for the curious: the "seekers" in this world.

Acknowledgments

Mindy Lake was the first person to notice the artist's symbolic use of a mother's womb in the **Last Judgment.** She edited a rough draft of the novel and offered encouragement. To Mindy, I express my sincere gratitude.

I am grateful to Jeff Lindstrom for suggesting that our protagonist hail from the Russian Far East. Without his suggestion, we would have not known about Maria's incredible childhood. Joshua Tallent provided professional technical assistance by uploading the novel to the Digital Text Platform. To Mindy, Jeff, Joshua—and all others who freely offered their expertise, advice and assistance—thanks. I offer my special appreciation to my son Todd Mikkelson and his daughter Maya Mikkelson who collaborated in the design and creation of the book cover and the outer-space graphic in the manuscript.

Finally, my deepest gratitude is reserved for the late Maharishi Mahesh Yogi—founder of the Transcendental Meditation Movement—whose relaxation technique for "going within" eliminated my decades-long bouts of depression and panic attacks. . . the day I started meditating. Before that day—34 years ago—I had made a promise to myself: that if I ever found a way to free myself from this debilitating disease, I would do something to share my luck with others.

This novel provides a platform for the fulfillment of that promise; it would not have been written had it not been for TM and recent divine revelations from two other sources: (1) the recently discovered Gnostic Gospel of Judas and the Gnostic Gospels found in the Nag Hammadi Library; and (2) Walsch's *Conversations with God,* which also emphasizes the importance of "going within" to save ourselves from the oblivion of not knowing who We Really Are—Divine Children of All That Is; it is to that Divine Being that I offer heart-felt gratitude that cannot be expressed—adequately—in words.